YEAR OF VICTORY

At last – the end of the war is in sight for the Adams family

Although the seemingly endless war was at last coming to an end, there were still many tribulations to be overcome. Flying bombs – the deadly V1 buzzbombs – appeared over London, causing dreadful destruction and the struggle continued to overcome the most powerful war machine the world had ever known. Amongst the Cockney community there were lighter moments – Felicity, Eloise and Lizzy knew their menfolk were safe and well. Daniel Adams and his American girlfriend even had a brief meeting with Winston Churchill himself. And as the Third Reich began to collapse, the scent of victory was in the air.

YEAR OF VICTORY

YEAR OF VICTORY

by

Mary Jane Staples

Magna Large Print Books
Long Preston, North Yorkshire,
BD23 4ND, England.

British Library Cataloguing in Publication Data.

Staples, Mary Jane
    Year of victory.

    A catalogue record of this book is
    available from the British Library

    ISBN   0-7505-1771-9

First published in Great Britain 2001 by Transworld Publishers
a division of The Random House Group Ltd.

Copyright © Mary Jane Staples 2001

Cover illustration © Nigel Chamberlain by arrangement with
Transworld Publishers Ltd.

Magna Large Print is an imprint of Library Magna Books Ltd.

Printed and bound in Great Britain by
T.J. (International) Ltd., Cornwall, PL28 8RW

3226159 4

All the characters in this book are fictitious, and any resemblance to actual persons, living or dead, is purely coincidental.

In fond memory of my sister-in-law, Doris Wake, a devoted fan, with my best wishes to her son Tony and her granddaughters Miranda and Lucy.

THE ADAMS FAMILY

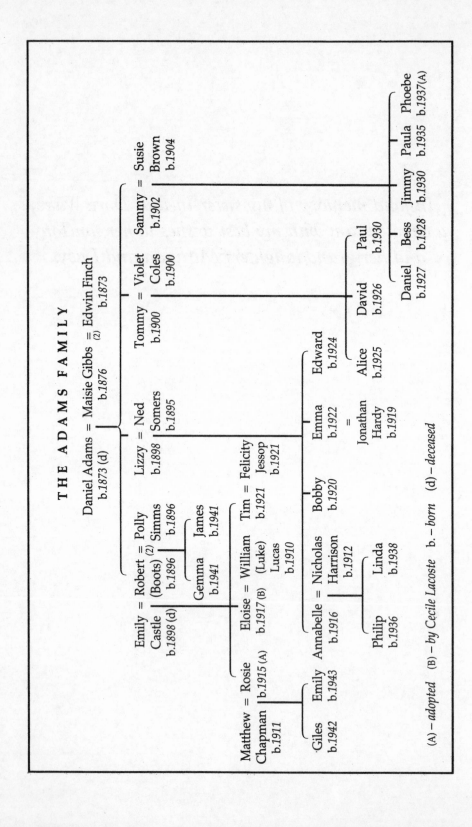

Daniel Adams = Maisie Gibbs = Edwin Finch
b.1873 (d)   (2) b.1876   b.1873

Emily = Robert = Polly   Lizzy = Ned   Tommy = Violet   Sammy = Susie
Castle (Boots) (2) Simms   b.1898 Somers   b.1900 Coles   b.1902 Brown
b.1898 (d) b.1896 b.1896   b.1895   b.1900   b.1904

            Gemma   James
            b.1941 b.1941

Eloise = William   Tim = Felicity   Emma   David   Paul
b.1917 (B) (Luke)   b.1921 Jessop   b.1922   b.1926 b.1930
           Lucas   b.1921   =
           b.1910   Jonathan
                                              Hardy
                                              b.1919   Daniel Bess Jimmy Paula Phoebe
Annabelle = Nicholas   Bobby   Edward   b.1927 b.1928 b.1930 b.1935 b.1937(A)
b.1916   Harrison   b.1920   b.1924
           b.1912   Alice
                                               b.1925
            Philip Linda
            b.1936 b.1938

Matthew = Rosie
Chapman b.1915 (A)
b.1911

Giles   Emily
b.1942 b.1943

(A) – adopted   (B) – by Cecile Lacoste   b. – born   (d) – deceased

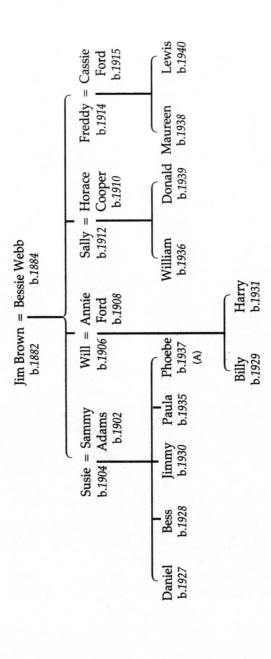

THE BROWN FAMILY

Jim Brown = Bessie Webb
b.1882   b.1884

Susie = Sammy Adams
b.1904   b.1902

Will = Annie Ford
b.1906   b.1908

Sally = Horace Cooper
b.1912   b.1910

Freddy = Cassie Ford
b.1914   b.1915

Daniel
b.1927

Bess
b.1928

Jimmy
b.1930

Paula
b.1935

Phoebe
b.1937
(A)

Billy
b.1929

Harry
b.1931

William
b.1936

Donald
b.1939

Maureen
b.1938

Lewis
b.1940

Chapter One

Mid-June, 1944

The flying object, high in the sky and heading directly north-west from the *Pas de Calais*, crossed the Channel, reached the coast of Kent and invaded the air space of the United Kingdom at tremendous speed. Members of the Royal Observer Corp spotted it but could not identify it except to say it was too small to be any known bomber, either Allied or German. The RAF fighter station at Manston was alerted, but the invader was moving too fast to be intercepted. Four hundred miles an hour.

It passed over the village of Brabourne Lees, over the town of Ashford, and with its power system, a tubular jet engine, loudly buzzing, flew on to Maidstone. Its noise heralded its visible arrival over the shopping area. People stared up at it, suspicious of its heavy buzzing noise while gaping at the speed with which it came and went.

On it flew, dark and squat, tearing through the sky over Swanley, Eltham and Lewisham towards the centre of London. Its loud buzzing flight caught the attention of Londoners. With straight front wings, and a small cross-section tail, it looked like a plane of rudimentary design, a black silhouette streaking fast and noisily against the canopy of high clouds. A group of people on the south side of Waterloo Bridge saw it coming and watched its approach. There was no great sense of alarm, for it obviously wasn't a lone German bomber. Comments were exchanged.

'Look at that, me old Dutch, what is it, some kid's toy plane that's escaped from Clapham Common?' asked a stout man.

'I saw my dad's shirt tails flying in the wind once, and Mum after him with the coal shovel,' said his old Dutch, 'but I never saw no toy plane from Clapham Common.'

'Take it from me, there's no toy plane that's as big or as fast as that,' said a soldier on leave.

They all stretched their necks as it began to pass overhead.

'Funny-looking, I call it,' said an off-duty bus clippie.

'I ain't laughing yet,' said the stout man cautiously.

'Christ, nor is the pilot, his engine's failed,' said the soldier, tensing.

'Blind O'Reilly,' breathed the stout man.

The engine had fallen silent. The machine, crossing the river, seemed to falter, and then it plunged earthwards, revealing the absence of either cockpit or pilot. The watchers held their breath as the mysterious flying object disappeared behind buildings on the north side of the river. It struck Aldwych, close to Fleet Street, and exploded with a tremendous roar. A bus, carrying several passengers, was blown over. Hundreds of windows in nearby buildings disintegrated. Shattered bricks showered the area like jagged missiles.

Hitler had launched his secret weapon, a jet-propelled flying bomb fashioned by his rocket scientists. The V-1.

At regular intervals, others followed the first. Since they could not be primed to strike a specific target, they were aimed at London generally as an instrument of terror. Devastation and havoc on an indiscriminate scale occurred, and was repeated daily.

Prime Minister Winston Churchill was suddenly aware that he had what he could have well done without at a time when huge efforts were being made to sustain the impetus of the successful invasion of Normandy – he had a major headache. This headache was no help at all to the programme he had been working on for years, that of ensuring Britain's war machine was formidable enough to compare favourably with the might of the Russian and American forces. His present endeavours consisted in assisting Russia to take Germany out of the war, and then smashing the Japanese, all with the massive help of the vigorous and dynamic Americans.

The advent of Germany's V-1, designed to win the war for Hitler at a time when Germany was beginning to sense defeat, was aimed at shattering the morale of the British people, particularly millions of obdurate Londoners, and thus reduce their long-standing determination to back Churchill all the way in his quest for victory.

Churchill sought new defensive measures.

RAF and USAF Fighter Commands, hugely supportive of the Allied offensive in Normandy, were forced to detach some squadrons and use them to patrol the Channel in a bid to intercept the V-1's, and by the end of June one thousand of these fearsome flying bombs had been blown up in mid-air. The defence offered by the fighter planes was augmented by ack-ack guns positioned along the coast between Newhaven and St Margaret's Bay, and the barrage balloons hung in clusters between Limpsfield and Cobham in Surrey. Fighter pilots quickly realized it was suicidal to shoot at a V-1 from close range. They improvised by allowing the missile to fly past and then giving it a burst from a safe distance, or, in a particularly daring fashion, by placing a wing tip beneath the buzz-bomb's wing tip and knocking it off course with a flip and a roll.

However, a discomfiting number were still getting through, and Churchill knew it was asking a hell of a lot of the people of London to put up with this new menace from the skies. Nevertheless, ask he did when he went among them. If some cockneys frankly and reasonably expressed themselves as being bleedin' fed-up with being bleedin' blown up, a heartening number responded with the two-finger 'V for victory' sign that Churchill himself had originated. In its own response, Allied Bomber Command made tremendous efforts to search for and destroy the V-1 launching sites.

Hitler was crowing. Not only did he announce that the V-1's were decimating London and tying down hundreds of Allied aircraft, he overcame his critical lack of a sense of humour by ending up with a funny ha-ha line.

'Our V-1 needs no fuel for a return flight.'

16

The 30th of June

Mr Sammy Adams, well-known businessman of Camberwell, stood looking at the ruins of his old Southwark Brewery, destroyed by a bomb during the time of the 1940-41 Blitz. His business manager, widowed Rachel Goodman, was with him. They were both forty-two, both worth a penny or two. Sammy was tall, well-dressed in a light grey suit and dark grey Homburg, blue eyes still reflective of his mental energy. Rachel, in a beige dress and a round brimmed hat defiant of wartime's severe lines, was vividly brunette, with large eyes of velvet brown. She was what Sammy called a well-preserved female woman. Born a Jewish cockney girl, she had been sent by her father to a finishing school when she was nearly sixteen, and she emerged a young lady. Her relationship with Sammy was that of a long-standing friend, and never at any time did she intimate she had always been in love with him. His marriage to Susie was precious to him, and no way was Rachel going to spoil that for either of them.

By his side, she surveyed the ruined premises, at the end of which stood a shop, closed and shuttered, but with two storeys of living accommodation above it. It was separated from terraced houses by an alley. It had been only slightly damaged when the adjoining brewery was destroyed, but the damage had been made good.

'There's your site, Sammy,' said Rachel 'but

you won't be able to think of development until after the war.'

'Right,' said Sammy, 'but what d'you think about me idea of erecting a three-storey block of good-sized flats for young couples to purchase?'

'Sammy, people here in Southwark don't purchase, they never earn enough for a mortgage.'

'I was thinking of starting a loan company and undercutting building society interest by a mouthwatering quarter-of-one-per cent,' said Sammy.

'A quarter-of-one-per cent is mouthwatering?' smiled Rachel.

'That's me fond conviction,' said Sammy, 'but first I'd like to extend the site, which we can do if we buy that shop.'

'Who could resist a generous offer, Sammy?' said Rachel. 'Who would want to live there if they could buy something far better?'

'You might well ask, not half you might,' said Sammy, 'and the answer's a lemon.'

'Lemon?'

'In person, a Mrs Delilah Harman, who owns the place, lives in it and is highly obstinate,' said Sammy.

'Delilah, Sammy? Delilah?'

'Well, Jessica, actually,' said Sammy, 'and one of your own.'

'You mean she's a Jewish lady?' said Rachel.

Sammy said yes, and that he'd made an offer, a generous one, a week ago. Well, any offer is generous, he said, considering that only some barmy geezer with no head would want to live in the place. It shook him to the core, he said, when

18

the old biddy turned him down flat on her doorstep. Didn't even invite him in for a cup of tea and a friendly chat. Be off with you, that was what she said.

'Pardon?' said Rachel.

'Fact,' said Sammy. '"Be off with you, yer saucy boy." That's what she came out with. Rachel, are you laughing?'

'My life,' gurgled Rachel, 'she called you a saucy boy?'

'Me, Rachel, yours truly. Me. I tottered, and she shut the door right on my hooter. I told meself I was having a bad dream, and that I'd got to let her know I'm Sammy Adams, not the local paperboy.'

'Sammy, I'm fascinated,' said Rachel, a picture of blooming life against the background of dead bricks. 'What did you do?'

'I stiffened me sinews, and knocked again,' said Sammy, 'and then what happened, you'll ask.'

'I am asking,' said Rachel.

'Well, old Delilah was upstairs by then,' said Sammy. 'She opened a window and poured a large jug of soapy washing-up water down over me. Fortunately, most of it missed, but me titfer caught a pint or so. There were words as well.'

'What words?'

'"Hoppit, yer saucy young monkey."'

'Oh, my life, Sammy, I'm having hysterics.'

'Help yourself,' said Sammy, 'but it's not funny, y'know.'

'No, Sammy.'

'Now you know why you're here, and why our old friend Eli Greenberg should turn up any moment. You and Eli, well, you're both related to old Delilah in a manner of speaking, and can talk to her in Yiddish. The place is only worth a couple of hundred smackers, but I'll go up to three. Start at two-twenty.'

'Sammy, I honestly don't want a jug of washing-up water poured over me and my hat,' said Rachel, 'but for you I'll risk it. And here's Eli. I'm sure he'll risk it too.'

A horse and cart drew up alongside the site, and Sammy let a smile show. There it was, Mr Greenberg's lifetime mode of transport. All the bombing raids, and now the flying bombs, had failed to deprive him of the horse and cart dear to his heart and his daily round. These days he was on the lookout for scrap metal that householders wanted to get rid of. There was an urgent industrial demand for it while the war went on.

'Here I am, Sammy my friend,' he said, climbing down and putting a feed bag on his nag's nose. 'And ain't I pleasured to see Rachel too? Vhy, I never saw you looking younger, Rachel, nor more expensive. Ah, expensive is high-class, ain't it, and vasn't you alvays high-class, my dear?' Mr Greenberg beamed. His ancient round black hat, rustier by the year, and his handsome black beard, flecked with white, were permanent features. He was sixty now, having entered the UK as a young boy in 1890, when Queen Victoria was aged and revered. His parents had brought him and his brother and sister out of Czarist Russia, away from the pogroms and the knout-wielding Cossacks, to face a new life of struggle and hardship in

20

London's East End. But there was freedom to be oneself, also good-natured bobbies and people who were resolute despite poverty. Before the war, Mr Greenberg had seen them pour into the streets to fight Mosley's blackshirted, anti-Semitic thugs. Such a pity, he often thought, that the German people of Berlin hadn't fought Hitler's thugs in the same way.

'Welcome, Eli old cock,' said Sammy.

'Sammy, vill you tell me vhat today's business is?' Mr Greenberg's tongue caressed the word he and Sammy cherished.

'It's about extending this site,' said Sammy.

'For a block of roomy flats, ain't it?' said Mr Greenberg.

'Right,' said Sammy, 'and I need to buy that shop and its premises, to knock it down and get the extension I require. But I'm having trouble with the owner.' He recounted details, which brought forth a rolling chuckle from Mr Greenberg. 'Eli, I've just had to tell Rachel I don't regard it as funny.'

'Sammy, there's tears in my eyes, ain't there?'

'I can't see any,' said Sammy, 'and it's to me regret that Rachel's still laughing.'

'But, Sammy, all that washing-up water and calling you a saucy young monkey,' said Rachel. 'I should lose my sense of humour about it?'

'Mine went for a long walk at the time,' said Sammy, 'and it's not come back yet. Probably fell off the white cliffs of Dover. But I'm not giving up. So you and Eli talk Yiddish to the old biddy to let her know you're her cousins, and that you're thinking of building a new synagogue on this site.'

21

'Sammy, Sammy,' said Rachel.

'All right, say a home for Jewish orphans.'

'Vhy not a block of flats for people in need?' suggested Mr Greenberg.

'Well, of course, people in need of a flat count as people in need,' said Rachel.

'I like it,' said Sammy. 'Right, I'll leave it to you two. Two's better than one, seeing the old girl's tough. Try to get her singing fairly quick, as I've got a busy day in front of me.'

Rachel smiled. The country was in its sixth year of war, but Sammy never let go of his business wheels and deals, and for some time now he'd been looking ahead. There had to be a rebuilding and development programme in every bombed city after the war, and Sammy was on to it, even if on a long-term basis. He'd made money already for the firm's property company by selling acquired bomb-sites to other companies with post-war development in mind. Capital was available for long-term investment simply because industry always boomed in wartime, and Adams Enterprises and its associated companies were banking their fair share of profits. Rachel knew that.

'Come along, Eli,' she said, 'let's see if we can get on the right side of Mrs Harman.'

'A Yiddish lady, you said, Sammy?' enquired Mr Greenberg.

'So I did,' said Sammy, 'which means you and Rachel can talk to her like fond relatives.'

'Sammy, it's a business deal or for friendship?'

'Call it a business deal for a fiver,' said Sammy.

'I'll be happy to, Sammy,' said Mr Greenberg.

'Friendship is precious, but a little hard on my pocket sometimes, ain't it?'

'Come along, Eli,' said Rachel again, and she and Sammy's old friend and business help made their way to the shuttered shop. Sammy put himself out of sight, but kept within earshot. Rachel knocked on the door at the side of the shop. After a little while, quick footsteps were heard, suggesting that Mrs Harman might be old but far from infirm. The door opened and the lady appeared, angular, grey-haired and sharp-eyed. 'Mrs Harman?' said Rachel with a friendly smile.

'That's me. What d'yer want? If you're selling something, I can't afford it, so be off with the pair of yer.'

'My dear lady,' said Mr Greenberg, 've–'

'I ain't your dear lady,' said Mrs Harman, and Sammy heard Mr Greenberg say something at length in Yiddish. That didn't please her, either, for she said irritably, 'I ain't spoke that language for fifty years, so talk English. No, yer needn't bother. I've lived 'ere all me life, as me father's daughter, me late husband's wife, the mother of me children, and the keeper of the shop till I had to close it for want of stock. So I ain't moving and I ain't selling. What's yer game, eh? I 'ad some young saucebox make me an offer last week, and I ain't liking you any more than I liked 'im. Who are yer? You ain't this young woman's husband, are yer? You're a disgrace if you are, seeing you're old enough to be her grandfather.'

That's made Rachel purr a bit, thought Sammy.

'Vell, missus,' said Mr Greenberg, 'I ain't her

23

grandfather, nor her husband–'

'I still don't like yer, nor yer face. Hoppit.'

'Mrs Harman,' said Rachel, 'our offer–'

'I told yer, I ain't selling to no-one, so take yerselves off.'

Sammy heard the door slam. I don't believe it, he said to himself, two old friends like Rachel and Eli can't make a Yiddisher momma sing? I've got serious problems.

'Sammy?' Rachel appeared, Mr Greenberg at her elbow. 'My life, you heard all that? She won't play.'

'I'll think of something,' said Sammy.

'Sometimes, Sammy, there's vun nut that von't be cracked,' sighed Mr Greenberg.

'I'll think of something,' said Sammy again. 'It might take a week or so – oh, hell, watch out.'

They were quite still then, tensing as they heard that which had become all too familiar, the powerful buzzing noise of a V-1, a 'doodlebug', invading the skies over Southwark. High up in the grey clouds, it passed on in the direction of Blackfriars Bridge, and they relaxed while saying a silent prayer for whoever was going to be close to the monster when it crashed and exploded. It actually fell in Finsbury Park, its blast reaching out just far enough to lightly scorch the heels of people who had begun to run as soon as they saw the monster nosediving out of the clouds.

Sammy and Rachel returned to the firm's offices in Camberwell Green, and Mr Greenberg went on his rounds with his horse and cart.

Life had to go on, and so did business.

Chapter Two

Early July

Some young ladies might have glanced into a mirror and given a light touch or two to their hair while on their way to answer a knock on their front door. Not Miss Alice Adams, the nineteen-year-old daughter of Tommy and Vi Adams. Such concessions to vanity did not enter her mind. A studious young lady, most of her thoughts related to the highly satisfying fact that she was due to enter Bristol University in September. Everything else was of a minor nature. Except the war, of course.

She felt it had been sensible of the Government not to have closed the universities because of the war, and to have allowed would-be students deferment from conscription into industry or the Services. Well, it was true, of course, that the country had never allowed any war to close down its places of advanced learning. She hoped to graduate with honours and become a university tutor. Meanwhile, she naturally took a serious interest in the progress of the present war, particularly in the way it affected the lives of close relatives, such as cousins Tim and Eloise and their father, Uncle Boots. To Alice, her Uncle Boots was the most admirable of the Adams men. She saw him as mature, sophisticated and cultured, and she saw herself as much the same in the years to come. Boots would have been amused to know she held such an opinion of him, since he considered sophisticated and cultured people were those whose practical talents began and ended with feeding pennies into a gas meter.

It was a fact, anyway, that Alice glanced at no mirror on her way to open the front door to a caller. She was, in any case, always quite satisfied with her appearance. While she wasn't as photogenic as her cousins Rosie and Eloise, her looks were by no means unattractive, her hair fair like her mother's, and her figure nicely shaped by her trim dark blue dress. But she lacked the air of animation that characterized so many of her cousins.

She opened the door. On the step stood a sinewy, lanky man with the dark looks of a pirate. She knew him, for she had encountered him before, several times. They had not been enjoyable meetings. He had an annoying habit of delivering opinions that weren't asked for, opinions that in the main suggested she was not to be taken seriously.

Fergus MacAllister was a Scot who had known wartime service with a famous Highland Division. Prior to the Dunkirk evacuation, the Division had fought a tremendous battle against overwhelming odds to prevent the whole of the British Expeditionary Force being trapped. That achieved, the Division found there was no way out for its own troops, and was eventually forced to surrender. Suffering a severe wound, Fergus had been stretchered out during the early stages of the battle, and thereby escaped being taken prisoner. However, his wound was of the kind that left tiny slivers of shrapnel in his body, and caused him to be discharged, much to his disgust. He was always hopeful that the shrapnel would expel itself through his skin and leave him fit enough to rejoin his regiment, although there was always the chance a sliver might slip into an artery. He knew that and lived with the threat of what that might do to him. Meanwhile, he had this job as a mechanic with the local Gas Board, and as such was invaluable. Vibrations affecting gas mains during past air raids eventually caused fractures that led to dangerous situations. And the flying bombs were inflicting new damage. Fergus had come to know Alice when attending to a gas leak in her mum's airing-cupboard, and the two of them had reached a point where they agreed to disagree. He did indeed think her far too serious for her age, and she thought him impertinent.

'Guid morning to you, Miss Adams,' he said, much more an outgoing Scot than a dour one.

'Oh, it's you,' said Alice.

'Aye,' said Fergus. He was on the doorstep of the Adams house on Denmark Hill in answer to a phone call from Alice's father, Mr Tommy Adams, who had informed the relevant department that the gas boiler which supplied the hot water was beginning to fail from old age. Tommy, in his cheerful way, had said he knew there was a war on, and that there were real emergencies, but if something could be done about his rackety old

27

boiler before it blew up, he'd make a donation to the Gas Board's favourite charity, whatever it was. The Gas Board clerk said that as there had been no serious flying bombs incidents in the area recently, he'd see if a mechanic could be sent sometime within the next two weeks. Have a heart, said Tommy. We're very busy, said the clerk. Tommy said all right, if the boiler does blow up, don't say you weren't warned. Don't use it, said the clerk. Tommy growled. Hence, the appearance of Fergus MacAllister.

'I don't know if we were expecting you again,' said Alice in her precise way. 'Are you the only mechanic employed by the Board?'

'I'm no' the only one, Miss Adams,' said Fergus, 'just the best, y'ken.'

'One must admire your modesty,' said Alice.

'True, I'm a quiet man on my own account,' said Fergus.

'Ha-ha,' said Alice.

'Am I to step in, Miss Adams?'

'I'm afraid my mother's out,' said Alice.

'Whisht, I've no' come to see your mother, but to look at your boiler.'

'I'm not sure I wish to be alone in the house with you,' said Alice.

'I'm thinking there's a risk in it for both of us,' said Fergus.

'Both of us? What d'you mean?' asked Alice.

'I mean, Miss Adams, how safe will I be alone in the house wi' you?' said Fergus.'

'That's ridiculous,' said Alice. They eyed each other, Alice straight of face and always inclined to dress him down a bit for his impertinence, and

Fergus, for some reason that didn't make sense to himself, quite taken with the hoity-toity miss. If she wasn't exactly sparkling, she was still a bonny young lady, with a fine, healthy-looking figure.

'Miss Adams, I'm still on your doorstep,' he said.

'Well, although you don't improve,' said Alice, 'you can come in and do what you have to do.'

'I'm obliged,' said Fergus, carrying himself and his bag of tools into the house. 'I'm hoping there'll be no doodlebugs chasing me off the job.'

'They're awful,' said Alice. In a matter of three weeks, she and her parents had learned how to cope with the menace, as had most Londoners. That was not to spend all day in a shelter, but to carry on with one's normal routine and dive for cover only when the engine of any approaching V-1 cut out, the signal that the explosive projectile was about to fall from the sky. 'Who thought up such ghastly things?'

'Hitler's ghastly scientists, I'm thinking,' said Fergus. 'It's a war against civilians he's been fighting since he bombed Warsaw and Rotterdam, and refugees on roads. I'll no' cry for him when the Allies hang him.' He moved towards the kitchen. Alice followed. 'I know my way,' he said, 'and I willna be bothering you if you're still at your studies.' He knew how committed she was to her academic future, and that she spent most days swotting. 'Run along, lassie.'

'Run along?' Alice took umbrage. 'Really, your impertinence gets worse, and isn't made any better by calling me lassie.'

'It's a fact that we're all a wee bit touchy about some things,' said Fergus, 'but it's no' my intention to upset you today, tomorrow or any time. You're a young lady much attached to your dignity, and I respect that.'

'No, you don't,' said Alice, and entered the kitchen on his heels. It was ten in the morning and, as usual, her mother had left everything clean and tidy before going out to the shops. Alice was never asked to do much more around the house than keep her bedroom tidy and make her bed. 'In any case, I'm not attached to my dignity, just my coming time at university.'

'I'm no' arguing with that,' said Fergus, putting his bag of tools down. He simply thought this serious-minded young lady gave the impression of being too old for her years. 'I never knew any lassie more addicted to learning.'

'You're very provoking,' said Alice. She might have saved herself this kind of dialogue if she had simply left him to his work and gone back to her books. But, as had happened before, more than once, his attitude aroused a compulsive urge to stay and make a fight of their encounters.

'What's this noise?' asked Fergus, and opened the door of the large cupboard housing the boiler. The boiler was thumping and coughing. 'Scale,' he said.

'Scale?' said Alice.

'Aye, and likely to be inches thick on a boiler as old as this,' said Fergus. 'Out of the Ark, I'd say, and probably a problem to Mrs Noah even then. I'll place a bet on it having heart failure any moment in trying to keep the water hot.'

30

'Sometimes it's not much more than luke-warm,' said Alice, 'and whenever anyone has a bath it takes ages for it to heat up again. Didn't my father tell your people that over the phone?'

'So I believe,' said Fergus. 'Were you thinking of taking a bath this morning, Miss Adams? If so, take it now, for as a start I'll be turning off the flow into this ancient monument and draining it.'

'Thanks very much, but I bath at night, not in the mornings,' said Alice.

'So do I,' said Fergus. He had his back to her, tapping the boiler with a spanner. 'So you could say we bath together.'

Alice supposed that was an attempt to show how witty he was. It failed miserably as far as she was concerned.

'Well, of course, you might say so,' she said, 'and so might most third-rate comedians. I'm going into the parlour to continue my studies, and I hope that boiler falls on you and makes a large hole in your silly head.'

'Whisht, is that how you feel, Miss Adams?'

'Yes,' said Alice. Out she went and into the parlour. The morning was quiet. There was a lull in the Germans' despatch of flying bombs. Allied bombers brought about periods of temporary relief by sustained attacks on launching sites. Alice sat down at the table on which books were spread. The top sheet of a writing block in front of her was covered with notes. She ripped it off, picked up her pencil and made a fresh start on analysing the literature of Thomas Hardy. At least, she attempted to, but she was too conscious that that provoking beast from the Gas Board

31

was in the house and probably having a snigger at her expense. After a while, however, she began to think she ought to excuse him because of his war wound. Some people, probably a great many, would think him a hero and excuse his every fault.

She fidgeted. She read a few paragraphs of *Far from the Madding Crowd*. Then she got up and returned to the kitchen. Lukewarm water was gushing from a tap into the sink.

'Hello again, Miss Adams,' said Fergus, 'I'm draining the boiler.'

'Yes, I see,' said Alice, and composed herself. 'Look, would you like a cup of Camp coffee?' Her mother had asked her to do that kind of thing for whoever turned up from the Gas Board.

'That's kind of you,' said Fergus, 'and I willna say no.'

Alice put the kettle on. The hot water tap stopped running, leaving the boiler empty. Fergus turned off the tap, then began to rap the boiler again with his spanner, creating dull booms.

'What do they mean?' asked Alice, putting coffee mugs on the table.

'Frankly,' said Fergus, 'they're no' the kind of sounds I like.'

'What kind would you like?'

'Clear and ringing, lassie,' said Fergus. 'It's the scale, y'ken, the inside of the boiler is thick with it. That's why the water takes a long time to heat up, and makes your gas bill a wee bit expensive, I dare say.'

'My father will pay for a new boiler,' said Alice.

32

'A new boiler?' Fergus took a pipe out of his overalls pocket, put it between his lips, sucked it, blew on it, took it out and looked at it. 'It's no' so easy, a new one.'

'You're supposed to be solving our problems, not adding to them,' said Alice.

'Dinna worry, Miss Adams, there's a solution somewhere,' said Fergus. 'By way of a salvaged tank at our depot. There's more than a few of those from bombed houses. Badly damaged ones go for valuable scrap. It's the copper they're made of, y'ken. New ones are in short supply because so much copper is required for armaments.'

'Yes, of course,' said Alice understandingly. The kettle boiled then, and she made two mugs of coffee from the chicory-based Camp liquid. She added a little milk. 'Do you take sugar, Mr MacAllister?'

'I willna take any of your ration,' said Fergus.

'We can spare a little,' said Alice, and added a small amount to each mug. She took one mug up. 'I'll leave you to have yours while I go back to my studies again.'

'Aye, you're a fine young lady wi' your books and your learning,' said Fergus, 'and I'm coming to respect that. Haven't I said so?'

'Yes, you've said so,' responded Alice, 'but I find many of your remarks more suspect than respectful.'

'No, I mean it,' said Fergus, 'but if you ever feel like a change from studying and would like to come dancing–'

'Mr MacAllister, I've told you before, I've no

33

time for that kind of thing.' Alice avoided all pursuits she considered trivial. 'I do realize you feel our practical needs, such as a roof over our heads, food to eat, clothes to wear, a transport system to get us to our places of work, and skilled men to keep everything in good repair, are more important than studying for a university degree, but some of us do have different feelings. Not everyone wishes to drive a train or farm the land, and I think there's room for all of us.'

Fergus picked up his mug of coffee, gave her a sorrowful look and said, 'Och, aye.'

'What does that mean?' asked Alice.

'That you've a fine way of delivering a lecture,' said Fergus.

'You've said something like that before, and it's objectionable,' accused Alice. 'I'm finding it very difficult to like you.' And she left the kitchen, carrying her coffee with her.

Fergus drank his own coffee, then finished his work and tidied up. He called when he was ready to leave.

'I'm away now, Miss Adams.'

Alice reappeared.

'What's going to happen?' she asked.

'First, you'll no' be getting any hot water,' he said. 'The boiler's empty, and I've turned off the flow and the burners.'

'Well, thanks very much, I don't think,' said Alice.

'Bide a wee moment, lassie—'

'Will you stop calling me lassie?'

'Aye, I will,' said Fergus. 'And as soon as I've found a reconditioned boiler at the depot, and had it loaded into a van, I'll be back with another mechanic. We'll dismantle your antique and fit the replacement.'

'And when will that be, next week?' asked Alice.

'If we're lucky, this afternoon,' said Fergus.

'Oh,' said Alice. Contritely, she added, 'That would please me and my parents, if you could manage this afternoon.'

'These are better times, Miss Adams,' said Fergus, 'wi' the Highland laddies back in France and giving Hitler's hairy Prussians a hot dose of their own medicine. Aye, this old kingdom's wearing a happier face, and if I canna help fit you a reconditioned boiler this afternoon, it'll no' be for want of trying.'

'Thank you, Mr MacAllister,' said Alice, deciding to be forgiving. 'As for the invasion of Normandy, wasn't the news exciting and wonderful? I'm sure every man was a hero.'

'You can be sure at least that every seasick man couldna wait to get on dry land, and didna give a hoot for what the Germans were going to throw at him,' said Fergus. His expression, thought Alice, was a little rueful, and she felt he would much rather have been over there in France with his Scots than here in her mother's kitchen. 'It's a fact, though, that these flying bombs are a wee bit upsetting to our home front.'

'Worse than upsetting,' said Alice.

'That's true, lassie,' said Fergus.

'You should know,' said Alice, feeling unexpectedly stimulated by this latest encounter, 'that Lassie is a Hollywood film star with four legs.'

'Aye, I'm sure I've heard of that wonder dog,'

said Fergus. 'I'll be on my way now, Miss Adams, but hoping to be back this afternoon. Guid morning to you, thanks for the coffee, and I'm tickled fine that our laddies are back in France. I'm thinking Hitler's now got his deserved fill of worries, for he'll no' push us into the sea this time. Aye, he'll be a worried man right now.'

'And I don't suppose his Germans feel too happy,' said Alice. 'Good morning, Mr Mac-Allister.'

Alice, along with most people in the United Kingdom had no idea whether or not Hitler was still a popular *Fuehrer*. Outside of Germany, few people knew that not everyone in Germany was pro-Nazi and pro-Hitler. Not everyone was in favour of the war, especially now that the Allies had established a firm foothold in Normandy. It meant Germany was under assault on three fronts, Russia, Italy and France. It was dangerous, however, to voice criticism either of the Party or Hitler. Over the years, thousands of men and women had been imprisoned or sent to a concentration camp, or summarily executed, for speaking out of turn. The Gestapo and the SS had cowed the nation, and even now, when it looked as if eventual defeat and devastation were unavoidable for Germany, there were no influential voices raised in public protest. More than a few suffering German people felt someone of standing should denounce the man who bore the major responsibility for the devastating nature of Allied bombing raids and for placing the Third Reich in crisis.

Hitler, supported by his gang of Nazi hellhounds, was that man.

Denouncing him was not enough as far as some people were concerned. Could no-one actually get rid of him and allow Germany to sue for a reasonable peace, at least with the Americans and British, if not with the Communist hordes of Russia?

It was a burning question which was beginning to occupy the minds of certain German generals and influential officials.

Chapter Three

Mrs Maisie Finch, known to her family as Chinese Lady because of her almond eyes and the fact that in days long ago she had taken in washing, was sitting at a table on the stone-flagged patio of her home in Red Post Hill, south-east London. She was just finishing a letter to her granddaughter Rosie, for whom she had a particular affection. Rosie was living down in Dorset with her children, Giles and Emily, and her sister-in-law, Felicity.

So your grandfather and me will be on holiday in Cornwall for the last week in July and the first week in August, which I'm sure will do your grandfather good as he's not been in the best of health this year. We'll be with Sammy and Susie and their children, and Daniel's young lady from America that you know about will be there too. Mind, I don't know if she's actually his young lady or if they're just close friends but I will say she's a nice respectable girl. Well, that's all for now, Rosie, except to say me and your grandfather hope your husband Matthew will come home on leave soon to be with you and the children for a while, and remember us to Tim's wife Felicity, we're glad she's still with you. I can't tell you how relieved I'll be when this blessed war is over and everyone in the family is back home safe and sound and in good health. Now that we've got these doodle-bugs to worry about, things don't get better. That man Hitler is more aggravating than the Kaiser ever was.

Chinese Lady signed off with love, then thought, as she often did, about where so many missing members of the family were at the moment. She knew where her eldest son Boots was. In France, with the army that had invaded Normandy. It was where he shouldn't be, considering he'd been there before, in the Great War trenches. He was nearly middle-aged, he'd be fifty in two years time, and didn't ought to have been in this war as well as the last one. It had to be worrying for Polly, his second wife and the mother of his twins. Polly ought to have him at home to help her bring them up, especially as she was nearly middle-aged herself. Chinese Lady would have rebutted any suggestion that Boots and Polly had passed the 'nearly' stage, that they were middle-aged now. To admit that would have meant she herself was old, and she resolutely refused to consider that as a fact. She didn't feel old and she was quite against looking old. Hence, she never wore granny bonnets, never sat with a shawl around her shoulders, never neglected her appearance or allowed herself to droop.

While Rosie's husband, Captain Matthew Chapman, an engineer, was in Italy, where the blessed war had been going on for ages, Boots's son Tim, who was one of them fighting Commanders – Chinese Lady meant Commandos – well, he was in hospital, recovering from a badly wounded arm. He said he'd been lucky to keep it, considering an Army surgeon wanted to chop it off and display it as a warning to the Army not to take the mickey out of German soldiers by waving at them, since they shot first and asked questions afterwards. Tim was married to Felicity, who'd been blinded in an air raid while on leave from the ATS, poor woman. And of all things, she was actually going to have a baby. Chinese Lady worried about how a blind mother could cope with an infant. Tim said she was going to manage by touch and feel, but Chinese Lady placed more faith in the fact that as Felicity was living with Rosie, her best help would come from Rosie.

Boots's other daughter, Eloise, an officer in the ATS, had just been moved to an Army supply base in the south of England. Mr Finch, Chinese Lady's husband, said the supply bases were helping to feed weapons and equipment to the Allied forces presently fighting the Germans in Normandy. Eloise's husband, Colonel Lucas, was out there, with the Army, and Chinese Lady wondered how long it would be before he got badly wounded too.

As for Lizzy and Ned's elder son, Bobby, no-one had seen him or his young French lady, Helene Aarlberg, for ages. They had both been overseas for goodness knows how long. It was like the Army had swallowed them up. It was a blessing that Lizzy and Ned's younger son, Edward, were still in England. But he was learning to be an RAF pilot, which Chinese Lady thought more than a bit dangerous for a young man not yet twenty.

Lizzy and Ned's daughters, Annabelle and

Emma, had both been lucky. Annabelle's husband, Pilot-Officer Nick Harrison, had been grounded after years of flying, and was now on the staff of an RAF training camp in Cornwall. And Emma's husband, Sergeant Jonathan Hardy, who had a crippled knee because of a war wound, was at an artillery training camp in Somerset, teaching recruits how to fire guns. Emma was working on a farm close by. In a letter, she said she was growing muscles, that she needed them at the moment, but hoped they wouldn't keep her company when the war was over, as she didn't think bulging biceps really suited a woman.

Susie's brother, Freddy Brown, was in Burma with the Army. Chinese Lady couldn't think how anyone could end up in a place like Burma, or how the war managed to get there. Mr Finch had informed her that the Japanese invaded the country with the intention of conquering India from there. British and Indian troops, he said, had recently prevented that by defeating the Japanese in a huge and prolonged battle, in which Freddy had probably earned himself some medals. Chinese Lady said never mind medals, it gave her the horrors thinking of a nice cheerful young man like Freddy in a place like Burma. I'd feel a lot happier, she said, if he was in Southend guarding the pier. And I'm sure his wife Cassie would feel happier too, and so would his mother, who never brought him up to be sent off by the Army to Burma. Mr Finch said he was sure few mothers wanted that for their sons.

Concluding her reflections, Chinese Lady

thought it a shame that Tommy and Vi still didn't have their sons David and Paul at home, but there they were, still down in Devon, David working on a farm and Paul still attending school. At least Tommy and Vi didn't have to worry about them being in the Army. That was a bit of a consolation, and so was the fact that David and Paul were out of the way of these blessed doodlebugs. And so were Sammy and Susie's eldest daughter Bess, and their younger son Jimmy. Sammy had been talking about bringing Bess and Jimmy home, but the doodlebugs had made him change his mind. It was worry enough for them that they had their younger daughters Paula and Phoebe at home.

Having mentally refreshed herself on the present whereabouts of absent relatives, Chinese Lady followed up her letter to Rosie by beginning one to Annabelle. Like most women born in the Victorian era, she was an inveterate letter-writer, especially when it came to keeping in touch with her extensive family.

'Alice, I'm having a cup of tea with your Aunt Lizzy this afternoon,' said Mrs Vi Adams over a simple wartime lunch.

'But Mum, that Gas Board man might be here again,' said Alice.

'Yes, I know, you told me,' said Vi, the most equable of wives and mothers. She was well into her forty-fourth year, and no more demanding of life and her family than she had ever been. Vi was a gentle and basically contented woman, and her husband Tommy considered her the best of the

Adams wives. Vi didn't even complain about their sons David and Paul still being far from home down in Devon, having been sent there as evacuees in 1939. They did go regularly to see them, and that seemed to keep Vi happy enough. As for Alice, their eldest, they both thought she was far too set on getting herself over-educated, and that she was missing out on the fun things that were all part of a girl's life. Of course, the war meant life had become more serious for everybody, but if one took a look at Sammy and Susie's elder son Daniel, well, what an example to Alice. Daniel worked his heart out very conscientiously at the firm's factory day in, day out, but enjoyed every minute of his spare time, especially in his new-found relationship with a girl. An American girl, of all things. Alice had no boyfriends, didn't think them necessary, and spent nearly all her time either studying in the parlour or at the local library. Tommy and Vi had dire thoughts of their daughter turning into a blue-stocking spinster, and anything more mortifying for the family they couldn't imagine. Chinese Lady wouldn't like it, either, she'd go as far as giving Tommy a look and asking if Alice had been dropped on her head as a child, and who was responsible. Tommy and Vi could only hope their obsessed daughter's life would take a turn for what was more natural.

'Mum, you know I don't get on too well with that Gas Board man,' said the obsessed young lady.

'With Mr MacAllister?' said Vi. 'Me and your dad haven't heard he's a difficult man.' Vi, a cockney, dropped a couple of aitches while making this observation, which pained Alice, who spoke well and precisely. Alice, alas, was a bit toffee-nosed. 'And you don't have to entertain him, just let him get on with his work and make him a cup of tea sometime, and do it with a good grace.' More aitches fell by the wayside.

'Well, all right,' said Alice. 'Mum, if you're going to Aunt Lizzy's, be careful about these flying bombs, they've started to come over again.' The morning lull had ended, and the V-1's were arriving at regular intervals and falling in various parts of London.

'And you, Alice, if you hear one coming this way, get under the Morrison shelter,' said Vi.

The Morrison shelter, a sturdy steel mesh frame fitted with a solid top was designed for indoor use, and could act as a table. It had superseded the Anderson garden shelter. The former was the brainchild of Herbert Morrison, the present Home Secretary, and the latter that of his predecessor, Sir John Anderson.

'Yes, I'll do that,' said Alice, resigned to another ordeal with Fergus MacAllister, although at the same time she experienced a little surge of spirited determination to hold her own with him.

However, before Vi went out, she received a phone call from the Gas Board to say that the right-sized reconditioned boiler wasn't available.

So sorry, but it might well be a few days before it could be delivered. Vi pointed out they had no hot water. The lady clerk dealing with the matter suggested, apologetically, that a large kettle should be used. Vi said they were having to do that already, and she could only hope the Board would come to their rescue in reasonable time.

When told of developments, Alice supposed she'd been given a reprieve.

A flying bomb came down in Peckham at that point, causing considerable damage but, fortunately, only one fatal casualty.

For these last three weeks, London had been under a new and sustained siege from the air.

In Germany, the people in high places who did indeed think it was time to get rid of Hitler, were beginning to ask questions of each other behind closed doors. Certain German Army officers were especially active in their approach to men of influence, men such as Admiral Canaris, head of Military Intelligence, and General Beck, who had resigned as Commander-in-Chief of the Army once he realized Hitler was going to take Germany into war.

There was also General von Stulpnagel, the Gestapo-hating Military Governor of occupied France, and Colonel Claus von Stauffenberg, a soldier of great courage and integrity who had recently been promoted to Chief of Staff of Germany's Reserve Army. Von Stauffenberg had long held Hitler in contempt.

Such impressive figures drew in other men, men of high position in the Army or civil administration. However, there was no co-ordination, no effective communication, and there were no arranged secret conferences, only the occasional discussion when one would-be conspirator found himself in company with another.

Something had to be done to bind them together, to organize them, and to plan the means
of eliminating Hitler, whose behaviour sometimes approached that of a lunatic. There were
suggestions that once the conspiracy was on a
firm footing, a search for the right kind of
assassin could begin. No, said Admiral Canaris,
when sounded out, finding the right man must
be the first step, not the second, since while he
remains merely a question mark, too many sup-
porters won't step out of the shadows.

'However, you agree, Herr Admiral, that Germany must be saved from the lunatic and total
ruin?'

'Germany should have been saved from Hitler
years ago. A pity Baron von Tresckow failed in his
attempt last year.'

Baron von Tresckow, a staff officer serving on
the Russian front, had indeed made an attempt
to kill Hitler in March, 1943, by placing a
packaged delayed-action bomb in the *Fuehrer*'s
plane just prior to take-off. The bomb's fuse had
been set, the explosion timed to occur while the
plane was in the air.

Hitler, appropriately, had the devil's own luck,
for the bomb failed to detonate, and the plane
landed intact.

This attempt on the *Fuehrer*'s life did, however,
mean that even fifteen months before the Allied
invasion of Normandy, there were some prominent German Army officers desperate to rid
their country of a leader with whom they were
completely disenchanted.

So, in the wake of the successful landing in

France by the Americans and British, that desperation surfaced again, this time among powerful men. The conspiracy began to take shape, and all that was needed to give it conviction and determination was the right kind of man, the would-be martyr.

Dr Carl Gordeler, Hitler's Price Control Commissioner, accepted the role of chief organizer, and he, along with his closest associates, looked around for such a man.

Chapter Four

Like everyone else in London, the people of Walworth thought Hitler's V-1's more than a bit much. Mrs Cassie Brown, who lived with her good old dad and her young son and daughter in Wansey Street, off the Walworth Road, thought them evil. She and her dad and the children had not long returned from Wiltshire, having spent three years there as evacuees, so she naturally felt it was downright horrible of Hitler to celebrate their return by aiming flying bombs at them. Her dad, Mr Harold Ford, said the perishing things ought to have been designed to turn round in mid-flight and buzz straight back to Hitler himself. After all, he said, the ruddy Germans and their scientists ought to know by now what Adolf had let them in for: war and ruination. So if anyone deserved to be on the wrong end of flying bombs, he did.

Mrs Hobday, a neighbour, was of much the same opinion. A large woman, she was formidable of bulk but good at heart, except on the occasions when she had Hitler on her mind, or Mr Hobday was making a nuisance of himself. Cassie, turning into the street one day, almost bumped into her. The large lady always advanced like a barque in full sail, and a positive collision could be damaging to the other party. Cassie, fortunately, took quick avoiding action.

'Oops, dearie,' said Mrs Hobday. 'Oh, it's you, ducks.' Liking Cassie, always lively, the lady dropped anchor for a chat. 'How's yerself and them lovely kids of yourn?'

'We'd all be fine if we didn't have to worry about these doodlebugs,' said Cassie. There was another lull at the moment, which meant Allied planes were on one more searching raid, which meant in turn that the launching crews were keeping their heads down. 'It's a mean way of making war, Mrs Hobday.'

'They get me shaking so much it's a wonder I don't come apart,' said Mrs Hobday, her fulsome body vibrating. 'It's a strain on me corset every time one comes over. Me old man says I need a suit of armour. He's full of bright ideas. 'Ere, he come home last night with some packets of tea that fell off a goods waggon that was being shunted at his depot, where he works. Would yer like a couple, Cassie?'

'Not half,' said Cassie who, in her twenty-ninth year, sported a wealth of shining black hair, appealing looks, and the cheerful resilience common to most Walworth people. 'You're a welcome friend, Mrs Hobday.' Her outsized neighbour frequently called to offer her a share of goodies that Mr Hobday brought home from Nine Elms. Mr Hobday apparently had a nose for always being in the right place when things fell off a goods waggon.

'Have you heard from yer 'usband lately?' asked Mrs Hobday.

'Not lately,' said Cassie. Her husband, Freddy Brown, was a sergeant in the East Surreys and had been serving with the British 14th Army in Burma and North-West India for longer than Cassie cared to think about. She never stopped missing him. She and Freddy had been an inseparable duo since she was ten years old, and had enjoyed a cherished companionship first as devoted friends and then as husband and wife. What worried Cassie most was the possibility of Freddy becoming one more fatal casualty of the land battles against the Japs.

The British soldiers of the 14th Army, along with their Indian and Gurkha comrades, had been engaged against the invading Japanese first in Burma, then on the North-West frontiers of India. The Japanese drive from Burma into India had reached a tremendous peak of warfare in their offensive against Kohima. There the 14th Army had made a great fighting stand to thwart the enemy intention to conquer India. The battle had begun early in March and lasted until June, by which time the 14th Army had inflicted greater losses on the Japanese than any they were suffering in the Pacific. Strangely, the Press and radio at home rarely headlined news from the Burma front, which caused the men of the 14th to see themselves as the Forgotten Army.

Sergeant Freddy Brown had been in the thick of things, operating with a group of Chindits, jungle guerillas, behind the Japanese front, sabotaging lines of communication, blowing up arms dumps and eliminating as many Japs as they could. It was a special kind of barbaric warfare, conducted on the principle of kill or be killed. It all helped to achieve the defeat of the hitherto invincible Japanese invaders, and to give Kipling's Tommy Atkins the chance to advance at last and to get back on the road to Mandalay.

It was doubtful if, towards the end of the decimating battle of Kohima, Cassie would have recognized Freddy – gaunt, bearded and sooty-eyed. Prior to his arrival in Burma, when the British were in dogged retreat, he had been a typically happy-go-lucky Walworth cockney, a character who had an ongoing faith in the blessings of tomorrow. The cockneys of his generation generally reckoned there was always a chance that Monday's worries would be offset by good news on Tuesday, like old Aunt Ada had snuffed it while she still had a few bob going spare in her Post Office Savings Bank account.

Now in his thirtieth year, Freddy could no longer afford to be happy-go-lucky. Life as a Chindit was deadly, and there was nothing to smile triumphantly about at the sight of a dead Jap, since it was often odds-on that the bugger wasn't dead. More likely than not, he was lying there waiting for you, his knife hidden in his hand beneath his body, and his friends close by. So you melted away, taking your own friends with you, to circle around and come at the backs of the silent enemy. And you all used your own knives then, in case a burst of fire brought a whole platoon of Japs down on you.

And sometimes you thought about your wife and kids, and wondered what they would think if they could actually see what the war, the Japs and the jungle had made of you.

51

There were no steamy jungles or murderous dog-eat-dog encounters in Dorset, only gentle green landscapes and an atmosphere of tranquillity. The latter, however, was deceptive. Irate farmers bawled at erring labourers or Land Army novices. Bulls bawled, cocks crowed, chickens squawked, geese honked, farm dogs barked, tractor engines kept going all day, village kids fought and yelled, and phones rang.

One rang in a cottage by the village of Bere Regis. Mrs Rosie Chapman answered it, exchanged some happy words with the caller, then turned.

'Felicity, phone!' Her voice sang its way around the cottage, and elicited a response from her sister-in-law, Mrs Felicity Adams.

'Who is it, Rosie?'

'Tim.'

'Hold on to him,' called Felicity, and made her appearance from the kitchen in company with Rosie's two-year-old son Giles, and her infant daughter Emily, nearly a year, trailing behind. Giles frequently kept close company with his Aunt Felicity, for she was often in need of a guide. But she reached the hall and the phone unaided, so well did she know the geography of the cottage. Rosie handed her the phone and ushered Giles and Emily back to the kitchen to allow Felicity some privacy.

'Hello? Tim?'

'Hello, little woman, baked any good cakes lately?' said Captain Tim Adams of the Commandos.

'No, not lately, little man, we've run short of

ingredients,' said Felicity. 'It must be this boring old war. Lovely to be talking to you, though. What's your news?'

'My arm's almost as good as new,' said Tim, a Commando veteran at twenty-three. 'I'll be frank, though, and say it doesn't exactly look new. In fact, it looks like a piece of old corrugated cardboard. Will you be able to live with it?'

'Easily,' said Felicity. 'I can't see for looking, can I?'

'I know, Puss,' said Tim. 'That's something you're having to live with every day, and it's a lot more savage than a scarred arm.'

'Stop making me feel sorry for myself,' said Felicity, 'I can get into that state without any help from anyone.'

'Well, look here, Mrs Felicity Adams,' said Tim, 'after the war, when we've settled down, if you still get into that kind of state and want to chuck things about twice a day, you go ahead. I'll pay for all breakages. Cheap at the price, whether it gets rid of your frustrations or not.'

'And if I chuck things at you?' said Felicity.

'Try not to miss,' said Tim, 'or your frustrations will stay with you.'

'What a sport,' said Felicity.

'How's our embryo?' asked Tim.

'Tucked up and coming along nicely, according to our friendly village doctor,' said Felicity. She was almost two months pregnant. It had been a compulsive wish, to have a child by Tim, despite her disability. 'Sickening hell, though,' she said by way of a PS, 'I think nature was in some kind of cursed mood when it designed nine months of

53

carrying for women. I wonder if a mistake was made, if nature had a clerk looking after its paperwork, and the clerk wrote down nine months when it should have been nine weeks. Do nine weeks make sense to you, Tim?'

'Totally,' said Tim 'and if I were a woman, I think I'd ask to see nature's original notes. I mean, it's reasonable to suppose there was a committee meeting with Adam and Eve to discuss the best way of reproducing their species, and so on.

'I'll go for Adam being the blighter who mucked up nature's final instructions,' said Felicity. 'He'd be bossy enough to write out the minutes, and slipshod enough to put down nine months instead of nine weeks, the hairy male ape. What was Eve doing, the silly woman, that she didn't correct the mistake?'

'Probably wasn't paying attention,' said Tim, 'probably thinking about the latest fashion in fig leaves.'

'And look what it landed her with, nine months of carrying,' said Felicity. 'Listen, lover, is this conversation for real?'

'You're real, Puss,' said Tim, 'and that's all that counts as far as I'm concerned. You and our infant.'

Felicity thought for the thousandth time of the bomb that had blinded her when she was caught in a London air-raid while on leave from her ATS unit. Since that traumatic event, Tim had been her lifeline. She had never imagined herself caring for a man as much as she cared for him, her lovely bloke.

54

'Darling,' she said, 'you're still the best thing that ever happened to me. Where are you exactly?'

'Still at Maidstone Hospital,' said Tim, 'but getting discharged tomorrow and accepting two weeks leave before rejoining my hairy lot in France. I'll be with you tomorrow afternoon and staying the whole fortnight. Rosie said OK. We'll have some fun, shall we, Puss?'

'I can't wait,' said Felicity. 'Listen, what about these bloody flying bombs? You mentioned in your last phone call that they're making Maidstone shiver and shake.'

'Maidstone's in the flight path of most of them,' said Tim, 'but none of them stop. They buzz the place, and it vibrates, but they carry on to London. Some secret weapon. Fiendish. Flying kippers would be kinder, and they'd land well-cooked and ready for the table.'

'Cut Hitler's head off when you reach Berlin,' said Felicity.

'Not until he's been boiled in oil,' said Tim.

The conspirators in Berlin were committing themselves, though not to boiling the Fuehrer in oil. The right kind of man had come forward to volunteer for effecting the swift despatch of Hitler. This was Colonel Claus von Stauffenberg, who had all the soldierly qualities so valued by the regular German Army. A tall, fine-looking officer with an exuberant personality, he had fought in the Polish campaign, in Italy and North Africa. In North Africa, he had been badly wounded by a land mine. He lost his right eye, part of his right arm and two fingers of his left hand. He recovered, overcame his disabilities to an extent that allowed him to stay in the Army, and when the first whispers of the conspiracy reached his ears by way of a friendly voice, he at once indicated his interest in any plot that could guarantee the death of the man he disliked intensely.

'We can hope, Herr Colonel, but can't issue guarantees, not until we find a volunteer who can get close enough to Hitler and use a foolproof method of killing him.'

'Give me time to think,' said von Stauffenberg. Days later, he announced by grapevine that he could find the opportunity and devise the method. Accordingly, he offered himself as Hitler's would-be executioner.

That gave a lift to the conspirators, and brought in some waverers, for the volunteer was a man respected and admired for his courage and intelligence. One could only admire him more in his willingness to undertake a mission plainly suicidal.

Von Stauffenberg, however, did not plan for a suicidal venture. He meant to survive and play his part in destroying the power of all those Nazis whose actions had shamed Germany and caused the Allies to declare they would be put on trial as war criminals as soon as Germany surrendered.

Hitler was at the top of the list.

Rosie was shopping in the village with Giles and Emily when Tim arrived at the cottage, and it Felicity who, in answer to his knock, opened

56

the door to him.

'Hello, Puss.'

'Tim?' As usual, dark glasses hid her scarred eyes, but her smile was very visible. 'Lovely to hear you're here.'

She was a living example of courage, thought Tim, in the way she had fought the shattering nature of her disability and rarely presented a bitter or downturned mouth. And she was a peach in her looks, her dark glasses even giving a touch of glamour to her appearance.

'I tried to phone you to let you know my arrival time, but couldn't get through,' said Tim.

'Oh, the damn thing's been out of order since your call yesterday,' said Felicity.

'Never mind, I'm here now,' said Tim. He put his valise down and took her into his arms. In her summer dress, she pressed close. He kissed her, ardently. Responding, she picked up the vibrations of his healthy body, which she knew comprised six feet of structured bone and whipcord muscle. But it was bitter to realize that the last time she had seen him was the last time she ever would. It made her want to fire burning arrows into the dark visage of the inimical fate that had destroyed her sight. However, she was not going to spoil the moment.

'I've really got you for two whole weeks?' she said.

'Not as exciting as me getting you,' said Tim.

'I'm not going to complain,' said Felicity. 'Rosie and the children are in the village, by the way. Rosie's shopping.'

'That's why you came to the door by yourself?'

said Tim. 'Well, I'm going to congratulate you for finding your own way. You're winning new battles all the time, you darling.'

'Come and watch me make a pot of tea,' said Felicity, 'then we'll get comfy and you can tell me all about what it was like on D-Day. I want to know.' She was firm about that. Having spent a year at Troon with 4 Commando, she had an affection for the rough, tough and fearsome exponents of total mayhem, and an abiding interest in all Commando operations. 'I can stomach the blood-and-thunder details.'

'But can our unborn infant?' asked Tim.

'Our unborn infant is only two months, and isn't receptive yet to war stories.'

They went through to the kitchen, Felicity leading the way, giving Tim the feeling that in surroundings she knew well, her blindness was no great handicap. She'd been fighting her good fight from the day she was admitted to that hospital near Farnham. What a girl.

'Felicity–' A knock on the front door interrupted him. 'I'll go this time, Puss,' he said.

The caller was a teenaged boy, accompanied by a bicycle. He wore a peaked blue cap and an earnest expression.

'Sir, asking I am if Mrs Chapman lives here,' he said.

'She does,' said Tim, 'but she's out shopping at the moment.'

'Ah,' said the boy, and extracted a buff envelope from his leather satchel. 'Telegram for her.'

Telegram? Oh, Christ, thought Tim, telegrams to wives in wartime usually meant only one thing.

'I'll take it,' he said. It was the last thing he wanted placed in his hand, but he had no option. The youth gave it to him.

'There we are, sir.'

Absently, Tim dug into his pocket, brought out a silver tanner and gifted it to the messenger boy as a tip. The boy thanked him profusely, mounted his bike and rode away. Your work on this commission is done, my lad, thought Tim. I've got to face up to doing mine, to giving this cursed thing to Rosie. Hell, is it going to inform her that Matthew's now a fallen war hero in Italy? Who'd be that kind of hero, a dead one? It'll devastate Rosie.

He returned to the kitchen, where Felicity had the kettle on, and had brought forth cups and saucers from the dresser, as well as a jug of milk and bowl of sugar from the larder. They were now set out in good order on a tray, providing another example of how well she could do some things without assistance. She was standing by the cooker, a teapot cuddled in her hands, the kettle steaming on a hot plate, and she was listening for the sounds that would tell her it was boiling. She heard Tim re-enter the kitchen.

'Who was at the door, Tim?' she asked, and Tim told her. 'Oh, my God,' she said, 'what else can be in a telegram in wartime?'

'I'm thinking of opening it, and telling Rosie what's in it,' said Tim. 'I might perhaps be able to break the bad news better than having her read it.'

'No, Tim, you can't open it,' said Felicity.

'Rosie would understand,' said Tim. He and

Rosie had always been close, always great friends.

'No, it's her telegram, Tim,' said Felicity, 'we'll just have to wait and agonize for her. Oh, hell, I feel ghastly, I don't think I can even fancy a cup of tea. It's too bloody bourgeois under the circumstances.'

'Leave it,' said Tim. He crossed to the cooker and switched off the hot plate control. At which point, a key was slipped into the front door lock. Seconds later into the hall came Giles and little Emily. Rosie followed with her shopping bag, and she and the children came through to the kitchen. There were terrible moments of discomfort then for Tim and Felicity, since Rosie's greetings for Tim were demonstrative, and Giles's pleasure at seeing his uncle was exuberant. It was difficult to cope with. Rosie, however, suddenly became aware that Tim wasn't too responsive.

'What's up, lovey?' she asked in the fashion of her late adoptive cockney mother, Emily. Rosie was a university graduate, intelligent and gifted, but identified first and foremost with her adoptive family and their values, and so had happily chosen marriage to her Dorset man, Matthew Chapman, in preference to a business career. Her corn-ripe hair, her deep blue eyes and her classical looks still made a striking woman of her at twenty-nine.

'I'd just like a private word with you, Rosie,' said Tim.

'Oh, dear, am I out of favour?' smiled Rosie, and went with him into the parlour. Tim closed the door to keep the kids out for the moment.

'Rosie, this came for you ten minutes ago,' he said, and showed her the telegram. Rosie looked at it, but did not take it. Her face tautened.

'Tim, I don't think I like the look of it,' she said through stiff lips.

'No, nor do I, Rosie love, but it's got to be opened,' said Tim.

Rosie took it, drew a breath and did what was necessary to extract the form. She read it.

THIS IS TO INFORM YOU YOUR HUSBAND CAPTAIN MATTHEW CHAPMAN ON LEAVE AND WILL BE WITH YOU JULY 10.

It was from a Captain J Roberts, officer in charge of records, the War Office.

Rosie stared at it, read it again, drew another breath and handed the form to Tim, her eyes brightly misty. Tim read the message.

'Bloody balls of fire,' he breathed, 'why the hell didn't he phone instead of sending a telegram?'

'It doesn't matter now,' said Rosie, eyes alight with blissful relief, 'doom, gloom and dread over, Tim, the tenth is tomorrow, and the phone's been out of order since you called Felicity yesterday.'

'Of course, yes, Felicity mentioned that,' said Tim.

'Someone from the GPO is coming to put it right. Oh, and I know Captain Roberts. I met him before he and Matt both embarked for Italy. He took a leg wound during a German air strike on the workshops, so Matt told me in a letter. It crippled him, but the Army found him a job at the War Office. Somehow, he must have got to

61

know Matt was on his way, and somehow Matt was able to signal him and to ask him to let me know. As he obviously couldn't get through on the phone, he sent the message.'

'God strafe all telegrams, though,' said Tim, 'this one gave Felicity and me a bad headache.' A bad headache. Could that compare with the Godalmighty stresses he and other Commandos had known during the fighting on D-Day and other days in Normandy? Yes, in its own way it could. The threat of what a telegram might do to his adopted sister had made its own traumatic mark on his mind. Tim cared deeply for Rosie. He loved his half-sister Eloise, but Rosie was pre-eminent in his family affections. 'I can do without any headaches at all,' he said.

'But everything's lovely now,' said Rosie. 'Matt will be home while you're here. We'll all get tipsy together on our store of cider. Our cider packs a punch, believe me.'

'Come on, let's tell Felicity and the kids,' said Tim.

'Oh, they all know about the cider, even little Emily,' said Rosie, heady with happy anticipation.

'Cider my eye, just tell them about Matt,' said Tim.

'Matt's going to have time to get to know Emily now,' said Rosie. 'Well, a week at least. Happy is the day, Tim.'

'Bless you, Rosie,' said Tim.

They rejoined Felicity and the children, and within a minute the kitchen took on an atmosphere of celebration.

Chapter Five

At five-thirty that day, Vi called Alice to the phone.

'Who is it?' asked Alice.

'Mr MacAllister,' said Vi.

'But it's Dad he needs to speak to about the boiler, not me,' protested Alice.

'Your dad's not home from work yet,' said Vi, 'and Mr MacAllister asked specially for you.'

Alice took the phone from her mum, who went back to the kitchen.

'Hello?' said Alice.

'That's yourself, Miss Adams?' said Fergus.

'Yes, it's me.'

'Sorry about not being able to get hold of the right-sized reconditioned boiler for you just yet,' said Fergus.

'Well, you must know how inconvenient it is having no hot water supply,' said Alice, 'but you should talk to my father about it, not me.'

'I'm not phoning about the boiler,' said Fergus.

'What, then?' asked Alice.

'About yourself,' said Fergus. 'Dancing no' being a favourite pastime of yours. I'm thinking the theatre's probably more your style, and that we might give it a go together.'

'Mr MacAllister,' said Alice, 'I'm thinking myself that you're trying to enter my private life. If I had encouraged you to, I could understand this phone call. But I haven't encouraged you in the least.'

'Aye, that's true,' agreed Fergus, 'but I'm a man with guid intentions, and when I'm able to offer help to a young lady in need of it, I'm no' too proud to offer.'

'I beg your pardon?' said Alice, and vibrations travelled into Fergus's ear.

'I'm willing to–'

'Mr MacAllister, all I'm in need of is an end to this war and a peaceful three years at university.'

'But there's playtime, y'ken.'

'Playtime?'

'I'll be frank,' said Fergus. 'I feel you're in serious need of some.'

'What?' said Alice, hardly able to believe this effrontery. The sublime cheek of the man. 'I'm in need of some playtime?'

'Aye,' said Fergus. 'All work when you're young will bring lines before you're thirty.'

'Am I hearing things?' said Alice. 'I must be. I mean, it can't be true, can it, that you're actually offering to take charge of my private life?'

'No, I'm no' offering that,' said Fergus, 'just a theatre seat. Is that your style, the theatre?'

'Do you mean Shakespeare?' asked Alice.

'No, I mean something to make you laugh,' said Fergus. 'The "Crazy Gang".'

'What?'

'Flanagan and Allen, y'ken, and other comedians like Nervo and Knox, and Naughton and Gold,' said Fergus. 'I've heard the audiences are rolling in the aisles, and I've two tickets for tomorrow evening's performance.'

Alice, of course, hardly saw herself rolling in the aisles, and neither did she feel she needed to.

'Mr MacAllister,' she said, 'how many more times must I tell you–'

'Dinna tell me again,' said Fergus. 'Will I call for you tomorrow evening and take you, or will I leave you to all work and no play?'

Alice calmed herself.

'Mr MacAllister, I suppose you're trying to be kind,' she said, 'but I really am too committed to my studies to find time to go to a theatre with you.'

'A pity,' said Fergus.

'No, you don't have to feel sorry for me, I assure you,' said Alice.

'Understood,' said Fergus. 'I'll take my land-lady instead.'

Alice had seen his landlady once. A full-figured woman in her thirties. Alice had thought her a bit tarty.

'Well, thank you for inviting me,' she said, 'and although I can't accept, I do hope you both enjoy the evening.'

'Aye, fair enough,' said Fergus, 'but dinna try too hard not to enjoy yourself now and again.' The pips went then. He was using a public phone box. 'Guid luck, Miss Adams.'

'Goodbye,' said Alice, and the line went dead.

That, she thought, had surely convinced the man she did not need playtime.

The matter came up over supper when Vi mentioned to Tommy that Alice had received a phone call from the man from the Gas Board.

'Fergus MacAllister?' said Tommy, at forty-four a man of healthy and vigorous appearance.

'Yes, him,' said Vi.

'Not about our boiler, was it, Alice?' said Tommy.

'No, Dad, about going to the theatre with him tomorrow evening,' said Alice.

'Eh?' said Tommy.

'Well, that was nice of him,' said Vi.

'Alice, you're actually going out with the bloke?' said Tommy, looking surprised but pleased.

'The bloke, Dad, is a Scotsman I believe to be quite kind basically, but he has a mistaken idea I'm in need of a social life. I'm really not in need of that at all.'

Tommy's expression changed, and he regarded his daughter in a puzzled way. Exactly how, he wondered, did Vi and me produce one like Alice? Even Boots with his education never talked like that when he was nineteen. It sounded like she was reading dialogue from some book. He exchanged glances with Vi, and Vi made a little face.

'Anyway,' he said, 'this theatre outing. I don't suppose it's the sort of thing anyone's actually in need of, but you might find you'll enjoy it.'

'Yes, I'm sure you will, Alice,' said Vi.

'Oh, I declined the invitation,' said Alice, 'and he's taking his landlady instead.'

Vi sighed, and Tommy looked at the ceiling in the hope of finding something to help him believe what he had just heard. Finding nothing, he said, 'Alice, you turned him down?'

'I thanked him for inviting me, Dad, but said my time was fully taken up with my studies.'

Tommy regarded the ceiling again.

'It's not natural,' he said. The ceiling offered no response. It just looked blank. He tried Vi. Vi made another little face. 'Well, I suppose it's her own life, Vi,' he said.

'Yes, she has to live it her way,' sighed Vi.

'Oh, come on, you two,' said Alice, 'I'm perfectly happy.'

'Pleased to hear it,' said Tommy, who would have had a word with Boots, if his elder brother had been available. You could always talk to Boots and get good advice from him. A bloke needed some real good advice when his only daughter at the advanced age of nineteen looked as if she was going to end up married to a set of books. Ruddy hell, books. I've read more than a few in my time, and so has Vi, but living with them? I ask myself, what sort of a life would that be?

General Ludwig Beck, retired but very much revered by the Army, took a phone call from Dr Carl Gordeler, the action man working feverishly to co-ordinate the conspirators.

'*Herr* General, I have news–'

'Wait. Should you be using the phone?'

'This phone, yes. It's quite safe.'

'Are you sure? Is anything safe from the eyes, ears and noses of Himmler's ferrets?'

'*Herr* General, the news I have for you concerns the attitude of the *Reichsfuehrer* himself.'

Reichsfuehrer SS was the official title of Himmler.

'Attitude? Attitude?'

'Towards our objective, *Herr* General. He consented to be interviewed, to listen to a resumé of events that clearly showed him that Hitler and his associates are leading Germany to disastrous defeat. Himmler offered us no support, but neither did he threaten to oppose us. He will stay silent and await the outcome.'

'I am to believe this of Himmler?'

'The *Reichsfuehrer*, *Herr* General, can see the light. You know and I know that Hitler is an abomination to the Allies. They will hang him rather than treat with him. Not that he will ever ask them for an armistice. Himmler will. He thinks, the self-deluded idiot, that he's acceptable to the Americans and British, and is ready to approach them. He'll ask for terms, and will do so as successor to Hitler in the event that the *Fuehrer* is eliminated.'

'In place of a madman, we are to have Germany's chief executioner?'

'I think not, *Herr* General. We have agreed to arrest the whole gang at the right moment. Himmler, Goering, Bormann, Goebbels... As our new head of Government, we shall ask you to approach the Allies. But it's a great help, isn't it, that Himmler is turning a blind eye to our endeavours?'

'Let me know who will be responsible for organizing the take-over of all important installations immediately the venture has succeeded,' said General Beck. Had he not been a man of failing health and no great powerhouse as a plotter, he might have pointed out that if the

68

attempt to depose or destroy Hitler failed, Himmler would at once turn on the conspirators and mastermind the arrest and death of all of them.

'Edwin,' said Chinese Lady to her husband on his arrival home from his Government job one evening, 'these doodlebugs.'

'These infernal machines, Maisie?' said Mr Finch, a key figure in British Intelligence, despite being seventy.

'They're getting to be a chronic nuisance,' complained Chinese Lady. 'I just don't know if I'm coming or going, if it's best to stay in and not go out or what. Does the Government know when they're going to stop?'

'I don't have that kind of information, Maisie,' said Mr Finch, whose fine head of hair was now silvery.

'Well, see if you can find time to ask the Government, Edwin.'

'Find time, yes, I'll make a note, Maisie.'

'I don't suppose you'll be able to ask Mr Churchill himself, but someone might know. Mind, I don't want you to do a lot of worrying.' Chinese Lady gave her distinguished-looking husband a little pat. He'd suffered a brief breakdown from overwork earlier in the year. 'Wait till it's convenient to ask.'

'Till it's convenient, yes, Maisie.' Mr Finch smiled.

'Only our neighbours, Mr and Mrs Rowlands, were telling me they're thinking they might have to live permanent under their kitchen table, which they've made their shelter. It's grievous for an old couple like them, Edwin.'

'I know, Maisie.' Mr Finch smiled again. Mr and Mrs Rowlands were both sixty. A man could smile about a wife who, at sixty-seven, had a conviction that she was not old herself. Having endured the privations and worries of the First World War for four years, she was putting up with this one in characteristically resilient fashion. There were, of course, the moments when she worried about the serving members of her family, and the all too frequent occasions when she carried on about Hitler. She had said he was worse than the monster she'd read about in her *Sunday Express* once, a warlord called Jungle Dan. Genghis Khan, Maisie, said Mr Finch. Yes, that was him, insisted Chinese Lady, I just said so.

That same evening, her youngest son, Sammy, profit-conscious businessman, faithful husband and doting dad, spoke to his wife.

'I tell you, Susie, these doodlebugs are blowing heads off. They're dropping like – yes, like what?'

'I know what you mean, Sammy,' said Susie, still an attractive woman at thirty-nine, and currently working on the problem of how to remain at that age for another five years, say. 'They're not like the gentle rain from heaven.'

'Blow me, Susie, that's a bit of high-class talk,' said Sammy.

'We all learned something about *The Merchant of Venice* at school, didn't we?' said Susie.

'Oh, Shylock and the other lot,' said Sammy. 'I

always reckoned Shylock was a good business
bloke who got unlawfully done out of the bargain
he made. Suppose Marc Antony did lose his
pound of flesh–'

'Antonio, Sammy.'

'Well, some Italian ice-cream bloke,' said
Sammy. 'If he'd had to give his pound of flesh
they could've filled the hole up with a bit of ox
liver and put sticking plaster over it, couldn't
they? A bargain's a bargain, once you've shaken
hands on it, Susie. Shylock didn't get gentle rain
falling on him, he got drowned by a bucketful of
legal codswallop. Well, that's what Boots told me
once in his educated way.'

'I don't think Boots would have talked about a
bucketful of legal codswallop, Sammy.'

'No, like I said, he used educated words, Susie,
and I translated. You have to do that sometimes
with Boots's wordage. Now, what I was going to
say was that life's getting a bit dangerous again,
so next time we take Paula and Phoebe to see
Bess and Jimmy down in Devon, it might be safer
to leave 'em there, and you stay too.'

'What?' said Susie.

'You stay on with–'

'Yes, I heard you, Sammy Adams,' said Susie.
'Nothing doing.'

'Susie–'

'Nothing doing,' repeated Susie, although she
couldn't disagree with the fact that people were
at risk again from bombs. Flying bombs this
time. One couldn't have said people were getting
used to them after three weeks, any more than
they could have got used to walking through a

minefield every time they went out. Everyone was on edge, everyone living on their nerves, and life was awful for confused and frightened old people. But most Londoners were facing up to the menace. Well, they simply had to, there was no alternative, and so they were going about their lives and their work as normally as they could. Women as well as men had their jobs to go to. They were needed in the factories as much as men were. Yes, thought Susie, we've all got to get on with our daily grind. Otherwise it meant living under Morrison shelters twenty-four hours a day. But children could be spared the dangers. 'Yes, we have to make evacuees of Paula and Phoebe,' she said, 'but Sammy, you old love, you didn't think I'd agree to stay with them, did you?'

'Susie, I regard you as highly valuable–'

'I'm not a grandfather clock or a Chinese vase,' said Susie, 'I'm Mrs Sammy Adams. I love our children, all of them, but I agree, we shouldn't keep any of them at home out of selfishness. We've got to see that none of them suffer in a war that's not theirs, poor darlings. It's ours, Sammy, our generation's. We'll see it through together, like Lizzy and Ned, like Tommy and Vi. Vi told me only yesterday that Tommy suggested she might like to go and join David and Paul in Devon, but she'd never leave Tommy. Sammy, marriage is for better or worse, for you being with me and me being with you in good times and bad. So don't talk any more about me going to live in the country, there's a love.'

Sammy coughed.

'Susie,' he said, 'I just thought–'

72

'I know, Sammy.' Susie adjusted the knot of his tie, which didn't need to be. She fiddled with it patted it, then gave him a light kiss on his cheek. 'I know, Sammy.' She smiled. 'Bless you. We'll have to talk to Paula and Phoebe.'

They did so. They put the prospect of going to Devon to Paula and their adopted daughter, Phoebe.

'Us?' said nine-year-old Paula. 'Me and Phoebe go away?'

'It'll be like a long holiday, darling,' said Susie. A few miles west, a flying bomb crashed down to devastate the evening for a number of people near Honor Oak park.

'Please, I don't want a long holiday,' said seven-year-old Phoebe. 'I like being with you and Daddy best.'

'Still, you deserve a holiday, you and Paula,' said Sammy. Susie was right. The war was no fault of the children, no fault of any children anywhere. In one way or another, it was his generation, here and in France and Germany, that had let the war happen, and if he thought Germany's generation was mainly at fault, the fact was it had nothing to do with kids. (He was, unlike Boots and his step-father, fairly ignorant about the militaristic attitude of indoctrinated German girls and boys, for whom enlistment in Hitler's youth organizations was compulsory). As far as Sammy was concerned, kids deserved to survive, kids everywhere.

Boots would have told him the war was not so much the fault of the British people as that of politicians who refused to heed the repeated warnings of Churchill, and went for the option of peace at any price in the belief that Hitler could be trusted. Lloyd George, Prime Minister during the '14-18 war, had actually declared Hitler to be a great man in all he had done for the resurrection of Germany. Churchill, however, had never lost his suspicions of Germany's *Fuehrer.*

'Daddy, I don't think me and Phoebe are very keen,' said Paula, 'especially as you told us our summer holiday's going to be with you and Mummy in Cornwall.'

'Well, me pets,' said Sammy, 'you know about these bombs, don't you?' One couldn't prevent growing children from knowing.

'Beastly,' said Paula.

'But I don't fink me and Paula's afraid,' said Phoebe.

'We'll see how it works out, darlings,' said Susie. 'We'll bring you back as soon as it's safe, I promise.'

'Mummy, I don't think me and Phoebe want to go,' said Paula.

'Must we?' said Phoebe, looking doleful. Then she brightened and said, 'Mummy, couldn't you and Daddy be with us?'

'Daddy's got his business to run,' said Susie gently.

'But me and Paula want to be where you and Daddy are,' said Phoebe.

We've got to think again about this, thought Susie.

'Well, we'll see, darling,' she said, and spoke to Sammy when the girls were in bed that evening.

74

'It's a problem all right,' said Sammy, 'but—'

'Sammy, on the wireless the other night,' said Susie, 'someone was talking about these flying bombs, and saying the chance of any house being hit by one was a lot less than by a concentrated bombing raid.'

'So?' said Sammy.

'I don't think we should send Phoebe to Devon unless she really doesn't mind,' said Susie.

'She minds,' said Sammy.

'I've a feeling that without us, she might begin to think she's lost her parents again,' said Susie. Until the time when she and Sammy assured the tragically orphaned girl she was theirs, Phoebe had suffered the problems of acute loneliness, made worse by believing her dead parents had simply gone away and left her. 'Sammy, shall we risk it, shall we let Paula and Phoebe stay?'

'Well, I tell you, Susie, I'm going to be a seriously deprived bloke without them,' said Sammy, who had a very special affection for Paula because of the courage she had shown throughout the many bombing raids. And his love for adopted Phoebe was returned in full measure by the girl. 'All right, Susie, we'll chance it.'

Which delighted Paula and Phoebe. Flying bombs might have been a disturbance in their young minds, but in this house they were with their parents, grandparents and brother Daniel, and no five people could have given them a happier sense of security.

Chapter Six

Miss Patsy Kirk, American girl with her seventeenth birthday coming up, was keeping house for her widower father, Meredith Kirk, a radio newscaster, who was reporting the war from London. It was a first-floor flat, actually an apartment, in a house in Danecroft Road, off Denmark Hill. At the moment, she was in argument with her caring parent.

'No way, Pa, no way am I going to be packed off to a backwater again,' she said. She had spent nearly three years in an English boarding school not long after arriving in the UK with her father. 'I'll turn into a country cabbage, as green as they come.'

'Patsy,' said Pa Kirk, a handsome specimen of American maturity at forty-five, 'these goddamned flying bombs have got me good and worried.'

'OK, Pa, we share that worry with everyone else in London,' said Patsy, dark-haired, bright-eyed and chirpy, 'but no-one's running, and I'm not going to. My stars, how can I run while Daniel's still whistling the blues away?'

'Now I get it,' said Pa Kirk, 'our problem's at that young man's door, is it?'

'Pa, that's not fair,' said Patsy. She had met Daniel, the elder son of Sammy and Susie Adams, several weeks ago, and he'd become her

English fun guy, her first boyfriend.

'Fill me in,' said Pa Kirk, 'what's not fair?'

'Mentioning Daniel.'

'I think that was you, Patsy.'

'Me? But I didn't mention his door being a problem. You did. Was that fair? I mean, what's his door got to do with it?'

Pa Kirk smiled.

'Just a well-used allusion, Patsy.'

'Pa, it's not a problem to me.'

'It might be if it leads to a flying bomb busting a hole in this roof and you're close by.'

'Well, Pa, I guess that could happen the other way about,' said Patsy. 'The bomb could drop on you while I'm out shopping. But I'm not asking you to start running.'

Pa Kirk shook his head at her, but couldn't hide another smile. His daughter, his only child, was gutsy, as gutsy as any of the fired-up GI's who had recently stormed and captured the port of Cherbourg, vital to the Allies' sea-going lines of communication. But this guy Daniel, the young man he'd met, was she hooked on him?

'Let's get this straight, Patsy,' he said. 'Is it Daniel who's making you dig your heels in?'

'He's not making me do anything,' said Patsy.

'All the same, honey, are you hooked on the guy?'

'Hooked?' Patsy looked disappointed in her good old Pa. 'Pa, is that the right word to use in the land of the Brits?'

'Isn't it?'

'No. They don't ask if you're hooked. They ask

a guy if he's sweet on a girl, or if he's barmy about her.'

'Barmy?'

'Yes, Pa. It means is he off his chump about her.'

'His chump, Patsy?'

'Sure. His head.'

'I see.' Pa Kirk tried to arrange his face in solemn lines.

'Pa, I'm surprised you don't know that after all your years in London.'

'Well, I hope you'll forgive my ignorance. I'll rephrase my question.'

'No, it's OK, Pa, you don't have to.'

'I'd like to. So can I ask if you're—'

'No, of course not,' said Patsy, and made a study of the living-room's old-fashioned lace curtains. 'Pa, could we run to some new curtains?'

Pa Kirk mused. She didn't want to be asked about her feelings for Daniel. Perhaps they were something she was wrestling with. Just coming up to seventeen, she ran rather than walked through life, joyfully independent. Had a crush on a young English guy floored her and left her confused?

'I don't think the lease allows me to change the furnishings,' he said. 'But I'll change my approach to wanting you out of the way of these hellfire bombs. I'll let you think it over, Patsy, instead of pushing you.'

'Thanks, Pa,' she said. As to her feelings, she only knew that if she disappeared out of Daniel's life, he might find some other girl. If he did, she'd get sick. That couldn't be right, not for an up-and-coming all-American girl. It was that feeling which she was fighting, since she'd always imagined herself marrying an all-American guy. Even so, there was no way she was going to run. 'I just think we ought to stay and stick it out with our friends here.'

'I don't think I can genuinely quarrel with that,' said Pa Kirk, 'but when the war in Europe is over, as it may well be this year, I'll be recalled, and we'll go back to the States together.'

'Yes, Pa, of course,' said Patsy, 'I won't feel we're running away then.'

A flying bomb, breaking through RAF evening patrols, crashed down in Blackheath. It blew an enormous hole in the heath and shattered windows of houses around. Pa Kirk and Patsy did not hear it, but both were acutely aware that London and its environs were under this new and nerve-racking siege from the air. However, it was some consolation to Churchill to receive reports stressing the fact that the incidence of loss of life was minimal compared with that suffered from conventional bombing raids. Further, a new device being mass-produced by the Americans for ack-ack and field guns would soon be ready. This was what was called the proximity fuse, invented by a British scientist. Fitted into shells, it effected an automatic explosion when a shell was in close proximity to a target. A direct hit was not necessary. It was confidently expected to play an important part in the defeat of the flying bombs.

'Time I left for my evening newscast,' said Pa Kirk.

'Take care,' said Patsy.

'Will you be seeing Daniel?'

'I guess I'll drop in, Pa. Daniel and his parents told me I'm welcome any time.'

'And do you feel welcome when you're there?'

'Like one of the family, Pa.'

'Cosy?'

'Happy,' said Patsy.

She was on the phone almost as soon as her Pa had gone. It was answered by her fun guy.

'Daniel here.'

'Hi, Daniel, I'm coming round.'

'Good-oh. Who are you, by the way?'

'I know who you are, Smarty-Pants.'

'How's things, Patsy?'

'Pa's worried about the flying bombs.'

'So am I,' said Daniel.

'He wants me to go and live in the West Country.'

'Well, my parents talked about taking Paula and Phoebe there.'

'Daniel, they're little girls. I'm not.'

'Who's arguing? Never seen a girl growing up better than you. You'll be a woman a bit later on.'

'Oh, sure, it happens to all of us,' said Patsy.

'If it happens to me,' said Daniel, 'I'll need an operation.'

Patsy's giggles travelled like rippling gurgles over the line.

'Daniel, you're a kook. Listen, you don't want me to bury myself in green grass hundreds of miles away, do you?'

'No, but if that's what your good old Pa wants, I don't have the right to argue with him, do I, Patsy?'

'You could want to.'

'Well, I do want to, you bet I do,' said Daniel, 'but as a respecter of parental rights, I've got to let your Pa do the talking.'

'What about my rights at my age?' demanded Patsy. 'I'll be seventeen on Saturday.'

'I thought twenty-one was supposed to be the turning point,' said Daniel.

'Daniel, if you don't stand up for my rights, I'm coming round to knock your fat head off.'

'That'll upset my grandma. She thinks you're ladylike.'

'Ladylike? What's that?'

'Nice behaviour, kindness to old people, not using naughty words, and not eating one of your American candy bars in church.'

Patsy shrieked.

'I'm coming round right now,' she said.

'Come round the back,' said Daniel, 'I'll be in the garden, looking at my new potatoes. If you see a flying bomb on the way, don't interfere with it. Let it pass on.' He paused to let a sober note introduce itself. 'Hell, Patsy,' he said, 'they're deadly. They come over, we see one and pray for its engine to keep buzzing for a while longer, and what we're praying for is that it'll drop on someone else, not us. I can't say I've seen one myself yet, but Mum has and she prayed like mad.'

'Well, of course she did, Daniel, it was natural,' said Patsy warmly. 'But you're staying to face up to them, and so am I.'

'Good on you, Patsy girl,' said Daniel. 'Don't forget you and me, and the family, will be

81

enjoying a two-week break from them down in Cornwall. Last week in July, first week in August. You haven't forgotten you're coming with us, have you?'

'It's in capital letters in my diary,' said Patsy. 'Daniel, I'm coming round.'

She found him in the garden, looking at his flowering new potatoes. Daniel, in his eighteenth year, was lean, lanky and the active, ebullient son of his dad.

'They'll be ready to dig in a couple of days, Patsy,' he said.

'Will you give some to us, to me and Pa?' asked Patsy. He seemed very sober this evening. She thought what clean regular looks and fine clear eyes he had. And although he was just a bit on the skinny side, he was all of a young man, a healthy kind of guy, who never groped or gave her wet kisses. 'I mean, will there be lots?'

'Of course, and you can have all you want,' he said. 'By the way, my grandma says she'll give you a tea party on your birthday, if you'd like.'

'Well, thanks to the sweet old lady, Daniel, but Pa says he'll be home for a couple of hours that evening, and you'll join us, won't you?' said Patsy.

'Love to,' said Daniel, and she took his hand, wanting to communicate an affectionate willingness to stand shoulder to shoulder with him against the enemy. They communed there together in the light of the early July evening, lifting their eyes to the clear but vulnerable sky.

From over the Channel, a flying bomb, having

slipped through the air shield, buzzed above the summer fields of Kent on its way to London. Two RAF Beaufighters, on inland patrol, spotted it.

'Dead ahead at six o'clock, Stinky!'

'Reading you, Fatso!'

They swooped, closed in, let it pass on and opened up with cannon shells from a safe distance. The flying bomb exploded in mid-air, and fragments fell on the green fields.

In France, the aggressive and robust Americans had not only captured Cherbourg after days of fierce fighting, but the greater part of the Cherbourg Peninsular was now in their hands. East of them, Montgomery's British and Canadian armies had thrust forward, taken Caen in a two-day battle with the help of some American divisions, and were now in a position to prepare for a powerful offensive aimed at driving the German armies out of France. The Germans, as Montgomery had anticipated, were bringing in divisions from other areas of the Normandy front, determined that, having lost Caen, their new line would be held. It meant weakening their army that was facing the Americans west of Caen. Monty wanted to claim the credit for that, but the American generals did not intend to feed his ego, which they considered was already over-inflated. Monty didn't think he had that kind of ego, simply a zest for being a front-runner. America's General Patton had the same kind of zest, and some observers felt he was going to play gutsy John Wayne all the way from Cherbourg to Berlin.

General de Gaulle, hero and Commander-in-Chief of the Free French armies, and the implacable foe of Pétain and his pro-Nazi clique, was back on his native soil, showing himself to the liberated people of Bayeux and other small towns. In these places, collaborators were being rounded up and summarily dealt with, and so were women who had taken German lovers. Their punishment was a haircut in public, which left them bald. It was not a pretty sight, the ruthless, humiliating shearing of their locks, but many French people had bitter memories of the shame collaborators had brought on France.

Although Churchill had been a staunch supporter of de Gaulle and his Free French from the time of the fall of France, the Frenchman, regrettably, was not in favour of Britain playing any great part in the liberation of his country. France and Britain were ancient rivals in their imperial quest for world power, and it would gall the French to be liberated by their old enemy. De Gaulle, therefore, strongly supported the Allied Command's plan for Montgomery's Army Group to take on the liberation of Belgium, Holland and Denmark, and to drive on to the Baltic. That would keep the British well away from Paris when that city was liberated. Churchill did not argue the point. He was mainly interested in the planned capture of Berlin, and so was Montgomery.

The skies above Normandy were commanded by the Allied bombers, fighter-bombers and fighters. *Reichsmarschall* Goering's *Luftwaffe*,

84

severely depleted by the transfer of squadrons to the Russian and Italian fronts, offered minimal resistance. German troop movements were constantly attacked from the air and thrown into confusion. Such was the awesome power and offensive capabilities of the American Air Force and the RAF, that some German commanders, including Field Marshal Rommel, were convinced that Allied air superiority was going to decide the outcome of all forthcoming land battles. Hitler, however, maintained a policy of no surrender, demanding that if the Allied invasion armies could not be thrown back into the sea, then no German divisions should yield an inch, and every German unit must fight down to the last man. The units composed of the *Fuehrer's* most loyal soldiers would probably do just that. Rommel saw such a policy as a useless sacrifice of fine fighting men.

Montgomery's Army Group, following the capture of Caen, was armouring itself for the new offensive against Rommel's army, the offensive which Montgomery predicted would lead to a great breakout of the Allied forces. British troops and their Canadian allies were snatching a brief rest after beating off furious enemy attempts to recover lost ground.

The headquarters of 30 Corps, spearhead of the planned offensive, were temporarily established in a chateau near a war-battered village some ten miles from Caen. Colonel Robert Adams, known as Boots to his family, was prominent as a logistics expert, one of a team of officers responsible for the movement and supply of troops. Headaches were numerous, for the steady flow of men and armour from across the Channel had cluttered up the beaches which were frequently shelled by German long-range artillery. However, at the moment, supplies were coming through satisfactorily, and Boots was taking time off from headaches to accept the job of interrogating eleven captured German officers one by one. He had the help of a fellow staff officer, Captain Ben Reynolds, an invaluable linguist. The Germans were stiff, polite and unforthcoming, giving only name and rank. Boots wanted to find out what their morale was like now that Germany was fighting on three fronts, in the east, in Italy, and in France. They refused to comment on the Allied landings or on the unpalatable fact that they had been unable to stem the invasion. They also refused to conduct themselves as if eventual defeat was on their minds, or to look as if it was, but Boots suspected they were shaken by events. He did not attempt to procure information which he knew would not be given. He did, however, put an out of context question to each of them, Captain Reynolds interpreting for the benefit of those who spoke neither French nor English. The question related to information Boots had received from a German soldier captured in Italy some months ago, and it was asked because the nature of the information was incredibly disturbing. The German, Corporal Hans Thurber, had spoken at length about what was being done to Jews at a concentration camp in Poland called Auschwitz.

Boots had never been able to get the horrific details out of his mind. So he asked his question of each of these captured German officers.

'What do you know of concentration camps run by your SS for the extermination of Jewish men, women and children?'

It was put unexpectedly but very deliberately, and with a steely glint in his eye.

Some answered briefly.

'Nothing.'

One officer said, 'I do not recognize questions based on a lie.'

The rest, including two officers of a *Waffen*-SS Panzer division, refused to make an answer of any kind. Boots noticed, however, a tightening of the lips of the *Waffen*-SS officers, both fine-looking physical specimens.

When all these prisoners were back under escort, Captain Reynolds asked Boots if he knew whether or not the more disturbing rumours about Jews and concentration camps were true. Boots said he believed them to at least be true about a particular concentration camp in Poland.

'What makes you believe that, Colonel?'

'Information from a German soldier, who received it from his brother, a member of an SS detachment running the camp,' said Boots.

'Doesn't that class as hearsay?' asked Captain Reynolds.

'Whatever, it bothered me, and it troubled the German soldier so much that he committed suicide,' said Boots. 'At the moment we've got our feet inside France. It's when we get them inside Germany that we'll find out the exact truth, and I've a feeling we're not going to like it one bit.'

Captain Reynolds regarded the Corps' logistics officer in curiosity. Colonel Adams, a fine-looking man of forty-eight, was known never to flap. He had a way of remaining unflustered in a crisis. Yet he seemed quite disturbed by what he knew of concentration camps, although he hardly needed to concern himself with something that would be handled by a special investigative unit.

'You sound as if you've got a personal interest in the matter, Colonel.'

'I have,' said Boots, thinking of the traumatized Hans Thurber and of the Jewish women and children of Poland, and what might have happened to the family of Rachel Goodman, a long-established Jewish friend, if Hitler had mounted a successful invasion of the United Kingdom in 1940. Germany's *Fuehrer*, however, had cancelled that and allowed Goering to use his bomber squadrons in an attempt to reduce Britain's cities to ashes. That having failed, he was now assaulting London with the V-2 rocket bombs. Boots had his worries about that, worries concerning the safety of those members of his family who were under daily fire.

The burly lieutenant in charge of the prisoners' detail put his head in.

'There's one more, Colonel Adams,' he said.

'Bring him in,' said Boots.

'It's a woman, sir.'

'What?'

'Female lieutenant of the German Women's Army Corps.'

'How the hell did a woman get taken prisoner?' asked Boots.

'Gave herself up, sir, by walking into the arms of a Somerset Light Infantry recce patrol.'

'Good God, she's a combatant?' said Boots.

'No, sir, just a bit peevish. Speaks good English and wants to talk to someone important. Says she's only come up against idiots so far.'

'Bring her in,' said Captain Reynolds. 'Colonel Adams is important enough.'

'Right, sir.' The lieutenant disappeared. He reappeared seconds later, escorting a woman in a skirted field-grey uniform. 'Lieutenant Trudi Lemberg, Colonel.'

Chapter Seven

The woman's uniform looked as if she had given it an unusually hard time, for it was badly creased and even grimy. Nor was she herself a picture to behold. She was without a cap, her corn-coloured hair was a dusty, tangled mass, her eyes sooty, her high cheekbones sharply etched against taut flesh, and she frankly seemed in need of a wash. Nevertheless, it wasn't difficult for Boots to imagine that if she hadn't been the worse for wear, she'd be worth a second look.

She came forward on supple, springy legs to stare down at him. He was seated at his desk, with Captain Reynolds standing beside him. There was an impatience about her, her sooty eyes dark with a suspicion that he was going to prove unsatisfactory.

In excellent English, she said, 'You are someone I can talk to, yes?'

'Wait,' said Captain Reynolds. 'Confirm your name and rank.'

'I have given my name and rank twenty times, each time to an English idiot who passed me on to the next,' she said. Her voice had a slightly husky note to it that some men would have found fascinating. Others might have said it spoke of late nights and too many fags. 'I have also given them to my escort, the fat officer, and he was an idiot too, telling me I had no right as a woman to

90

be in a combat zone. But very well, I am Trudi Lemberg, with the rank of lieutenant, and have been working with the administrative staff at the headquarters of General von Stulpnagel, Military Governor of France. I speak Russian, German, French and English, and wish to talk to Mr Churchill.' She eyed Boots challengingly. 'Are you important enough to arrange that?'

'I doubt it, but in any case, I think Mr Churchill's busy at the moment,' said Boots. 'Let me see, your General's headquarters are in Paris, so how did you come to be so far from there, and for what reason?'

'You are in command here?' she enquired.

'Lieutenant Lemberg, you're out of order,' said Captain Reynolds. 'Colonel Adams doesn't answer questions, he asks them.'

'What a fool you are,' said Lieutenant Lemberg irritably. 'What you want most from prisoners is information, yes? I have information.'

'Which you'd like to give to Mr Churchill?' said Boots.

'Of course.'

'You'll have to make do with me for the moment,' said Boots. 'Could you find the lady a chair, Captain Reynolds?'

Captain Reynolds supplied one, and the grimy, worn-looking woman sat down.

'Is there a cigarette?' she asked.

Captain Reynolds supplied that too, together with a light. She drew in smoke, expelled it and regarded Boots with female interest replacing suspicion. He was a distinguished-looking man with a very masculine appeal for women. He had

91

never been promiscuous, however. He had been completely faithful to Emily, his late first wife, and was just as faithful to Polly. He regarded promiscuity in husbands as an idiotic and certain way of killing a marriage, and as his mother's son he regarded marriage and the family as the stabilizing strength of society. Polly, knowing that, was an unworried wife.

Now he returned Lieutenant Lemberg's interested look with a slight smile, and asked, 'So how did you get here?'

'I walked,' she said.

'Walked?' said Captain Reynolds.

'Of course. Do you think I was given a car and a driver? Let me tell you.' She was, she said, from the Soviet of White Russia, her father's native land, although her mother was from Kiev in the Ukraine. Her father had German ancestry, and like herself, was fair-haired. When Hitler's armies invaded the Soviet Union three years ago, they quickly overran White Russia, and it was not long before men of the Gestapo and SS were clearing whole villages of their inhabitants and murdering them.

'Murdering the men?' said Boots.

'Did I say only the men? No, no. They exterminated whole families to make room for German settlers. Are you ignorant of Hitler's ambitions to colonize the Baltic countries, the Ukraine, White Russia and so on?'

'Do you mean they exterminated whole Jewish families?' asked Boots.

'Ah, they went first, the poor Jews. They were taken away, and they disappeared.' Lieutenant

92

Lemberg went on to say that her own family might have been murdered, but Himmler's SS found out that her father was of German descent, so he was sent to Germany to work in a factory, and she went with him because she had his German blood. Because the Germans needed workers, they were sending all White Russians of German descent back to where they said such people belonged. Her mother had no German blood, so they took her away and undoubtedly murdered her. She herself, twenty-one and suffering an interrupted university career, was separated from her father when they reached Germany, and after a prolonged medical examination, which humiliated and infuriated her, she was told she was a natural German with no diseases and could volunteer to join the Women's Army Corps. Volunteer, what a sick joke, when it meant either that or entering an establishment for breeding purposes. Or, as a third option, working for a *gauleiter* who was intent on bedding her, with or without her permission. During his final attempt to rape her, she pushed him off the balcony of his apartment bedroom in Cologne. Much to her pleasure, the fall smashed his head and his body and killed him. If she despised Stalin's commissars, as did most White Russians and Ukrainians, she hated Hitler's murdering Nazis. She left the apartment, returning to the hostel in which she was living with other approved foreigners, and from there she departed the following day for the Women's Army Corps training centre. With her went women of German blood from places like

93

Estonia and Latvia. They were escorted by Ukrainian Nazis. Many Ukrainians were fighting alongside the Germans against the Russians or working with Gestapo or SS police units. Concerning the death of the *gauleiter*, no Gestapo hyenas came after her, and she learnt from a newspaper that the man was judged to have committed suicide by jumping from his apartment. Ah, well, it could have looked like that and the end of the beast was well-deserved.

Her exposition was being given in her excellent English, but was punctuated frequently by little hissing imprecations in Russian or German or French, and Boots suspected she had all the erratic temperament of a true Slav, not a stoical German.

It was not necessary, she said, to describe her experiences in the Women's Army Corps, except to say nothing lessened her hatred of Nazis. Eventually, she was transferred to General von Stulpnagel's headquarters in Paris, where her linguistic talents earned her a commission. General von Stulpnagel was at least a correct German, and he had an intense dislike of the Gestapo and its brutal use of power when dealing with French Jews and dissidents.

Time went by and everyone in Paris began to wonder if the Americans and British would ever open a Second Front.

'Ah, then at last your armies invaded!' She put a kind of ferocious triumphalism into this statement, although almost immediately she fixed Boots with an accusing and belligerent eye, and said, 'What took you so long?'

'The right kind of preparations,' said Boots.

'It was very trying to my patience,' she said, 'but the Germans in Paris, ah, how pale and fearful they turned when they knew your landings were successful and that Cherbourg had been captured.'

Captain Reynolds coughed, and Boots said mildly, 'Pale and fearful? The Germans? Are you sure?'

'I concede, of course, that it was a feeling I had, and not what was actually visible.' Lieutenant Lemberg crushed her cigarette to extinction in the ashtray. 'Every German knows that Mr Churchill is a great warlord who will execute every criminal German officer on the day of victory and perhaps personally shoot Hitler.'

Captain Reynolds regarded the woman as if uncertain about her mental state. Boots was not thinking along those lines himself. She was theatrical, yes, but he was not yet prepared to disbelieve her and dismiss her.

'Are you sure?' he asked again.

'Of Mr Churchill and what he will do?' she said. 'Yes. He is the one man the Nazis have always worried about. I wish to go to England, to talk to Mr Churchill, and to stay there, free from Communists and Nazis. I am willing to marry an Englishman, if one can be found for me, one who is not an idiot or deceitful. I have heard the English are a perfidious race.'

'We have quite a few faults, as anyone who isn't English will tell you,' said Boots. 'Lieutenant, you still haven't explained how you arrived in this combat zone.'

'I told you, I walked.' Lieutenant Lemberg fidgeted, then said that as soon as it was obvious the Allied armies were preparing a massive offensive against the Germans at Caen, she left her desk at the end of her day's work and began a walk to Normandy.

'With a hundred and fifty miles in front of you?' said Captain Reynolds sceptically.

She insisted that was nothing, and less than nothing to any White Russian. She had a map and by constant reference to it was able to select routes that kept her off roads crawling with German Army traffic. She travelled mainly by night and rested by day. She discarded her cap, stole an old waterproof from a farmhouse, and wore it to hide her uniform. She could not risk being picked up and taken back to Paris as a deserter. They would decide she wasn't a good German, after all, and almost certainly shoot her.

She slept rough in her daily hiding places, and grubbed around for farm food, mostly carrots. She became aware of much daytime air activity, and sometimes the noise of swarms of planes kept her awake when she was trying to sleep, which was very irritating, but also uplifting, for she was sure they were the planes of the Allies. The Allies, British and American, were her fixed objective. They were people who encouraged neither Nazism nor Communism, political systems whose chief weapons of oppression were torture and death. At this point, Lieutenant Lemberg issued a spitting imprecation in Russian, which Boots supposed was to do with how she felt about Stalin. Either that, or it was part of an act. But no, he was still willing to reserve his judgement.

No-one, she said, was a greater upholder of political freedom than Mr Churchill. That was true, yes?

'It'll please him to have you say so,' said Boots.

'I will say so,' she declared, and resumed the recounting of her journey. She reached areas thick with German troops, and that made her more cautious than ever. But she triumphed, she said, for this morning she emerged from a wood and saw not Germans, but a patrol of British soldiers. She threw the waterproof away, and in her uniform delivered herself up to then. They gaped. They were thick in the head, not knowing whether to believe her and what to do with her. She was hustled toward the rear area by being passed from one group of soldiers to another, and the were all fools in the way they gaped and showed suspicion, but a least none attempted to rape her. Finally she was brought here. She hoped Colonel Adams was not like most of his soldiers, slow in the head.

'I hope so too,' said Boots. 'Tell me, am I to believe you worked at General von Stulpnagel's Paris headquarters?'

'Of course. I have said so, yes. Ah, but even there, and even with papers identifying me as German, I could not have spoken out of turn without running the risk of being sent to a concentration camp. In Paris, the Gestapo hover. They have ears against every wall, and it is an occupational pleasure to them, sending people to concentration camps.'

'What do you know about concentration camps?' asked Boots.

'That they are Himmler's best-kept secret,' said the travel-stained woman.

'What else?' asked Boots, and Captain Reynolds wondered if the Corps' logistics expert was stepping into territory officially exclusive to the Security Services. He was only required to establish the credentials of a prisoner, and to obtain anything in the way of useful military information if he could. A prisoner volunteering information of a different kind was passed on to Intelligence.

'Such camps are everywhere in Poland and Austria,' said Lieutenant Lemberg, 'and are places where the Nazis practise extermination.'

'Of Jews?' said Boots.

'Jews from everywhere, and dissidents from everywhere.'

'Is this what you wish to talk to Mr Churchill about?' asked Boots.

'About concentration camps?' Lieutenant Lemberg looked disgusted. 'What can Mr Churchill do about such places? Nothing until the war is over. No, no, I have something else to tell him, something truly important.'

'Important?' said Boots. He paused as a flight of Allied fighter-bombers, low in the sky, hit the chateau with shock waves of thunder. He waited until the noise died away, then said, 'How important?'

'It is for Mr Churchill alone, it is for him to say who else should know.'

'I see.' Boots gave her a straight look. 'Well, Lieutenant Lemberg, nine people out of ten here would be highly suspicious of exactly what brought you here, and why you're so set on seeing Mr Churchill.'

'I am a liar?' Lieutenant Lemberg was on her feet and waving angry hands about.

'What Colonel Adams means,' said Captain Reynolds, 'is that perhaps if we were to arrange for you to see Mr Churchill, you might push him off a balcony too.'

'Ah, that is his meaning?' Surprisingly, the woman from White Russia showed a smile. White teeth gleamed. 'Good. I like Colonel Adams, I think. Although he is insulting me, he is not another fool. He is wise enough to see that I might be an agent for the Gestapo with orders to kill Mr Churchill. But I am who I have said I am, the daughter of Gregor Ivanovich Lemberg, and I have survived Stalin's disgusting Communists and the ordeal of being surrounded by revolting Nazis for three years. Everyone in Europe who opposes Hitler thinks of Mr Churchill as the warlord capable of freeing them from the tyrant. I wish him to use his majesty to help me find my father when he has won the war.'

'His majesty?' said Captain Reynolds.

'His great state.'

'I think President Roosevelt of America might point out that his is the greater state,' said Boots. 'He has more of everything than Britain or Mr Churchill, and the war can't be won without all he has.'

'But it is Mr Churchill who has led the fight against Hitler, not Mr Roosevelt.' Lieutenant Lemberg glanced at Captain Reynolds. She was aware his attitude was sceptical. 'I am wasting my time talking to people who don't believe me.' She looked at Boots. He responded with an encouraging smile. 'If I could talk to you alone?' she suggested hopefully.

'Not possible,' said Captain Reynolds.

'We'll stretch the rules a little this time,' said Boots. 'Give me ten minutes with her.'

'It's on your head, Colonel, not mine,' said Captain Reynolds, and left the office.

'Lieutenant, I'll respect your confidences,' said Boots, although he knew he was not entitled to make promises of the kind she was after.

'I will trust you and tell you,' said the White Russian woman, 'and then you will understand why I must also tell Mr Churchill.' She leaned forward to address Boots in low, discreet tones. 'Colonel Adams, some German generals are arranging for Hitler to be assassinated, and General von Stulpnagel is among those at the head of the plot. It will happen quite soon, and then these generals will ask the Allies for peace terms. Field Marshal Rommel will go along with the decision to negotiate. How do I know this? I am sometimes compelled to share the bed of one of General von Stulpnagel's leading staff officers, and now and again he drinks too much and talks too much. You understand that, yes? And you understand that there is no need for the Americans and British to sacrifice their soldiers in an offensive, but to wait for Hitler to be killed and for the German generals to then ask for an armistice? And that Mr Churchill must be told so? Yes? Colonel Adams?'

Boots was staring in wordless disbelief. Lieutenant Lemberg no longer rated in his mind as credible. Second thoughts, however, suggested there was something very credible about her passionate outbursts, her expressed hatred of Nazis and Communists, and her several references to General Stulpnagel. He knew at this point that he was no longer entitled or qualified to examine her further, that she belonged to Intelligence headquarters.

He called for Captain Reynolds to return, and asked him to see that Lieutenant Lemberg was allowed to freshen up, and to be given food and drink.

'Then arrange for her to be driven to Bayeux with escort, would you, Ben?'

'Bayeux?' said Captain Reynolds. Boots nodded, and Captain Reynolds knew the destination was to be Intelligence headquarters.

'Why am I to go to Bayeux?' demanded the lady.

'From there,' said Boots, 'you can look forward to being taken to London.'

'Ah, so? Good,' said Trudi Lemberg.

An hour or so later, Boots handed a sealed letter to the escort, the burly lieutenant, and then said goodbye to the White Russian woman.

'But you should be coming with me,' she said.

'Unfortunately, my duties won't allow me the pleasure.'

'But you could make love to me tonight.'

'I think not, Lieutenant Lemberg, I'm happily married.'

Trudi Lemberg sighed.

'How disappointing,' she said, and left with her escort to enter the waiting car. She had entered Boots' life on a note of drama, and she departed with regret.

Boots, thinking her a slightly dangerous woman to have around, returned to his office with Captain Reynolds, to whom he had recounted her words about a plot to assassinate Hitler.

'I wonder, will Churchill and Eisenhower fall for her suggestion to postpone the offensive?' asked Captain Reynolds.

'Well, who knows what Intelligence will make of her, but I'd have thought the answer to that is "not bloody likely!"' said Boots.

Chapter Eight

While Boots was dealing with the White Russian woman, his wife Polly was entertaining Mr Tod Dowling in the kitchen of her wartime home in Dorset. Polly, soon to be forty-eight, nevertheless still retained a natural elegance and a sleekness of body that made her a woman of silky movements. Boots often thought she could be bracketed with Greta Garbo, whose movements, even on screen, exuded sexuality, although he had read once that this Swedish lady had rather large feet. Another difference was that Polly had an infectious and unfailing air of vivaciousness, while Garbo always seemed to be brooding on the difficulties of survival. Polly was a constant reminder of the Bright Young Things of the wild and restless Twenties. She had been one of them.

Mr Tod Dowling thought Polly a lady, since she always treated him like a gentleman.

'A brace, Mrs Adams?' he said.

'Yes, as a present to relatives of mine, Mr Dowling.'

'Ah,' said Mr Dowling, a wiry old country codger with a permanent expression of wishing to please, which he wore below the brim of his permanent headgear, an old tweed cap originally grey but now indeterminate. 'I won't say I can't run to a brace.'

'You're always so reliable, Mr Dowling,' said

Polly, grey eyes remarkably innocent at the moment.

'Say Sunday?' offered Mr Dowling.

'In the late evening, as usual?' said Polly.

They were talking about pheasants.

'Best, don't you see?' said Mr Dowling, who always delivered after dark.

'I do understand,' said Polly.

They were talking about poaching, and Polly, who could always stretch a principle or two, was as much in favour of opportunism as Mr Dowling was.

'Well, there's the durned old war and shortages,' said Mr Dowling, 'and there's eyes.'

'Yes, much the best not to deliver in broad daylight,' said Polly, 'or you'd have Constable Robbins knocking on your door.'

'Ah, that's a fact, that is,' said Mr Dowling. 'By the way, I hear one of they German prisoners of war escaped from a working party yesterday. Slipped away like a river eel from a pike.'

'I only know there are working parties this side of Creech village,' said Polly. 'I haven't had the doubtful pleasure of seeing them, or the one who's escaped.'

'Best for a lady like you to keep your distance from him, I reckon,' said Mr Dowling.

'With a spade in my hand, I could forget I'm a lady,' smiled Polly.

Mr Dowling chuckled and said, 'Well, I'll do me best for you regarding your order, Mrs Adams.'

'Thank you, Mr Dowling,' said Polly, 'and if you'd like to take a fresh crisp lettuce away with you, help yourself to one from my kitchen garden. I've grown some prize-winners this year.'

'Mrs Adams, you're a lady all right, and look it, that you do.'

'Well, don't ever catch me in my gumboots and my gardening smock,' said Polly, 'or you might change your mind.'

Mr Dowling departed with his opinion and his goodwill unchanged, and richer by one crisp lettuce.

Polly was due to take herself and her twins to Bere Regis in a few days, to see Rosie and Felicity and their husbands, both of whom were on leave. She intended to treat them to the pheasants. She was looking forward to the visit, for she hadn't seen Matthew or Tim for ages. Great balls of fire, she thought, look what marrying an Adams has done for me. It's turned me into a woman with countless relatives, and I always told myself that was something to avoid. But I've fallen into the trap, I'm a relative myself, an Adams relative. Ye gods, in time to come I'll be old scratchy Aunt Polly to scores of Adams kids, all little beggars, I'll be bound. And it doesn't bother me, I really am looking forward to seeing Matthew and Tim again.

It's hell, though, without Boots. The Army has first claim on him. I'm a woman deprived, and day after day I'm getting older and more haggard. Haggard? God, I hope not. Haggard is first cousin to skinny, and if there's one thing I'm sure of it's that Boots won't go overboard for a wife who slips through his fingers. He's old-fashioned. He believes in bosoms. I think I like that kind of old-fashioned belief in a man.

She and the twins just had each other for company these days. Her erstwhile companion and help, Kate Trimble, a lively and imaginative young woman, was now in the WAAF and no doubt within sighting distance of the war's most glamorous heroes – dashing fighter pilots. Polly smiled reminiscently, remembering the far-fetched stories Kate had weaved around them.

She heard Gemma and James yelling at each other in the garden, as they often did, but that never affected the fact that they were inseparable. Who would have thought she and Boots were going to produce such little darlings?

Little beggars?

Not my two.

The day also marked Miss Patsy Kirk's seventeenth birthday. Her affectionate Pa had given her a silver bracelet adorned with lucky charms, had hugged her, kissed her and then departed for town where, along with other war correspondents, he was to head for SHAEF (Supreme Headquarters of the Allied Expeditionary Force) to be given details of when they might be able to join the team of top newsmen already in Normandy. He hated leaving Patsy on her birthday, but had promised faithfully that he'd be back from town to spend a couple of hours with her and Daniel from six until eight this evening. Would that do? Love it, Patsy had said. True, in Boston a girl on her seventeenth birthday could expect to have a guy in a tuxedo call for her, give her a bouquet and a box of candy, then take her some place special. But this was England, where families had old-fashioned birthday tea parties, baths were still used, showers a rarity, central heating still a million light years away, and the country well into the fifth year of the war.

There were greetings cards from Daniel's family, and one from Daniel himself, together with a little packet containing a present. She read the card.

Happy Jolly Great Rapturous Seventeenth Birthday to my one and only American girl guy. Kisses from Daniel.

In the packet was a colourful and quite exquisite enamel brooch of two crossed flags, the Union Jack and the Stars and Stripes. Patsy loved it. She phoned Daniel early in the afternoon, when she knew he would be home from his Saturday morning's work.

'Hi, Daniel.'

'Happy birthday, Patsy.'

'Thank you, Daniel, and for the card. And the brooch... It's lovely, I'll keep it for ever, to remind me of the time when we licked Hitler together, which we will, won't we?'

'You bet!'

'Daniel, when a girl gets a brooch like that from a guy does it mean he likes her a lot?'

'I should think so.'

'What d'you mean, you think?'

'Well, I do think.'

'You think you like me a lot?'

'Not half.'

'Yes, but aren't you sure?'

'Sure I'm sure.'

'That's not the same as only thinking you do.'

'Well, I do.'

'Daniel, do you like me a lot more than any other girl you've ever met?'

'I should think so,' said Daniel.

'You only think?' said Patsy. 'Look, I'm not starting that stuff again.'

'Nor me.'

'But you tried to.'

'I only said—'

'I know what you said. Listen, you comic, do you or don't you?'

'Do I or don't I what?'

Patsy giggled.

'Daniel, you're a smarty-pants. But I love the brooch, I really do. Don't forget you're coming here at six, when I'm doing birthday eats for us. You, me and Pa.'

'I'm not going to forget, Patsy,' said Daniel.

'But I'll come round this afternoon and see you and your family for an hour, shall I?' she said.

'Good, wear something nice,' said Daniel.

'Daniel, I'm not dressing up.'

'I hope you will, Patsy. Grandma's old-fashioned, and she'll faint away if you turn up in just your birthday suit.'

Patsy gave a little yell, which travelled fast over the line and landed in Daniel's ear.

'That's the worst joke you've ever made, d'you know that?' she said.

'No joke, Patsy, Grandma's—'

'Daniel, shut up.'

'Is something wrong, Patsy?'

'Yes, your gobbledegook.' Patsy suppressed her fits. 'I'll be round in a while.'

'It's a fine day. I'll be in the garden, so come round the back, as per usual.'

'Daniel, I'm touched that you like me a lot.'

'I should think I do,' said Daniel.

Patsy shrieked and banged the phone down.

She was on her way to Daniel's home in Red Post Hill a little after three. The afternoon was warm and bright, white clouds high and running. Generally, however, the weather over Europe had been sadly indifferent, causing problems for the Allied invasion armies from D-Day onwards. That they had done so well was due to superb planning and execution, aggressive outlook of the commanders and men, and the unlimited courage of so many. Hitler had hoped to fling a spanner into the works with his flying bombs, but was failing. London was taking the flying bombs and carrying on. So was Churchill. Patsy, faithful to the eminence of President Roosevelt and the mighty aura of the Stars and Stripes, had nevertheless developed a happy admiration for Britain's Prime Minister, who had suffered some catastrophic setbacks without ever faltering in his leadership. Patsy felt she would always remember her years in England, the years when Churchill and his people had their backs to the wall. They'd be the kind of memories you simply couldn't forget.

Turning into Red Post Hill, she heard one of the buzzing monsters, the first over this area today. She stopped. So did an elderly gent on the opposite corner. They both looked up. The projectile could not be seen. It was high above the screening clouds. But they could hear that continuous buzz. Patsy glimpsed it after ten seconds or so as it came out of the thick curtain of white. It was a little east of Denmark Hill, coming from the Dulwich Village area, and travelling directly north to the heart of London.

'There's the bugger,' called the elderly gent.

'Hate it,' said Patsy.

'Devil's work, young lady, devil's work.'

The V-1 disappeared.

'I sure hope no-one gets in the way of it,' said Patsy.

'They'll be running all ways somewhere.'

'So would I be with that thing on my tail,' said Patsy.

'It won't win the war for Hitler, though, not now the lads are at him with their bayonets.'

'Bayonets?' said Patsy.

'Nasty things, bayonets, y'know. Keep going, young lady, keep ducking.'

'I sure will,' said Patsy.

She arrived at Daniel's home ten minutes later, her body alive from the walk, her dark hair a picture of springy curls. She wasn't into the wartime style of manufactured rolls. She went round to the back of the house and into the garden. There was Daniel, up by the vegetable plot. His family, like many others, helped to dig for victory by growing a fair amount of their own produce. He was talking to a fair girl in a light summer dress of blue. She was laughing, he was

110

smiling. Patsy checked at the totally unexpected. Daniel had never mentioned other girls. None in particular, at least. Who was this one?

The girl turned then and came down the garden as Patsy made her way up.

'Hi,' said Patsy.

The girl, much too pretty for Patsy's liking, stopped and smiled.

'Hello,' she said, 'I think I've heard about you, I think you're Patsy. I'm Philippa Wells. Pippa. Got to dash, but hope you're not going to carry Daniel off to America and the Wild West just yet. Cheerie-bye.' Off she went, a fleet nymph, leaving Patsy a little taken aback.

'Patsy?' called Daniel, and she joined him. A spade in his hand, his face touched by the sun, his blue eyes alert, he looked as if he belonged as much to the far-flung fields of America's Middle West as to an urban garden in London. Nearby was a trug containing light-skinned new potatoes. Others had just been unearthed.

'Hello, Patsy, Merry Christmas.'

'You're goofing. It's not Christmas.'

'No, right. Happy Birthday, Patsy.'

'I saw a doodlebug on my way here.'

'I think we heard the cursed thing,' said Daniel, and grimaced.

Patsy put the compulsive question.

'Excuse me, but who was that girl you were mooning over?'

'Mooning?'

'Yes. Who is she?' Patsy was green-eyed and couldn't help the demanding nature of her question.

111

'Oh, that's Pippa, a neighbour from across the road. She's at a private art college in Sydenham then she's going into the Wrens. There's only about six pupils. It's the war, as if you didn't know. Oh, yes, and her mother's having trouble with her electric steam iron. It's boiling over or something, and I've promised to pop across and have a look at it later to see if it's turning into a kettle. I've inherited my dad's interest in how things work, including domestic appliances.'

'She's not a girlfriend?' said Patsy.

'Who? Pippa? Not much, considering she's keen on a Navy bloke built like a battleship.'

'Daniel, you'd tell me, wouldn't you, if you had other girlfriends?' said Patsy.

'In this family,' said Daniel, 'you only have one at a time. Grandma wouldn't allow harems. She thinks they're heathen.'

'Well, good for Granny,' said Patsy. 'Listen, d'you know what that girl said to me? That she hoped I wouldn't carry you off to America just yet.'

'Oh, I suppose she meant not before I'd looked at her mum's electric steam iron,' said Daniel. 'I like the sound of America, by the way, but you're not actually thinking of doing that, are you?'

'Carrying you off? To Boston?' Patsy shook her head. 'You're too English for Boston. It's loaded with Irish-Americans, and they'd crowd you.'

'Jasus, is it me that's upset them?' said Daniel with an Irish accent.

Patsy laughed.

'Daniel, don't get too smart. Just be a nice simple English guy.'

'Simple. Right, got you, Patsy,' said Daniel.

Patsy laughed again.

'Daniel, I really do like my birthday present,' she said.

'The brooch?'

'Yes.' Patsy opened her handbag and extracted it. 'There, see how cute it is in the sunlight?'

'What's it doing in your handbag?' asked Daniel. 'It's for wearing.'

'I know that, you dummy. Pin it on for me.'

'Where?'

'On my dress, of course.'

'Where?'

'You choose, it's your present, your privilege.'

Daniel surveyed her bodice. It was very close-fitting, and Patsy knew it. Well, at seventeen, no-one could say she wasn't as well-developed as an all-American girl ought to be.

'Er – well,' said Daniel.

'What's with "er well"?' asked Patsy.

'Er – your bumps,' said Daniel.

'Bumps? Bumps?' Patsy struggled to keep one more fit at bay. 'What d'you mean, bumps?'

'I'm not complaining, Patsy, but they seem to me to be in the way.'

'Oh, you mean my boobs,' said Patsy.

Daniel coughed, very much like his grandpa did whenever grandma went unknowingly over the top. He knew about boobs, of course, and that they'd originated in America. It was bosoms that had originated in the United Kingdom, under the auspices of Queen Victoria. His Uncle Boots had said so, years ago. The regal old lady was firmly against legs being mentioned or seen, but she sanctioned bosoms. Boots had said that too, and Grandma had given him all kinds of looks, none of which he seemed to notice.

'Er – Patsy, you don't say words like that out loud unless you're ten miles away from my grandma. I told you, she's old-fashioned.'

'Daniel, you're a scream, and so's your granny. Come on, decorate me.'

Her dress had a white collar, so Daniel pinned the brooch at the neck, where it sparkled in the light.

'How's that?' he said.

'You're a nice guy,' said Patsy, touching the brooch. 'Have you been digging potatoes?'

'Yes, for you, I promised,' said Daniel. 'You'll like them for flavour.'

'Lovely,' said Patsy. 'Thank you, Daniel.' Her eyes, looking him over, flickered. 'Digging potatoes makes you look like a yeoman of England.'

'Where'd you get that from?'

'Books,' said Patsy. 'Don't you know your history? It's all about your yeomen. Ours is all about our fight for our inalienable rights and Henry Ford.'

'Well, good for good old Henry,' said Daniel. 'Come a bit closer and I'll give you a birthday kiss.'

'I'm dressed up,' said Patsy.

'Yes, I noticed,' said Daniel, and kissed her. Patsy's eyes shut tight, and she held on. So Daniel gave her another. She still held on.

'Patsy?'

'Yes, Daniel?'

'You're standing in the potatoes.'

'Who cares?'

'The potatoes, probably. Come and have a cup of tea and meet my cousin Edward. He's on weekend leave from the RAF and he's here paying a call on us. His girlfriend Leah is with him, so come and meet her too. She's a stunner.'

'A stunner?' said Patsy.

'A beauty,' said Daniel.

'So what am I, then?' demanded Patsy.

'You're my one and only American girl guy,' said Daniel, 'as mentioned heretofore.'

'Get you,' said Patsy.

A buzz-bomb dropped and exploded near Greenwich then, but as with so many others, they didn't hear it. They went into the house and there Patsy met Edward and Leah. She thought Edward a fairly serious young man, but he still had a sense of humour. They all had that. Daniel, his dad, his grandpa, his mother and his Uncle Ned and Aunt Lizzy, and now his cousin Edward. She supposed it was a family trait. As for Edward's girlfriend, Leah Goodman, Patsy thought her quite beautiful, a vivid brunette with marvellously melting brown eyes. No-one mentioned she was Jewish. No-one thought they needed to.

Chapter Nine

When Patsy was back home and had stored her new potatoes in the larder, Pa Kirk phoned to say he'd be with her at six pronto, and would be bringing an old friend.

'Pa? You mean an old flame of yours?'

'No, Patsy, an old friend of the family.'

'Who?'

'A pleasant surprise. So there'll be birthday drinks for four, Patsy.'

'You, me, Daniel and the pleasant surprise, Pa?'

'Right. By the way, one of those damned V-1's dropped into the Thames this afternoon and almost blew the river to blazes.'

'That could have been the one I saw.'

'As long as all you see keep going, seeing's safe enough, Patsy, but we'll have to think about getting you—'

'See you later, Pa,' said Patsy, and hung up.

Pa Kirk and the pleasant surprise arrived from town at ten-to-six, the latter in the form of an American GI, Private Michael Brady.

'I found him in the Irish pub in Victoria Street,' said Pa Kirk.

Private Michael Brady, whose Irish-American family ran an auto breakdown service in Boston, had been known to the Kirk family for years. Mike, a bit of a wild one up to the time he became

116

an enlisted man in 1942, was twenty-four, a typically large Yank with a round Irish face, round brown eyes, and the beguiling smile of his kind.

The smile leapt hugely at his reunion with Patsy. He'd last seen her just before she and her father sailed for the UK. She'd been close to fourteen then. Now, at seventeen, she was very easy on the eye in a dress of green, Irish emerald green, for sure. He confessed himself mightily taken with her, wished her a happy birthday along with the luck of the Irish, and presented her with a bunch of flowers, scented stocks.

'Oh, gee whizz, thanks for ever, Mike,' said Patsy.

'You're welcome,' said Mike. 'Patsy, you sure have grown up.'

'It happens to all of us,' said Patsy.

A double knock on the front door of the house startled Mike.

'Say, who's that rattling your porch?' he asked.

'I'll make a guess that it's an English friend of mine,' said Patsy, sure that Daniel had arrived.

'I'll go,' said Pa Kirk, and down he went. Patsy asked Mike what outfit he was in. Mechanical maintenance with an armoured division, said Mike, which was due to embark for France in a week or so. He was on leave right now, staying in an American-run London hostel for GI's. He sure hoped he wouldn't be in it, he said, if one of those hellfire flying bombs dropped on it. They were kind of unfriendly. Patsy said none of the English people around here would invite one to tea. Mike laughed. Noticing the brooch pinned to her dress, he said he was mighty fond of the

117

Stars and Stripes, and was trying to get to like the Brits.

'They're our allies now,' she said.

'Sure they are, Patsy, I've met some, and I'm over here, with a million other guys, to help win the war for them.'

'Oh, they need us, sure,' said Patsy, 'but we need them too, and their little old island. It's our springboard.'

Pa Kirk returned, accompanied by Daniel, and introduced him to the GI.

'Ran into this guy in town, Daniel. Old friend of ours from back home. Mike Brady. GI private. He's on leave. Mike, meet Daniel, a new friend of ours.'

'My pleasure,' beamed Mike, and shook Daniel hugely by the hand. Daniel had a firm, dry hand with a good grip of his own, but his fingers suffered torture from Mike's bone-crusher, then numbness.

'Mutual,' he said.

'Sure is,' said Mike.

'What d'you think of our island?' asked Daniel.

'Kinda small,' said Mike.

'It's a bit flat too,' said Daniel, as an oblique reference to the bombing raids and the V-1's.

Patsy thought he looked even leaner beside barrel-chested Mike. Still, he was just as tall, and he kind of equalled out with his self-assurance. He had any amount of that, and so did his family. His grandpa, his dad and his mother. Yes, and even his little sister, Paula.

'You ain't enlisted?' said Mike.

'I will be, in the New Year,' said Daniel. He'd be

118

eighteen then, and eligible for call-up.

'I gotta feeling General Patton might have finished the Krauts off by then,' said Mike.

'I've got a feeling of my own', said Daniel, 'that you might be right and that he won't wait for me. How will that rate, Patsy?'

'Lucky,' said Patsy, and laughed.

Mike's smiling eyes kept turning her way, which made her wonder if it would raise a few sparks in her English guy. If so, that would mean he had pretty deep feelings for her. Did she want that? She knew what she didn't want, competition from that girl he called Pippa.

'You're cuddling flowers,' said Daniel.

'Yes, they're from Mike for my birthday,' she said.

'I'll pour the birthday specials, Patsy,' said Pa Kirk, and he attended to the liquor while Patsy darted into the kitchen, taking her bouquet with her. The liquor turned out to be two bottles of Californian pink champagne, acquired by means happily known to American news hawks. The cork popped and hit the ceiling, and the champagne bubbled and fizzed. Pa Kirk said that as Patsy would have only one seventeenth birthday, it had to be OK for her and Daniel to enjoy a glass or two.

Patsy returned with a tray containing a platter of hamburgers, the main ingredients supplied by her Pa through another happy connection with American sources in London.

'I'm looking at hamburgers in this quaint old Limey apartment?' said Mike in heartfelt pleasure.

119

'They're hamburgers?' said Daniel.

'Spiced,' smiled Patsy. 'Have one, Daniel. There's more in the kitchen. Mike? Pa?'

'This is my first ever,' said Daniel.

'Your first hamburger?' said Mike. 'You've been missing out, and I'm sad for you.' He shook his head in sympathy.

'Don't be sad,' said Daniel. 'Well, what you've never had you've never missed, as the doctor said to the complaining hundred-year-old bachelor bloke just before he croaked.'

'A hundred-year-old has-been was worrying about dames on his deathbed?' said Mike.

'Well, I suppose he had long-delayed regrets,' said Daniel, and Patsy yelled with laughter. Pa Kirk smiled, and Mike showed a broad grin.

They munched their way through spicy hamburgers to which sliced tomatoes and lettuce had been added. They drank the champagne, and Patsy joined in the toast to her birthday.

'The champagne's getting up my nose,' said Mike. 'Is there a beer, Mister Kirk?'

'Sure,' said Pa Kirk.

The little party went on until Pa Kirk had to leave for town again. He took Private Mike Brady with him. Mike said a breezy goodbye to Daniel, and then exercised his privilege as a family friend by giving Patsy a bear hug and a kiss. He aimed for her lips, but Patsy turned her head and it landed on her cheek. He promised that as she'd made a great job of growing up, he'd look out for her when the war was over and they were all back in Boston. Patsy said that would be kind of nice.

'You all right, Daniel?' smiled Pa Kirk.

'I'm fine, and thanks for the champagne,' said Daniel. 'I'll stay and help Patsy clear up, shall I?'

'I guess that'll be OK,' said Pa Kirk.

When they had the apartment to themselves, Patsy asked Daniel what he thought of Mike Brady. Daniel said he thought he could get to like the bloke. Patsy said everyone liked Mike, and Daniel asked if that included President Roosevelt. Patsy, laughing, looked as if she and the sparkling champagne had achieved affinity at first go.

Daniel busied himself gathering up plates and glasses, and placing them on a tray. He knew Pa Kirk expected him to be a good guy. Pa Kirk was a caring and responsible dad, and had told him once that what went on at some American co-ed colleges was a hell of a worry to parents of female students. Daniel got the message, which he thought fair enough.

'Come on, Patsy, let's do the chores,' he said.

'OK,' said Patsy, and together they cleared up, washed up and dried up. Patsy then said they could listen to the radio if he'd like to stay on a while. Daniel said he'd get off home and see her tomorrow. She went down to the hall with him to see him out. 'Daniel, thanks for coming, for being with me.'

'Thanks for inviting me,' said Daniel. 'It's the first time I've sampled hamburgers and champagne.'

'Help, I'd better see to Mike's birthday bouquet and find a vase for it,' said Patsy. 'Well, it sure was sweet of him to think of me.'

'Very welcome from an old friend who's going

121

to look out for you after the war,' said Daniel. 'So long now. Great birthday party. See you tomorrow.' He gave her a light kiss, opened the front door and away he went.

Patsy felt that wasn't at all satisfactory. Had she made a mistake in mentioning Mike and his bouquet? She actually began to worry. She couldn't settle, so after a while she phoned. Daniel answered.

'Hello?'

'Daniel, it's Patsy. Listen, I want to say something about the flowers from Mike. When I said it was sweet of him, I didn't mean it was especially personal to me.'

'Patsy, it's not a problem, is it, a bunch of flowers from an old friend? It's not to me.'

'Sure?'

'Sure, What makes you think otherwise?'

'You didn't kiss me when you left.'

'Didn't I? Half a mo', yes, I did.'

'Daniel, could you honestly call that a kiss?'

'Honestly, yes. What did you call it, then?'

'A peck in passing,' said Patsy, and heard him laugh. 'What's funny?'

'You are, Patsy.'

'Oh, sure, I'm cute. Daniel, can I come to church with you and your granny and the others tomorrow?'

'Yes, come and join us,' said Daniel. 'Grandma wants to give thanks that the Allies are in Hitler's backyard, and that they'll be knocking on his front door in a month or so to deliver him back to his dad.'

'His dad?'

'Satan himself,' said Daniel.

'Just for the hell of it?' said Patsy, and they both laughed. However, after she'd put the phone down, Patsy wondered if she was getting deeper into her relationship with Daniel than she'd envisaged. She still had dreams about an all-American guy, but something was interfering with the picture. Like getting upset about a peck in passing. And wanting to give a poke in the eye to a girl called Philippa Wells.

In Dorset, Captain Matthew Chapman was home from the war in Italy and enjoying a reunion with Rosie and his children. He was also getting to know Felicity, and to discover how devoted she and Tim were to each other. He marvelled at the way Felicity had learned to cope with her blindness, and at the fact that she had chosen to have Tim's child. He wondered just how she would manage. Rosie told him not to worry, that Felicity would manage very well, and that she herself would help if any little difficulties happened along.

She had asked Matthew a very pertinent question on the morning after the night of his homecoming.

'Matt, what have you been up to in Italy?'

'Repairing engines and keeping my head out of the way every time the flying Jerries hit us with low level attacks.'

'And?' said Rosie.

'And what?' said Matt, relishing the luxurious comfort of the bed and the delight of being in it with his one and only Rosie.

123

'And what? Yes, that's the burning question,' said Rosie. 'Your performance, my word, I can only think there was something brazenly Italian about it.'

'Brazenly? Let's see,' murmured Matt, 'I don't think that's a word well-known to us Dorset folk, us being a simple lot.'

'A good try, lover,' said Rosie, happy to have him home at last, even if only for the length of his leave, 'but I don't believe any of it, you shocker. There was nothing simple going on in this bed from the moment you climbed in.'

'A man can only do his best, Rosie.'

'My word, not half, you dog,' said Rosie.

'All my own work, Rosie, believe me.'

'I like hearing you say that. Incidentally, can I expect a similar performance tonight?'

'How about now?'

'Don't you dare, the children will be out of their beds and in here any moment.'

'Tonight, then,' said Matt.

'Tonight,' said Rosie, 'I'll be wearing armour.'

'There's an answer to that,' said Matt.

'Such as?' said Rosie.

'The can-opener,' said Matt.

Chapter Ten

It was still the evening of Patsy's birthday when Lizzy and Ned's younger son Edward took Leah Goodman to her home in Brixton after their visit to Daniel's family. He talked about the enormous raids being mounted on France by the RAF and American Air Force. The training of RAF pilots was at full steam here and in America and Canada, he said.

'Well, I'm glad you're here and not over there,' said Leah. She and Edward were addicted. To each other. They intended to become engaged when Leah was eighteen, providing her mother and grandfather raised no final objections. Edward was a young man earnest and principled, but his sense of humour saved him from being stuffy, something Patsy had noticed. Leah, inheriting her mother's lush velvety looks, was modest about her appearance but took pride in being totally supportive of her war hero, Prime Minister Winston Churchill.

'Leah, are you dreaming?' said Edward with a smile. 'We're there.'

Leah came to. Their tram was at the Brixton stop. They had enjoyed the visit to his grandparents, who always showed her the kind of affection that touched her deeply. She and Edward had also enjoyed meeting his cousin Daniel's American girlfriend, an engaging extrovert from the land of the free.

They alighted from the tram to walk to Hayter Road, which led to Leah's home in Winterwell Road. Brixton was relatively quiet, most shops shut, the time eight o'clock. In pre-war days, many would have still been open.

'Edward?'

'Yes, Leah?' said Edward, whose manly feelings were all committed to this lovely girl.

'Did you think Daniel's girlfriend attractive?'

'Why d'you ask?'

'Well, you spent a lot of time talking to her.'

'Listening, mostly,' said Edward. 'Well, she did a lot more talking than I did, and I liked her accent.'

'She's quite pretty,' said Leah.

'Not in your class, though.'

'D'you think Daniel's in love with her?'

'Well, if he is, Grandma won't allow him to go off to America with her.'

'But she couldn't stop him, could she?'

'She'll think of something.'

'She's a dear really, your grandma, isn't she?'

'I like her for liking you,' said Edward. 'It means she won't stop me going off with you.'

'Going off where?'

'Oh, somewhere just round the corner from her own home.'

'My life, we're going to live nearly next door, Edward?'

'Not really,' said Edward. 'But you'll see that when we start making our marriage plans–'

'Edward, we're not even engaged yet.'

'Well, we did say next year if we both felt the

same as we do now, and if that would give your mother and grandad time to be in favour.'

'Oh, Mama isn't going to mind, and although Grandpa isn't totally in favour, he'll accept it. I did tell you.'

'So you did, Leah, and I appreciated the way you confided the news.'

'Edward, you don't have to talk like a solemn old owl.'

'Yes, I do, Leah. Our forthcoming hopes are based on what will be a very solemn undertaking.'

'Oh, my life,' said Leah. 'But we can still have some happy laughs together, can't we?'

'Yes, let's say at four o'clock every Saturday afternoon,' said Edward.

'Just Saturdays at four o'clock?'

'Four o'clock all right for you?' said Edward.

'I hope it's all right for me to laugh now, because I'm going to,' said Leah.

'OK, just for now,' said Edward. Leah made do with a smile. 'Let's see, where was I? Oh, yes, when we start making plans for our marriage, the first thing Grandma will ask is where we're going to live.'

They turned into Hayter Road, walking in harmony.

'Edward, do I get a say on where we live?' asked Leah.

'Of course. It's your say as much as mine. But if we agree on Timbuctoo, watch out for ructions from Grandma.'

'I should want to live in Timbuctoo? I should say not. Edward – oh, listen!'

They turned at the sound that was now all too recognizable. The distant buzz of an approaching flying bomb. People in the main road, Brixton Hill, stopped and stared. As the noise increased, Edward and Leah saw the thing resolve itself in the sky, black, fizzing and awesome, and heading straight for the centre of Brixton. Seconds later, its power unit cut out and its frightening noise was gone, replaced by a silence that in its portent was even more frightening. Its nose dipped and it angled steeply earthwards. People ran. Somewhere, anywhere.

Edward and Leah, transfixed for a moment, saw it coming their way, low, lower, lower. It passed like a diving black monster over their heads, and they turned again, watching in horror as it plunged down over the roofs of houses on the left side of Hayter Road and, at about a hundred yards from them, exploded in a street. The roar was cataclysmic to the ear. It stunned the young people for a moment, but houses protected them from any blast. Edward came to and shouted.

'Oh, my God!'

He began to run, Leah with him. She knew, as he did, that the explosion had taken place within the area of her home. Her mother was there, and so was her grandfather. Billowing smoke soared into the sky. They ran fast, hearts pounding, feet pounding. It seemed like a race in which life or death could be determined by the time of their arrival. They turned into Bonham Road, and saw damage to windows and roofs. People were coming out of their houses and shouting. Edward and Leah raced for Winterwell Road, and checked on reaching it. The flying bomb had landed in the street itself. A huge hole gaped, smoking and smouldering. Houses were down, collapsed ruins. Dust eddied over the ruins and the street. Leah's home was at the far end. She and Edward ran again, they ran around piles of shattered bricks, slates and glass, and as they approached Leah's home out of the house came her mother and grandfather, Mrs Rachel Goodman and Mr Isaac Moses, a businessman of distinction. The windows of the house were shattered, and tiles were loose, but apart from that it was undamaged. However, in awful grimness, the adjacent house was now only half a house. Its top had been cleanly chopped off by the blast, and only the ground floor was standing. What was left of the top half was a huge pile of rubble behind the bottom half.

Leah ran into Rachel's arms.

'Oh, Mama!'

Rachel was a woman not only of rich looks, but of human warmth and sterling character. She had been bombed out during Goering's greatest blitz on London, and was now standing up to the nerve-racking experience of having her new home escape destruction by a mere whisker.

'We're fine, darling, your grandfather and myself – it's the old couple next door. I've phoned the ARP post.' It was an effort to be so calm, for the devastation midway down the street was appalling.

Edward, in company with Mr Moses, was staring at the half of a house. Its front door was

129

hanging from its hinges, and the interior seemed full of floating white dust. Elsewhere, people were staggering about around the rubble of ruined houses.

'There's an old couple in there, Mr Moses?' said Edward.

'Mr and Mrs Pascoe,' said Isaac in a strained whisper, the dust of the street settling on his silvery hair and on Edward's RAF forage cap. 'They rarely go out in the evenings, they prefer listening to their wireless.'

'Where's the wireless?' asked Edward.

'In their parlour,' said Isaac. 'Edward, we must take a look. We can't wait for rescue services to arrive.'

'Mr Moses, I'll go, you stay here,' said Edward, and ran at the hanging door. He pushed it aside and it fell with a crash.

'Edward!' screamed Leah, but he was already in the dust-laden passageway. He stared. The ceiling was gaping in places, joists uncovered, the evening light showing through. A door to his left was strangely quivering. He suddenly realized that all that was left of the house was similarly affected. Everything was quivering.

'Edward!' Rachel was at the front doorway, Isaac behind her.

'Stay there,' said Edward, 'stay there.' Christ, he thought, what's that? The sound of music? Music? He opened the quivering door, and there was the parlour, dust-laden, its furniture covered with shattered plaster. There were two people, a man and a woman, each in an armchair, bodies dust-covered, with bits of plaster in their laps, their heads slumped forward. On the mantel-piece was a wireless set, battery-powered, and the music was of a Saturday evening concert.

Edward pushed his way into the room. Ragged gaps in the ceiling revealed timbers split, cracked and creaking. He reached the woman. He made no attempt to examine her, not while the creaking and quivering were so portentious of new disaster. He lifted her. She was thin, and no weight. He carried her, stepping carefully over lumps of plaster.

'Edward?' It was Isaac's voice.

'Coming. Stay outside, outside the front door. The place is rocking.'

'I know, I know. Edward, be quick.'

Edward appeared, the old lady in his arms. He stepped gingerly through the passage. Rachel and Leah were outside, just beyond Isaac. Rachel, glimpsing Edward and his burden, ran forward. Together, she and Isaac gathered up the unconscious woman, whose dusty forehead showed a huge bruise.

'Lump of plaster must've hit her,' said Edward, and turned back for the old man.

The street was live with noise, with shouts, with people doing what they could for others. Men and women of the local ARP were appearing. A fire engine was racing up from the main road, its bell clanging. At which point, a flame shot up from the ruins of a house.

Edward, conscious of shuddering timbers and unsteady brick walls, went back into the parlour. The evening concert was now in full swing. The old man in an armchair slowly lifted his head and spoke in a husky whisper.

'Martha? Martha?'

'Come on, old feller,' said Edward, 'Martha's outside, waiting for you.'

He lifted him, a heavier weight than the woman, and it was a swine of a job to step over and around the litter and reach the parlour door. The cracked plaster at the centre of the ceiling split apart and fell with a muffled crash amid the music.

'Edward!' screamed Leah.

Edward, in the passage, trod grit and bits. Behind him, half of what was left of the passage ceiling fell in. At the rear of the place, the back wall collapsed. The rest of everything shuddered. Edward rushed forward, kicking stuff aside, and he almost catapulted himself and his burden through the doorway. At which point, all that was still standing broke up and fell. The wireless, falling with it, became silent.

The police were in the street, with ARP wardens and firemen. And the first ambulance had arrived. The moment Edward was released of his burden, Leah flung her arms around his neck and spilled tears on his chest.

'It's OK, lovey,' said Edward.

'No, it's awful.'

'Not so much for you and me,' said Edward, his forage cap with the white flash of a cadet smothered with plaster dust.

'Yes, that's what I mean,' said Leah, 'all those neighbours and their ruined homes. Oh, how many dead, Edward, how many?'

Fatal casualties were fortunately few. Just two,

as it turned out. It was Saturday evening and many people had been in cinemas, theatres or dance halls. Neither conventional bombs nor the V-1's could keep London's pleasure-seekers indoors on Saturday evenings. Two deaths, however, were more than enough to distress Leah anew. After a while, Rachel did the only thing that could steady shaken nerves.

She made a pot of tea. Over the welcome cups, they talked involuntarily of Germany's infamous war fanatic and his abominable lack of humanity. Rachel and Isaac were thinking not only of his flying bombs, but of his suspected elimination of Europe's Jews. One day, thought Rachel, when the Allied armies are inside Germany itself, some of our soldiers will come across the first signs of the exact truth. That thought coincided with the fixed belief of a man Rachel had always regarded as a treasured friend. Boots.

Rachel phoned Lizzy and Ned. Ned answered.

'Ned, my dear?'

'What's up?' asked Ned.

'We've had a flying bomb come down in our road,' said Rachel.

'Oh, my God,' said Ned, and swore bitterly under his breath. Forty-nine, his artificial leg a permanent memento of the '14-18 war, he was living through this present conflict with what endurance he could muster, while keeping to himself his feelings of hatred and contempt for all those people who in one way or another had brought it about. 'Oh, my God,' he said again.

'May He preserve you and yours, Ned,' said

133

Rachel, quiet and sober. She gave him the details. Four houses completely wrecked, several others damaged, and her own with almost every window blown out and a number of tiles shattered. Tragically, two of her neighbours had been killed.

'But you, Rachel, and Isaac, what about you two?'

'We're only shaken, and–'

'Listen, d'you know where Edward and Leah are? They were with Edward's grandparents this afternoon.'

'They're here, Ned, and quite safe.' Rachel explained that the young people had been in Hayter Road when the V-1 struck, that they'd actually seen it come down. She also told Ned how Edward had brought her immediate neighbours, an elderly couple, out of their wrecked house. 'Ned, my life, you can be proud of Edward. He's also been helping other people, with Leah. We can be proud of both of them. I'm letting you know he'll be a little late getting home to you and Lizzy.'

'Rachel,' said Ned, 'you're a gem for thinking of us in the middle of all your trouble. Let me say something now. If all your windows have gone, and you've lost tiles, you can't stay there. The Government's repair gangs will replace your windows and make sure the roof doesn't leak, but until then you and Isaac must come and stay with us, and I know Edward's grandparents will find room for Leah.'

'I would love that, Ned, staying with you and dear Lizzy, but my father has already made arrangements for the three of us to be with friends in Streatham until the repairs have been done.'

'You're happy with that?' said Ned.

'Yes,' said Rachel, 'and I must ring off now, I've so much to do. Goodbye, Ned, love to Lizzy.'

'Goodbye, Rachel,' said Ned, 'my regards to your dad.'

He recounted the conversation to Lizzy. Lizzy was aghast at the narrow escape of their son and Leah, and of Rebecca and her father. She was a bundle of nerves until Edward finally arrived home tired out but all in one piece. The family was as vulnerable as all other families in this kind of war. The death of Emily from a bomb in 1940 had proved that. Lizzy prayed that the successful invasion of France would bring the war to a quick end, and release her elder son Bobby and his French lady friend from their endeavours, wherever they were. Ned had long suspected they were working for the French Resistance movement, and Lizzy had finally begun to suspect the same.

Chapter Eleven

At Alençon, seventy miles south of Caen, the railway junction had been feeding German troops into night trains scheduled for the front. Its busy operations stopped one night, when all lines leading north to the Caen area were blown up in several places by three French Resistance groups which had joined forces – not always a popular move, since by and large most groups suspected the others had been infiltrated by Communists. German-occupied France was a country of many bitter political differences.

Two SOE agents took part in the crucial act of sabotage; Captain Bobby Somers, elder son of Ned and Lizzy, and Lieutenant Helene Aarlberg, FANY, a Frenchwoman. Both were explosive experts, and when their work was done at Alençon, they withdrew with the help of their Resistance friends to wait for London to keep its promise to bring them out. If the news of the successful Allied invasion of Normandy had exhilarated them, it had also persuaded them to accept a request from London to participate in putting out of action a rail link vitally important to the Germans. Sabotage of this kind was far more damaging than a hit-and-miss bombing raid. London promised to bring them home after that. Well overdue for a much-needed rest, the news that flying bombs awaited them did not reduce their longing for a break.

Now, in a retreat between Alençon and Mortagne, they were expecting a radio message that would offer them details of a flight home in a Lysander. They were holed up in an ancient, crumbling farmhouse, and members of the local Resistance group were keeping in touch with them. The night was clear, they were outside the place, sitting on an old bench against the wall, and sharing a bottle of red wine after an improvised meal, supplied by their contacts, a meal which Helene said only a starving dog could possibly have enjoyed. She herself, she said, had never been a starving dog, she'd been a woman all her life.

'That needs thinking about,' said Bobby, broad of shoulders, hard of muscle and quick and decisive in thought and action. Also bossy, in Helene's opinion. Even so, she would not have changed him. She was not in favour of dithery men, fat men, weak-boned men and bookish men. She was bossy herself, and accordingly there was sometimes a clash of wills and opinions. She found that kind of thing enlivening. Bobby found it gave him a chance to point out that men, being men, had to do what they had to do, and that women, being what they were, delicate, had to take note of same. That always made Helene yell with laughter. 'Is what you said strictly true?' asked Bobby.

'True that I'm a woman?' said Helene. She was twenty-three, strong, robust, and good-looking rather than pretty, with nothing of a coquettish Parisienne about her. A farmer's daughter – no-one could have disbelieved it. Bobby thought her a French Boadicea, and very much as head-strong as that ancient Iceni Queen. For all that, she was the woman with whom he wanted to spend the rest of his life. He might have to calm her down a little, but that need not be unenjoyable. 'Of course I'm a woman,' she said. 'Do you think you have been making love to a cabbage?'

She was on edge. So was he. They had been in France for many months. It was their fifth mission, and each had been a prolonged en-counter with the nerve-racking trials and dangers of Resistance work. Nor was every member of the Resistance a committed friend. Some were sus-picious of the political aims of the SOE, and considered it patronizingly English. Helene had no patience with such people.

'Idiots,' she would say, 'the SOE isn't English simply because its headquarters are in London. It's made up of all kinds, and will recruit anyone who can offer what is needed to help you lift France out of its despair.'

'All the same, London is too self-important.'

'London is necessary, you imbecile.'

Bobby passed the wine bottle to her. She drank from it.

'Wasn't there a time when you were a small girl?' he asked, teasing her.

'If you don't understand me, don't talk to me,' she said. The conversation was in French.

'I'm beginning to feel we've spent too much time together,' said Bobby.

'What do you mean?'

138

'We're getting on each other's nerves,' said Bobby.

'Is it my fault you are an unimaginative Englishman?'

'No more than it's my fault your father didn't smack your bottom when he should have done.'

'Ah, now you are insulting my father, who took you in when you were running from the Nazis and did much for you.'

'I'm not insulting him, I'm only suggesting he should have put you over his knees now and again.'

'That is an insult to think he would have ever done such a thing. I'm beginning to hate you. What an idiot I was to agree to marry you.'

'You needn't keep the agreement if you'd rather not.'

'Good. I've decided you are the last man I would want to marry.'

'Well, let's leave it at that, then,' said Bobby.

Silence for five minutes. In front of them, deserted fields were full of scrub, unseen in the dark night. France seemed to be at slumber. At their backs, however, in the north, the opposing forces were restless in their expectation of morning conflict.

'Bobby?'

'Helene?'

'You didn't mean that, did you, that you don't wish me to marry you? You promised it would happen as soon as London brought us back to England.'

'I thought you said–'

'How do I know what I'm saying when you're

139

upsetting me so much?'

'Well, to be fair–'

'Is it fair to tell me you've stopped loving me?'

'I didn't say–'

'You said you didn't wish me to marry you.'

'Jesus Christ,' said Bobby in English, 'stop turning me upside-down. God, what a woman. Don't fool yourself, you're going to marry me, even if I have to tie you up and bundle you into the church.'

'Bundle me in? What an idiot you are. No-one could do that to me.'

'Don't you believe it. And once the knot is tied, you madam, I'm going to chain you to the bedpost and feed you bread and milk. That'll calm you down.'

'Never. I'll break the chain, smash the bed and throw it out of the window.'

'I know you will,' said Bobby. 'I can look forward to that kind of marriage, can I?'

'Oh, but we shall be very happy, Bobby.'

Bobby laughed in low key, then stiffened. There were movements in the scrub. Someone was out there. Was it Pierre, their main contact as the local Resistance leader? Was he coming to deliver the expected radio message? Helene drew a sharp breath. They picked up their Sten guns lying on the bench, and came to their feet. From out of the night rushed a dog. With eyes used to the darkness, Bobby saw the animal as it made straight for Helene. He brought his Sten down hard and fiercely, smashing the dog's skull as it leapt.

Booted feet clattered over the hard ground, and

light sprang from a battery-powered torch. Bobby darted, bent double. Helene ran, but directly into the path of two SS men, who knocked her down. One man delivered a kick to her ribs. She gasped in pain.

Bobby was away. Two Gestapo men swivelled, one casting the beam of the torch in every direction. It failed to illuminate the fugitive.

'Let him go,' said one Gestapo officer. 'He's heading for the road. Our SS colleagues there will give him a welcome, while we get the woman to talk.'

The torch cast its light on Helene, prostrate on the ground, the SS men standing over her. The Gestapo duo advanced, and hauled her to her feet with brutal roughness. With blows and kicks, delivered more as a custom than a necessity, the four Germans sent her staggering into the ancient farmhouse. There, with the light flashing in her face, the Gestapo officers began to interrogate her in French.

'Who are you? A damned partisan, of course. You're a curse, all of you, here in France and everywhere else. Speak up, who are you?' A blow to her head caused her to expel a gasp, but she said nothing. 'There was someone with you. Who is he?' Another blow. 'Speak up, you whore.'

Helene faced them, all four of them, each one turned by the war and Nazi indoctrination into pigs capable of horrendous and terrifying acts, as she and Bobby well knew by now. Most people who worked for the Resistance were aware, for instance, of the barbarity of the SS officer, Klaus Barbie, who masterminded the activities of the

141

Gestapo from his headquarters in Lyons.

Where was Bobby? She felt terribly alone and frighteningly vulnerable. The back of a hand slashed across her face.

'Did you hear me, bitch? I told you to speak up.'

'I don't talk to pigs,' she said, and the hand struck her again, violently.

A shadow was suddenly framed by the open doorway. The door itself had long been used for firewood. A burst from a Sten gun sent bullets ricocheting off the stone floor.

'Drop! Drop! On your faces!'

The SS men reached for their machine pistols. Bobby fired at their legs. They crumpled and fell, and they writhed. Helene snatched the torch from the hand of one of the Gestapo officers, and turned the light on him and his colleague. They stared at Bobby, standing in the doorway, his Sten pointing at their legs.

'Go to hell!' one hissed, cursing the fact that they had mistaken the flight of this man for an act of lily-livered desertion of his female colleague.

'Drop on your filthy faces,' said Bobby, and the two Gestapo men went down on their knees, then flat on their faces. Nearby, the SS men were groaning, wounded legs fiery with pain. Bobby looked at Helene and gestured. She came to stand beside him. Below her beret, her forehead showed a livid bruise, and a similar bruise marked her left cheek. 'Who hit this woman?' rasped Bobby.

No answer. Helene pointed the torch first at the

Gestapo officers, then at the SS men.

'All of them,' she said.

'The mark of Himmler the angel?' said Bobby, addressing the Germans in searing French. 'Your New Order permits savagery towards women, does it? Yes, common knowledge. Do you have no bloody rules at all when taking a prisoner? How many have you murdered between you? How many include your own mothers? You're all quite capable of that. Well, your time will come. It's on its way, the promise of the Allies to deal with your kind. Here's something to be going on with, you animals.' And he fired a deliberate burst into the legs of the Gestapo officers. They jerked and screamed.

'My God,' breathed Helene, but Bobby, toughened mentally and physically by the war and sickened by what he knew of Gestapo and SS savagery, had suffered not a single qualm in pulling the trigger.

He and Helene were well away minutes later, hurrying through the scrub to make contact with Pierre in a village west of Mortagne, to let him know what had happened and their need of a new hiding place. Pierre obviously had a traitor in his group, someone who had informed the Gestapo of the farmhouse location. And that someone was a menace to Pierre and his whole section. Pierre, in fact, might by now have been taken.

'Are you hurting, Helene?'

'My ribs are sore, my head is sore, and I'm bruised in many places, so yes, I'm hurting.

Mother of God, how those Nazi Boches can kick.'

'We've a few kilometres to go. Can you manage?'

'I can manage, Bobby. I'm ashamed to say that for a moment I thought you'd deserted me.'

'It was the most practical thing to do, to separate when they rushed us. I tell you, we both need a long break. I hope to God that London can bring us out soon.'

'My hopes are consuming me. My God, how fierce you were with those Nazi pigs. But if they bleed to death, will anyone weep for them? Not even their mothers, of whom you spoke so dramatically.'

'They won't bleed to death if they crawl about and bandage each other, or their headquarters send men to find out what's happened to them. Go carefully now, their vehicle may be some-where around when we reach the road, and someone might be in it. Stay silent, my French chicken.'

They hurried on to the road, some half a mile from the farmhouse, and sure enough there was a vehicle, an open car, two SS men standing beside it. They were muttering and fidgeting, giving Bobby the impression that any moment they were going to investigate. He savoured the shock that would hit them when they reached the place. He and Helene veered silently away and disappeared into the darkness.

Pierre had not been arrested. He was blas-phemous when told of what had happened, and swore to find out who had betrayed the farm-

144

house location. Bobby asked if he had heard whether there had been any arrests among his group. Pierre said he had received no messages or signals to that effect.

'So, it was only us,' said Helene. 'The traitor picked on us because we're attached to London?'

'Perhaps,' said Pierre. 'I can't deny some Resistance men resent the people who sit on their backsides in London and give orders.'

'That's the attitude of collaborators, natural traitors to the Resistance,' said Helene.

'I'll find those in my group,' said Pierre. 'Meanwhile, another hideout must be found for you.'

Bobby said they would find one for themselves, that in fact they knew of one, from where they would keep in regular daily contact with Pierre until they were flown back to London.

'And you must find another place for yourself, since the traitor, whoever he is, might now think about pointing the Gestapo at you,' said Helene.

'A man can trust no-one these days,' said Pierre.

'Nor can a woman,' said Helene. She glanced at Bobby. 'But there are some exceptions, and that makes staying alive worthwhile.'

She and Bobby bivouacked under the sky that night. When she asked him why he had turned down Pierre's offer to find them a new hideout, he said, 'Something occurred to me at that moment, something he put into words a few seconds later.'

'What words?' asked Helene.

145

'That a man can trust no-one these days.'

'We can't even trust Pierre himself?' said Helene.

'After what happened tonight, we can't take chances, my French chicken.'

'Pierre is a good Frenchman, I think,' said Helene, 'but I agree, we can't take chances, Bobby.'

'I'm against anything that might mean we'd miss our wedding,' said Bobby.

'Oh, I'm as much against that as you are,' said Helene, and cuddled up to him.

The plot in Berlin was set. Colonel von Stauffenberg was the one conspirator who could get close enough to Hitler to kill him. Nothing could have been more propitious than his promotion in June to Chief of Staff, Reserve Army, for this required him to attend Hitler's full staff conferences at his headquarters in Rastenburg, East Prussia. Deep in a forest, these headquarters were known as the Wolf's Lair. From there, Hitler pursued his dictatorial conduct of the war, issuing orders that made no sense to his harassed field commanders. Colonel von Stauffenberg intended to carry out his mission at the next full conference, scheduled for the twentieth of July.

He was going to use the same kind of delayed-action bomb that Baron von Tresckow had used in the failed attempt last year. This time, however, the timing mechanism would be perfected to ensure failure was not repeated. Accordingly, at Army Reserve headquarters in Berlin, he waited with controlled nerves for the arrival of the day that would mark the end of the despot who had caused Nazism to become symbolic of terror and corruption. He had used thuggery and terror from the beginning of his rise to power.

Dr Gordeler, the co-ordinator, hurried about, seeking to establish which conspirators would be responsible for taking over Berlin's sources of Nazi power as soon as Hitler was reported dead. An enthusiastic worker for the cause, he was unaware that the Gestapo were keeping a suspicious eye on him. His enthusiasm took an indiscreet turn at times.

Himmler sat like a silent spider, making no move one way or the other.

He knew the proposed date.

The 20th of July.

Ten days away.

Chapter Twelve

After a dismal and howling morning of wind and rain, the inclement weather had blown itself out. The afternoon became warm and sunny, and at evening Dorset was bathed in soft summer twilight. Polly's twins were in bed and sound asleep, tired out after one more harum-scarum day. She wondered how two infants, not yet three years old, could summon up such a zest for life. They were a delight to her father and step-mother, who loved to see them regularly, but as things were at the moment, with London under siege from the V-1's, there were no weekend visits to Polly's parental home in Dulwich. On no account would she risk their precious young lives.

Hand-washing soft woollens at the kitchen sink, she began to turn her thoughts on her own life as it was at present. She had never imagined herself being enslaved by the demands of domesticity and parenthood at her age. Twins and kitchen-sink chores in her late forties, ye gods, what grinning little imp of fate had fashioned that for her? She should be feeling hard done by, but she wasn't, far from it. If that imp was still grinning, he was hitting the wrong note, for she was laughing. Well, as good as, and if only those frightful Huns of Hitler would give in so that Boots could come home, she would ask for nothing more than the span of three score years and ten for both of them.

The kitchen window, overlooking the back garden, gave her a view of colour softening in the twilight. When darkness fell, Mr Dowling would deliver the promised pheasants. He never failed.

Someone knocked on the front door at that moment. Had Mr Dowling arrived in advance of the night? He had never done so before. Polly dried her hands, took off her apron, and answered the knock. There was, however, no-one on the step. Very odd. The knock had been quite positive. She stepped out, advanced along the path and looked around. The leafy lane, leading to the road into the village of Corfe Castle, was empty. A suspicion rushed at her, and she hastened back into the house and through to the kitchen. The back door was open, framing a man, a man in a cap and an old overcoat that reached to his feet. An overcoat in July? He removed it then, and the cap, dropping them on the floor, and giving a little sigh of relief at being rid of them. Polly noted a worn field-grey uniform with sergeant's stripes. His head was cropped, his face weatherbeaten, his body lean, and his chin stubbled. For all that, he was a handsome swine. Damn, she thought, she should have locked the back door, but one didn't lock any doors in quiet Dorset villages.

'Good evening, madam,' said the intruder in good if accented English.

'You're a German,' said Polly, 'and a damned crafty one. You knocked on my front door and then let yourself in by the back door.'

149

'It was the best way, I think,' he said, closing the back door quietly. 'It avoided an argument at the front of your house.'

'I'm grateful, of course,' said Polly, cool and sarcastic on the surface. 'You're the escaped prisoner of war, aren't you?'

'That is so,' he said. 'But I mean you no harm. So do not worry that you're alone.'

'I'm not alone,' said Polly, and went ironically over the top with her next remark. 'My husband, parents and two cousins are all in the house.'

'Of course.' The German sergeant showed a faint smile. 'Have you a glass of water you could give me?' He made the request politely.

'I can give you a glass of water, yes,' said Polly, 'on condition you leave and give yourself up.'

'A glass of water isn't much to ask for,' said the German, 'or to give without making conditions.'

Polly filled a glass from the tap and placed it on the kitchen table. He moved then, quickly, taking up the glass and draining it at one go. Polly watched him, thinking of the twins upstairs, and of the threat he posed to them. In his position, he might not hesitate to use her children to coerce her into giving him help.

'You're now going to ask for food?' she said.

'I haven't eaten for two days,' he said. 'I've been hiding in the ruins of your castle, at the very top, from where I've watched the search parties.'

'Sit down, if you wish,' she said. 'You have the advantage, and I accept that. I'll give you bread, cucumber and apples, and wrap them up for you. You can take them away with you.'

'Thank you, madam,' he said, but did not sit

150

down. He was watching her as keenly as she was watching him. 'With your permission, I will eat now. Thank you.'

'I hope you're going to be sensible,' said Polly. 'I dislike people who make nuisances of themselves. The sensible thing would be to go and to take the food with you.'

'Ah, so?' The German nodded. '*Ja*, of course. But I hope you will permit me to stay until it's dark. Then, if you will drive me to a certain place–'

'Drive you?' said Polly.

'There is a car outside. Your children can come with us.'

'Well, damn you for a godforsaken swine,' said Polly, 'you've been watching this cottage.'

'It was the car that caught my eye and interested me more than an hour ago. Yes, I've been watching, sometimes from outside your back windows. Madam, I am still very hungry.'

Polly, thoughts on the twins, opened the larder door and brought out a loaf of bread and a bowl of apples, which she placed on the table. A cucumber from her vegetable garden followed. She took a bread knife out of the dresser drawer and looked at it. The German sergeant smiled.

'This knife is a killer,' said Polly.

'Yes, I can see, but you are not going to be foolish, eh?'

'You're the foolish one,' said Polly, the knife firmly gripped, its blade of bright, sharp steel glittering. 'You can't escape this country, you must know that. It's an island.'

'I have a friend, a contact, and hope you will be

151

kind enough to drive me to a place called Wey-mouth.'

He had to be referring to a German agent, thought Polly, or an agent for Germany. Some-one who could help escaping prisoners of war, or turn them into resident agents themselves.

She returned to the table, and cut slices from the loaf. They lay there, along with the cucumber and the bowl of apples. The German sergeant seized a slice and stuffed it into his mouth. He picked up the cucumber and bit it with crunch-ing bites. He was obviously very hungry indeed. He wolfed four slices of bread, demolished the cucumber and attacked the apples. In between he kept saying, 'Thank you, madam, thank you,' although his words were muffled by his mouthfuls.

'You really would be better off giving yourself up,' said Polly. 'The war is lost for Germany.'

He swallowed munched apple and said, 'Never. Germany will always fight on. We know our *Fuehrer* has ordered no surrender ever.'

'Your *Fuehrer* is a stinker and a monster,' said Polly. 'There's too much coming out of German underground movements not to know he's condoned murder and torture.'

'All lies, madam, all lies.'

'My husband who's an Army officer, has told me of a German soldier taken prisoner in Italy, who spoke of the activities of his brother, an SS guard at a concentration camp called Auschwitz in Poland. His brother confessed that thousands of Jews have been gassed and cremated there.'

'If your husband believed that, he was deceived.

152

Jews have had to leave Germany, yes, but to be resettled, not murdered. They are a miserable race. Hitler, I must tell you, is the greatest man who ever lived, and while he remains in command, Germany will never lose any war.'

'I feel sorry for you,' said Polly, 'for I'm sure you're going to be dreadfully disillusioned.'

'Our *Fuehrer* will never forsake the German people, and the German people will never forsake him.'

'You speak very good English,' said Polly.

'We have English lessons at the camp, given by one of our own men. It is to prepare us for the time when we shall conquer and occupy England.'

'You are living in fairyland,' said Polly.

'The camp is a fairyland?' said the German in smiling disbelief.

'No, your dreamworld of conquest,' said Polly, 'and your devotion to a monster. Don't you know Germany is seen as a nation of war criminals?'

'Ah, so? Seen by Churchill and the Americans? A joke, I think. Please to sit, madam, and let us pass the time until dark without quarrelling, when I will ask you again to drive me to the place called Weymouth.'

Polly knew what she was up against. A Hitler fanatic. She realized all too well that she must play for time in the hope that a search party would arrive. It was surely possible that he was being tracked down. He must have left some clues of his trek from Corfe Castle. Somebody must have noticed him and his impossibly long overcoat, worn on a warm July day and making an eccentric figure of him. But there had been rain, gales of rain, during the morning, of course. That was when he would have taken the risk of coming out of hiding.

'Very well, let's sit and talk,' she said.

They seated themselves, Polly opposite him, the bread knife still in her hand, her only real worry directed at her twins. She conversed with the German sergeant as calmly and as rationally as she could, but he proved impossible to reason with. He refused to give himself up and to accept any criticism of Hitler and the Nazi regime. He stood fast by his conviction that concentration camp horror stories were Allied propaganda, that Hitler was infallible, and the only Western leader who had been brave enough to have taken on the threat of Stalin and Communism. Polly pointed out that Stalin had not threatened Germany, but signed a peace pact with her, that Hitler broke the pact and attacked Russia without warning.

'That was to make sure Stalin did not attack Germany first,' said the German. 'Germany is fighting to save the world from Communism, and is being stabbed in the back by Britain and America. Madam, I don't wish to offend you, but that is cowardly and disgraceful.'

'So are your flying bombs,' said Polly.

'You think?' He smiled. 'An unpleasant surprise, yes? It is one of the reasons why Germany will never lose this war. Our scientists are superior and will help us win the last battles on both fronts.'

I'm talking with an idiot, thought Polly. A brainwashed one. If all we hear about concen-

154

tration camps is true, it's probably because Germany is full of brainwashed morons who do exactly what they're told, even murder. The superior have a right to eliminate the inferior, that kind of stuff. Ghastly. And what would this particular moron do to my children if I refused to help him? He seems civilized, but I think if he received an order to bludgeon a Jew to death, he'd do so, shouting 'Heil Hitler!' as the final blow fell.

'I think you're underrating the Allies,' she said. 'Tell me, when you meet this friend of yours tonight, how will he get you out of the country and back to Germany?'

'Did I say he would do that?'

'No, you didn't say,' said Polly, thinking she might be right in suspecting his contact would make him an accomplice in espionage work. 'But it's reasonable to suppose that that's what you're after, a return to Germany.'

'I can tell you nothing about that.' Regarding her in a friendly way, he said, 'You are an attractive woman.'

'I would appeal to Hitler?' said Polly.

'Hitler lives apart from women.'

'Well, I'm decidedly glad he lives apart from me,' said Polly.

'Your husband, what kind of a man is he?'

'A hundred times the man that Hitler is.'

'Ah, so?' A smile. 'A god?'

'A man in the best sense of the word,' said Polly.

'You are lovers as well as husband and wife?'

'Don't be impertinent,' said Polly.

155

'Madam, could you give me a little more bread?'

Silently, Polly cut two more slices, thick ones, and he ate them as if he was still ravenous.

They talked some more, the German alluding to the greatness of the Third Reich, and Polly declaring herself sceptical of such convictions. Time went by. Twilight turned to dusk, and dusk slowly invited the onset of darkness. When Polly suggested she should switch the kitchen light on, the German said not to do so yet.

'You intend to sit here in the dark?' said Polly.

'In ten minutes we can have light,' he said. 'Then I will ask you to bring your children down so that they can be with us in the car. You would not wish to leave them here alone, of course.'

'It's possible they would be safer here alone than with you,' said Polly.

'I am unarmed, madam. See, I don't even have the knife. You have it.'

Polly was still holding it.

'But you are bigger than I am,' she said, 'and less scrupulous, I fancy.' She jumped at the sound of the front door knocker. Mr Dowling?

'Don't answer it,' hissed her uninvited guest.

'I must. I know who the caller is. A local poacher, bringing me pheasants by appointment. He will know I'm in with my children and waiting for him. You can believe that, it's true.'

'Answer him, then, but I shall be at your back, and if you betray me, you will regret it. That is something for you to believe.'

Polly got up, switched on the kitchen light and walked into the hall, towards the front door, the

German following. He placed himself behind the door as she opened it.

'Ah, there you be, Mrs Adams, and here I be, with the goods, as you might say,' said Mr Dowling, a shadowy figure in the darkness.

'Well, thanks, Mr Dowling,' said Polly, 'but I can't invite you in, I've an unexpected visitor.'

'Ur?' said Mr Dowling, who never hung about, anyway, preferring to vanish as soon as he had delivered the goods to Polly or any other customer.

'I'll have to pay you tomorrow,' said Polly. 'Goodnight, Mr Dowling.' She closed the door on the confused countenance of the cheerful poacher.

'Well, durn me,' he said, regarding the blank door in disbelief. The lady hadn't even taken possession of the cardboard box containing two plump pheasants. And what was she doing with a knife in her hand? He had been able to see that much, although the hall was in darkness.

Polly returned to the kitchen, the German on her heels.

'Good,' he said. 'In a few minutes now, bring the children down.'

'And if I refuse?' said Polly.

'We will go up and bring them down together.'

'I am beginning to dislike you intensely,' said Polly, and sat down at the table again. He took the chair opposite her. His calmness made her uneasy. It spoke, she thought, of determination. How dangerous was the determination of a fanatic?

The handle of the back door slowly turned, and

quietly the door opened. The German had his back to it. Mr Dowling stepped in soundlessly, and Polly saw his stock-in-trade, a shotgun. He levelled it.

'Get your hands up, mister,' he said.

The German sergeant swivelled fast, and the chair crashed as he came to his feet. Mr Dowling poked the shotgun forward and curled his finger tightly around the trigger.

'Be careful with that,' said the German, seemingly resigned. But Polly thought he was ready to spring.

'Git 'em up, Adolf,' said Mr Dowling, 'or durned if I don't blast your head off.'

The German raised his hands high, but aimed a lightning kick. Mr Dowling, wiry and elusive, as befitted a man of his calling, hopped out of the way and swung his shotgun. It smacked hard against the German's forehead and downed him. He fell heavily.

'Bloody good show, Mr Dowling, you old darling,' said Polly.

'You use your phone, Mrs Adams, and I'll keep Adolf quiet,' said Mr Dowling. 'Thought it weren't like you, shutting your door in me face on account of an unexpected visitor. Unexpected, right, I thought, go round the back and see what's what.'

'What a lovely old sport you are,' said Polly, and went to phone the police. The police contacted the army, the army reacted speedily, and Sergeant Fritz Koeller, bruised and defeated, but still quite calm, was subsequently taken away by two military policemen backed up by the local constable.

158

Polly gave Mr Dowling a generous measure of whisky, and treated her nerves to the soothing effect of a helpful brandy. The twins had slept throughout, thank God.

'Nasty for you, Mrs Adams, worn't it?' said Mr Dowling.

'Illuminating,' said Polly.

'Ur?'

'If that German sergeant is typical of Hitler's Germans generally,' said Polly, 'I now know why the war has lasted so long.'

'It were brave of you, Mrs Adams, to face him out all evening.'

'I had no option,' said Polly, 'and he was never violent at any stage, only determined. He did nothing to actually frighten me. But his conviction that Germany will still be victorious was astonishing. More whisky, Mr Dowling? You deserve all that's left in the bottle.'

'I'm thanking you, but no, Mrs Adams. I'll be on my way now. The – er – the required goods are in that there cardboard box.'

'What a good friend you are,' smiled Polly, 'and a saviour for arriving with your shotgun in the nick of time.' She paid him, and he left with the comment that it was a privilege to know such a brave lady.

Polly drew a breath and slowly expelled it as she closed the door behind him. That moment she longed for Boots to be there.

The twins slept on.

Chapter Thirteen

Friday, the 16th of July

Mike Brady phoned Patsy.

'Hi, there, Patsy, how d'ya feel about a date?'

'A date?' said Patsy.

'Sure. Tomorrow evening. I'll pick you up at seven, say, and we'll shake a leg together. I know where the bands play here in town.'

'Well, that's nice of you, Mike,' said Patsy, 'but I've already got a date for tomorrow.' It was no special date, simply that she'd be going round to see Daniel, as usual.

'Patsy, I ain't having to believe it's that skinny guy, is it?' said Mike.

'It can't be,' said Patsy, 'I don't know any skinny guys.'

'Not the one I met on your birthday?'

'I don't rate Daniel as skinny,' said Patsy, 'just kind of slim, but with muscles in all the right places.'

'OK, Patsy, some other time, then, eh?'

'Say when we're back in Boston,' said Patsy, who saw that as a long way off.

'Sure,' said Mike, 'I'll stay in touch.'

'Take care when you get to France,' said Patsy, and rang off.

Trudi Lemberg was still in Bayeux, much to her

160

disgust. She was complaining bitterly about passing time, insisting that she knew the assassination attempt was to be made before the month was out, although she did not know the exact date.

Certain quarters and certain people in London had been made aware of her astonishing story.

In the bombproof basement of a certain Whitehall building were a number of makeshift offices. The deputy director of a branch of British Counter-Intelligence entered one. It was small, and in the absence of a window, ventilation was provided. A touch of comfort for one's feet was offered by a brown carpet, on which stood a desk and two chairs. If the room was not spacious, it was cosy, and cosiness was quite to the liking of its occupant, Mr Edwin Finch, the husband of Chinese Lady. The transfer of staff from the offices above had taken place a day or so after the first V-1's began their indiscriminate assault on London.

Mr Finch looked up from his desk at the entry of Sir Andrew Kerr, who brought with him his habitual air of geniality. He could, however, be rough and tough whenever inefficiency dented the reputation of his department.

'Morning, Edwin,' he said breezily.

'Good morning,' said Mr Finch, a compact decoding machine on his desk. 'To what do I owe the honour of this visit?'

'Pleasure of your company to begin with,' said Sir Andrew, pulling a pipe and tobacco pouch from his jacket pocket. Filling the pipe, he sat down and said, 'And to ask if you've heard about this plot by some German generals to thump Hitler.'

'I've heard, yes,' said Mr Finch. 'Thump meaning blowing his head off in some way or other?'

Sir Andrew put a match flame to his pipe and sucked. The tobacco glowed, and through wraiths of blue smoke he regarded Mr Finch thoughtfully. Mr Finch, seventy, was silver-haired now, and had been serving British Intelligence since the end of the First World War. Well past retirement age, he had elected to stay in harness until the war with Germany was over, and the department was happy to make full use of his experience, his talents and his unshakeable loyalty. His file was a comprehensive history of his life, and Sir Andrew knew he was German-born, had served as an agent in Britain for Imperial Germany before and during the '14-18 conflict, that he slipped back into Germany in 1916, only to realize he had been in the United Kingdom too long. His allegiance to Germany had undergone a radical change. He found himself critical of its Prussianized culture, and he was drawn back to Britain, returning by devious means in 1918 to offer British Intelligence information on Germany's great spring offensive that was designed to finally smash the armies of Britain and France. It failed, but the information made a credible figure of the German who had lived in England for many years under the name of Edwin Finch. All the same, he was thoroughly investigated before being accepted into British Intelligence and receiving, two years after his return to Britain, what he most coveted, docu-

162

ments that made him a naturalized subject of HM King George V. Since then he had been an invaluable cypher expert, as well as a field operative on occasions. An appealing characteristic of the man was that he had become more English than the English. He spoke the language like a native, dressed as impeccably as a West End clubman, and was completely devoted to the English family he had acquired through marriage.

'Do you know, Edwin, that the information was given by a woman claiming to be a White Russian?'

'I only know what has come through official channels as Top Secret,' said Mr Finch, 'that Hitler's life is being threatened by a clique of German officers. More than that, I don't know.'

'It seems', said Sir Andrew, 'that the woman, according to her story, was removed to Germany from White Russia with her father, who had German antecedents. She was subsequently invited to join the German Women's Army Corps, and eventually posted in an admin capacity to General von Stulpnagel's headquarters in Paris. There, apparently, through a drunken staff officer who had made her his mistress, she learned of the conspiracy. How does all that sound to you?'

'Imaginative,' said Mr Finch, 'but how did we come to lay hands on her? I presume we did.'

Sir Andrew puffed on his pipe, took it out and examined it.

'Apparently, she deserted her post when she knew our invasion armies were securely estab-

163

lished, made her way to our front line, gave herself up and was taken to 30 Corps headquarters'.

'30 Corps?' said Mr Finch, who knew full well that Boots was on the staff at headquarters.

'She was interrogated there by a staff officer, a Colonel Adams.' His pipe having gone out, Sir Andrew lit it again. 'Not one of your many Adams relatives, is he, Edwin?'

'I think you know Colonel Robert Adams of 30 Corps is my eldest stepson,' said Mr Finch.

'Ah, yes,' said Sir Andrew without batting an eyelid. 'What's he like?'

'Whimsical,' said Mr Finch. That the wild improbability of Boots's involvement was reality frankly intrigued him.

'Whimsical?'

'He not only tolerates fools and idiots,' said Mr Finch with a smile, 'he can find them amusing.'

'What's he like apart from that?'

'You can take my word for it, he's one of the finest men I've ever had the privilege of knowing,' said Mr Finch. 'Moreover, he's intelligent, and if there's a suggestion that he was taken in by this woman, allow me to be the first to dispute that.'

'The suggestion is,' said Sir Andrew, 'that the woman should be interrogated by someone who speaks both Russian and German, has a firsthand knowledge of Russians and Germans, and can therefore look deeper into her mind than the rest of us. Well, by God, a German Army plot to eliminate Hitler demands some attention. It seems the PM declared that although he disapproves in principle of the assassination of Heads of State, he won't shed any tears over the elimination of Germany's abominable *Fuehrer*. By the way, how's your general health, Edwin?'

'In a state of excellent recovery,' said Mr Finch.

'Would you accept an invitation to buzz over to Normandy and interrogate the lady yourself? I can't think of anyone else here better qualified to come up with a profitable examination of her credibility.'

Mr Finch smiled.

'A profitable examination of her credibility?' he said. 'The comprehensive nature of the English language,' he murmured, 'still entertains me. I'll go, of course I will, Sir Andrew. But why hasn't she been brought to London for interrogation?'

'Our contact with the Cabinet wants her to be kept where she is for the moment, on the grounds that you can work on her keenness to come here. Apparently, that's what she most wants, to come to London, to be given asylum and to see the PM.'

'Only the PM?' Mr Finch smiled. 'When am I to go?'

'We'll get you over this afternoon,' said Sir Andrew.

'I call that short notice,' said Mr Finch.

'You don't mind, do you? We'll drive you to your home in, say, ten minutes, where you can pick up the few things you might need, while letting your wife know there's a problem at the Government's Civil Service offices in Bath that needs your expert attention. You'll be away for two or three days, say. How's that?'

165

'I'll survive,' said Mr Finch, 'although my wife will consider the Government is heartless to send me all the way to Bath.'

'Give Mrs Finch my regards,' said Sir Andrew.

'Well, I just don't know,' expostulated Chinese Lady. 'What's the Government up to, might I ask?'

'It's only for two or three days, Maisie,' said Mr Finch.

'And he might find time to enjoy some of the sights,' said Susie. Sammy and Daniel were at work, and Paula and Phoebe at school.

'But all the way to Bath,' protested Chinese Lady. 'Susie, where is it?'

'In Somerset,' said Susie.

'I knew it,' said Chinese Lady. 'That's hundreds of miles away. Why couldn't the Civil Service people have rented extra offices in Clapham instead of Somerset? Edwin, you'll have to talk to the Government. Edwin? Susie, where's he gone?'

'Upstairs, Mum, to pack an overnight case,' said Susie.

'The way husbands disappear when you're talking to them, there ought to be a law against it,' said Chinese Lady.

'Don't I know it,' said Susie. 'That Sammy, he's as slippery as an eel sometimes. I don't know how many times I've found myself talking to a blank wall. Still, they've got their uses, Mum. And even if there was a law against them disappearing when you're talking to them, they're all crafty enough to get round it.'

'The trouble is, they're born not listening,' said

166

Chinese Lady, but with a twitch of her lips.

'Yes, can't help laughing, can we?' said Susie.

However, when Mr Finch reappeared with a small luggage case, Chinese Lady warned him that if the Government kept taking advantage of his good nature, she'd go up to Whitehall and talk to someone about it herself. She didn't suppose she could get to talk to Mr Churchill, but she'd insist on someone of some importance.

'Like Mr Attlee?' said Susie.

'Who's he, have I heard of him?' asked Chinese Lady.

'He's the deputy Prime Minister,' said Susie.

'Oh, he is, is he?' said Chinese Lady. 'He'll do. Are you listening, Edwin?'

'Maisie, you always command my full attention,' said Mr Finch. 'Must be off now, the car and driver are waiting.' He kissed Chinese Lady's cheek. He caught Susie's smile and kissed her too. 'I'll be back in a few days. 'Bye now.'

'Edwin, you just tell someone you're not to be sent off anywhere else hundreds of miles away,' said Chinese Lady. 'Susie, you're listening to me, I hope, you're hearing what I'm saying?'

'Yes, Mum.'

'Well, there you are, Edwin, Susie knows I mean what I'm on about, so I hope you do too. Edwin? Well, I just can't believe it, Susie, he's gone again.'

'Talk about blank walls, Mum,' said Susie.

A flying bomb fell and exploded adjacent to Clapham Common. If Chinese Lady had known she might have looked at Somerset more favourably.

Evening

Daniel was in the garden, doing some sterling work with the mower. He enjoyed a spot of gardening. So did his grandad, and the two of them were often at work together. Not this evening, however, for Grandpa had been called away. To Bath, according to Grandma, and she wasn't in favour. Like most places more than five miles from London, Bath was foreign to her. Southend was all right, and so was Margate, but Bath, well, she didn't think that would do Grandpa much good. In Daniel's opinion, however, the old lad was actually a picture of health these days.

In the house, young Paula and little Phoebe were shrieking and yelling. Sammy was having one of his games with them, and as usual Susie was asking for a bit of peace and quiet. A hopeless request. But Susie was never too insistent. She knew how close Sammy was to his sons and daughters, to Bess and Jimmy, still living in Devon, as well as Daniel, Paula and Phoebe here at home. The longer the destructive war went on, the more he saw all young people as the hope of the future. He had ambitious plans for Daniel, the brightest of their children.

As there were no troublesome flying bombs disturbing the evening at the moment, Daniel was enjoying his work with the mower. Susie, answering a knock on the front door, admitted a caller. Moments later she was at the open kitchen door, lifting her voice.

'Here's Pippa to see you, Daniel.'

'Honoured,' called Daniel, and out stepped Philippa Wells, the daughter of a neighbour. She advanced on Daniel, and he stopped mowing.

'Daniel, can you help?' she asked.

'Only modestly,' said Daniel. 'I don't repair roofs or chimneys.'

'Oh, nothing as tricky as that,' said Pippa. 'It's just that Mum wants to cut the lawn and our mower won't start, and Dad's away.' Her dad was someone who travelled about for the Ministry of Food, and was often out of sight for days. 'Can you come and get it going?'

Daniel was not only set on giving his grandad's back and front lawns a good going-over this evening, he was also expecting Patsy.

'I'll pop over on Sunday morning, Pippa,' he said. 'Will that do?'

'Oh, thanks a lot, we can wait till then,' said Pippa. 'You're a darling. There.' She kissed him. It was no more than a friendly kiss, but it happened just as Patsy entered the garden from the side path. 'See you Sunday morning, Daniel,' smiled Pippa, and went back into the house.

Patsy, carrying a linen bag with wooden handles, wasn't a bit pleased with her English guy, and approached him darkly. There was no other word for it.

'I saw that,' she said.

'Saw what?' said Daniel.

'You kissed that girl.'

'No, I didn't.'

'Yes, you did, you creep, and right in front of my eyes.'

169

'I dispute that.'

'Listen, Smarty-Pants, you can dispute an opinion, you can't dispute a fact. I hate sly guys, d'you know that?'

'I hate 'em myself,' said Daniel. 'One sort of crept up on Dad's market stall years ago, and nicked a bit of porcelain. Mind, I wasn't there myself at the time, not having been born yet, but Mum was, and often tells the story of how it happened and how Dad got the piece back. Actually, I wasn't only not there, I wasn't even a twinkle at the time. Well, Mum and Dad weren't yet married, or even engaged, so of course I–'

'Do you mind not trying to talk me into the ground?' said Patsy, distinctly upset and not prepared to disguise it. 'I object to you kissing other girls in front of my eyes. In fact, I object to you kissing other girls full stop. Does that sound unreasonable?'

'No, not a bit,' said Daniel, 'except it wasn't like that. Pippa came over to ask me to do something about their mower, and when I said I'd pop across Sunday morning, she landed a smacker on my nose. Or somewhere near my nose. Does it show?'

Patsy tried to keep her hot fires burning, but how could a girl stay like that when a guy with a sincere look on his face was inviting her to inspect his nose? It was a gag, a hoot, and she ought to sock him, but elected instead for an armistice.

'Daniel,' she said, 'you know I like it best when it's just you and me.'

'I like it that way too,' said Daniel. 'At least, I

think I do.'

'You only think? Can't you – oh, you're doing that again. Again.'

'No, I'm sure, Patsy.'

'You sure you're sure?'

'I think so.'

'Get this,' said Patsy, and she did sock him then, with the linen bag.

'Point taken,' said Daniel. 'What's in that bag, by the way?'

'A tapestry kit,' said Patsy, 'and I'm sitting with your mother and grandma to discuss the most suitable coloured wools for the pattern. Your mother says she has a boxful of unused tapestry wools and that I can take my pick.'

'What pattern is it?' asked Daniel, and Patsy smiled.

'Oh, it's a picture of General Washington and his horse celebrating victory over the British at Yorktown,' she said.

'That's it, is it?' said Daniel.

'Yes,' said Patsy. The punch line arrived. 'At least, I think it is.'

Daniel yelled with laughter.

'Good on you, Patsy,' he said. 'Listen, I've been thinking. How about if we put our bikes on a train to Westerham in Kent tomorrow afternoon, and cycle around the country lanes there?'

'Daniel, could we do that, you and me?' said Patsy.

'Easily,' said Daniel, 'we just need legs, and I've got mine and you've got yours. Yours are better-looking, but mine still work fairly good. And around Westerham, it's Churchill country. He's

171

got his home there.'

'Oh, great, I can't wait,' said Patsy.

'Good,' said Daniel. 'I'll finish the lawns now while you go and talk to Mum and Grandma about your knitting.'

'Tapestry,' said Patsy, 'tapestry.'

'Oh, yes, George Washington and his horse,' said Daniel.

'But don't be surprised if it turns out looking more like a scene of Venice,' said Patsy, and went into the house while the satisfaction of having the last word was still with her. A girl had to have the last word sometimes. She said so to Daniel's mother.

'Sometimes, Patsy?' said Susie. 'No, sometimes won't do. Don't settle for anything but every time. Now, let's have a look at your tapestry design.'

Chapter Fourteen

Earlier that day the promised reconditioned boiler from the Gas Board had arrived in a van at the house of Tommy and Vi Adams on Denmark Hill, and was unloaded by two men. Vi was at home, which allowed Alice the relief of staying in the background. The men went to work releasing the old boiler from its mounts, and fitting the replacement. It all took time, and Vi provided them with a pot of tea and some plain cake made from a wartime recipe.

Alice appeared while they were drinking their tea and having a sit-down. She looked at the men, who said good afternoon to her.

'Excuse me,' she said, 'but isn't Mr MacAllister here?'

'He would've been, miss, but wasn't able,' said one man.

'Wasn't able?' said Alice.

'No, nor capable, like,' said the other.

'Took a bit queer yesterday morning,' said the first.

'No, not queer, Percy,' said the second, 'painful.'

'Well, painful makes yer feel queer, Charlie,' said Percy.

'What kind of pain are you talking about?' asked Alice.

'Cruel,' said Charlie.

'In his back,' said Percy.

'Low down,' said Charlie, 'where you get lumbago.'

'Me old dad used to get that,' said Percy. 'Used to catch him bending, and took him hours to straighten up again.'

'Do you mean Mr MacAllister had an attack of lumbago?' asked Alice.

'No, not lumbago,' said Charlie, 'red-hot pins and needles, according to his landlady, who went and called the doctor, and the doctor called an ambulance and off went Fergie to King's College Hospital.'

'Where about six ounces of iron filings jumped out of his lumber yard,' said Percy.

'Lumbar region, Percy, lumbar,' said Charlie 'and I don't remember his landlady telling us they jumped out, did she?'

'Well, she got all the details from one of the hospital doctors,' said Percy.

'Me and Percy went enquiring, like, Fergie being a working mate of ours,' said Charlie, 'and his landlady told us they cut him open, and out come all those bits of shrapnel he's been carrying around with him ever since Dunkirk. Funny they all ended up in the one place, like.'

'He was glad to get rid of 'em,' said Percy. 'So would I 'ave been. Not good for yer, a load of iron filings in yer lumber yard.'

'Lumbar region, Percy,' said Charlie, 'don't I keep telling you?'

'Does it mean that Mr MacAllister is all right now?' asked Alice.

'Well, he's got some stitches, but he's not

174

feeling queer no more,' said Percy.

'What's happening to him?' asked Alice. 'Is he still in hospital?'

'He'll be out in a day or so, according to his landlady,' said Charlie.

'And right as rain,' said Percy, 'with ideas about going back in the Army. I'd join up meself, only me trouble and strife won't let me. Says I'm too old.'

'Well, we're both going on a bit,' said Charlie.

'Me?' said Percy. 'I ain't fifty yet.'

'Mr MacAllister's leaving the Gas Board and rejoining his regiment?' said Alice.

'He's hoping to, according to his landlady,' said Charlie.

'He's still a young man,' said Percy.

Alice went back to her studies, but stopped on the way to speak to her mother in the living room.

'Mum, you knew about Mr MacAllister being left with shrapnel in his body, didn't you?'

'Oh, yes,' said Vi, 'but there's been a change, he's had it removed. The men told me when they arrived.'

'You didn't mention it to me,' said Alice.

'Well, Alice love, I didn't think it was something you wanted to know,' said Vi.

'But I was naturally sorry about his kind of wound,' said Alice. 'I've read that a lot of wounded men in the last war were left with shrapnel in their bodies, and that it could be fatal. So I felt for Mr MacAllister.'

'Yes, he's a nice man,' said Vi, 'even if you didn't get on with him. The men told me he hopes to

175

get back to his regiment.'

'Yes, they told me that too,' said Alice, 'but one would have thought Mr MacAllister would have let us know himself instead of us finding out in a second-hand way.'

'Well, I'm blessed, I can't make any sense of that,' said Vi. 'How could he have let us know himself when he's still in hospital?'

'He could have sent a note,' said Alice, 'especially as he knew we were expecting him.'

'Expecting him?' said Vi, mystified.

'Yes, he said he'd help to fit the replacement boiler himself.'

'I still can't make any sense of what you're saying,' said Vi. 'You can't really think Mr Mac-Allister should have sent us a note from his hospital bed to tell us he was sorry he couldn't be fitting our boiler on account of having an emergency operation, can you?'

Alice fidgeted. She was pleased at the way things had turned out for Fergus MacAllister, of course, but for some reason she felt frustrated.

'Oh, well, perhaps not,' she said, and went back to her studies. Her frustrated feelings, however, interfered with her concentration, which put her into a bit of a paddy, for there was simply no reason why she should have such feelings.

Sammy was upset by the damage done to Rachel's house, and he didn't feel too good, either, about what had caused it, a different kind of air blitz. Since Rachel and her late husband, Benjamin, had been bombed out during the devastating raid on London in December, 1940, he considered Hitler's Huns had been guilty of a diabolical act of malice in landing a flying bomb on the doorstep of her new abode, or almost on her doorstep.

In the office, he had commiserated with her and Leah when they returned after he'd insisted on their taking a few days off. Rachel, as his general manager, and Leah, on his clerical staff, were both invaluable. Further, both were likely to become relatives on account of his nephew Edward's declared intention to become engaged to Leah next year. Next year would see him reach twenty-one, by which time Sammy reckoned Hitler's Germany ought to be well and truly sunk, and the young couple could enjoy a peacetime wedding.

'Sammy, we should be crying over some damaged tiles and our broken windows?' said Rachel. 'Think of the unhappy people who have had their homes destroyed, and those who have lost dear ones to these terrible flying bombs. Leah and my father and I have been giving what help we could to shocked neighbours. Ourselves, we've been fortunate, Sammy.'

'Yes, we have really,' said Leah, 'and we want to get back to work, Uncle Sammy.' She and her sister Rebecca had always regarded Sammy as an honorary uncle.

'Well, I won't say we're not up to our elbows,' said Sammy, 'or that we can do without you. So if you could help catch up on invoicing, Leah, and I could point your mum at the mountain of paperwork on her desk, I'd nearly be a happy man.'

'Only nearly?' said Rachel.

'Well, that doodlebug in your street has upset me considerable,' said Sammy. 'It might only have knocked some tiles off your roof and smashed windows, but I'm still not rapturous about it. It makes me feel Fatty's following you about.'

'Fatty?' said Rachel.

'Goering,' said Sammy. 'He's still in charge of Germany's air war, I suppose. He did a lousy job on you in the big London blitz, and he's just had a go at finishing you off. He must have had a look at your family's identity cards.'

'Sammy, he's following us about with his bombs because we're Jewish?' said Rachel with a slight smile.

'All the buggers in Berlin have got a nose for the people of Abraham and Moses,' said Sammy. 'Excuse my French, Leah.'

'Oh, I like your kind of French on this occasion,' said Leah.

'Well, don't you worry about Fatty, Leah,' said Sammy, 'he's coming to the end of being a headache to all of us. As my respected stepdad says, there's no way Germany can win the war now. Fatty's going to get the chopper, along with the rest of the gang, when our tanks roll into Berlin. So let's get cheerful and do some work, eh?'

'My life, Sammy,' said Rachel, 'I should believe there's something not cheerful about working for Adams Enterprises?'

'It's your business as well, Rachel, you being an important shareholder, and also a handy shifter

178

of Government forms in triplicate,' said Sammy. The firm's contracts with the Army, the RAF and the Ministry of Supply brought all kinds of forms into the office.

'One has to accept that although the war's caused shortages of many things, Sammy,' said Rachel, 'Government forms in triplicate are multiplying, but–' She checked, and they all froze at the sound of a flying bomb, the huge buzz penetrating offices and ears. Sammy thought at once that it had to be travelling just above rooftops, so huge was the noise. With Rachel and Leah, he stayed frozen for long seconds. While they all knew one only dived for cover when the power unit cut out, the vast buzzing sound seemed so close that they felt the projectile must be scraping chimneys and would touch and explode any moment. But it passed on. They did not know it was actually careering crazily on a low trajectory by reason of a developing fault. It roared on, the noise faded, and they expelled relieved breath. The V-1's faulty mechanism took it down, down, down, to crash and explode by the grace of kind Providence close to some desolate ruins of bombed buildings in South-wark. A pile of rubble danced crazily, bricks hurtled about, the blast raged on and a nearby residence shuddered and collapsed, taking roof, walls, glass and furniture with it. Fortunately, the sole occupant was out shopping.

In his office, Sammy expelled another breath.

'Jesus Christ,' he said, 'we're still alive, but what's it going to do to other people? It sounded so low that it's probably going to crash into

179

buildings while it's still buzzing, if it hasn't happened already.' He looked at Rachel and Leah, pale, shaken but bravely calm. Bloody hell, he thought, I'm near to actually believing Goering the Hun really is using his boxes of fireworks to follow them about.

'We're not going to run around with our heads covered, Sammy,' said Rachel quietly.

'No, my life we're not,' said Leah. 'So come along, Mama, and let's start work.'

She and Rachel did just that, while Sammy delivered a few words of encouragement to the rest of his slightly disorganized staff before settling down at his own desk. He had a natural aptitude for making work much more of a happy recreation than a chore. Well, providing a man of business correctly estimated the overheads, there was always a pleasing margin of profit looking up at him. On this occasion, however, pleasure was not confined to estimations of profit for this current month. It kept taking in imaginative pictures of Hitler, Goering and all other top Nazis burning in hell.

Sammy had a visitor at noon. His old friend Eli Greenberg knocked on his door and put his hat and his head in.

'Sammy, my boy, might I have a vord or two?'

'Hello, Eli old cock,' said Sammy, 'I'm up to my ears, but when did I ever ask you to drop in only by appointment? Come in, take a pew and let's hear what's on your mind.'

Mr Greenberg, long a friend to the Adams family as well as an invaluable help to Sammy on many occasions, came in, closed the door and sighed. He took a chair, and as he sat down he shook his head mournfully.

'It's a sad day, Sammy,' he said.

'Don't tell me your business has been hit again, this time by a ruddy doodlebug,' said Sammy. Mr Greenberg's long-established yard at Blackfriars had been destroyed by a bomb during the air raid that had made Rachel homeless, and he had acquired new premises in Camberwell.

'That vould be painful, Sammy, but not as painful as grief,' said Mr Greenberg. 'Ah, my sad lady vife, there is grief for you, and for me too.' He had married a widow some years ago, a widow with three sturdy sons. She had said they needed a father on account of wanting to run while they were still walking blindly, and Mr Greenberg had become a very wise and dutiful stepdad to them. And a fond one.

'What's happened?' asked Sammy.

'I have spoken to you of my three sons, Sammy?' Mr Greenberg never referred to them as his stepsons.

'You have, Eli, and I can't say you haven't.'

'Three fine boys, Sammy, and haven't I vatched them grow into fine young men? Moshe, Michal and Jacob. Moshe in the Navy, and Michal and Jacob in the Army. And didn't I ask Moshe at the time, vhy does he choose the Navy? And didn't he say he vas alvays admiring of Lord Nelson? And didn't I ask him vhat he vould do if his ship vas sunk? And vhat did he say to that? He said svim for the shore. How sad, Sammy, how sad.' Mr Greenberg sighed again, deeply.

181

'Eli?' Sammy, very sober, was sure he knew then what the likeable old rag-and-bone merchant was going to tell him.

'The shore vas too far, Sammy. His ship vas torpedoed in the Atlantic. The telegram from the Admiralty vas delivered yesterday, vasn't it? Sammy, such grief my lady vife suffered, and I am sadder than I have ever known. I have loved Moshe and his brothers like my own, ain't I?'

Sammy was silent for a few seconds, seeing the pain in the eyes of his old friend, a man whose word had always been his bond, and who had never failed him in their business dealings.

'That's a hard one for me to take, Eli, that piece of news. You go back a long way in my life, but it's not easy to find the right words, even for an old friend like you. I'm simply sorrier than I can say. I feel for you, Eli, and for Mrs Greenberg. I'm sad myself, and you can believe that.'

'Vell, Sammy, it's a comfort talking to you, ain't it?'

Sammy looked at his watch.

'Eli, let's have what we both need,' he said, 'let's go across to the pub. Would Moshe mind us doing that, if we remembered him over a noggin or two, always recommended by Boots as a warm friend to sorrows?'

'You're speaking, Sammy, of a glass of Johnny Valker?' said Mr Greenberg.

'Under these kind of circs, Eli, it won't do us any harm,' said Sammy, 'and you might like to tell me all about Moshe.'

'Sammy, it von't be respectful to his memory or to my sad lady vife, to get drunk,' said Mr

Greenberg, 'but a glass or two, and some more talk, vell, I don't have a better idea myself. And Moshe vouldn't disapprove.'

'Right, let's go across, then,' said Sammy.

He gave Eli over an hour of his time in the pub's saloon. Scotch was in short supply, but Sammy was a regular and a favoured one, so the barman obliged with two glasses to begin with, and an encore later on.

Sammy listened while Mr Greenberg talked about Moshe, the eldest of his sons at twenty-four, how he'd grown from a sturdy, ambitious youth into a fine young man, and how proud he'd been to put on the uniform of the King's Royal Navy.

'He vas born in this country, Sammy, ain't that a fact? And vasn't Lord Nelson a hero of his, like I said? And vasn't he set on doing vhat he could in the fight against Hitler's U-boats? Ah, so young, Sammy. Gone at tventy-four, vhich is no age. But vhat more could a young man do than serve his country in such a fight as this?'

'Well, Eli, the rest of us can be proud of Moshe and all other young men like him,' said Sammy. 'We owe them, and I hope we never forget that. Ruddy politicians might, like they forgot the men of the trenches and their widows, and let down those that came out alive. But you and me, and the people, we won't forget our lot. That's another fact.'

'Sammy, vill you now have another Johnny Valker, this time on me?' offered Eli, his accent as pronounced as it always had been since his early days of learning the language of the United

Kingdom, the country that had received him and his immigrant parents, and never sent police to knock on their door in the middle of the night.

'My shout again, Eli,' said Sammy.

'Already ain't you shouted tvice, Sammy?'

'Well, I'm on those kind of shouting terms with Joe, the barman, so let me do the honours again, eh?'

'You're my very good friend, Sammy, and the years have been happy, ain't they?'

'A pleasure to know you, Eli,' said Sammy, and went to the bar. The barman again obliged him. He and Eli sipped reflectively at their third noggins.

'Sammy, vhat about the nut that von't be cracked?' asked Eli.

'Mrs Harman? I tell you, Eli, she's tough all right.' Sammy went on to say he had called on the old biddy again. She opened her door to him, looked at him like he was a dog's left-over dinner, listened to him for only ten seconds, and then, bang, she slammed the door on his hooter again.

'Vell, that ain't promising, Sammy,' said Eli.

'Granted,' said Sammy, 'but there's got to be some way of making her sing, and I'm still working on it.'

They returned to the subject of the Navy's war against the U-boats, and the young seamen who were giving their lives to the cause. Nothing was said about Hitler. Probably a million more spitting words had been aimed at the Nazi leader than at the German Kaiser during the First World War. Sammy and Mr Greenberg didn't bother to add any on this occasion.

Count von Stauffenberg, a monarchist, was confident he could take care of Hitler. Repeated experiments, each one with the type of bomb he had in mind, were all successful, made so by a different fuse, a British-designed one that he was sure was totally reliable.

Chapter Fifteen

Saturday afternoon

The train heading for Westerham, in Kent, was carrying a number of passengers. Patsy and Daniel had a compartment to themselves, which Patsy thought really cute, since most trains were packed. People, and not just men and women of the Services, always seemed to be on the move.

Patsy and Daniel had their bikes aboard, in the guard's van at a cost of a tanner per bike. They were getting out of London for the afternoon to enjoy a wandering cycle ride around the leafy lanes that were a feature of the Westerham area. Daniel had said they could actually cycle past Chartwell, Winston Churchill's country home. Oh, gee whiz, said Patsy, is that a fact, Daniel? Sure is, said Daniel, and Patsy asked him if he had to talk like a cowboy. Daniel asked was that cowboy lingo, then? He thought, he said, it was the way she talked sometimes. Yes, said Patsy, but I like you talking English mostly. We both talk English, said Daniel. I mean the way you talk it, said Patsy. Well, I like the way you talk it, said Daniel. It's no great shakes, said Patsy. I still like it, said Daniel. Daniel, do you really? Sure do, said Daniel, and Patsy, giggling, bopped him one.

Now, on the train, she watched the fields of Surrey passing by, the Kent border a little

186

distant. She looked a treat, thought Daniel, in her Hollywood-style cream-coloured sweater and short brown pleated skirt, comfortable for cycling. She was a sweet girl, a treasure to her fond Pa, and she had rattling good legs too. Daniel was appreciative of any girl's good-looking tent pegs.

'Daniel?'

'Yes, Patsy.'

'What're you looking at?'

'You,' said Daniel, sitting opposite her.

'Me? You sure?'

'Certain sure. Are those American fully-fashioned stockings you're wearing?'

'Yes, Pa gets them for me from some American PX supply source in London. Daniel, is it my legs you're looking at?'

'Well, I can't tell a porkie—'

'A porkie?'

'Pork pie. Cockney slang for a lie.'

'Cute,' said Patsy. 'Listen, what kind of a guy are you?'

'Saucy?' suggested Daniel.

'I mean, what's on your mind about my legs?'

'Oh, nothing very much,' said Daniel.

'What d'you mean, nothing very much? Don't my legs rate, then?'

'Top of the class, Patsy.'

Patsy smiled, and studied the passing scene again, the farmlands, the hedge-bordered fields, the varied shades of green, and the softness of gentle hills.

'Daniel, I do like your country,' she said.

'It's a bit knocked about, Patsy.'

'It's not showing here. I'm really glad Pa brought me over with him, even if he did pack me off to some stuffy English boarding school.'

'I'm glad myself,' said Daniel. 'I'd never have met you if he'd left you behind in Alabama.'

'Daniel, I'm happy you're glad too – hey, what d'you mean, Alabama?'

'I've got it wrong? Buffalo, then?'

'Buffalo? Buffalo? It's Boston, you kook, you know it is. You're making fun of me, and if you keep it up, I'm going to sock you. I don't want to keep doing that, but if I have to, I will.'

'Sock away,' said Daniel.

Patsy, motivated by a kind of happy exhilaration, leapt up and reached to tug at his hair. Daniel slid away, she overbalanced and finished up sitting on his lap. Daniel decided that when opportunity offered, he'd be daft to turn it down. So he kissed her.

'Daniel?'

'Patsy?'

'You're kissing me.'

'You're sitting on my lap.'

'Yes, but we're on a train.'

'What's the answer to that?' smiled Daniel. 'That there's always a first time for a girl to be kissed on a train?'

'Oh, I guess so.' Patsy wondered why his kisses gave her a happy melting feeling. She wasn't actually in love, was she? Was she? 'OK then, do it again, while I think of the Stars and Stripes.'

But the train slowed then and came to a stop at the last station before Westerham. People began to board, including women with shopping bags.

188

Patsy hastily returned to her seat. An elderly couple entered the compartment, and that meant a change of chat and a change of behaviour for the rest of the journey.

They walked their bikes through the ancient market town of Westerham so that Patsy could take a tourist's look at it. Daniel, knowing the place, drew Patsy's attention to the statue of General James Wolfe, conqueror of Quebec and the French Army of General Montcalm.

'My stars,' said Patsy, 'that's the guy, Daniel?'

'Not in person, Patsy, in statue.'

'Oh, I wouldn't know that, would I? I'm retarded, so I naturally thought it was him in person, standing on a lump of rock and waving his sword. I guess I'll have to see a brain surgeon and get him to make some kind of a hole in my head.'

'Don't do that, Patsy, I like you just as you are. Who cares that you're not all there? Better that than a hole in your head. If you're a bit barmy, and me too, well, as my Uncle Boots says, we can all take comfort from knowing that so is everyone else.'

Patsy shrieked with laughter. People looked, and she and Daniel moved on, Patsy observing shops and name-boards and window displays, the latter kind of lacking substance. Patsy, far from being retarded, had more than her fair share of sense and perception, and she had long been aware that the war was slowly draining Churchill's old island of its wealth and materials. Her own country, with its vast resources, its high

189

productive levels, and its security from the bombs that had destroyed so many of London's and Liverpool's factories, knew little of shortages. She might have felt guilty about that if she hadn't sensibly realized it was America's resources, industrial strengths and limitless manpower that were going to drive the final nail into Hitler's coffin. All the same, she sometimes felt quite sad that a fun guy like Daniel couldn't go into a shop or store and buy something he or his family needed, but which simply wasn't available. Her Pa could get all kinds of things from American supply sources in London, but on the whole he didn't mind going along with the Brits and their shortages. Nor did she.

She noted the attractive width of this thoroughfare in quaint old Westerham.

'Daniel, this is Main Street?'

'High Street.'

'It's kind of English.'

'It so happens, Patsy, that—'

'Yes, I know, Smarty-Pants, it is English. Daniel, I've got to tell you you're getting into the habit of acting the superior male. You do realize that, don't you?'

'Well, no, I don't.'

'Well, you are.'

'Oh, I suppose I owe my superiority to my dad. He's famous for his.'

'His superiority?'

'Yes, how did you guess?'

'You've just told me.'

'Well, believe me, Patsy, you can't touch my old man—'

'He's your Pa, and he's great, so you shouldn't call him your old man.'

'Oh, it happens a lot over here, Patsy. Anyway, you can't touch him for brain power, so yes, I suppose I've inherited some of it. But don't let it bother you, you'll catch up.'

Patsy gave him a look. He was grinning, of course.

'How would you like my bike wrapped round your big fat head?' she asked.

'No, don't do that, Patsy, waste of a good bike. Let's ride 'em, and I'll lead the way to Winston Churchill's country home.'

They cycled out of Westerham, and Daniel took her up and down the hilly byways towards Crockham Hill. The afternoon was fine, the vistas mellow in the summer light, the atmosphere one of uninterrupted quiet. Patsy, supple of limb and always on very friendly terms with physical exercise, made light of the ups and took the downs in singing style.

'What's going on behind me, all that yelling?' called Daniel.

'Yelling nothing, you dope, I'm yodelling,' called Patsy.

'You only yodel in the Swiss Alps, don't you?'

'Well, I'm yodelling in the Alps of Kent, so there. Daniel, you sure you know where you're going?'

'What's that?' called Daniel.

'When do we get to see Mr Churchill's country castle?'

'In about fifteen minutes.'

'Is there a drawbridge and ye olde English

191

knights in armour?'

'If there are, Patsy we'll both be seeing things.'

'Giddy-up, Daniel, ride those wheels, cowboy.'

Patsy's sense of happiness was high and infectious, and Daniel's grin was huge. Patsy, sure the war against the Krauts and the Japs was going to be won, felt there was reason to be happy, and there was nothing that contributed more to such feelings than being with Daniel. Daniel was very English, so was his old-fashioned grandma, and she found that really side-splitting sometimes. Daniel and his family actually had sit-down Sunday tea every week, war or no war, rationing or no rationing, at which his grandma presided like Queen Victoria, in company with a large teapot. She knew that because she had been an occasional guest. Imagine marrying into a family like that, you'd be kind of stepping back in time, and life was really all about looking ahead and going along with progress.

All the same, Daniel was sweet. She was growing more and more attached, and she realized it. He was getting to be her first thought on waking each morning.

The hill leading up to Chartwell beat them both. They dismounted and pushed their bikes, side by side.

'Daniel?'

'What's up, America?'

'Daniel, have you ever been in love?'

'What, me at my age?' said Daniel, plodding.

'No, I guess not,' said Patsy, 'but what kind of a girl would you like to marry?'

'Well, I mostly fancy Rita Hayworth, but I'd

192

settle for some millionaire's daughter as long as she'd buy me a sports car.'

'Daniel, you rotter, you wouldn't marry a girl for her money, would you?'

'Yes, if I was mad about her and couldn't live without her, and let's be frank, Patsy, her money would be useful.'

'Daniel, if I thought you really would marry a girl for her money, I'd get to hate you forever.'

'I wouldn't like that,' said Daniel. 'All right, then, cancel the millionaire's daughter, but why are we talking like this?'

'Talking about how one sees one's future is always interesting,' said Patsy. 'I mean, wishes and hopes grab us all, don't they? How far now to Churchill Castle?'

'Only about another quarter-mile – hello, someone's up the pole.'

Patsy, who knew that was an English way of referring to a person a bit screwed-up, said 'Who? Where?'

'Up there,' said Daniel, pointing, and Patsy lifted her eyes to a man literally perched close to the top of a high telegraph pole, seen against a dense bank of trees. He seemed quite comfortable, a large works bag dangling from a strap around his waist. He had heard their approach and was looking down at them.

'Hi!' called Patsy.

The man smiled and gave them a wave.

The road was quiet, devoid of any kind of traffic, and Patsy felt she and Daniel had been given this lovely area of countryside all to themselves. They remounted their bikes when the incline was more favourable, and cycled past a red van parked well off the road. A few minutes later they reached Winston Churchill's home, Chartwell, a redbrick Victorian country house that was handsome but unpretentious. They stopped outside the gate that fronted the entrance. Apart from that, tall hedges hid the rest of the property and its gardens.

'There, it's no castle,' said Daniel.

'But oh, my stars, it's an important landmark now, Daniel, it has to be because of Churchill,' said Patsy, feeling that Britain's war leader would have his permanent place in history alongside President Roosevelt. They were both great leaders. 'Doesn't it give you a thrill, just being here and looking? Mr Churchill couldn't be here now, could he?'

'I don't think he can spare the time to leave London,' said Daniel, 'not with the war hotting up in Normandy every day.'

They both felt there was something very atmospheric about the place, although they could detect no people, no movement. Daniel supposed servants were present in the house, looking after it, and somewhere in the grounds there would be a gardener or two.

Movement did occur then. A man materialized, almost out of nowhere, a man in a dark suit and bowler hat. He stood observing them from just behind the gate.

'Hi there,' called Patsy. He didn't respond, he stood silently watching them, hands behind his back, and his attitude discouraged Patsy from asking if Mr Churchill was home.

'Come on, Patsy, let's press on,' said Daniel, and they remounted and rode on. They saw another man as they approached a second entrance that seemed to lead to the gardens. The man, dressed like the first, was standing at the entrance, and he watched them just as silently as they cycled by.

After a while, when they were riding side by side, Daniel said, 'I've got a feeling Mr Churchill's there. Well, I'm guessing those men were bodyguards, security people. They wouldn't be around if the place was empty, or if there were only servants.'

'Well, that's great, Daniel,' said Patsy, 'we'll always be able to remember the day when we were outside Mr Churchill's country castle and he was actually there.'

'Would that make us famous, I wonder?' said Daniel.

'Get you,' said Patsy, and they cycled on until a lovely green field and a five-barred gate invited them to stop for tea. In his cycle bag, Daniel had a flask of hot tea and two enamel cups. In her own bag, Patsy had peanut butter sandwiches, the butter obtained by her Pa.

They found a sunny spot in the field, beside a hedge, and there they drank the tea and ate the sandwiches.

'Did you say peanut butter?' asked Daniel.

'Sure I did,' said Patsy. 'How'd you rate it?'

'Good question,' said Daniel.

'Well, come on,' said Patsy.

'It tastes of peanuts,' said Daniel.

'You sure?' said Patsy. 'Not marmalade?'

195

'Peanuts,' said Daniel.

'What a guy,' said Patsy to the sky. Little white clouds hovered in the west, edging east into the blue. At which point the heavens began to vibrate. Patsy's back stiffened. Was one of those horrible V-1's on its way to London? She watched the sky. 'Daniel?'

'It's planes,' said Daniel.

They arrived above them, at a height of five hundred feet and with a great burst of engine power, a flight of twelve new fighters, incredibly fast. Daniel watched spellbound, Patsy in awe, both swamped by the tidal waves of sound. The planes, sharp with sunlight, flashed across the sky in perfect v-formation, and were gone in seconds.

'Daniel, did you ever see anything so magnificent?' breathed Patsy.

'I think they came up from Biggin Hill,' said Daniel. 'It's an RAF fighter station not far from here.'

'Biggin Hill?'

'Yes, Patsy, and famous for its part in the Battle of Britain. Some of your American pilots came over to fly for the RAF in that battle of the skies.'

'Gosh, so they did. I remember Pa telling me. He was proud of that, and so was I. Daniel, did you see how those planes flew through the sky, in v-formation? Don't you think that has to be V for Victory? We will win now, won't we?'

'We sure will, Patsy.'

'Daniel, I did ask you not to talk like a cowboy.'

'Did you?'

'I sure did,' said Patsy, and they looked at each other, laughed together, and sank back to lie in

196

the caressing light of the sun. 'Daniel, I know the war's still going on, and that these horrible flying bombs are kind of crucifying London and the people, but I feel very happy, don't you?'

'I'm never down in the dumps when I'm with you, Patsy.'

Patsy turned on her side to regard him. He seemed very relaxed, arms folded behind his head, and he looked just about the nicest guy ever.

'Daniel, we'll always be great friends, won't we?'

'It'll be hands for ever across the sea when you get back home, Patsy.'

Patsy felt that wasn't the answer she wanted.

'Daniel, I don't want to go home yet, not until the war's over.'

'Well, the longer you stay, Patsy, the better I'll like it.'

'Is that right, Daniel, you mean that?'

'Sure do,' said Daniel, and she laughed. She edged closer and leaned over him, looking down into his eyes, which were warm with the good humour of his smile. She dipped her head and put her lips to his, kissing him with ardour. 'What's happening?' he asked, as she lifted her head and showed a flushed face. He was always very careful with Patsy, knowing her likeable Pa trusted him not to behave like a promiscuous American college bloke, who thought a campus was where a guy laid a girl.

'Oh, that was just to show you how much I like you,' said Patsy, a little catch in her voice.

'Well, I'll say what I've said before, that I like it

197

that we like each other,' said Daniel.

'You don't mind that I'm American, and that we licked you in our War of Independence?'

'I wasn't there myself, so why should I mind?' said Daniel.

'Well, I feel the same,' said Patsy. 'I mean, I like it that we like each other so much. It's – well, kind of meaningful, I guess.'

Daniel smiled. He wasn't eighteen yet, but he wouldn't have been Sammy's bright son if he hadn't realized he and Patsy were having flights of fancy. Patsy was a winner, with all kinds of prospects waiting for her back in thriving, bustling America. His dad reckoned the United Kingdom was going to find itself threadbare when the war was finally over, and that it would take years for young people to achieve a decent standard of living. However, the firm's new property company was going to prove a profitable venture, either short-term or long-term, his dad was sure of that, and had promised him a special position. Sammy, in fact, wanted Daniel out of the factory and to make an executive of him.

'Let's see.' Daniel gazed thoughtfully up at her. 'Yes, let's see, how much money would you have by the time you were twenty, say?'

'What? Oh, you stinker, you think that's funny?' Patsy was laughing, however. She really was at her happiest, in this quiet little world all their own, from where the views of the Weald of Kent were beautifully soft. She didn't need Boston or an all-American guy, not at this moment.

'Time to go, Patsy, we've got a train to catch,' said Daniel.

'OK, Mister Superior, you're the boss – you think.'

'You're a nice girl, Patsy, but don't give me any sauce.'

Chapter Sixteen

They took the descent with care. Passing Chartwell, they glimpsed the two men they had seen
earlier. They were outside the entrance gate,
talking, but spared a quick glance as Patsy and
Daniel rode by. It made Daniel feel that Mr
Churchill might really be at home, giving himself
a bit of a break from all that hedged him about in
London.

A little later, they also passed the red van
parked way off the road. And of all things, the
man at the top of the telegraph pole was still
there. Daniel and Patsy, arriving silently, looked
up at him. The man had field glasses in his hand,
and was looking down at them. Daniel spotted
something with a dull blue glint poking up out of
his works bag.

He let his bike run fast then. Patsy, catching
him up, called, 'Daniel, not so fast – we
shouldn't, not downhill.'

'I'm riding for the Westerham police station,
Patsy, I think there's a rifle in that bloke's bag.
And he's been using binoculars, didn't you
notice?' The wind tugged at Daniels's words.

'Daniel, stop, I can't hear what you're saying –
Daniel, stop.'

They braked hard and pulled up. Everything in
front of them, the fields, the copses and the
landscapes, offered nothing in the way of war and

its deadly machines. On the face of it, the late afternoon existed in peaceful companionship with summer as Patsy asked Daniel what was on his mind.

'I'm going to the Westerham police station,' said Daniel. 'That bloke up the pole was using binoculars, and I think there's a rifle in his bag.'

'Yes, and I saw the glasses,' said Patsy.

'He's watching Chartwell,' said Daniel, 'and that makes me feel he's hoping to sight Mr Churchill.'

'You really think Mr Churchill's there?' said Patsy, sun-kissed face expressing a kind of affectionate hope that Daniel knew what he was talking about.

'Those two men we saw were security blokes with big feet, that's my guess,' said Daniel, 'and I daresay the Chartwell grounds are alive with them, which would surely mean our old lion is in residence. But none of the men could stop a rifle bullet.'

'But, Daniel, that man can't see Chartwell, not even from the top of the telegraph pole. It's hidden by trees and hedges all the way up from there. He's down below the house, not looking at it from above.'

'Patsy, you're right, of course he can't,' said Daniel. 'Wait a bit, though, he can see the road, he could see a car coming down, and give himself enough time to get to the ground and use his rifle as soon as the car reached him.'

'Daniel, yes, he must have seen us riding down, or we might have caught him actually using the binoculars,' said Patsy a little breathlessly. 'Oh,

201

my stars, you think he means to put a bullet through one of the car windows and into Mr Churchill?'

'We've got to suspect that, Patsy.'

'How long would it take us to get to the police station?' asked Patsy.

'Say twenty minutes.'

'We could get back to Chartwell in ten minutes, and talk to the security men.'

'Patsy, you're not just a pretty face.'

'Oh, tell me more,' said Patsy.

'We'll discuss it on the train going home,' said Daniel. 'Right now, let's get back to Chartwell, and let's make ourselves heard when we're near the telegraph pole. It'll be a way of making the bloke believe we don't suspect him. Right, about turn, Patsy.'

'Oh, righty-oh, guv,' said Patsy, thrilled to be involved, but still humorously responsive to her fun guy. 'I got yer, guv.'

'I like your lady cowboy talk best,' said Daniel, as they began the ascent, pushing their bikes. They saved their breath for the moment, waiting until they knew they were within hearing distance of the man up the pole, when Patsy piped up.

'Daniel,' she said, 'why are we going back to look at the field?'

'I told you, that's where I'm sure I left the camera,' said Daniel.

'I don't see why you're dragging me back,' said Patsy.

'Because we can cycle back the other way, we can go straight on,' said Daniel.

'OK, tire me out,' said Patsy.

They carried on their conversation in that way. They passed the telegraph pole. The man was still in position, and looking down at them again. There was no sign of the field glasses or of any rifle, although the bag was still in evidence.

'Hi, still there, mister?' called Patsy.

'Must finish,' he said, and Daniel felt the brusque words were thick with an accent. He and Patsy went on, pushing themselves hard, along with their bikes. They reached Chartwell once more. One of the dark-suited men appeared, giving them a look that was plainly suspicious of their third appearance. They walked across to him, outside the entrance gate.

'Excuse me,' said Daniel, 'but—'

'You two keep turning up like bad pennies, so what's on your minds?'

'If you're a security guard, we believe that means Mr Churchill's at home,' said Daniel.

'You're wrong.' The guard was sharp-eyed. 'But if you were right, so what?'

'There's a man perched at the top of a telegraph pole about a quarter of a mile down on the right,' said Daniel.

'It happens.'

'He was there when we came up two hours ago,' said Daniel, 'and he's still there, and there's a plain red van parked near by. Shouldn't the van have GPO markings on it?'

The security man visibly alerted.

'What else d'you want to tell me?' he asked.

'He's been using binoculars,' said Daniel, 'and I think – in fact, I'm pretty sure – he's got a rifle.'

'It's true,' said Patsy, 'and we thought we'd better let you know just in case Mr Churchill is here.'

'You sound like an American girl.'

'So I should,' said Patsy, 'I *am* American, and no-one's ever complained. Look, we think this is urgent.'

'Take your time,' said the guard, and Patsy and Daniel guessed Mr Churchill, if at home, wasn't due to leave just yet.

'Daniel, my English guy, was going to the police station,' said Patsy, 'but changed his mind when I said we could get here quicker.'

'Sensible. We don't want a lorryload of police rushing up here. But hold on, I'm not listening to a leg-pull, am I? I'd better not be.'

'I should say not.' Patsy spoke firmly.

'It's a fact,' said Daniel. 'By the way, the bloke can't see the house from where he is, but he can see the road, and I think that's what he's watching, the road. One more thing, he spoke to us when we called up to him, and he didn't sound English.'

'Or American,' said Patsy.

'I think we'd better investigate,' said the security bloke. He put two fingers between his lips and whistled. In seconds, men seemed to appear from everywhere.

The security guards, making a detour from Chartwell, came at the man on the telegraph pole from out of the woods. They did so at a rush. He made a grab, and a rifle appeared in his right hand.

'Don't use that,' warned the top security man. 'If you do, you can bet on a hanging. So come down and we'll have a friendly talk with you.'

The suspect flung a curse or two, but came down and allowed himself to be disarmed.

Patsy and Daniel were in the main kitchen of Churchill's home, and at the gentle mercy of the staff. Tea and cake were being pressed on them, the cake as delicious as any pre-war equivalent. It melted in the mouth.

'Bless us, you two livened things up for some of the men here,' said a rosy-faced woman. Daniel thought her the cook, or one of the cooks. Servants surrounded them, smiling and intrigued servants. They were even more intrigued to know Patsy was an American girl.

'How did you two find each other?' asked an elderly bloke.

'Oh, we kind of met one day,' said Patsy, 'and Daniel's been ringing my doorbell ever since.'

'Initiative, that's what he's got,' said an admiring young lady. 'If I had me own doorbell, he'd be welcome to ring it every time I was off duty.'

'When are your off-duty times,' asked Daniel, and received an under-the-table kick on his ankle from Patsy. 'No, never mind, can anyone tell us what's been happening?'

'Oh, they've picked up a certain person,' said the elderly bloke, who might have been the butler, thought Daniel, on account of his air of importance. 'The selfsame person is now answering questions.'

'We heard about you,' said the admiring young

lady, addressing Daniel. 'My word, you've got initiative all right, Daniel. You don't mind me calling you Daniel?'

'Help yourself,' said Daniel, and received another unseen kick. Patsy was beginning to fume. 'But it's a fact, they've got the bloke down from the telegraph pole?'

'You have my word,' said the dignified elderly bloke.

The top security man entered, his bowler hat in his hand.

'Miss Kirk? Mr Adams?'

'We're here,' said Daniel.

'So you are, but crowded out, I see. Would you come with me?'

The kitchen staff seemed to emit a concerted sigh. They had found the young couple very entertaining. They receded reluctantly, to allow Patsy and Daniel to join the security man. He took them through to the hall, and at once the aromatic smell of a cigar preceded the appearance of a chubby gentleman, ginger hair slightly awry and a beaming smile on his face, the large cigar in his hand.

'Miss Kirk and Mr Adams, sir,' said the security man. There was another in the background.

'Haven't time to address myself at length to you young people,' said the chubby gentleman in rolling, gravelly tones, 'but permit me to say well done. Yes, very well done. May your future be blessed with years of peace. We have the Nazi tyrant by the throat. Thank you. Goodbye.' He waved his cigar benevolently at them, put it into his mouth and disappeared as quickly as he had presented himself.

'Blind old Aunt Amy,' breathed Daniel, 'that was actually him, Patsy.'

'Oh, my stars,' said Patsy, gulping, 'it was.'

The security man smiled.

'Yes, he insisted on seeing you,' he said. 'Now, you'll be wanting to get home.'

'We need to catch a train,' said Daniel.

'I need a long sit-down on one,' said Patsy, 'I'm giddy.'

'There's a jeep waiting to take you all the way to your homes.'

'All the way with our bikes aboard?' said Daniel.

'Yes, all the way. We have your addresses, and you live close to each other, it seems.'

'That's handsome of you,' said Daniel.

'No more than you both deserve.'

'Can we be told who the bloke up the pole was?' asked Daniel.

'I can tell you that was an appropriate place for him. He's a Germanized Pole who slipped into this country during the Dunkirk evacuation.'

'And was he going to take a potshot at Mr Churchill?'

'Can't tell you that, Mr Adams. By the way, you're strictly forbidden, you and Miss Kirk, to retail an account of today's events to anyone until such time as you hear from a certain Government department. I hope you understand that.'

'I guess you mean no-one is to know Mr Churchill's life may have been in danger from a Polish Nazi who slipped through your hands at the time of Dunkirk,' said Patsy.

'And was sitting on a telegraph pole all day,' said Daniel.

'Which makes us look ridiculous?' said the security chief.

'Bit of a laugh in its way,' said Daniel.

'Yes, there's that aspect, and also the fact of not spreading a sense of alarm about the safety of the Prime Minister.'

'Right, we understand,' said Daniel.

'I'm sure you do. Goodbye, Miss Kirk, goodbye, Mr Adams.' The security man shook their hands warmly. 'Glad to have met you.'

They were both home an hour later. The jeep driver dropped Patsy off first.

'Daniel, call me sometime this evening?' she said.

'Just to make sure you're over your giddy spell? OK, I'll phone, Patsy.'

She touched his hand and walked to the front door of the three-storeyed house converted into flats, which Americans called apartments. She let herself in with her key and climbed the stairs to the first floor.

Pa Kirk was in, having just finished a meal he had made for himself.

'Hi, Pa, sorry I'm kind of late.'

'I question "kind of", Patsy. You *are* late.' Pa Kirk took a keen look at her. The sun had touched her face, and there was a little hint of excitement about her. 'By a couple of hours.'

'Oh, we got carried away by our bikes and some lovely spots for lazing about,' said Patsy. 'By the way, I don't think Daniel is too crazy about peanut butter.'

'The English are conservative about food that doesn't bear some resemblance to their own,' said Pa Kirk.

'Daniel wasn't conservative about my birthday hamburgers,' said Patsy. 'He's not really like that.'

'Patsy, what's going on between you two?'

'Going on? What d'you mean?'

'I'm wondering exactly why you're late home by a couple of hours.'

'Shame on you, Pa, for thinking those kind of thoughts.'

'Patsy—'

'I never would, not with any guy, not even with Robert Taylor, my favourite film star, And I certainly wouldn't with Daniel, I know it would spoil things for us, and I don't want them spoiled. Daniel comes of an old-fashioned family, and he's never once groped me.'

'Patsy, how do you rate that young man now?'

'Pa, don't you have to make tracks for London Town?'

'I do, yes, and I'll have to get going in a few minutes. Patsy, answer up.'

'What was the question, Pa?' asked Patsy, examining her neatly pared fingernails.

'Exactly what are your present feelings for Daniel?'

'Pa, I just like him a lot, you know that.'

'Patsy, he's not fully adult yet, and nor are you.'

'That's irrelevant, Pa.'

'It's what?'

'It doesn't count, and we're both old enough, anyway, to have minds of our own. Look,

209

Daniel's my boyfriend, and girls have boyfriends. It's one of those things that make the world go round, isn't it? You had girlfriends when you were young, didn't you?'

'Sure I did, but I never made any of them two hours late getting home.'

'My two hours late don't have your kind of meaning,' said Patsy. 'Pa, have you got something against Daniel?'

'No, I simply don't think your future's here, in the United Kingdom,' said Pa Kirk soberly. 'It's been a gallant old country, it's fought the battles of its life on land, sea and in the air, but it's worn out. Post-war, it's not going to be able to offer any great prospects for young people. Your prospects are back home in Boston.'

'Yes, I know that, but not with someone like Mike Brady,' said Patsy.

'I wasn't thinking of Mike Brady.'

'Pa, I'll go back home with you when the war's over. I said so, didn't I? But I want to stay here until then and enjoy my time with Daniel. That's fair, isn't it?'

Pa Kirk smiled, his worries eased.

'Sure, that's fair, honey,' he said. The familiar sound of a high-flying V-1 intruded, and they both tensed for the few seconds it took to pass over the area. The V-1's were another worry. 'Damn those infernal machines.'

'I know, Pa, they're scary, but there are hundreds of American men and women in London, and they're sharing the risks with the London people, like we are. We can't run, Pa.'

'No, but let's see, you're off to Cornwall with

Daniel and his family at the end of this month aren't you? said Pa Kirk.

'I'm looking forward to it,' said Patsy.

'Well, it'll keep you out of the way of these goddamned bombs for two weeks,' said Pa Kirk. 'Patsy, I've got to shoot now.'

'So long, Pa.'

He left. He might have said that because Patsy was his only child, a daughter he cherished, he simply couldn't accept the possibility of a situation that would put the Atlantic between him and her. He was a fair man, a caring father, but was quite against losing Patsy, which was what a divide of two thousand miles would amount to.

As far as she felt about Daniel, Patsy was sure of one thing, that she wanted him all to herself between now and the time she went home.

He phoned an hour later, as promised.

'How's yourself, Patsy?'

'Listen, Daniel, how are you going to feel when Pa takes me home to Boston at the end of the war?'

'I thought we'd already talked about that,' said Daniel.

'Yes, but I'm asking now about how you will feel when I'm gone.'

'Ruin my day, that would,' said Daniel.

'Just your day?'

'The best part of my life.'

'Am I really that to you, the best part of your life?'

'Of course you are, Patsy, but the end of the

211

war isn't going to happen just yet.'

'But it could be only a few months if the Allies make it with their big break-out, which Pa says is sure to happen any day now.'

'So you might be the best part of my life for only a few more months, Patsy?'

'Would it kind of kill you if I left then and we never saw each other again?'

'I can't tell a porkie, Patsy, I'd fall ill. But friends like you and me, well, we could keep in touch with letters across the sea. I know there's a lot of sea—'

'Letters? Just letters? Daniel, I don't think much of that.'

'It would be one way of keeping in touch, of letting each other know how we were getting on.'

At her end, Patsy made a face, at the same moment both phones seemed to carry rumbling vibrations to ears as a hugely noisy V-1 hurtled through the sky towards the Pool of London.

'I hate these flying bombs,' said Patsy a little intensely.

'Same here,' said Daniel.

'Daniel, do you have post-war prospects? I mean, good prospects?'

'Not half,' said Daniel. 'Dad formed a property company some time ago. He's already made handsome profits from buying and selling bombed commercial sites. Those sites have got to be developed sooner or later, Patsy, either by rebuilding the original premises or putting up something new. Anyway, Dad's offered me a good position in the company, providing I take a course in property law when the war's over.'

'Will that really be a great prospect, Daniel?'

'Dad doesn't go in for anything that only offers piffling prospects to his relatives, and I'm one of his closer relatives.'

'Daniel, I'm very happy for you, then, and you do like it that we're such great friends, don't you?'

'Not half,' said Daniel.

'Well, I'm just not going back home in a hurry, I'm not. Didn't we have a lovely time together today? I'm still dizzy that we met Mr Churchill his very own self.'

'Just for your ears alone we really could get famous if our next meeting was with President Roosevelt,' said Daniel. 'Is he likely to come over and ring your doorbell?'

'Speaking of doorbells–'

'You don't have one,' said Daniel, 'just a common knocker.'

'Speaking of doorbells, Daniel Adams, what was the idea of getting fresh with that floozie who said screwy things about your initiative?'

'Floozie?'

'A female you English guys would call a tart. Daniel, you wouldn't ring the doorbell of a floozie, would you?'

'I'd get into serious trouble with my grandma if I even stood on a floozie's doorstep,' said Daniel.

'How would she know?'

'Ask my dad, and he'd tell you what I'm telling you now, Grandma knows everything about all of us. She's got family second sight.'

'I think she's a lovely old lady.'

'She's still got second sight.'

213

'Daniel, I didn't realize Mr Churchill was so tubby.'

'That doesn't count with a bulldog. It's his jaws. They never let go once they've got hold of your leg.'

'Mr Churchill's jaws have got Hitler by the throat. He said so. Daniel, thanks for calling me.'

'Good luck, Patsy, and good night.'

'Good night, Daniel, stay with me.'

Neither of them ever suggested they were in love. Well, they were desperately young and untried in this world of tough fighting Servicemen and adventurous Servicewomen. In any case, theirs was a relationship of light hearts, something not to be disturbed or interfered with by anything serious. Everything in the garden was lovely, thank you.

Except that Patsy felt there wasn't room in Daniel's garden for girls other than herself. Especially there wasn't room for the one called Pippa.

Chapter Seventeen

Mr Finch was in Bayeux, interviewing Lieutenant Trudi Lemberg. The young woman, very fretful indeed about the idiots who were keeping her confined, found this new interrogator almost soothing. She supposed him to be a typical English gentleman in his courtesy, kindness and fine manners. Most certainly, he had the handsome, distinguished appearance one expected of such men. And, although he was silver-haired, he still owned the kind of appeal that could find favour with many women. Further, he spoke Russian and he knew White Russia, that country whose huge dark forests were sheeted with the purest white in winter.

Mr Finch was at his intelligent best in his interrogation, applying faultless tact and old-fashioned charm in his quest into the mind of this volatile woman. The interested men in London, as well as the American and British Intelligence officers here in Bayeux, were sure that if she knew as much as she claimed, then she must also know the date of the planned assassination and the name of the assassin. She had always insisted she did not know.

She responded willingly to Mr Finch's comments and questions, taking no notice of the man standing by. He was merely one of the idiots who, since her arrival here, had been interrogating her, always with a measure of suspicion and disbelief. This English gentleman was a most welcome change.

She talked about the time when her drunken lover, one of General von Stulpnagel's staff officers, told her that a number of German generals were planning to kill Hitler, that they would engage in armistice negotiations consequent on his death and thus make it unnecessary for the Allies to expend lives in any July offensive. Mr Finch listened for pauses, pauses indicating she was having to think carefully about what she said next, which could mean her story was an invention. But there were no pauses, no hesitations. Her words flowed freely, and matched the picture built up for him by Sir Andrew Kerr.

He changed direction and, using Russian, began to examine her family background. She responded without reserve, giving him details that left him in no doubt of her identity as a White Russian. He returned to the revelations of her lover, Colonel von Dressler. That produced a typical flash of fire.

'I am to say everything he said all over again?' she demanded, astonished that this mellow-voiced English gentleman seemed about to join all the other idiots in asking for repetition. Only her first interrogator, Colonel Adams, had been an exception. But he was a man of sense, and an exciting one. 'That is crazy.'

'No, I merely want to ask two questions,' said Mr Finch gently. 'First, is it strictly true that you are unable to give us the name of the man

216

selected to kill Hitler because Colonel von Dressler did not know it himself?'

'Yes, of course that is true.'

'And Colonel von Dressler did not tell you the date of the proposed attempt on Hitler's life?'

'He did not because he could not. He did not know. He said only that he thought it was to be late this month. As for the man who will attempt the assassination, I cannot tell you what I do not know myself. But I have never said the German generals will select him. He will be a volunteer.'

'A volunteer?' said Mr Finch.

'That is what Colonel von Dressler told me when he was dribbling these things.'

Mr Finch smiled. Of course. If this woman had invented the story, or German Intelligence had invented it for her, a name would have been thrown in to add conviction. Any name would have sufficed. A date too might have been given. But because Lieutenant Lemberg had dealt in the truth, she had automatically excluded everything she did not know.

'My dear young lady,' he said, 'forgive us if we have taken our time to examine you, but I think we can now firmly accept all you have told us.'

'Then I can be permitted to come to London and live there?'

'I've heard, of course, that that is what you would like,' said Mr Finch, and thought of the day long ago, in 1918, when he had been back in Germany for eighteen months and experienced an emotional longing to make a permanent home for himself in London, preferably not too far from a family he had come to cherish. This woman from Stalin's White Russia knew nothing of the United Kingdom and its people, but there it was, a wish to seek asylum there. His terms of reference enabled him to make a promise to her if he found himself satisfied with her story and her character. 'Lieutenant Lemberg, as soon as I return to London tomorrow, I will see that arrangements are made to bring you over.'

'I can believe that?' said Trudi Lemberg.

'It's a promise you can rely on,' said Mr Finch.

'I think you most kind,' she said. 'It would be to my advantage, yes, if I had an English husband?'

'Granted asylum, you wouldn't need a husband.'

'But it would help, I am sure,' she said. 'Are there many unmarried men in England?'

'There are hundreds of unmarried American soldiers,' said Mr Finch.

'Ah, so?' Trudi looked delighted. 'An American, yes, he would do. Are Americans very rich?'

'Yes, a great many.'

'Good,' said Trudi. 'Rich Nazis or rich Russian Commissars, no. But a rich American? Yes. I would much have liked the first officer who interrogated me. He was Colonel Adams. I am sad to know he is already married.'

'My dear young lady, I'm sure you'll get over it,' smiled Mr Finch, and wondered, in a quite irrelevant way, if Allied transportation would get him home in time for Sunday tea tomorrow. It was very irrelevant considering he was now convinced that a plot to kill Hitler definitely existed, that the attempt would be made before July was out, and that this, if successful, would be

218

followed by a request for an armistice.

All the same, Sunday tea at home ranked high on his list of pleasant English customs.

At the Berlin headquarters of the Reserve Army, Colonel Count von Stauffenberg looked at his calendar.

The seventeenth of July.

Three days to go.

Well, he was ready, so was the bomb, and his planned course of action was clear in his mind.

And his fellow conspirators were ready too. Theirs was the responsibility for taking control of Berlin. They were to act as soon as news of Hitler's death reached them. In Paris, General von Stulpnagel would round up and arrest SS and Gestapo leaders.

Montgomery's Army Group, probing at the German defences, and reconnoitring the enemy's strong points, was still massing for the offensive designed to open up France. Monty intended to go hell for leather at Rommel's army, favouring a huge hammer blow on a narrow front. The opening of the British attack was to coincide with an American attempt to break out of the Cherbourg Peninsular, for which purpose Monty's tactics had been to draw the bulk of the German forces into the Caen area. He had succeeded. The Germans had the greater part of their Normandy army facing the British and Canadians and the Americans were to be given the opportunity of hurling themselves at an enemy that might be comparatively thin on the ground.

Eisenhower was confident that the Americans, with a greater sense of aggression and drive than the British, would achieve the kind of breakout that would put them on course for Paris.

Hitler, who regarded himself as a master tactician and most of his generals as incompetent, was ratty about the fact that neither the Americans nor the British had been thrown back into the sea. He had given specific orders for this to be done, but the reverse had happened. The Allies had strengthened their hold on Normandy, and Hitler had had to issue new orders, commanding his troops to stand their ground down to the last man until a German offensive could be launched.

At his headquarters in Rastenburg, East Prussia, he was in a state of irritation about what he saw as the increasing failures of his generals. Developments on the Russian and the Normandy fronts, all convinced him that too many of his field commanders were floundering. Dismissals of those judged guilty of incompetent leadership were frequent.

The drawback, of course, to being a general, was that even the best sometimes lost a battle. That was not only inevitable, it was a fact of history. Unfortunately, Hitler could not see why any kind of failure could attend a battle as long as his orders concerning dispositions and tactics were faithfully carried out. He insisted at the top of his voice that the terrible tragedy of Stalingrad would not have happened if only his original orders had been properly implemented. In fact, it was his orders alone that had resulted in the German Sixth Army being ringed and trapped.

He refused to believe this.

He had to go.

Von Stauffenberg's foolproof bomb was ready and waiting.

Daniel and Patsy were strolling in Ruskin Park that afternoon, Patsy looking a charmer in a summer dress of fine pre-war printed cotton. The cotton had been supplied with the compliments of Sammy, the dress made up by good old Gertie Roper at the factory, and Patsy had been touched by the gesture and the thought that inspired it.

The park was still a popular venue on Sundays, and people escaped to it from their four walls. It was open to the skies, and there were no bricks and mortar to be turned into missiles by the impact of a flying bomb. Except, that is, for the public convenience and the tea rooms.

There was a conspicuous absence of young men and women. Some teenagers were larking around, and there were a few little boys and girls running about under the eyes of their mums. Middle-aged couples sauntered, and old people who lived in houses that had no gardens sat on benches and mused on the greenness of the grass.

'I like our park,' said Patsy. It wasn't her first visit with Daniel.

'I like it that you think it's ours,' said Daniel.

'Oh, that's how I'll remember it,' said Patsy. 'By the way, Pa's in uniform now.'

'He's joined your Army?' said Daniel.

'No, it's just that accredited war correspondents are entitled to the uniform of the Press Corps,' said Patsy. 'It saves them being taken for spies if they fall into enemy hands.'

'Is your Pa going to the war zone, then?' asked Daniel.

'Yes, any day now, it seems,' said Patsy.

'That'll leave you on your own,' said Daniel.

'You remember Mike Brady?' said Patsy.

'I sure do,' said Daniel

'Daniel, I've told you, talk English,' said Patsy.

'English, right, got you, Patsy. But what about Mike Brady?'

'He phoned this morning when I was home from church,' said Patsy. 'He has relatives in Dublin, a whole lot of Bradys who go back years, and after talking to Pa, he offered to get in touch with them and arrange for me to go and live with them until Pa gets back from France. I guess that won't be until the Germans have been licked.'

'You're going to Dublin?' said Daniel.

'Excuse me?' she said.

'You're going to Dublin?' repeated Daniel.

'Hey, you're not trying to say I should, are you?' said Patsy. 'What do I want to go there for?'

'I suppose your Pa feels that living with the Dublin Bradys means you won't be alone,' said Daniel, 'and it'll also mean you'll be out of the way of the flying bombs.'

'Let's sit down before I go off pop and start to hate you,' said Patsy, and they seated themselves on a vacant bench. 'Now see here, Daniel Adams, what kind of friend are you? Yes, and look me in the eye when you answer.'

'Right, look you in the eye, Patsy,' said Daniel, and did so. The confrontation was steady, Patsy's bright eyes challenging, Daniel's blue eyes unwavering until the right one winked.

'Don't do that,' said Patsy, 'I want to examine your true feelings. True feelings can be found in the eyes, did you know that?'

'Right, found in the eyes,' said Daniel, and the confrontation began again. This time, Patsy's eyes were searching, although Daniel doubted if anyone could read all that much in someone else's mince pies. Bit of a lark, really, being eyeball to eyeball with his American girl guy. Still, he held her gaze. An elderly couple passing by smiled as they caught a young man and a young lady staring fixedly at each other, faces close.

Daniel's right eye winked again.

'I told you not to do that,' said Patsy.

'Listen,' said Daniel, 'if you keep looking at me like that, and I keep looking at you like this, I'll end up kissing you.'

'You can't do that, not in a public park,' said Patsy.

'I can, but I suppose you mean I shouldn't,' said Daniel. 'Um, how about behind the gardener's tool shed?'

'Certainly not,' said Patsy. 'Um, where is it?'

'On the far side of the park,' said Daniel. 'Anyway, did you find my true feelings?'

'Yes, and they're telling me you don't want me to go to Ireland,' said Patsy, 'and you don't, do you?'

'Frankly, no,' said Daniel.

'Honest?' said Patsy.

'I'm not keen on having you swallowed up by a whole lot of Mike Brady's Irish relatives,' said Daniel, 'and I'm not keen on having him suggest it.'

'Oh, I guess he meant well,' said Patsy, 'Daniel,' she said, 'I'm just not going anywhere until the war in Europe is over. I don't want to keep on repeating myself, but I have to ask you again if you'd like me to stay here. You would, wouldn't you?' If she didn't know it, or wouldn't admit it, she was asking for a commitment.

'I could speak to your Pa,' said Daniel, who was sensibly keeping his feet on the ground. 'I mean, I can understand he wouldn't want you to live in that flat alone. How about if you moved in with my Aunt Lizzy and Uncle Ned, or my Aunt Vi and Uncle Tommy? Neither house is far away.'

'Daniel, would they have me?'

'One or the other,' said Daniel, 'you can bet on it. Aunt Vi and Uncle Tommy's home might be the best for you. Well, their daughter Alice is with them, she'd be company for you, and the two of you might get to be – um – buddies.'

'Daniel, you keep talking American.'

'What's American, then?' asked Daniel.

'Buddies.'

'Well, let's say bosom chums, then.'

'Bosom chums?' Patsy gave a little yelp of laughter. 'Daniel, you're killing me.'

'Sorry about that, Patsy, but I daresay your Pa would prefer you to be with my aunt and uncle to having you in our second floor back room.'

'Your second floor back room?'

'Yes, it's next to mine,' said Daniel, 'and we might occasionally bump into each other in our pyjamas.'

Patsy looked him in the eye again, and this time saw the amateur comedian. Amateur or not, she liked his jokes.

'Daniel, you're sweet,' she said.

'If that means cute, count me out,' said Daniel. 'Come on, time we went home for tea.'

'Your grandma's Sunday tea?'

'In the garden today,' said Daniel. 'Not so formal. All the same, it's still Sunday, so don't lark about, and don't cross your legs. Grandma will have fifty fits if you flash your stocking-tops.'

People looked. A young lady rising up from a bench with a young man was shrieking with laughter.

It was a welcome change from the sounds of war.

They were in the garden, the afternoon warm, the weather an improvement on that which had made the invasion of Normandy so difficult, not only at the beginning but for days on end.

Chinese Lady sat at a table with Sammy, Susie, Ned and Lizzy, the latter two being there by invitation. Lizzy was always happy to be present at one of her mum's Sunday teas, and Ned had long accustomed himself to the ritual. Ned was not unlike Boots in his easy-going nature, which meant falling in with the whims and wishes of the ladies.

Daniel and Patsy sat at another table with Paula and Phoebe, and everyone was eating bread and

225

jam, home-made blackberry jam. Chinese Lady, Lizzy and Susie all specialized in the domestic art of jam-making. In the autumn, Lizzy and Susie, with their husbands in tow, often went out to places like Woldingham in Surrey, where the hedgerows offered a profusion of blackberries ripe for picking. They returned with laden baskets, whereupon Lizzy would go to work on Sammy, who had what he called a nodding acquaintance with geezers who were useful, but not the kind of blokes he'd invite home. He meant spivs, and he also meant Susie would carry on a bit if she ever found one on her doorstep. Susie disapproved of spivs and the black market. So it was always Lizzy who'd go to work on Sammy. She was sure God would forgive her if she stretched her own principles a bit in these days of harrowing shortages. The result was that Sammy would suddenly come into possession of large packs of sugar. Susie, for the sake of appearances, would demand an explanation, and Sammy would readily supply one, such as the packets had fallen off the back of a lorry and couldn't be left lying around. They'd get run over, he'd say, and he just happened to know the bloke who picked them up. Susie would say well, I'm not sure I like it, but all right, I suppose it wouldn't have made sense to let them go to waste. Thus she would salve her conscience. Sugar for blackberry jam was, after all, very acceptable. She and Lizzy would share the supply, make their jam and give some to Chinese Lady and Vi.

Patsy, of course, thought it a hoot that everyone

had to eat bread and jam before arriving at the cake. But at least, as Daniel had said, it was less formal, tea in the garden. As for the English being reserved and insular, Patsy always found everyone in this family, from the grandparents down to the two young girls, completely out-going, even if so much about the way they lived was old-fashioned. Rachel Goodman could have told her that they were Londoners and that most Londoners were extrovert far from being reserved.

The blue sky was dappled with playful little clouds that had no need to look askance at buzzing black monsters from the pits of hell, for those pits were again under attack from Allied warplanes, and the rocket scientists and their mechanics were keeping their heads down deep in their carved-out burrows.

'Would anyone like more tea?' offered Chinese Lady, lifting the cosy off the large pot just as someone stepped out of the kitchen onto the stone-flagged patio.

Little Phoebe spoke up in a spasm of surprised delight.

'Crikey, it's Grandpa!'

'Welcome home, Dad,' said Lizzy, who had always shown affection for her mum's second husband. It was an affection that went back many years to the time when he lodged with the family in Walworth before and during the First World War.

Chinese Lady turned in her chair and looked up into the smiling face of her husband. A distinct flush of pleasure coloured her face.

227

'Lord, is that you, Edwin?' she said.

'I believe so,' said Mr Finch, and Chinese Lady, examining his appearance, saw with relief that there were no signs of tiredness. He looked full of well-being.

'Bless me soul,' said Sammy to his girls, 'look who's here, me poppets, your grandpa.'

'Daddy, I already seen him,' said Phoebe.

'So did I,' said Paula.

'He's back from his Bath,' said Daniel.

'And just in time for tea,' smiled Susie.

'Sunday tea,' observed Mr Finch, seating himself. 'Might I beg a cup, Maisie? And a slice of bread and jam?'

I don't believe it, said Patsy to herself, I can't believe it. At their Sunday teas they're all living as if Queen Victoria is still alive. Look at Daniel, he wouldn't dream of asking if coffee and hamburgers couldn't be served for a change.

If Patsy thought the Adams' version of Sunday tea was a hoot, German-born Edwin Finch's belief that it was among the most civilized and enjoyable of English customs was confirmed at this moment.

In France several days ago, the German Army command structure had suffered a crippling blow. Field Marshal Erwin Rommel was being driven back to headquarters after an extensive inspection of the German front lines. He was travelling in his open staff car. It was spotted by a Hunter, an Allied fighter plane that launched an immediate low-level rocket attack that blasted the car off the road. Rommel sustained serious injuries and was rushed to hospital.

The conspirators in Berlin were stunned by the news, for Rommel, while disapproving of assassination and wanting no part of it, had pledged his support for the overthrow of Hitler and his tyrannical Government of National Socialism. Rommel's name was one to give lustre and integrity of purpose to the conspiracy, which needed the backing of the German people as soon as the Nazi hierarchy had been broken, one way or another.

Although Rommel was now out of danger, the plotters were wavering. Not the vigorous and determined Count von Stauffenberg, however. There were only three days to go to Hitler's full staff conference, and von Stauffenberg would attend, with his bomb.

Chapter Eighteen

'I don't like it,' said Bobby that night. London had delivered a message concerning a flight home through a BBC broadcast, and Pierre had given him the details when meeting him at the daily rendezvous, a village cafe. Helene was never present. She kept watch from a distance, ready to whistle if the Gestapo showed up anywhere in the village. It wasn't so much a question of distrusting Pierre, a likeable and very co-operative man, as of taking absolutely no chances. It was always possible that one day he'd be tailed.

All three of them met later, by arrangement, when Pierre led the way to a landing venue agreed with London. There, Bobby and Helene were to await a promised Lysander at two in the morning. They had arrived early, in twilight, and Pierre said he would be back later with some of his men to see them safely away. He left with them a sack containing sticks and torches for marking out the landing area. It was now one-forty and the Lysander was due to touch down in twenty minutes or so.

'No, I don't like it,' said Bobby emphatically.

'You don't like waiting, you mean?' said Helene. They were crouching on their knees just inside a stretch of bushes not far from the landing area, their every instinct compelling them never to make visible targets of themselves.

230

'Who does in a France full of Himmler's filthy SS and his disgusting Gestapo?'

'I meant I don't like the set-up,' said Bobby. 'Where's Pierre and some of his Resistance group? He told us he'd be back with them, but they're not here yet. There's always some Resistance people to safeguard the landings and take-offs of Lysanders. Also, my French chicken, he agreed someone must have informed the Gestapo about our farmhouse location, but he hasn't found the bugger. Have the stinking Gestapo pounced since we last saw him? Has he been taken, along with his group? If so, you know who might turn up any moment, don't you think?'

'The stinking Gestapo?' said Helene.

'Along with the traitor,' said Bobby.

The moon was full, intermittently flooding the land with light as it appeared and disappeared amid swirling clouds. They looked at the landing area they had marked out in the shape of the letter 'L' with torches attached to sticks. They had not yet switched on the torches.

'Bobby, we can't miss our chance, we have to put the lights on,' said Helene.

'Yes, we have to,' said Bobby, and they came out of cover, ran to the landing strip and switched on the torches. The time was now fifteen minutes to two. 'The Lysander will be safe. It won't land unless we give the signal.' It was to be four quick flashes.

They began a new wait, a fraught one. The minutes crept by. The light faded and went as clouds ran under the moon.

'Maurice!' Helene hissed his code name. The

moon reappeared, and into the light rushed five men and a woman, all armed with Stens and all members of Pierre's group.

'Lynette! Maurice!' The code names burst from the woman. 'You're in trouble. Pierre is betraying you. He'll be here with the German Security Police in a few minutes. We were able to get ahead of him. He and – ah, listen!'

They heard the humming vibrations of the Lysander.

'They will let you give the signal, then take you, the Lysander, its pilot and the new agent he's bringing,' said the woman.

'Pierre said nothing about a new agent,' hissed Bobby.

'No, that was to make you ask a few questions when the plane arrived and to delay the take-off.'

Helene let go an imprecation in descriptive French.

'Give the signal,' said one of the men, 'we will hold them off to allow you to get aboard.'

Oh, bloody hell, thought Bobby, can I believe this? Yes, I must. Not all these six people can be traitors. I have to believe it's Pierre.

The Lysander, descending, was heading for the landing strip. Bobby turned and flashed the all-clear signal. In came the plane. The Resistance members separated into two groups of three and rushed to form an ambush, going to ground fast. The Lysander touched down, bumping gently. At which point men rose up from cover forty yards away and headed at sprinting pace towards the illuminated landing strip. They were uniformed men of the security branch of Himmler's SS. Two

SD men, members of the Gestapo's Security Service. They ran into bursts of fire from each side. They flung themselves down. Among them was the Frenchman called Pierre.

Bobby and Helene were at the plane. The door was open, a man there, a returning SOE agent. He was ready to jump off, the plane still slowly moving.

'Stay aboard!' shouted Bobby. 'Keep going!' he yelled at the pilot. He helped Helene to scramble up. The man at the door hauled her in, and Bobby took a grip of the door with one hand and hurled himself upwards. Helene and the startled SOE agent took hold of him and brought him bundling in. His head took a bruising bump.

The pilot saw flashes of automatic fire ahead. The aircraft taxied, slewing round, and he began to race for take-off over the rough ground, his passengers thrown about by the bumping, shaking run for the skies.

The Resistance group ceased fire and melted away while the going was in their favour. Two SD men lay wounded and cursing. The rest were intent on reaching the Lysander, and they charged forward, firing at the tail of the receding aircraft as it careered over the ground. It took off like a bird gliding upwards on spirals of hot air.

It flew away in the light of the moon, with its passengers trying to right themselves as they tumbled about. Thoughts scrambled around in Bobby's bruised head. The whole incident represented one narrow squeak too many. Who the hell was it who said, 'Fight for death or glory, boys,' and made a virtue of it? Running for one's life might not be virtuous, but it made bloody sound sense.

The Lysander, on a north course for home, flew high in the sky to avoid any anti-aircraft fire. The German flak batteries in Normandy were very active at night. By day, it was suicidal for their gun crews to show their heads, such was the ferocity of low-level attacks launched at them by Allied fighter-bombers.

Bobby and Helene, comfortable now, talked to the other man, discovering he was an established SOE agent, code name Victor, who had been due to meet up with Pierre. Bobby said it was fortunate the meeting had been aborted, since it was almost certain Pierre was in the nature of a double agent. But his time was up, said Bobby, for his group, having found him out, would set their dogs of retribution on him, drag him down, take him out of circulation and find a hole in the ground for his body. No quarter was ever given by French Resistance members to those who betrayed them and France itself.

'Pétain and Laval will join him there one day,' said Helene, fiercely loyal to her native country, 'and Pétain will have to answer for his role as Hitler's willing puppet.'

'A hell of a lot of people are going to have to answer for all kinds of treachery, all kinds of war crimes,' said Bobby.

'Laval, I imagine, is already shaking in his shoes,' said Victor, 'although he knows and we know that we've got to grind the Germans deep into the ground first. That won't be easy, my friends. The German Army isn't a pushover.'

'Don't spoil my tea,' said Bobby.

'Tea?' said Victor. 'What tea?'

'Maurice is making a joke,' said Helene.

'I see.' Victor smiled.

'You're lucky if you do,' said Helene. 'All his jokes are terrible.' She laughed. She was very happy for herself and Bobby. 'He has made hundreds, I tell you, every one worse than the one before.'

'Then why are you laughing?' smiled Victor amid the sound of the Lysander's busy engine.

'Because his terrible jokes have made an imbecile of me,' said Helene and laughed again.

'The German Army, though...' said Bobby, 'it's got to be beaten flat this time.'

'Yes, and there are enough holes in the ground for all the swines,' said Helene, a woman of little tenderness towards the enemies and despoilers of France, but with bucketfuls to spare for Bobby, except when he was in argument with her or trying to boss her about. He had a strange idea that men were born to give orders to women. What an idiot. But what a lover. And, after all, most men were idiots, so most women ended up marrying one. Some were lucky. They married exciting and entertaining idiots.

Marrying Bobby was going to make her one of the lucky ones. Helene Aarlberg was sure of that.

The Lysander was over the moonlit Channel, and making a gradual descent.

Bobby whispered to Helene, 'Home's coming up.'

'Your home and our wedding,' said Helene.

235

All had gone so well since the rushing take-off and the landing was only a matter of minutes away.

Fate dealt its blow as the plane approached the coastline of Sussex when, without warning, sparks began to dart and fly from its tail. Bullets from the charging Germans had struck home, and if reaction to the damage had been long delayed, it now showed itself. Tiny flickers of flame developed, and the machine became unsteady in its flight. Sparks multiplied and showered, the flickers of flame turned into red-gold tongues, and as the sea below gave way to the shores of Sussex, the pilot began to fight for control and to use the moonlight in his search for terrain on which to make a forced landing.

He shouted warnings to his passengers, and opened up his radio to signal his station. Bobby, Helene and Victor froze as down went the Lysander, rocking and shuddering, its tail now visibly burning. From the land below, the machine was a black shape spewing flames against the canvas of the moonlit sky. It rushed down and looked as if it would nosedive into a field. The pilot managed to straighten it out at the last moment and the Lysander crash-landed, plundering grass and earth, and running crazily on until it ploughed into a hedge. Its nose, propeller and cowling smashed through thick bramble, and its burning tail sheered off and hurtled away like a whirling Catherine-wheel firework.

Of the four people in the body of the wrecked plane, one was dead, three were unconscious.

Chapter Nineteen

Monday

At mid-morning Sammy, receiving a phone call from Mr Greenberg, asked him if he was feeling a little better about the son he had lost.

'Vhy, ain't it kind of you to ask, Sammy, and if I said yes, a little better, that vould be true. And if I said the sorrow is still painful, that vould be true too. Ve are all born to die, Sammy, in God's good time, but for some that time is sadly short. Ah, and vasn't it so for poor Emily? But vun must carry on, for vhat is the point of living on grief and dying of hunger? No, ve can't allow grief to turn us aside from our daily vork, Sammy, and I am phoning on a matter of business, ain't it?'

'Well, I'm pleased to hear you say so, Eli,' said Sammy, 'and let me invite you to spell it out.'

'You remember the nut ve couldn't crack?' said Mr Greenberg.

'Do I not,' said Sammy, 'I'm still thinking about how to make the lady see I'm her best friend.'

'Sammy, in passing by your old brewery site this morning, vhat d'you think my old eyes blinked at? A new pile of bricks and tiles. So I stopped and there she vas, the poor voman, mourning her old shop and living accommodation. A flying bomb dropped not far from your site on Friday, Sammy, and down her place

237

came, didn't it?'

'Blind O'Reilly, I didn't pray for that to happen to her,' said Sammy. 'Eli, was she in at the time, is she hurt?'

'Vell, I had a little talk vith her, Sammy, and can tell you she vas shopping vhen it happened,' said Mr Greenberg. 'Ah, a nasty shock vhen she came back, vhich is still paining her, but vhat's bricks and mortar compared to vun's life? Sammy, vhy don't you pop down there now? I can tell you she'll be there, vaiting to see you, a lady that had a property up to a few days ago, and now only has a ruin, ain't it? Can you go?'

'You bet, Eli, right away,' said Sammy.

'I von't ask you to treat her kindly,' said Mr Greenberg, 'for I know you vill, don't I?'

'I'm not going to grind her into her ruins, believe me, Eli old cock,' said Sammy.

'It's a hard var, Sammy, and a hard life,' said Mr Greenberg, 'and vouldn't God shake a sad head at us if ve didn't do vhat ve could for each other?'

'So would my dear old Ma,' said Sammy. 'I'll make Mrs Harman a fair offer, and for your contribution, Eli, will a tenner do?'

'A tenner, Sammy?' said Mr Greenberg. 'Vasn't it a fiver?'

'Eli, blokes like you don't happen every day,' said Sammy, 'and a tenner it'll be.'

'Sammy, that ain't business, that's happy friendship.'

'You're welcome, Eli.'

She was there, Mrs Harman, sitting on a rescued

chair on this warm but cloudy day, with London a capital grieving for its ruined buildings and its dead people. Her shop and living accommodation and the old brewery were one now, a united heap of rubble. But other pieces of furniture had been brought out by ARP workers, as well as some personal valuables, and all were stacked close to the stiff, angular lady. A few neighbours were there, sifting around in search of other things. Mrs Harman looked up as Sammy arrived. She spoke.

'The old feller said you'd come.'

'Mrs Harman, you've got my sympathy,' said Sammy.

'I don't have nothing to offer you, young man. Look at it. All gone.'

'The site's still yours,' said Sammy. 'Will you take three hundred quid for it?'

Mrs Harman stared at him in astonishment.

'If that's a joke, I should be laughing?' she said. 'Well, I ain't.'

'It's no joke,' said Sammy, and talked kindly to her, at the end of which it embarrassed him to watch her eyes turn moistly wet. They parted the best of friends, the old lady with fifty pounds in her hand as a deposit and a surety of good faith in her promise to sell. Nor did Sammy ask for a receipt. He knew the type. Straightforward, blunt-speaking and sound as a bell.

'Young man,' she said, as he shook hands with her.

'Yes, missus?'

'I think I could get to like yer.'

The flying bombs were still coming over, and however many were being destroyed in the air, those that slipped through fell out of the sky like silent thunderbolts. Silent, that is, until they hit the ground. Or a shop, or a house. Then the explosive roar of sound was ear-shattering. The suffering cockneys, referring to the V-1's as bleedin' doodlebugs, expressed their feelings in the ripest of Anglo-Saxon adjectives.

Chinese Lady, getting off a bus at Camberwell Green with Susie, did so in a spirit of stiff defiance of the menace from the skies, her mouth set, her back straight, her hat sitting firmly on her head. Some days her hat stayed on her head all day until suppertime, whether she was indoors or out. She had a fixed conviction that it was a sign of well-dressed respectability. She still used a hatpin. Lately, she had taken to using two as an extra guard against the possibility of having her hat blown off by one of these blessed buzzbombs.

Susie was in a summer dress of mid-blue, designed to grace her as a woman approaching forty, but at the same time not to advertise that unwelcome fact. Sammy saw to it that most of her clothes were made at the factory from fine pre-war materials, and under the expert eye of good old Gertie. Her hat today was of dark blue, and in wartime fashion it sat on her fair hair rather than over it, and looked as if it hadn't made up its mind whether or not it really was a hat. Chinese Lady had her own opinion about it. She thought it might just as well have been placed on top of the family piano to serve as some kind of ornament. In other words, it definitely wasn't a hat as far as Chinese Lady was concerned. Sammy wasn't too keen on it, either, and had said he wasn't sure that the wife of a businessman in the rag trade ought to wear it in public. Susie, with a glint in her expressive blue eyes, said did you say something, Sammy Adams? No, I was only mumbling to meself, Susie, said Sammy, who had an unthinking tendency to put his foot into his mouth, but could at least recognize the consequent danger signals. Mr Finch, when asked for his opinion, tactfully said he thought the hat unusual. Susie queried unusual. Unusually fetching, said Mr Finch who, like Boots, was adept in his ability to avoid being backed into a corner by the ladies of the family. Chinese Lady was happy to have her husband home again. He had said very little about Bath, apart from admitting his work for the Government had prevented him from enjoying its links with Regency culture. Chinese Lady asked what Regency culture was. Oh, that which is associated with the Prince Regent and his times, said Mr Finch. Chinese Lady's next question was predictable. Who's he, have I heard of him? He's long dead now, Maisie, so don't let's worry about him, said Mr Finch. Well, just make sure the Government doesn't send you to any more places that are as good as foreign, said Chinese Lady.

She and Susie were meeting Cassie Brown and Vi in Lyons tea shop for morning coffee. Lyons tea shops still served coffee of a sorts, and so did their rivals, the ABC. And they were still well patronized, especially by lady shoppers who liked to pop in for a cup of tea. Lyons tea was notable

241

for being consistently refreshing, and if a cup had gone up from tuppence to threepence, well, no-one complained. Further, the atmosphere was always welcoming. If many pre-war Nippies were now doing their bit for the country in uniform or in factory overalls, and if the wartime waitresses were middle-aged, the service was still good.

The Lyons tea shop at Camberwell was a favourite place with Chinese Lady. She often met old Walworth friends there, and was looking forward to seeing Cassie, who was married to Susie's younger brother Freddy.

Cassie and Vi were already in the tea shop, seated at a table for four. Cassie, in her exuberant way, waved when Chinese Lady and Susie entered, then came to her feet and gave each a kiss on their arrival at the table.

'Ever so glad to see you both,' she said. 'Vi's ordered the coffee, and they'll bring it as soon as we're all sitting.'

The coffee did indeed arrive without delay, and it became as welcome an accompaniment to conversation as a piano to a vocalist. Chinese Lady, Susie and Vi all wanted to hear from Cassie about Freddy and their children. Cassie said her son and daughter were fine, but were having nervous times because of these evil flying bombs, and she was having to take them back to Wiltshire. She and her dad would stay there with them, of course, and her dad had written to his sister Win about putting them all up again. She herself had written to let Freddy know.

Susie asked if Freddy was still in Burma, and Cassie said yes, he was, and she wouldn't be

242

surprised if he'd got lost in the jungles, because she hadn't heard from him for ages. Chinese Lady and Vi exchanged the kind of looks that suggested they were both thinking the worst might have happened. Susie, however, said that from what she'd read in the newspapers, lots of the soldiers in Burma did sort of disappear for ages, that they were sent behind the Japanese lines to make raids on things like ammunition stores. Chinese Lady said a fine young man like Freddy, who'd been brought up to be a good husband and father, ought not to have to do that kind of thing, which sounded a lot too dangerous. Still, she added on a hasty and more encouraging note, Freddy was much too sensible to get himself into trouble, that if he had got lost he'd soon find himself again, and that she was sure Cassie would hear from him soon. And along came a touch of reassurance to the effect that she thought she'd heard Burma wasn't covered all over with jungles, that there were some very nice views and walks, and things like pretty villages with shops that sold rice puddings and parrots.

'Rice puddings?' said Cassie.

'Rice puddings?' said Vi. 'You sure, Mum?'

'Well, it's only what I think I've heard,' said Chinese Lady, 'and I know I heard there's a lot of rice in Burma. Mind, about the parrots, I don't know I'd want one myself. I did have one once that Boots gave me. You should of heard the things it said. I couldn't repeat them, especially not in Lyons.'

'I wouldn't trust any parrot that came from

Boots,' said Susie. 'It would be bound to be a shocker.'

'Oh, I like Boots,' said Cassie.

'So do I,' said Susie, 'but he could turn any parrot into a shocker without hardly trying.'

'Still, he's got his good points,' said Chinese Lady.

'Yes, a lovely bloke, Mum,' said Susie. After Sammy, Boots was her favourite Adams man.

'Imagine him fathering them twins of Polly's,' said Cassie.

'There you are,' said Susie, 'that's what a lovely bloke like Boots can do to a woman, even a highclass one like Polly.'

'Susie, Susie,' said Chinese Lady, 'not here, love, not in Lyons.'

Cassie looked at Vi. Vi, nearly forty-four, was giggling. Cassie, only twenty-eight, joined in.

The Lyons establishment didn't seem to take offence.

Cassie talked again about Freddy, about how he was missing the growing years of their children.

At this particular moment, two veteran Chindits of Burma were leaning on the rail of a ship gliding slowly through the strongly defended Suez Canal. There were other men of the 14th Army aboard, men who like themselves had been hospitalized on account of debilitating exhaustion, a condition that in the climate and demands of war-torn Burma could reduce a man to physical and mental decrepitude if treatment was delayed. While recovering, they'd been

244

advised that on discharge they were to be granted home leave. Home leave was something they hadn't known for two years and more. The men at the rail, in khaki drill uniforms, were both sergeants, and both silent as they gazed out at the Egyptian heat haze and the clusters of ack-ack guns and rockets. Sergeant Freddy Brown was thinking there was no way he could let Cassie know he was on his way home. He had written to her from the hospital, when he knew he was going to get home leave, but in his disoriented state he had omitted to have it posted. Not until he was on the home-going ship did he discover he still had it.

Freddy, formerly a fresh-faced, cheerful character who had few quarrels with the world, had become very much the primitive jungle fighter with a ferocious hatred of the Japanese. He had seen what they could do to a village and its inhabitants. A pallor had emphasized his gaunt look on the day he embarked for home, but the sea air during the voyage had cured that and given him a weatherbeaten look. However, nothing could disguise the fact that he was as lean as a starved wolf, particularly now that his beard was shaved off.

Sergeant George 'Dusty' Miller, his fellow Chindit, spoke.

'If I don't feel a lot bloody better about Lily than I do now,' he said gratingly, 'I think I might strangle the bitch.'

'Well, start feeling a whole lot better,' said Freddy, 'or you'll get strangled yourself, by the hangman. You'll get a trial first, of course, but you won't like it.'

'That's it, cheer me up, you bugger,' said Sergeant Miller, who hailed from East London. He was one of the many 14th Army men who had received 'Dear John' letters from their wives or sweethearts, asking either for a divorce or for the engagement to be broken on account of each said wife or sweetheart having fallen in love with an American GI. Sergeant Miller, twenty-five, had been married only six months prior to departing with his company for the war against Japan in March, 1942. His wife, Lily, was a good-looking young blonde, a 'smasher' according to Sergeant Miller, although Freddy, having been shown two snaps of her, thought that with her crimped hairstyle she was slightly brassy.

He and Dusty Miller had come to know each other during various Chindit operations. They had both earned their three stripes fighting the Japs, and both had become harder of body and soul. Dusty Miller was four years younger than Freddy, and Freddy, as his elder, offered terse advice when shown the bombshell of a letter Dusty received from his wife.

Dear George,
   I don't know how to write this letter but I've got to. I know I've not said anything about Elmer, an American soldier I met at the Lyceum Ballroom...

The Lyceum Ballroom, formerly the Lyceum Theatre, was a place where hundreds of English girls and women, attached or otherwise, had met their American fate.

That was six months ago, and I know I shouldn't have but I kept meeting him, well, you having been away such a long time it's not been much of a proper life for me as your wife, and Elmer helped me not to feel lonely. I'm ever so sorry but we're in love and want to marry, so I'm having to ask you if you'd give me a divorce. I don't mind having to take the blame. I really am ever so sorry, but you and me not having seen each other for over two years we'd probably be like strangers if we met. Hoping you're well and not wounded or anything, and that you'll understand.

Lily.

Freddy, having read it, refolded the letter and returned it to Dusty, who at that moment was still rigid with rage and shock. They were back at base for a brief rest following one more Chindit strike.

'Can you bloody believe it, can you?' ground Dusty.

'Stuff her,' said Freddy.

'What?'

'When you get home, if some of us ever do, stuff her up the chimney, leave her there for a weekend, then pull her down and dump her in a pond.'

'Christ,' breathed Dusty, 'there's me, hit with a bleedin' chopper by me own wife, and you give me that kind of advice, you played-out jungle wallah?'

'I can't do better,' said Freddy. 'A pond's the best place for her.'

'Can't you be more of a bloody help?'

247

'No, I bloody can't,' said Freddy.

Dusty wrote to his wife. He sent her a letter full of anger, disbelief and a total refusal to do anything that would help her and her fornicating GI.

Now, on the gliding ship, he considered Freddy's reference to the hangman.

'Is she worth swinging for, you mean?' he said.

'Well, is she?' said Freddy, thinking of what he'd feel like if he'd received a similar letter from Cassie. He'd feel he'd been hit by a train. 'Didn't I tell you first off to give her a good hiding and chuck her in a pond?'

'You told me to stuff her up the chimney first,' said Dusty, 'but take it from me, if I start manhandling her, I'll finish up breaking her neck.'

'Listen, mate,' said Freddy, 'you've earned yourself a future, not a dance on a rope. Let me give you some new advice. Keep away from her. What's your dad like, what's he do?'

'He's a council navvy, but he's been working in a fact'ry for the last three years.'

'Sounds like a useful muscleman,' said Freddy. 'Tell him to take care of your wife's GI, to go round to your house when he knows the bloke's there. Tell him to take a couple of mates with him, just in case the Yank's a bit hairy. Then do a heavy job on him. Enough to make sure he won't be able to fornicate for a year. Is your dad a close friend of yours? I mean, are you mates?'

'Too bloody true,' said Dusty.

'That's it, then. He'll do the job for you. You stay away, you got that?'

'Don't chuck your stripes at me, I've got three of my own, and I can sort out my own problems.'

248

'Suit yourself,' said Freddy. He knew that if he'd been in Dusty's shoes, he'd be planning an accident for the GI, not blonde Lily. As far as she was concerned, or any other back-sliding wife, dumping her in a pond would be enough.

That, and shutting the door permanently on her.

Cassie arrived home at ten minutes to twelve, and went straight to her kitchen, where she applied a match to the burners of the gas oven, and turned the flames low. In the oven she then placed a lidded crock containing a stew made from vegetables and a scrag-end of mutton, something the butcher had let her have as a bit of a gift. That is, at the marked price but without deducting the weight from her weekly ration. Maureen, her daughter who was called Muffin, and Lewis, her son, lapped up stews and wouldn't ask questions about the scrag-end. Cassie had made the stew first thing after taking the children to school. The school had reopened following the cessation of heavy air raids and the return home of many evacuated children. Cassie always took her two and brought them home, especially since the appearance of the flying bombs. Although the entry age was five, the school had accepted Lewis at four.

While the oven slowly reheated the stew, Cassie went to meet her girl and boy.

Over the meal of tasty stew, with dumplings, six-year-old Muffin said, 'Mummy, isn't Daddy ever going to come home?'

'Of course he is,' said Cassie. 'We'll get a letter from him one day telling us he's on his way.'

'I ought to 'ave a dad,' said Lewis.

'What d'you mean, you ought to have?' asked Muffin who, from the time Lewis was two, had made it clear she was boss.

'Well, so I ought,' said Lewis.

'Soppy boy, you've got the same dad as me,' said Muffin. 'He's a sergeant in the Army, and he always says things to us in his letters to Mummy.'

'Yes, but I can't remember 'im,' said Lewis.

'But we've got photographs of him that you've looked at,' said Muffin, chasing half a dumpling around her plate. Having caught it, she rolled her eyes at Cassie. 'I don't know what we're going to do with that boy, Mummy,' she said.

'Oh, he'll always pass with a push, won't you, Lewis love?' said Cassie. 'You have to remember, Muffin, he was very young when Daddy had to go abroad.'

Muffin, eyeing her brother as if not sure she could accept that as an excuse for him, said to him through a mouthful of dumpling, 'Yes, but what I mean is how can you say you ought to have a dad when you've got Daddy?'

'Muffin lovey, don't speak with your mouth full,' said Cassie.

'Yes, I wish she hadn't,' said Lewis, ''cos I fink I've got most of it all over me face.'

The first V-1 of the day passed over nearby Bermondsey then, and its noise spread just far enough for Cassie and her children to hear the diminishing vibrations. Muffin and Lewis winced, and went quiet for a short while before resuming their little argument. Because none of the flying bombs had dropped near their home or the immediate area, they were living with the menace, but Cassie knew it was right for all of them, including her dad, to go back to Wiltshire the day after tomorrow. Her dad, a good old stalwart, had said much the best thing for the kids, Cassie.

She hated the war. She hated it for what it had done to people, to families, and to the country. And as much as anything, she hated it for separating her from Freddy.

She couldn't wait for the day he'd be home. She thought about the fact that she hadn't heard from him for ages. Immediately, she pushed to the back of her mind the worst that that might mean.

'Mummy, you're looking worried,' said Muffin.

'Bleedin' doodlebugs, that's why,' said young Lewis, and Muffin gave a little yell of outrage.

'Mummy, did you hear that?' she cried.

'Lewis, where did you pick up that language?' asked Cassie.

'From Ginger Stubbs,' said Lewis, a picture of genuine innocence.

'Well, lovey,' said Cassie, 'anything else Ginger Stubbs says is out, out, out.'

'Out?' said Lewis.

'Yes, not to be repeated and not to be brought home,' said Cassie.

'Oh, all right,' said Lewis, even if he had no idea what was wrong with Ginger Stubbs's language. There was a lot like it around Walworth.

Chapter Twenty

Bobby came to. Vaguely, drowsily, he took in the smell of antiseptic. He murmured. He heard a woman's voice.

'He's coming to.'

'Not for long, Matron.' A man's voice. 'He'll be away again any moment.'

What the hell were they talking about? He asked himself that question in a kind of mental slow motion. Such as it was, it was his first fleeting moment of consciousness for many hours. He struggled to open lazy, heavy lids, but his mind clouded over and he drifted down again into the waiting abyss.

'Oh,' said Miss Alice Adams on opening her front door in the afternoon. That man was on the step, looking as dark-visaged as ever, his air of good-will emphasized by a smile of a positive kind.

'Guid afternoon, Miss Adams,' said Fergus MacAllister.

'Oh,' said Alice. 'Oh, hello.' The learned daughter of Tommy and Vi was slightly flustered.

'I thought I'd call to let you know I've been passed fit to rejoin my battalion,' said Fergus, as cheerful as a cockerel on the happiest of terms with a galaxy of fine-feathered hens. 'You've heard, I believe, that I'm empty of my wee bits of tin?'

'Yes, I heard from two of your workmates,' said Alice,' and I'm very glad for you.'

'I'm also here, Miss Adams, to acknowledge I owe you some recompense for giving you a few upsets,' said Fergus. 'I willna deny my impertinence, and to make up for it, I'd like you to have these wi' my best wishes.'

He handed her a white cardboard box. Slightly confused, Alice lifted the lid. Inside, encased in cellophane, were a dozen red roses.

'Oh!' she said, now really off balance.

'To be truthful,' said Fergus, 'I felt I couldna go on my way without offering you an apology for my bad manners, or without saying guidbye to you. I wish you great guid luck, Miss Adams.'

'Oh, but you don't have to go this minute, do you?' said Alice, overcome by the roses.

'I'm no' actually leaving until tomorrow evening,' said Fergus, 'when I'll be catching a night train to Edinburgh. I've to report to the barracks in two days, where I'll have a final medical.'

'Come in, you must,' said Alice. 'The roses are lovely, the first real bouquet I've ever had. Come in, Mr MacAllister, and share a pot of tea with me.'

'A pleasure, if you're sure I'm not interrupting your studies,' said Fergus.

'Why, Mr MacAllister, how can you say such a thing?' Alice sounded reproachful. 'Even my most serious studies can accept an interruption when someone brings me a dozen red roses. Really, I'm overwhelmed.'

Fergus stepped in, closing the door, and Alice

253

led the way to the kitchen. She glanced in the hall mirror as she passed it. The mirror seemed to blink in astonishment at such an unusual happening.

Alice was quite taken up with a sense of relief. She had actually felt she would like the chance of seeing Mr MacAllister again, so that she could let him know she was sorry for being unfriendly, and glad that he was now quite well.

She put the kettle on and she talked. Not about university or her studies, but about the welcome operation that had removed the residue of shrapnel from his body. Fergus stood listening and looking, hearing and seeing a different young lady, not a bit aloof or starchy, but actually animated. She went on about how pleased she was that he was now able to rejoin his Scottish regiment, which she was sure would do its part in helping to win the war against the Germans, who were a beastly lot for bombarding London with these flying bombs.

Having stood the roses in a bowl of water for the time being, she made the tea, placed the pot on a tray with cups, saucers, milk jug and a plate of plain wartime biscuits.

'Now,' she said, 'let's have it in the living room, it's more comfy there, and you can tell me about your happy time in King's College Hospital.'

Fergus followed her into the spacious living room. It spoke of an affluent family in that its carpet of thick pile covered almost the whole of the floor, around which was fine furniture based on polished rosewood, even if two attractive sofas had been favoured over modern settees. Fergus saw sofas as representative of a family with one foot still in the past. They could still be seen in his family home in Aberdeen. He commented in appreciation of this living room without mentioning the sofas. Alice said that her father, as a director of Adams Enterprises and efficient manager of the Belsize Park factory, had really done very well for himself and his family, but was very modest about it.

The day was warm, and the open French windows gave a view of a well-kept garden and the rooftops of houses showing amid leafy trees in the area on the west side of Denmark Hill.

'Och, aye, I like a man who can be modest about his success, Miss Adams,' said Fergus, who could have told her that his own father owned an Aberdeen factory manufacturing precision instruments. It had prospered by reason of wartime contracts, but he couldn't have said his old man was modest about it, or that his strong Protestant beliefs didn't make life difficult for his family on occasions.

'Well, sit down,' said Alice, placing the tray on a table. Fergus seated himself in a deep armchair. He knew Tommy Adams as a customer of the Gas Board, and as a stalwart-looking cockney whose daughter was more representative of the middle class. Alice poured the tea, handed him a cup and saucer, and offered the biscuits. He took one. She was still talking, this time about an old family friend, a Mrs Rachel Goodman, who had not only been bombed out during the original Blitz on London, but had recently had her new house damaged by a V-1.

'That's no' just bad luck,' said Fergus, 'that's no' fair. One bomb is enough for any family.'

'More than enough,' said Alice, and referred again to his time in hospital. Fergus said all it amounted to was a whiff of gas, a touch of the knife, and some stitches. He was now feeling fine, he said. 'But isn't it a bit soon to be going up to Edinburgh?' asked Alice, seating herself.

'It canna be too soon for me,' said Fergus, 'but they'll no' be sending me off to France until they've polished up my drill and given me new weapon training?'

'Well, I do wish you luck,' said Alice, and talked about how long the war had gone on, how it was beginning to tire people out, and all the worries her parents had had to suffer from air raids and other unpleasant happenings. Fergus couldn't help showing a little smile at times. It was as if Miss Alice Adams had suddenly found there was more to life than preparing herself for Bristol University.

From the direction of the *Pas de Calais*, a V-1 crossed the Channel. Eluding air patrols in its speed, it was soon within sight and hearing of the people on the streets off Herne Hill. They lifted their heads to stare up at the pilotless machine of destruction.

People in the Denmark Hill area heard it. Alice heard it, came quickly to her feet and went to the open French windows to search the sky.

'It sounds frighteningly close,' she said.

'Come away, lassie,' said Fergus, and stiffened as the huge buzzing noise stopped. The winged bomb dipped and nosedived. Alice saw it, and stood rigid and paralysed as it rushed down towards the rooftops of houses in the near distance. Fergus, glimpsing it himself, leapt towards Alice. Reaching her, he took hold of her and flung her down on the carpet, himself with her, just as the V-1 disappeared and struck a clump of trees at the back of a garden in Ferndene Road. It smashed into them, and the instant splintering of a trunk produced a sound like the crack of a rifle. Gasping, Alice tensed for the explosion. But none came, the mechanism failed on impact, and the huge bomb rolled and settled at the foot of the smashed trees.

'Oh, my God,' gasped Alice, fighting to get her breath back, and quite sure that an explosive blast would arrive any moment and take the roof off the house, 'what's happening?'

'I'm thinking Jerry's fired a dud,' said Fergus, 'a one-in-a-thousand dud, thank the Lord.'

He sat up. Alice lay on her back, shockingly disordered of dress and slip to the eyes of the prim and proper. Not being of that species, Fergus blinked happily. Alice uttered a little scream, blushed to her roots, sat up and covered herself.

'Oh, no, I don't believe it,' she gasped.

'Whisht, it's no' so bad compared to what might have been,' said Fergus. 'It was only your legs, Miss Adams, and we've all got legs, y'ken. I willna say, however, that I've seen any better-looking than yours.'

'Oh, you ungallant beast,' said Alice, 'you did that to me, you put me on the floor.'

'Had to,' smiled Fergus, 'in case you forgot to

257

duck. When bombs or shells are flying about, there's only one way to save your head being blown off, and that's to duck down and go flat on your face. And a carpet's kinder to the face than hard ground. Further, you canna take the risk of a shell or a bomb being a dud.'

'I have to point out that you threw me down,' said Alice heatedly, 'and I landed on my back, not on my face.'

'Aye, throw you I did, but haven't I just argued we couldna take the risk of that bomb being a dud?' said Fergus. 'It's lying there somewhere in Ferndene Road, I'm thinking, and the residents will be wondering if it's going to explode any moment.'

Alice shook off personal feelings.

'Shouldn't we go round to see if anyone is hurt and needs help?' she asked.

'No, lassie, we shouldna do that.'

'I'm not afraid,' said Alice.

'Then you should be,' said Fergus. 'I'd be feared to go walking into a possible explosion mysel'. It's a job for the police, the wardens, and the other air-raid services. There's the fire service, they'll arrive for a beginning. The police will get people out of their houses and call up the Army's bomb disposal squad to neutralize the V-1.

'How will they do that?' asked Alice.

'By touch, feel, expertise and the kind of courage not many of us have,' said Fergus. 'It'll be a matter of first getting the nose-cone off, and I'd no' like to be too near it while that's happening. We're fortunate in being where we

258

are, far enough away not to have to do some running.'

'But you fought in the battles during the retreat to Dunkirk,' said Alice. 'That must have taken some courage.'

'Fighting for your life in a battle that heats the blood can't compare with having to disarm one of these devilish doodlebugs when the blood's cold,' said Fergus.

Alice looked at him, his expression soberly reflective. She conceded that her feelings towards him were changing, and that she wasn't disposed to fight the change.

'Fergus, we've let our tea get cold,' she said.

'Och, aye, but that's of no importance,' said Fergus. 'Cold tea at the North Pole, that would count as depressing, y'ken, but here, at this moment, no, dinna think anything of it.'

'I'll make a fresh pot,' said Alice.

'No, I'll no' put you to that trouble,' said Fergus.

'It's no trouble, and you don't have to go yet, do you?' said Alice.

'I've time to spare, Miss Adams.'

'I'm Alice, and I'd like you to stay for a while.'

'It'd be a pleasure,' said Fergus. He smiled and Alice changed her mind about labelling his looks villainous. 'A pleasure I'll remember, for I'm thinking we'll no' meet again.'

'That's negative thinking,' said Alice.

'Ah?' said Fergus.

'Well, after sharing that moment of fright and terror,' said Alice, 'we can hardly be distant with each other.'

'I'll no' easily forget our time on the floor,' said Fergus.

'I didn't mean that, far from it!' said Alice.

'It's still something I'll no' forget,' said Fergus.

Alice shook her head and laughed. It was the first time Fergus had heard that kind of sound from her, the first time he had seen how it made her eyes light up.

'Fergus, it's time we became friends,' she said.

'I'd like that,' he said.

'I'll make fresh tea,' she said.

When Vi arrived home after spending time with Lizzy, Alice was just saying goodbye to Fergus at the open front door. Vi, walking up the drive, stopped in curiosity.

The Scotsman, the Gas Board mechanic so disliked by Alice, was saying something to her, and Alice was all happy smiles, the kind she would never have shown to someone she didn't approve of.

Well, I'm blessed, thought Vi, has our Alice got a springtime fancy at last, and in the middle of summer? Wonders just don't cease, not even in this unhappy world. Tommy'll be pleased if it means his only daughter won't end up as one of them blue-stockinged old maids, and I will say Mr MacAllister is a nice, cheerful man, the kind Tommy gets on with.

'Alice?'

Alice turned her head.

'Oh, hello, Mum,' she said. 'Fergus called and brought me some lovely red roses, and he was here, thank goodness, when a doodlebug

260

dropped in Ferndene Road. But a miracle happened, it didn't explode, and Fergus said not to go round because the police wouldn't want us to, or anyone else. We think a bomb disposal team is there now. Fergus said they'll be trying to defuse it.'

All those words came easily from Alice's lips. And more followed, rather overwhelming Vi, but she took in the information that this man from Scotland was going up to Edinburgh tomorrow night to rejoin his regiment, and that Alice was very glad for him in his wish to get back into uniform.

Well, thought Vi, perhaps she has got a springtime fancy at last. At the age of nineteen and going on for twenty, no-one could say that was too soon.

'Well, come on, Mum, say hello to Fergus,' said Alice.

'Oh, pleasured to see you, I'm sure, Mr MacAllister,' smiled Vi. 'We've all heard about your successful operation, but I didn't know about any doodlebug in Ferndene Road. Lord, that's a bit too close for my liking. I'm only thankful you were here to be a comfort to Alice.'

'Comfort?' said Alice. 'Mum, he threw me to the floor.'

'Beg pardon?' said Vi, startled.

'Aye, so I did, Mrs Adams,' said Fergus, 'but only as a precautionary measure. Alice was standing at the open French windows as the V-1 dropped. We both glimpsed it, so down we went on your floor to avoid any blast. It occurred to me you wouldna have liked your daughter to have had her head blown off, and I never feel I want to lose my own too easily. Mind, Alice wasna too pleased wi' me, for I daresay it's uncommon for her to end up on a floor.'

'Thanks very much for working that out,' said Alice, but with a smile.

'Are we worried that this bomb might still go off?' asked Vi.

'I've a feeling, Mrs Adams, that the bomb disposal unit must be winning,' said Fergus, 'or the police might be asking for the whole of Denmark Hill to be vacated, although I doubt if the blast from as far as Ferndene Road would do more than make your roof tiles quiver a wee bit.'

'Oh, that's all right, then,' said Vi. 'I must say I'm pleased things have turned out nice for you, Mr MacAllister, and I'm sure we'll all want to know how you get on when you're back in the Army.'

'I'm touched,' said Fergus. 'Guidbye now. Guid luck to you, Alice, and to you, Mrs Adams.'

He shook Vi's hand, then gave a light touch to Alice's arm, a touch that was a gesture of appreciation for her friendliness and hospitality. It was also to let her know he would like to keep in touch with her. Alice Adams was as bonny a young lady as any Scots girl. He had a rival, of course, in Bristol University, and if it looked like becoming her first love, he'd have to blow it up. Well, he knew a thing or two about explosives.

'Goodbye, Fergus, do take care,' said Alice, 'but wait a moment, what's that funny smile doing on your face?'

'Funny?' said Fergus.

'Och, aye, funny, y'ken,' said Alice, imitating his Scottish brogue.

'I'm thinking of walls tumbling down,' said Fergus.

'Goodness,' said Vi, 'what walls?'

'Oh, I just had a thought,' said Fergus, 'it's gone now. Guidbye, and guid luck again.'

Alice and her mother watched him leave, his walk swinging and easy. He turned at the gate, and smiled and waved. They waved back, and Alice impulsively called.

'Write to me.'

'Gladly,' said Fergus, and went smiling on his way.

'Alice?' said Vi, as she entered the hall with her daughter.

'Oh, I think I like that man, after all,' said Alice.

'Well, your dad and me aren't going to complain, love,' said Vi.

'I don't mean it's serious,' said Alice, guarding herself against the possibility that her happy fixation on university might actually come to take second place to something else. Such a possibility had to be impossible.

'Not serious, no, all right, love,' said Vi. But I just don't know, she thought, it still seems that our Alice might have found an interest she likes more than her books. What kind of interest? An exciting one, like a tall dark man?

'Mum, you're making a funny noise,' said Alice.

'Beg pardon, love?'

'Mum, you're actually giggling, at your age.'

'No, just a bit of a cough, and it's gone now.'

'So it should have, giggles are for little girls,'

said Alice, and gave her mum a look.

Vi couldn't help herself. Alice and a tall dark man. Something like another giggle trembled in her throat. What a day. Well, she'd had a bit of a giggle in Lyons during the morning, when Susie said only a bloke like Boots could turn a high-class woman like Polly into the mother of twins. She'd have to tell Tommy that.

'I suppose I'm forgetting my age, Alice,' she said.

Alice laughed.

My, that girl of ours sounds much more natural, thought Vi, and she hasn't got her nose in a book, for a change. I'll have to tell Tommy that too.

'Eh?' said Tommy, when he was home from work and Vi had his ear to herself. 'Susie said *what* in Lyons?'

'Yes, in Lyons,' said Vi, 'and your mum, of course, hoped no-one was listening.'

'Tell me again what Susie said, I ain't sure I got it right first time,' said Tommy.

'That Boots was a bit of a shocker, and the only man who could've turned a high-class woman like Polly into the mother of twins,' said Vi.

Tommy grinned.

'Got to hand it to Boots, putting Polly in the club at his age and her age,' he said. 'Got to hand it to Susie as well, for sort of putting it on record in Lyons.'

'Even your mum laughed,' said Vi. 'Well, she nearly did, and Cassie nearly split her sides. And I had a good old giggle.'

'No harm in that,' said Tommy, pouring himself a glass of light ale from a bottle of Watney's. 'Here, d'you know what Gertie told me today?'

'That she's leaving?' said Vi.

'What, good old Gertie?' said Tommy, and took a mouthful of ale through the rim of foam. 'Don't give me that kind of worry, Vi. If Gertie packed it in, the factory would fall down dead.'

'Oh, dear,' said Vi.

'The roof would go first, then the walls, and all the bricks and tiles would follow Gertie home. No she's not leaving, and what she told me is that the Yanks get their own beer shipped over in cans. She got that from a niece that's walking out with a Yank. Cans. I ask you, Vi, beer in cans? Cans are all right for baked beans, condensed milk and corned beef, but beer?'

'I suppose bottles coming all the way from America might get broken,' said Vi.

'Well, one thing's for sure,' said Tommy, 'beer in cans won't ever take on here. I'd fall down dead meself if it did.' He took another gulp of the bottled ale. 'Listen, did Susie really say that about Boots?'

'Yes, she came right out with it,' said Vi.

'Susie's a card,' said Tommy. 'Always was, even when she first started working for Sammy on his stall and was skinny all over on account of not getting enough to eat. Look at her now, figure nearly on a par with Lizzy's.' Some more ale went down. 'Lizzy'll have to get measured for a new corset by Christmas, I reckon. She's getting what you call buxom.'

'Tommy Adams, that's your loving sister you're

talking about,' said Vi, 'and she's fretting about where Bobby's got to.'

'Bobby's got sense and stamina,' said Tommy. 'I told Lizzy last week he'll turn up, even if right now Jerry's chucking things at him in Normandy. Where's Alice?'

'In the garden,' said Vi.

'With her nose in a learning book, I suppose,' said Tommy.

'No, she's taking the dead buds off the rose bushes,' said Vi.

'Eh?' said Tommy.

'I think roses are a bit special to her today,' said Vi. 'You'll never believe, but Fergus MacAllister brought her a dozen lovely red ones this afternoon.

'Eh?' said Tommy again, so Vi told him about Alice's new attitude towards Fergus, and her admission that she liked him, and that she'd asked him to write just when he was leaving.

'Well, roll me over, I'm hearing things,' said Tommy. 'Our Alice has got feelings for a bloke?'

'It must be because she's suddenly realized Fergus is tall, dark and handsome,' said Vi.

'Skin me alive,' said Tommy, 'I think I'll treat meself to what's left in that bottle of Watney's. Alice interested in a tall, dark and handsome Scotch bloke, Susie talking saucy about Boots in Lyons, and beer in cans? What kind of a day am I having?'

'I've been having an entertaining one,' said Vi.

Through the evening sky at speed, one more V-1 appeared, passing over Nunhead, to roar on towards Central London out of sight and sound of Tommy, Vi and Alice. It fell silent above Bermondsey and nosedived into the Thames near Blackfriars Bridge. Exploding on impact, it created great eruptions of water. The river was not amused. For long minutes after the eruptions subsided, it swirled angrily around the large pool of restless bubbles.

At his headquarters deep in the forest at Rastenburg, East Prussia, Hitler was receiving encouraging news from Dr Goebbels in Berlin of how effectively the V-1's were pounding the people of London, reducing huge areas of the capital to rubble and panicking the British Government. Very satisfying that was to the *Fuehrer*, whose own capital was being cruelly knocked about by the Allied bombing squadrons.

He chose to ignore the fact that his propaganda minister was prone to exaggeration.

Chapter Twenty-One

Bobby came to for a second time. He opened his eyes and in vague curiosity examined a white ceiling. His mouth was dry, his palate execrable, his head painful, his body inert. He tried to think. His mind refused to co-operate. He tried to lift himself. The pain that stabbed at his head made him gasp. Someone came rustling up. So did someone else. Whispers floated about.

Arms slid under his back and gently lifted him. A glass containing a liquid reached his lips, and his lips parted. The glass tipped and he drank thirstily. The arms relaxed and he sank back, the pain in his head slowly ebbing away as he was taken by the sedative into blissful unconsciousness.

'Tomorrow,' said Sister Yates of Lewes Hospital, 'he should be a little better.'

'Hopefully,' said Nurse Wickford, 'tomorrow will be another day.'

'Yes, we've all seen Scarlett O'Hara in *Gone with the Wind*,' said Sister Yates. 'Check the temperatures of the other two, will you, Nurse?'

'Of course, Sister.'

Bobby had no idea the plane had crashed close to Lewes in Sussex, that the noise had awakened a farmer and his family, and brought them running to the plane. The farmer had rushed back to his house to phone Lewes Hospital, requesting an ambulance and a medical team. The team was needed to get the people out of the plane. They were injured and unconscious, and the farmer said he and his family were against getting them out themselves in case they worsened the injuries. He then rang the police station. The ambulance subsequently arrived with a medical team. The pilot was found to be dead. The three injured survivors of the crash were carefully removed on stretchers and rushed to hospital. The police meanwhile had made contact with the nearest RAF station.

In London, Colonel Buckmaster, head of SOE (French), was now in possession of the facts, and intending to go to Lewes as soon as possible.

Later that evening

A spate of V-1's had crashed down near the Pool of London, causing the old rubble mountains of destroyed wharfside buildings to spew disintegrating bricks like eruptions from volcanoes.

In their apartment, Patsy and her Pa were having one more argument.

'No way, Pa, no way am I going to be parcelled off to Dublin,' said Patsy.

'It's time to be reasonable, honey,' said Pa Kirk.

'When being reasonable means being freighted to Ireland, it's jolly unreasonable,' said Patsy.

'It's what?'

'Can I help it if I picked up some English expressions at that la-di-da boarding school you sent me to?'

'La-di-da?'

'Oh, come on, Pa,' said Patsy, 'you know that's English for swanky.'

'Patsy, by this time next week I'll be some place in the Cherbourg Peninsular with other war correspondents.'

'Sure you will, Pa, and I'll be right there with you in spirit.'

'I was hoping Mike Brady could persuade you to think positively about taking up his offer of staying in Dublin,' said Pa Kirk. 'But he wasn't persuasive enough, it seems.'

'Pa, there was never any chance he was going to get me to go to Dublin. You've got to do what you've got to do, be a gritty war correspondent, and I've got to do what I've got to do, stick it out here with Daniel and his family and our neighbours. Pa, you can understand that, can't you?'

'Patsy, you're asking me to leave you here in this apartment, in the path of these goddamned V-1's, while I'm safely moving about behind the American lines in France?'

'Oh, have I told you Daniel wants to talk to you about getting me to move in with his Aunt Vi and Uncle Tommy?' said Patsy.

'No, you haven't told me,' said Pa Kirk.

'Well, he does want to see you,' said Patsy. 'He mentioned that his aunt and uncle's daughter lives with them and that she and I might get to be buddies.'

'Buddies?' Pa Kirk, for all his maturity and his worldliness, was floundering a bit.

'The very word,' said Patsy. 'My English fun guy is beginning to talk like an American cowboy.'

'Your English fun guy?'

Patsy took on a firm look.

'Yes, Pa.'

'Meaning?'

'I don't want to lose him by going off to Ireland.'

'Patsy, we've been through all this before,' said Pa Kirk, 'and each time you've left me unsure of your exact feelings for Daniel. Come clean, honey, or I'll have to think about pulling a few strings and booking you a berth on a homegoing ship.'

'Pa, you wouldn't do that, you couldn't!' Patsy was in sudden distress, and Pa Kirk actually saw wetness in her eyes. That tugged at his heart-strings. Patsy, endearing and lovable, was his one real treasure.

'There's something, is there, Patsy, that means more to you than a return to Boston?' he said gently. 'I did tell you this old country doesn't hold great post-war prospects for young people.'

'Pa, Daniel has prospects, he really does.' Patsy was emphatic. 'His father is big in business, he has a property company as well as shops and factories, and he's promised Daniel a major position in the property company after the war.'

'And that's important to Daniel, of course,' said Pa Kirk.

'Well, it naturally is, isn't it?' said Patsy.

'Here's the crunch question, Patsy. How important is it to you?'

'Well, I guess it could come to mean a lot,' said Patsy. 'It could.'

'Jesus,' said Pa Kirk. 'Patsy, he's not eighteen

271

yet, is he? He's not even among the UK's newest enlisted men. Has he said or intimated he's in love with you?'

'No, Pa.' Patsy made a little face. 'Honest, he's kept off anything like that, and so have I. I think we both realize we've got a year or so to go before we can be adult in our conversational exchanges.'

'Before what?' said Pa Kirk, not sure whether to laugh or worry. 'Patsy, say that again.'

'Now, Pa, you know what I mean,' said Patsy.

'Do I? It seems to me I'm listening to something coming out of the top of a young head.'

'Well, this young head, Pa, belongs to someone who's keeping house for you,' said Patsy.

'Ah,' said Pa Kirk. He rubbed his chin. 'You've made a point, honey.'

'Pa, I have to have time,' said Patsy. 'Right now I feel there's no-one I could be happier with than Daniel. But I'm willing to wait and see if I've just got a crush. I guess you're thinking that. But don't send me home, Pa, give me time to work things out.'

'That's what you want, honey, time?'

'Yes, Pa,' said Patsy.

'I think you mean time for both of you, don't you?'

'Yes, Pa.'

'OK, Patsy, you've got it,' said Pa Kirk.

'Pa, oh, thanks.' Patsy hugged him. 'You're the best ever, and I love you for being that.'

'But I'm not going to have you living here alone, even if you have got friends and neighbours in the other apartments. If the offer's good, move in with Daniel's relatives.'

272

'Oh, I sure will,' said Patsy happily, 'I'll ask Daniel if he can fix that for the day you go to France.'

'Do that,' said Pa Kirk. 'Now, there's just one more thing. I know this damn' war is hastening the disappearance of all kinds of conventions, but if you find out you've more than a crush, let Daniel make the running, don't throw yourself at him.'

'Throw myself at him?' said Patsy. 'Pa, don't you think I know the value of self-respect? Besides, I guess I'm all in favour of the kind of conventions you're talking about. And on top of that, Daniel's grandma wouldn't approve of anything else.'

'His grandma? How would she know?'

'Oh, she knows everything that happens to her grandsons and granddaughters. Daniel said so, and knowing her as I do, I believe him.'

'Some lady,' said Pa Kirk and laughed, and Patsy felt how great it was for a girl and her father to be the best of friends.

'Pa, thanks for being my dad,' she said.

Later that evening, when her Pa was up in town, she rang Daniel. Susie answered.

'Oh, hi, Mrs Adams, it's Patsy. Is Daniel there?'

Susie smiled. Few were the days when Patsy and Daniel didn't meet, or talk to each other on the phone.

'He's across the road, mowing Mrs Wells's lawn, Patsy. She couldn't manage it herself after he put her mower right yesterday morning, so Pippa asked if he could do it this evening.'

'But, Mrs Adams, it's nearly dark,' said Patsy.

'That means he'll be back any moment, and I'll get him to ring you, Patsy.'

'Thanks, Mrs Adams.'

Patsy sat fuming after hanging up. That girl Philippa. She might have some guy in the Royal Navy breathing heavy over her, but she was homing in on Daniel. Patsy was sure of that.

I'll get real sick if he falls for that flirty creature.

It was a little while before the phone rang. Patsy jumped up, then steadied herself before picking it up.

'Patsy Kirk. Who's this?'

'Hello, ray of American sunshine, Daniel here. Mum said you rang.'

'Daniel, where've you been, and what have you been doing?' Patsy could hardly believe how sick she was already.

'I've been cutting Mrs Wells's lawn–'

'With that girl Philippa?'

'No, with her mum's mower. Anyway, Pippa's GI called for her, and out she went with him.'

'What? But I thought you said she was dating a sailor.'

'Oh, he's sort of optional,' said Daniel.

'Well, I think that's low-down, especially if she's got her eye on you as well.'

'If she has, I'll do some running. And I might have to do some from her Ma too.'

'Her Ma?'

'Sure thing,' said Daniel. 'After I'd finished mowing her lawn, she invited me in. She had a gin and tonic and I had a shandy.'

'Shandy?'

'Ale in a glass topped up with ginger beer. Anyway, she sat over there and I sat over here, if you get me, and we both said to hell with Hitler's doodlebugs. Then she crossed her legs and there was a flash of elastic.'

'Elastic?'

'Something like that. Nearly ruined my eyesight, I can tell you.'

'Daniel, you're sexy, d'you know that?'

'Me?' said Daniel. 'Patsy, I don't cross my legs and flash my—'

'Daniel!'

'Now what?'

'Think what you're saying. And listen, when I said you were sexy, I meant you were talking sexy.

'Is that good?' asked Daniel.

'Ask your granny,' said Patsy.

'I don't think I'd better,' said Daniel. 'Anyway, about Mrs Wells. I panicked.'

'I don't believe that,' said Patsy.

'No, it's a fact,' said Daniel. 'Well, I've lately suspected that Pippa's Ma fancies me—'

'Fancies you? It's indecent, talking about someone's mother like that.'

'Oh, this one's not old or churchgoing, so instead of staying, I finished my shandy and made a beeline for home and safety. Well, I put it to you, Patsy, what chance would I have had if there'd been a crisis?'

'What crisis?' Patsy wasn't sick any more, she was having fun over the phone.

'Patsy, with her figure, she's a lot heavier than I am, and if she'd jumped on me—'

'Daniel, now you're being disgusting.'

'All I know is that I chose safety first,' said Daniel.

'And all I know is that I don't believe a word of it,' said Patsy.

'You can believe one thing, that it's a relief to find myself talking to you,' said Daniel. 'Why did you want me to phone you?'

'So that you can listen to something that's not disgusting,' said Patsy.

'Go ahead.'

'Oh, thanks. First, you're not to go across the street to that house any more.'

'Eh? Oh, right, Patsy, leave that house alone. Right.'

'You don't mind I'm playing bossy?' she said.

'No, I think you just don't want me to get flattened.'

'So stay away.'

'Stay away. Right, Patsy.'

'Listen. Daniel, Pa's going to let me hang on here indefinitely. He said I needn't go back to Boston until – oh, I guess until my feelings change.'

'What feelings?' asked Daniel.

'That's if they ever do,' said Patsy.

'But what feelings?' asked Daniel.

'Are you pleased Pa's going to let me stay indefinitely?'

'Rapturous,' said Daniel, 'but these feelings of yours, you haven't–'

'Oh, by the way,' said Patsy, 'Pa's going off to France next Saturday with the other war correspondents, and he doesn't want me to be alone here, so could you ask your aunt and uncle if I really could move in with them?'

'Of course, Patsy, I'll talk to them, and I'm sure you'll be able to move in as soon as we come back from the holiday in Cornwall. The holiday's only next Saturday.'

'Oh, yes, I can't wait,' said Patsy. 'Thanks for promising to speak to your aunt and uncle. Daniel, I really am glad we met that day, but I'd better hang up now, I've got all sorts of things to do.'

'Patsy–'

'I'll come round tomorrow evening, shall I? Good night, Daniel.' Patsy hung up.

I still don't know what feelings she was talking about, thought Daniel, but what I do know is I'm happy she's not going home to Boston just yet.

His dad came into the hall.

'Dreaming, Daniel?' said Sammy.

Daniel looked at his dad, a tall man, like Uncle Boots and Uncle Tommy, and still full of energy. Electric was what people called him. It kind of showed in his blue eyes whenever he had a new idea or a new challenge. Although he was over forty, and getting on a bit, poor old Dad, he was still the active kingpin of the family business.

'I've just been talking to Patsy.'

'I'm admiring of that girl,' said Sammy.

'She's staying indefinitely, with permission from her Pa,' said Daniel.

'Not going back to America?' said Sammy. 'No wonder I'm admiring of her, considering there's times when these perishing doodlebugs sound as if they're chasing people up and down their stairs. Well, good as.'

'You're right, Dad,' said Daniel, 'I've had moments when I was sure one was climbing up my shirt-tail.'

Sammy turned sober. The day hadn't been quiet.

'A joke or two helps, I suppose,' he said, 'but let's face it, me lad, no-one's laughing out loud. On the other hand, look at it this way. America's a bit of a dubious place for a girl like Patsy, so she might be safer here. You've heard of Al Capone, I suppose?'

'Yes, and I think he's dead,' said Daniel.

'But there's a lot more like him that have come up out of the ground,' said Sammy. 'Not the sort of geezers young Patsy ought to get introduced to. You've heard of gangsters' molls as well, I suppose?'

'Dad, you're over the top if you're suggesting Patsy would ever get to be a gangster's moll,' said Daniel.

'I agree, not a chance,' said Sammy. 'I'm only saying gangsters and their molls don't happen to be the kind of people we'd want her to get mixed up with.'

'Give over, Dad, you're falling off your horse.'

'What I mean, me lad, is that it might work out better over here for Patsy,' said Sammy. 'I'm glad she's staying on. Your mum and me have taken to her, so have your grandparents.'

'Dad, are you telling me something?'

'Not my place to,' said Sammy, 'except it's up to you to see she doesn't get shipped back to America and land in the soup. I mentioned Al Capone, didn't I?'

'Yes, Dad, sort of loudly,' said Daniel.

'Very dodgy geezer,' said Sammy, shaking his head. 'I came up against a bloke like him once. Large and round, and known as the Fat Man. Dead evil, believe me, but your Uncle Boots sorted him out on my behalf.'

'Pity Uncle Boots was never given the chance to sort out Hitler,' said Daniel. 'By the way, what d'you think of Mrs Wells across the road?'

'Tarty,' said Sammy. 'It's all right you mowing her lawn for her, but if she ever invites you into her parlour, start running.'

Daniel's grin was broad and wide.

Chapter Twenty-Two

The 19th of July, early morning

Riding to the factory in Uncle Tommy's car, as usual, Daniel brought up the subject of Patsy and her need for a new roof over her head when she came back from Cornwall.

'You and Aunt Vi did mention, and so did Aunt Lizzy and Uncle Ned, that–'

'That you only had to ask?' said Tommy, keeping an eye on the road and the traffic, and an ear open for the noisy animosity of V-1's. You couldn't set your clock by their arrival. Sometimes hours went by without sight or sound of any. At other times they came in intermittent spates like April showers. 'Ask away, Daniel.'

'Ta muchly,' said Daniel. 'Could you and Aunt Vi give her a room?'

'Three, if she wants,' said Tommy. 'There's only Alice at home. David and Paul are staying in Devon for the time being. David's got his farm work, and while these ruddy doodlebugs keep coming, Paul might as well stay to finish his schooling. No problem about Patsy, we'll like having her. Vi and me, we're taken with your American girl.'

Just what his parents and grandparents felt, thought Daniel, according to what his dad had said. If everyone else in the family felt the same,

Patsy would eventually be asking questions about what was happening to her. It would be in the form of an invisible family embrace. And what could he do about that until the war was well over and his prospects were turning out to be as promising as expected? A bloke couldn't take any prospects for granted, he could only hope.

'Thanks, Uncle Tommy, you're a sport, and so's Aunt Vi.'

'A pleasure, me lad,' said Tommy, then drew a hissing breath. 'Jesus Christ, look at that, Daniel!'

Clearly in their sights was one of the jet-propelled monsters, buzzing high above Camberwell New Road, heading for Kennington Oval and Vauxhall, travelling in a straight, undeviating line that would take it across the river to Hyde Park.

'Oh, gawd blimey,' breathed Daniel in the cockney lingo that belonged to the years the family had spent in Walworth.

Tommy kept going, passing pedestrians who had stopped to stare. The V-1, size diminishing to the eye, could still be seen. Suddenly it dipped, and Tommy and Daniel knew its power unit had cut out.

'It's going to hit Vauxhall Bridge!' gasped Tommy.

'I'm praying for the bridge and the people caught on it,' breathed Daniel.

'God, I hope they'll make a successful run for their lives,' said Tommy.

The black monster had disappeared. Tommy drove on, passing the Oval to enter Harleyford

Road, which led to the bridge. He and Daniel, teeth clenched, awaited the traffic hold-up that would indicate the bridge had been hit. But the traffic was moving on, slowly. It was always slow on the approach. The bridge came into view. People were lining it on one side, and other people were hurrying and scampering to join them.

The Thames had received another explosive strike, and its waters on the south side of the bridge were heaving and boiling. Tommy, now on the bridge and driving very slowly, called to a man from his open window.

'What happened, mate?'

'Fell in the bleedin' drink and drowned itself, didn't it?'

'Ta, old cock, you've made me morning a happy one,' said Tommy.

'Bleedin' painful one for the fishes, though,' called the man.

Tommy drove on, whistling a song.

Daniel thought of Patsy staying on to face these flying bombs in company with the people of London.

What a girl, what a poppet.

A small convoy of six merchant ships and two troopships, escorted by a Royal Navy destroyer and corvette, was passing through the Strait of Gibraltar, the Rock a heavily fortified bastion guarding the Strait. Aboard one of the troopships were a number of 14th Army veterans.

'Won't be long now, Freddy,' said Sergeant Dusty Miller.

'Just three more days,' said Freddy, his thoughts on Cassie and his kids.

'Then it's the gloves on for me and me loving wife,' said Dusty.

'Forget it,' said Freddy.

'Give over, I'll never forget it.'

'I mean forget it till you get there,' said Freddy. 'You're beginning to be a pain in my bloody elbow. And my ears.'

'Well, bloody hard luck,' said Dusty, as bitter as vinegar.

'Now look,' said Freddy, the lower deck heaving beneath his feet as the ship churned through the notoriously choppy Strait, 'I've got sympathy for you, and I feel for you. But if you don't calm down, you'll blow it, you'll boot both of them to kingdom come and swing for it. Get wise, Dusty. They're not worth it.'

'You're right, I know it, but—'

'Have a fag,' said Freddy, offering his free tin.

'Ta, don't mind if I do.'

They smoked their gaspers as they tramped the crowded deck, and Freddy thought again of Cassie and his kids.

Cassie.

If he too was bitter about some things, he was only ever in reflective praise of Cassie. And grateful for the son and daughter she had given him.

Freddy, as a Chindit, was tough and hardened, much as Tim Adams was as a Commando, but both held resolutely on to what meant most to them. Both knew that however drained and tired their country would be post-war, there was going to be no place like home and family.

Bobby was conscious. His head, swathed in bandages, was aching, but for the first time he was able to talk coherently. His bed had been wheeled into a private room, at the request of Colonel Buckmaster, who was sitting beside him, pleasant features typically sympathetic.

'You know now you've got a fractured skull?'

'I know just from the feel of it,' said Bobby.

'The operation relieved all pressure,' said Colonel Buckmaster. 'So you'll be able to hang on to your thinking apparatus, your use of which has earned the firm's gratitude.'

'I've heard better jokes,' said Bobby.

'You also know, don't you, what happened to Lieutenant Aarlberg?'

'I know,' said Bobby.

'Concussion, fractured shoulder blade, and a broken arm.'

'I know.' Bobby's voice was dry and husky. 'But I don't think I'm up to visiting her yet.'

'She's comfortable, and happy to know you're going to recover. Victor sustained a cracked rib-cage, a fractured wrist and a broken leg. Pilot-Officer Gregory never stood a chance, of course. We've lost an accomplished and fearless Lysander man.'

'I know that too, and that the crash was all due to that stinking weasel Pierre,' said Bobby.

'Pierre was hanged not long after he got back to his house that night.'

'Not by the Gestapo,' said Bobby.

'No, by the Resistance,' said Colonel Buckmaster. 'They were waiting for him.'

'So they hanged him. Is that a consolation?'

'Very little consolation exists for friends or relatives of the victims of this war. Would you like me to let your parents know you and Lieutenant Aarlberg were injured in an accident in Sussex, say, when your car collided with another?'

Bobby, under orders from the nursing staff to lie quite still, said, 'One day all my relatives, and Helene's, are going to know how we spent most of this war.'

'We'd still like all that to remain exclusive until the war's over.'

'I thought you'd say that,' said Bobby. 'But about a car accident, which of us are you going to put at the wheel?'

'I thought Lieutenant Aarlberg. As a FANY officer, that would be appropriate. Many of them take the wheel.'

'She won't like the implication that she might have been at fault. But go ahead.'

Colonel Buckmaster came to his feet.

'Captain Somers, my friend, I do have to return to London now, but on behalf of everyone concerned, let me thank you and Lieutenant Aarlberg for the many missions you have successfully undertaken, every one at great risk to yourselves. I shall keep in touch with your progress, and see you both again sometime in the future. Not to ask you to go to France again, but to renew friendship and perhaps to offer you useful work at our New Forest establishment.'

Bobby lay relaxing after his visitor had gone. His eyes gradually closed and he slept, much to

285

the satisfaction of Nurse Wickford, who slipped in to take a look at him.

'I want to see Captain Somers,' said Helene to Sister Yates.

'Unfortunately, Lieutenant, neither of you is allowed out of bed yet.'

Helene, her left arm in plaster and her fractured shoulder blade throbbing, was hardly in the best of tempers, even if the effects of concussion were receding.

'Is there anywhere in this world one can escape rules and regulations?' she said, which put a smile on the faces of the other patients in the ward.

'Rules and regulations are necessary to any society,' said Sister Yates.

'I did not ask to get out of bed to walk to Captain Somers,' said Helene. 'Nor did I ask for him to walk to me.' Having been wheeled into an adjacent room for the visit of Colonel Buckmaster, she asked. 'What is wrong with wheeling our beds to a meeting-place?'

'Later, perhaps,' said Sister Yates.

Helene stared at her in suspicion and alarm.

'You are hiding something from me,' she said, 'something terrible.'

'Captain Somers is injured but recovering,' said Sister Yates. 'The gentleman who called to see both of you told you so, and I assure you it is so. Relax, please, Lieutenant.'

'That is easy to say,' said Helene. Longing to see Bobby, she lay complaining to herself in muttered French.

Sister Yates spoke to the matron, and the matron spoke to the surgeon. He gave the matter some thought, then suggested that Lieutenant Aarlberg be transferred to the room that was serving as a ward for Captain Somers. Matron Wellings, shocked, expostulated. Such a thing, patients of opposite sexes in the same ward, was against every rule and, moreover, an infringement of their dignity, especially the dignity of women patients. The surgeon said that in this case, perhaps a blind eye could be turned to the rules, and that such a move could well prove in the interests of these two patients. Matron Wellings still objected, so the surgeon informed her that Lieutenant Aarlberg and Captain Somers were engaged to be married, that the Frenchwoman had told him so today.

Matron Wellings yielded to the extent of agreeing one could join the other for an hour.

'That is all, one hour in Captain Somers' room, perhaps morning and afternoon,' she said.

'Of course, Matron. Will you arrange it?'

'Yes, but only if neither patient objects to the move.'

Neither did. Helene, of course, was delighted, not caring a French sou for rules or infringements. When she found herself with Bobby, his bed in one corner of the room, hers in the other, only the sensitive condition of her fractured shoulder blade kept her where she was.

When they were alone, but under strict instructions not to move, she said, 'Bobby? *Cheri?*'

'Hello, my French chicken.' His voice was still

287

husky, his bandaged head damnably sore and tender, but he made himself heard.

'Bobby, I love you.'

'So do I.'

'You love you?'

'No, you. That's what I meant.'

'Can't you look at me?'

'Not yet. Not allowed to move my head.' He had a welter of pillows beneath his head, which was at grateful rest on the heap.

'Bobby, your bandages are enormous.'

'How are yours?'

'Oh, I have no bandages, only some heavy plaster and a painful shoulder. One can't have plaster on a shoulder, so I am ordered ten times a day not to move it. How can I move it when my arm is strapped to my body?'

'That's so the fracture will knit,' said Bobby.

'Yes, I know. Bobby, are you in pain?'

'No, not now, but I think I'm bruised all over and suffering hell about the death of our pilot.'

'Bobby, we must remember never to forget him. He brought the plane down so bravely, fighting to make the best landing he could. Such a fine man, so much more of a man than Pierre.'

'The Resistance hanged Pierre,' said Bobby.

'Yes, Colonel Buckmaster told me. He said Pierre knew by then he'd been found out, and had two SD men protecting him. But the Resistance laid an armed ambush at his house, demanded him and the SD men handed him over. Bobby, you and I, we are still alive, despite Pierre. How lucky we are, and how grateful, yes? I thought when our plane was going down that we should never be married, after all.'

'Someone smiled on us,' said Bobby. His own last thought before the plane crash-landed had been that he had left it too late to marry Helene, his courageous comrade, his French love. If any people had taught him that marriage was worthwhile, for all its ups and downs, it was those of the Somers and Adams families. His parents, Lizzy and Ned, had survived all setbacks to achieve compatability and companionship of an enviable kind. As for his Aunt Vi and Uncle Tommy, and Aunt Susie and Uncle Sammy, not the worst kind of figurative thunderstorm could wreck what they had made of their marriages. Then there was Uncle Boots, the most worldly member of the family. He had enjoyed his marriage to Aunt Emily so much that he had entered a second one, with Polly Simms. Perhaps Aunt Emily could take posthumous credit for making marriage so acceptable to him. If so, perhaps she didn't rest too unhappily in her grave, the grave that was regularly visited and tended by the family. Aunt Emily was out of this world, but not forgotten.

'Bobby?'

'I'm here, Helene.'

'Why are you so quiet?'

'I was thinking what a privilege it is for a man to have a wife, and to be given the chance to have one like you.'

'Bobby darling, not even the most civilized Frenchman could have said anything so touching to me.'

'Well,' said Bobby, voice croaking a little by

289

now, 'could you do something for me? If there's a bell by your bed, could you use your sound arm to ring it for me?'

'Bobby, oh, no,' said Helene, 'you aren't feeling terrible, are you?'

'No, I'm just in need of a bottle.'

Helene struggled to repress her first laugh for days. Laughing would do her shoulder no good at all.

She rang the bell.

Chapter Twenty-Three

The bustle of activity at 30 Corps headquarters in Normandy was reaching a peak. The attempted break-out was only a few days away. Consolidation of the forward areas was almost complete, despite periodical attacks by German infantry and armoured units, all of which continued to be beaten off, such was the mounting strength of Monty's army, of which 30 Corps was an aggressive part.

Boots snatched enough time to accept and read mail from home. Polly, Sammy, Rosie and Eloise had all written.

Polly's letter concerned the fact that while she was a happy mother of his adorable twins, thank you very much, she was a starved wife and would like him to do something about it. Then she recounted the frightful arrival one evening of an escaped German prisoner of war, who proved to be a typically fanatical Nazi and a threat to herself and the twins in his determination to get her to drive him to Weymouth. Fortunately, lovely old Mr Dowling and his shotgun appeared in the nick of time and floored Hitler's Hun. Now then, you dear old love, she finished with, when are you coming home to comfort me and your twins?

Boots dashed off a quick and comforting reply. Sammy's letter was mainly about business, especially the property company, which had already earned Rosie a good return for her investment. Rosie, left twenty thousand pounds by her late natural father, had invested the lot in the property company.

Sammy wrote regularly to Boots to keep him informed of business developments. His main purpose in this was to ensure that Boots's interest in Adams Enterprises and its associate companies didn't suffer want of information. Boots, of course, had his Army responsibilities, but Sammy wasn't inclined to let these restrict his letters to *'How are you and good luck, mate.'* He was set on having Boots back as general manager and wise old owl. However, having outlined the present state of business affairs, he devoted a few lines to Daniel's growing relationship with the American girl, Patsy Kirk.

Boots had heard about Patsy. From Chinese Lady. Now Sammy was informing him that the family was taking very kindly to her. Boots smiled to himself, wondering if the girl knew she was being gathered to the family bosom, and that escape might be more than she could manage.

Rosie's letter was warm, affectionate and chatty. At the time of writing, husband Matt was still on leave from Italy. His reunion with his children, Giles and Emily, had been famous to behold. Well, he hadn't been able to spend any time at all with them since going overseas, and the only way he could convince little Emily he was her father was to go down on all fours, turn himself into a donkey and give her rides on his back. Emily was gone on donkeys, far more than horses or camels, and Matt was having to live with that.

Tim was still there, still on sick leave, although his wounded arm was almost as good as new, apart from looking like a piece of hoary brown bark, and Felicity was very responsive to his presence. She was healthily pregnant, and still coping wonderfully well with the handicap of her blindness. Everyone there, however, had worries about the flying bombs and what they were doing to London. She phoned Chinese Lady regularly, as well as Susie, Vi and Lizzy, and she was sure Boots would be happy to know, if he didn't already, that they were all proving very expert at ducking, dodging and diving into safety, although Chinese Lady had said having to crawl under a Morrison indoor shelter didn't improve her opinion of Hitler.

Eloise's letter opened on a note of despair.

Dearest Papa,
I am without hope. I am sure my husband is lost to me.

Her husband, Colonel Bill Lucas, called Luke by his friends, was a Commando officer.

I haven't heard from him for suffering weeks, weeks, and you know the kind of war he and his Commandos fight, in direct and dangerous combat with the enemy. I don't wish to be a nuisance to you, but could you help your devoted daughter by making enquiries about him? I feel sure you have the kind of important influence that can command information.

Boots doubted if Luke had been engaged in action recently. The Commandos had done their work on D-Day and following days, their own special kind of work. They had suffered inevitable and severe casualties before their invasion operations ceased, and were then withdrawn for the groups to be made up to strength again and prepare for other hazardous missions. Such preparations often meant a blanket of silence was thrown over them.

Boots dashed off a reply to Eloise as well, telling her in effect not to worry, since she would have heard from the War Office if anything serious had happened to her husband.

Eloise at this time was working at a supply depot in the south of England, and the depot was often in a state of rush and hurry, for it was serving the ports carrying the necessities of war across the Channel to the British forces in Normandy. Eloise, now an ATS lieutenant, no longer projected an air of self-importance. The invasion of Normandy, the battles, the casualty reports, and the realization that her husband and other Commandos in their special assignments were at risk in a way she never was, sobered her considerably. Her husband was constantly on her mind, her wishes and hopes directed always at his survival, and that of her brother Tim, needed so much by Felicity.

Today, she was outside one of the enormous sheds containing all kinds of equipment. Army trucks were being loaded, and she was looking for a sergeant, needing to place a new order in his hand. A rugged-looking Army officer, striding through the shed after visiting the despatch office, emerged into the light and came up behind Eloise.

'Get your shoulder bag, Lieutenant Lucas, I've a car waiting to take you to a hotel for lunch and a spot of dalliance.'

Eloise swung round and shrieked.

'Luke!'

There he was, as formidable as ever in his aggressive self-assertiveness and his muscular physique, the little scar above his right eye a memento of Dunkirk. He was brown, commanding and smiling.

'Hello, Frenchy.' He called her that sometimes in recognition of the fact that she was the daughter of her French mother, and had provocative French ways.

Eloise jumped into his arms. Well, that was what it looked like to a body of busy RAOC men and women of the ATS. They stared. Female officers weren't supposed to jump into the arms of male officers, not in broad daylight. However, as neither Eloise nor Colonel Lucas cared a great deal for every rule and regulation, any more than Helene and Bobby did, they kissed warmly and positively.

'Luke, I haven't heard from you for weeks.'

'Sorry, but couldn't be helped. I'm here now to take you to a hotel in Chichester. I've spoken to your senior officer, and you've got permission to have the day off. Come on, get your bag and let's motor off.'

'Oh, how happy I am,' said Eloise.

'Glad to hear it, but don't waste time standing about.'

They were at the hotel in the lovely old market town of Chichester forty minutes later. Colonel Lucas had signed the register, ordered lunch and afternoon tea, and they were now in the room he had reserved for the day. He had to leave at six to get back to his base by eight.

'We'll go down for lunch at one,' he said. 'What's the time now, you sexy woman?'

'Nearly noon,' said Eloise, a little flushed, 'and should you call me a sexy woman?'

'Well, I don't know anyone sexier.' Colonel Lucas removed his jacket. The devil's own smile accompanied his next words. 'Get that lot off, Mrs Lucas.'

'Get that lot off? Really, Luke,' said Eloise, 'that isn't the language of love.'

'Take it from me, the language of love is on its way and it'll make itself heard in a few minutes.'

'Heavens, how demanding you are,' said Eloise. She looked at him. They looked at each other, she trimly attractive in her well-fitting uniform, he ruggedly masculine in his shirt and trousers. The devil in his smile faded, and the light in his blue eyes became warm with affection. Eloise experienced a little dart of painful emotion. For years now he had been fighting as a Commando, and every mission had put his life at risk. He was the kind of soldier who aroused excitement and admiration in her, but how many more times could she now expect him to survive those specialized operations that brought him face to

296

face with the enemy?

She said then what she had never said before.

'Luke, please take care of yourself. I'm sometimes afraid for you.'

'Afraid?' he said.

'Yes.'

'My very dear girl,' he said, 'because of you I always take care.' That was more of a reassurance than a fact.

'Love me, then,' said Eloise.

'I want to, very much,' he said.

And that was that.

When they came down for lunch, they both looked as if they had won the war entirely by themselves, and thus brought peace to the suffering world. They wore the same look when they came down for tea, after which they sat in the hotel's little garden and examined the dreams in each other's eyes. Or so it appeared.

They booked out at six o'clock, and Colonel Lucas drove Eloise back to the ROAC depot, where he said goodbye to her and promised that from hereon he hoped to be able to write to her regularly.

'And if I'm a little like a bear at times,' he said, 'never think I don't love you.'

'Oh, but if you weren't what you are, you'd be an ordinary man,' said Eloise, 'and you're not. Luke, I'm very happy that you love me.'

'Well, I'm damned glad you married me.'

'Well, dearest husband, I'm sure you deserved your good fortune,' said Eloise, which sent him on his way laughing.

Lizzy received a phone call from a man who introduced himself as Major Fry, the officer commanding Bobby's unit. While there was no need for her to worry unduly, he wished her to know that her son, Captain Bob Somers, had been involved in a car accident, together with his driver, Lieutenant Aarlberg of FANY. Both were hospitalized, but were already recovering, and would be given leave as soon as recovery was complete, perhaps in two weeks. Lizzy who, along with Ned, had felt there was a worrying reason why a letter from Bobby was long overdue, asked for the location of the hospital. Lewes, Sussex. Lizzy then asked if visitors were allowed. Yes, of course. And was it really true she had no need to worry? Major Fry said absolutely true, and that a visit next Sunday, perhaps, would reassure her. Lizzy said she and her husband would make the visit, then. What were the injuries?

'Your son suffered a crack on the head and a bruised body, Mrs Somers, but no bones broken. Lieutenant Aarlberg has a cracked shoulder bone and a broken arm. I assure you again, nothing to worry about.'

'Well, I must say it's kind of you to let me know,' said Lizzy.

'I've had worse things to do. Goodbye, Mrs Somers.'

'Goodbye,' said Lizzy. Not wanting to wait until Ned came home, she rang him at his wine premises in Great Tower Street. Ned counted himself lucky to have the premises still standing.

He listened to Lizzy's outpourings.

'A car accident?' he said. He wasn't necessarily going to believe that himself.

'Yes, Ned.'

'But they're all right, you say?'

'I'm sure they are. Well, Bobby's officer was very positive about us not having to worry. He said we could visit them. Oh, and he also said Helene was driving – lor', suppose the accident was her fault, would she be charged? Mum would say that's what comes of making women drive cars, which they weren't born for.'

'Some women are driving trams.'

'Yes, they're the trams Mum won't ride on,' said Lizzy. 'Anyway, I told the officer we'd go and visit on Sunday.'

'We'll do that,' said Ned.

'I'm so relieved they're recovering,' said Lizzy.

'I'm thankful, and I'll enjoy seeing those two lovers again, even if they are bandaged up,' said Ned.

'Ned, d'you really think they're lovers?'

'I'm sure they are.'

'But they're not married,' said Lizzy.

'No, but they're young and healthy,' said Ned, 'and there's a war on. And they're in it.'

'I suppose we've got to be understanding,' said Lizzy.

'We can't be anything else, but don't tell the vicar,' said Ned. 'And most of all, Eliza, don't tell your Mum.'

Lizzy's baptismal name was Eliza, and Ned had always called her that. He liked the name. It conjured up for him his early recollections of her in her school boater and pinafore frock. And London's perky flower girls used to wear boaters.

Sammy was seeing Paula and Phoebe into their beds that evening. They shared the same room these days, simply because that was how they liked it.

'Daddy,' said Paula, cosily tucked up, 'are Daniel and Patsy you-know?'

'You-know-what?' said Sammy.

'Well, sweethearts,' said Paula, not yet up with the parlance of teenagers. 'Are they dating?' was the parlance of teenagers.

'I'll ask your mum,' said Sammy.

'Oh, does Mummy know?' asked Phoebe, as Sammy tucked her in.

'Mums see more than dads,' said Sammy. 'And hear more, so don't lark about once my back is turned.'

'I fink it's Granny that knows mostest,' said Phoebe, dark of hair and eye, and winsome in her prettiness.

'Well, blow me, you clever sausage,' said Sammy, 'you've found that out, have you?'

'No, I told her,' said Paula.

'So you're the clever one, are you?' smiled Sammy.

'Yes, me and Mummy's the same,' said Paula, 'we're both clever.'

'I fink I'm like Daddy,' said Phoebe.

'How are you like Daddy?' asked Paula.

'We're both nice,' said Phoebe, looking up at Sammy from her pillow. He winked. She giggled.

300

'Anyway, I think Paula's got the answer,' said Sammy. 'If anyone knows about Daniel and Patsy, it'll be Grandma.'

'Grandma knows everything,' said Paula.

'Who told you that?' asked Sammy.

'You did,' said Paula, 'and so did Daniel.'

Sammy departed grinning. Who'd have girl kids? I would, ten of them. Mind, I'm not sure how Susie could manage that lot. If only one more was on the way, she'd have crippled my credentials as soon as she knew.

He went down to the parlour to talk to Susie. Chinese Lady and Mr Finch were listening to light music on the kitchen wireless. Patsy had visited earlier and was now enjoying a summer evening walk with Daniel.

'Susie?' said Sammy.

'Yes, Sammy?' said Susie, busily embroidering.

'Susie, did you know Paula and Phoebe want to know if Daniel and Patsy are lovey-dovey?'

'Oh, the pets,' said Susie, 'but don't you have the answer?'

'I don't feel what you might call definite,' said Sammy, 'but I did suggest to Daniel that Patsy was the kind of girl he ought to hang on to.'

'Now, Sammy, don't start pushing,' said Susie, 'it counts as not minding your own business. Let Daniel make up his own mind.'

'Susie, would I ever do any pushing?'

'Yes, all the time,' said Susie.

'Susie, you grieve me occasional,' said Sammy.

'Oh, I am sorry, Sammy, what a shame.'

'It's sad, y'know, being misunderstood,' said Sammy.

'That's what the burglar said when the police-man found him at a jeweller's shop window with a brick in his hand,' said Susie.

'Fair cop, I suppose, but nothing to do with the good intentions that come over me sometimes,' said Sammy.

'Sammy, we both know Daniel's a bit too young to make up his mind about any girl yet.'

'Nothing wrong, though, in working up to it gradual,' said Sammy.

'Working up to what exactly?' asked Susie, applying her needle with dexterous finesse.

'To a bit of lovey-dovey,' said Sammy.

'You can talk,' said Susie. 'If I remember right, you took years to have some of that with me, and there I was, thinking you never would.'

'Well, Susie, you being a dream girl, I felt I had to make me fortune first,' said Sammy. 'I wanted to make sure you collected a handsome amount of me worldly goods and still left me enough to look after me overheads.'

'Sammy, I didn't marry you for your worldly goods,' said Susie, taking a critical look at her embroidered forget-me-nots.

'I'm touched,' said Sammy. 'Excuse me, but what's that you're embroidering?'

'Never you mind,' said Susie.

'Susie, is it your Sunday knickers?' asked Sammy, who knew that embroidery generally was missing from ladies' lingerie these days, that everything was fairly cheap and plain, and issued under a 'Utility' label.

'Don't get ideas,' said Susie.

'I'll come round on Sunday,' said Sammy.

302

'We'll be in Cornwall then,' said Susie.

'Yes, that's when I'll come round,' said Sammy.

'Daniel,' said Patsy, as she strolled with him along East Dulwich Grove towards Red Post Hill. 'Pa wants to meet your Aunt Vi and Uncle Tommy.'

'Only natural, seeing they're going to be your guardians while he's doing his war correspondence bit in France,' said Daniel. 'I'll ask them to come with me to your flat one evening before Saturday.'

'And before eight,' said Patsy, 'he always leaves for town at that time.'

'Noted,' said Daniel. 'Patsy, what d'you miss most about America?'

'July the Fourth, going with Pa to see the Boston Red Sox in a baseball game, and ice cream parlours and soda fountains,' said Patsy. 'A corporation called Howard Johnson has a chain of ice cream parlours where you can take your pick of about thirty different flavours.'

'Thirty?' said Daniel. 'Don't you get confused about what to choose?'

'Oh, choosing is all part of the enjoyment,' said Patsy. She paused to give the matter more thought. 'It's great for the kids, an ice cream parlour, but for myself, oh, I guess I can live without them these days.'

'I've almost forgotten what ice cream looks and tastes like,' said Daniel, 'and I've never seen a baseball match. Girls play it in this country, only they call it rounders.'

'Do they get the ball pitched at them at ninety

miles an hour?' asked Patsy, standing up for the real game.

'Not unless there's a doctor standing by,' said Daniel. 'Anyway, sorry we've got no ice cream parlours. Nor any ice cream. I think the country's nearly broke.'

'Daniel, I can live without ice cream all through this war,' said Patsy, 'and I could always lend Mr Churchill a few dollars if things get real bad.'

'You're a great girl, Patsy,' said Daniel. 'What else d'you miss?'

'Oh, nothing important,' said Patsy. The driver of a van passing by gave her the eye and a whistle. 'Daniel, did you see that guy getting fresh with me?'

'Yes, but don't wave at strange men, Patsy.'

'I didn't, and wouldn't,' said Patsy. She smiled. 'I'm kind of old-fashioned, like some English people I know.'

'Don't know any myself, except for Grandma,' said Daniel.

Patsy laughed, then said, 'Daniel, don't you miss some things about your own country? I mean the things you took for granted in peacetime?'

'Like ice cream?' said Daniel.

'Daniel, we can both live without that, can't we?' said Patsy, as they turned into Red Post Hill. The evening was quiet, the massed branches of trees lush with the green leaves of summer, and white clouds from the west infiltrating the darkening blue of the sky at twilight. 'I mean important things, like dating girls without having to worry about bombs or having to enlist, or being able to go into a store and buying just whatever you want. Daniel, I get really sad sometimes about everything your country and its people have had to suffer all these years.'

Daniel, touched, said, 'I like you for that, Patsy, but I don't suppose we've suffered half as much as the people of Hitler's Europe.'

Patsy stopped. Daniel stopped. The laden branches of a pavement tree sheltered them. They gazed at each other. Patsy thought how adult he looked in his tallness, and his fine firm features. Mr Finch would have told her that Daniel was like his cousins Bobby, Tim, Edward and David, in that all of them seemed to have missed the awkward adolescent stage and simply jumped from youthfulness into manliness. Mr Finch had known similar development in their fathers.

'Daniel, I won't ever leave before the war is over, and perhaps not even then,' said Patsy. 'I'll perhaps stick around until ice cream comes back again.'

'Patsy, you're the best girl I know.'

There was no-one about in this residential area, simply no-one. So they kissed. Bliss, thought Patsy, and wondered how they could just call themselves friends when they kissed like this?

'Daniel, you're a really nice guy.'

'Mutual, Patsy, and I hope you're sorry now that you licked us a few years ago,' said Daniel.

'A few years?' said Patsy. 'It was over a hundred and fifty.'

'A hundred and fifty?' said Daniel. 'No wonder I can't remember what I felt like at the time.'

'Oh, man, you're touched in the head,' said Patsy.

'So's Hitler,' said Daniel, 'but in a different way from the rest of us.'

They walked on, back to Daniel's home, hand in hand.

Later that evening, when Fergus MacAllister was on his way to catch his train to Edinburgh, he had a letter in his wallet, hand-delivered. It had been written by Alice.

Dear Fergus,

I had to write to wish you the very best of luck and to tell you again how sorry I am that I was so unfriendly to you. I'm very glad we're on better terms now, and I shall be looking forward to hearing from you, and to know if being put through your paces at your Edinburgh barracks means you'll end up fit enough to be taken back into your regiment.

I do hope so, as I know that's what you want. I think what you also want is to help drive the Germans back into Germany. When that day arrives, try to give them a message from me. Tell them to stay there!

My very best wishes to you.

Very sincerely,

Alice.

For Fergus, that little letter reposing in his wallet was a good luck charm.

He'd had a second letter that day. From his father, expressing pleasure and relief that he'd had a successful operation, and hoping he would now leave the land of the heathen Sassenachs and come back to Aberdeen. Idolatrous London was no place for a MacAllister.

That letter wasn't in his wallet.

In Dorset, Rosie and Felicity were feeling bereft. Matthew was on his way back to Italy, and Tim had returned to 4 Commando carrying an armful of scars.

'Is there a gin and tonic going spare?' asked Felicity.

'There could be,' said Rosie, 'but not for you in your condition.'

'It's not the thing for pregnant women, of course.'

''Fraid not,' said Rosie.

'Well, curse it,' said Felicity. 'I need bucking up.'

'So do I,' said Rosie. 'I think I'll have a gin and tonic.'

'Rosie, you beast,' said Felicity.

'And you can have a glass of Somerset cider,' said Rosie.

'One's best friend ought to be able to do better than that,' said Felicity.

'It'll buck you up,' said Rosie.

They sat with their drinks, listening to wireless music while waiting for the ten o'clock news.

'I feel deprived,' said Felicity.

'I know,' said Rosie.

Their thoughts were on Tim and Matthew.

The ten o'clock news offered no promise of an early return of their husbands into their lives.

Chapter Twenty-Four

The 20th of July

Colonel Count von Stauffenberg, minus his right forearm and with only three fingers to his left hand, was nevertheless in secure possession of his briefcase when he boarded the plane that would carry him on the 350-mile flight to Hitler's headquarters in East Prussia. The bomb was safely lodged in the briefcase. The plane left at seven in the morning and arrived at the headquarters airfield at ten. Von Stauffenberg ordered the pilot to be ready for take-off back to Berlin at any time after midday.

Hitler's headquarters, set deep in a pine forest, were surrounded by a minefield and a high barbed wire fence. SS men with machine-guns manned several watchtowers, and the single entrance could only be reached through three checkpoints. It was virtually impossible for any person other than Hitler's closest associates or his staff officers to enter this fortress. He was a man obsessed by fears for his personal safety.

His full staff conference was due to begin at twelve-thirty, and von Stauffenberg, with the authority to attend all such conferences, was admitted by the SS guards into the fortress, where he was received by Field Marshal Keitel, Chief of Germany's High Command, and several high-ranking men. After a protracted discussion on the present state of the conflict with Russia, followed by talk on a variety of critical matters, he excused himself and thus procured an opportunity to set the bomb. Then he followed Keitel towards the conference room. He politely turned down an offer from a sympathetic staff officer to carry his briefcase for him.

'Thank you, but I can manage.'

He entered the conference room, a long wooden hut in temporary use while alterations were being made to the concrete bunker complex. If his heartbeats were erratic and his nerves taut, he showed no sign of being anything but his usual vigorous and outgoing self. No sweat stood upon his brow.

Hitler was present, examining maps spread out on the surface of a large oak table. He was a shadow of his former self, a stooping, pasty-faced figure who suffered the trembles and tremors associated with Parkinson's disease. His lifestyle was unhealthily sedentary. He rarely went to bed before three or four in the morning, and slept until midday. He kept his cronies up with him, regaling them with reminiscences of the old days, when his Nazi party was fighting for recognition as a political force, and his Brownshirts were beating out the brains of Communists. He could talk the hind leg off an elephant, let alone a donkey. What genius he had was corrupted by his unprincipled and vindictive use of power. He trusted very few people. Himmler, perhaps, and Goebbels, and one or two others. Goering he had come to despise.

Von Stauffenberg noted that neither Goering nor Himmler was present. A pity. He had hoped the bomb would take them to hell along with Hitler.

Hitler, listening to a report concerning the situation on the Russian front, hardly noticed the entrance of von Stauffenberg, whose formal greeting went into the wastepaper basket of the unacknowledged. With a simulated casualness that drew the attention of no-one, the Count placed the briefcase down on the floor and against one of the table's supports close to Hitler. Inside the briefcase, the timing mechanism of the snugly enclosed bomb was at silent work.

Von Stauffenberg realized that the timber-built hut was hardly bomb-resistant, especially as its windows were open, but he knew the blast would be more than enough to pulverize the life out of Germany's lunatic *Fuehrer*.

The Count stayed only a few moments before excusing himself on the grounds that he needed to phone his Berlin headquarters. When he left, there were seventeen officers around the table, representing the Army, Navy and Air Force, and all eyes were on Hitler. The bomb was due to explode in ten minutes.

Von Stauffenberg walked smartly but without undue haste to join his aide, a young officer called Haeften, who was waiting for him beside their staff car. Haeften had the motor idling. The walk took time, too much time, and the bomb went off with an almighty roar just as the Count reached the car. He and Haeften rushed themselves into it and went away at speed. Smoke was rising from the shattered hut.

They still had to get through the checkpoints, and because of confusion among the guards, whose first impression was that the Russians had bombed headquarters, von Stauffenberg used the power of his personality to bluff his way through.

He and Haeften raced for the airfield. The plane was waiting. They boarded it, and when it took off for Berlin, they were in a state of triumph and exaltation, leaving behind them the shattered conference hut and taking with them a conviction that Hitler had been blown to pieces.

Unfortunately, the fox had cut loose a few moments before the bomb went off. That is, Hitler had moved well away from the briefcase, which itself had been moved by a staff officer who found it too close to his feet. These actions saved Hitler's life. He was badly shaken, but his injuries were superficial. The blast, however, had killed four officers.

Von Stauffenberg, anticipating that news of Hitler's death would quickly reach the conspirators in Berlin, confidently assumed a takeover of the capital would begin while he was still in the air.

He was actually flying towards his summary execution.

That evening, Tommy and Vi, in company with Daniel, arrived at the house in Danecroft Road to meet Patsy's father. Daniel introduced them to Pa Kirk.

'Hello,' said Tommy.

'Hello,' said Vi.

'My pleasure,' said Pa Kirk, noting Tommy's stalwart look, and Vi's soft-eyed smile. A good-looking lot, the Adams men and women, he thought. He had met Daniel's parents weeks ago. 'So you're the aunt and uncle of this young feller.'

'That's us,' said Tommy.

'I understand you've offered to take Patsy into your home while I'm away,' said Pa Kirk, who was having to come to terms with his conviction that his daughter's attachment to Daniel was no light thing.

'Mr Kirk, we'll be happy to look after her,' said Vi.

'That's a fact,' said Tommy.

'Pa, I'll be happy myself to stay with them,' said Patsy.

'Let's have a drink before I skip off to town,' said Pa Kirk. The time was seven-thirty.

Vi didn't drink. Well, not beer or spirits. So she and Patsy each had a Coca-Cola, which Patsy called a Coke, and which Tommy blinked at, because it came in cans. He and Daniel opted for beer, and Tommy almost fell about when that too came in cans, and ice-cold from Pa Kirk's English fridge and his usual American supply sources in London. Ruddy mermaids, thought Tommy, it's true, then, the Yanks can their beer. It was light and weak, and its ice-cold condition knocked any flavour out of it. Still, a bloke had to be polite, even if cans were hard to believe. Pa Kirk had one himself, and spent half-an-hour summing up the people who were going to take care of Patsy. He noted she was very much at ease with them, and that Daniel was taking a back seat, refraining from pushing the credentials of his aunt and uncle as temporary guardians of Patsy. In that respect, the young man was showing wisdom. In general, in fact, he had a maturer outlook than Mike Brady, still very much a big kid at times. Pa Kirk admitted that to himself, but not without a sigh. He could actually see himself losing Patsy to this Adams family.

However, he shook hands warmly with Vi and Tommy when he left for town.

'Let me thank you for finding a place for Patsy in your home,' he said.

'Mr Kirk, we really will take good care of her,' said Vi.

'You can bet on that,' said Tommy.

'Daniel'll give us a talking-to if we don't,' said Vi.

'He's good at that, aren't you, Daniel?' said Patsy.

'Sure am, sugarpuss,' said Daniel.

'Get you,' said Patsy, then excused herself to go down to the front door with her Pa. 'Are you happy about the arrangement?' she asked.

'I tell myself philosophically that what will be will be,' said Pa Kirk, 'which means that whatever makes you happy, I'll do my best to go along with.'

'Well, I guess being philosophical is something we all ought to cultivate,' said Patsy. 'So long, Pa, don't stay out all night with ladies from the Windmill Theatre.'

'You know about the Windmill Theatre ladies,

313

do you?' smiled Pa Kirk.

'Sure I do,' said Patsy. 'They keep the troops happy by not wearing very much during their song-and-dance routines.'

'Sleep easy,' said Pa Kirk, 'I'm not acquainted with any.'

Upstairs, Tommy was expressing disbelief that the Americans put beer into cans.

'Tommy, you saw it with your very own eyes,' said Vi.

'I'm still not believing it,' said Tommy.

'I could've told you,' said Daniel.

'Glad you didn't,' said Tommy, 'or I'd have lost me faith in your eyesight. Gertie actually handed me the bad news a few days ago, but I thought she'd just had a drop too much gin the night before. Canned beer, I ask you, and near frozen at that. Ruddy 'orrible shock to a bloke's stomach. Stand it up against a pint of old ale out of the barrel, and what've you got, me lad? A canful of baby's water that's been left out in the cold.'

'Tommy, I expect you're speaking of something the Americans are fond of,' said Vi.

'Um – baby's water, Aunt Vi?' suggested Daniel. Vi sort of spluttered. 'Aunt Vi?'

'I'm going backwards with all me fits of the giggles lately,' said Vi, and Patsy returned then.

'Who'd like a piece of blueberry pie?' she asked.

'Blueberry pie?' said Tommy. 'I've heard of that.'

'Is it your own, Patsy?' asked Vi.

'No, Pa brought it home from London,' said Patsy.

314

'I like your Pa, Patsy, for knowing where American blueberry pies hang around in London,' said Daniel.

'He brought two home.' said Patsy. 'One's for your aunt and uncle to take with them, if they'd like.'

'Patsy, that's really nice of you and your father,' said Vi.

'Oh, you're welcome, Mrs Adams,' said Patsy. 'Shall we all have a piece of the other? It's been keeping warm. I'm sure you'll like it.'

'I won't say no,' said Tommy.

'I'm saying yes, please,' said Vi.

'I'm saying is there custard?' said Daniel.

'No pie for difficult people,' said Patsy.

'Forget the custard,' said Daniel.

They had all finished their supper over an hour ago, so Patsy introduced them to the pie, and it pleased her that no-one complained. Far from it, although being English they ate it with a spoon and fork. Patsy played the gracious hostess by following suit. Tommy looked as if he'd been introduced to something he ought to have discovered as a kid. Privately, he considered this American speciality had a lot going for it. It was well and truly believable. Canned beer wasn't. Shame, really, he thought. Any large body of people, like the Americans, who could originate blueberry pie, ought to be able to find a way of getting their beer into barrels or bottles.

Out loud, he paid the pie generous and sincere compliments, and Vi declared she loved it, much to Patsy's pleasure. Daniel said something through a mouthful that she failed to catch. Vi

315

thought this lively and intelligent American girl wanted Daniel's opinion as much as anyone else's, and she wasn't surprised when the young lady asked him right out if he liked it or not.

'Could you do me a favour?' asked Daniel, attacking the last segment on his plate.

'What favour?'

'Well, is there any more pie? I mean, are there seconds?'

'Oh, you really like it?' said Patsy, delighted.

'Not half,' said Daniel, which Patsy knew by now was a Londoner's most affirmative expression of approval. 'It's on a par with Bramley apple pie, and I can't say fairer.'

'Nor me,' said Tommy, 'and I'll go for a second helping, Patsy.'

She cut them seconds, and an atmosphere of happy sociability prevailed.

At home, Alice answered the ringing phone.

'Hello, Alice Adams here. Who's that?'

'Edinburgh,' said a voice she now knew well.

'Fergus, it's you?'

'Aye, it's me.'

'All the way from Edinburgh?' said Alice.

'I'm using the phone in the barracks' orderly room,' said Fergus.

'Have they found you desk work, then? Aren't you fit enough to be considered for active service, after all?'

'Oh, I'll be on the square tomorrow,' said Fergus, 'but just now the orderly room's empty. The night duty sergeant's on his rounds, and he'll no' be back for a wee while. I couldna resist calling you. I hope you dinna mind.'

'Of course not,' said Alice.

'I wanted to thank you for your letter,' said Fergus.

'It was to wish you lots of luck,' said Alice.

'Any demon bombs near you today, Alice?'

'No. Not one near here,' said Alice, 'but some elsewhere.'

'Well, remember what I said, if one does come your way, go down flat on your face. If you stay standing up, the blast will blow you through your parlour wall.'

'I'll remember,' said Alice. 'If the postman should be around, I wouldn't want him dashing in to bowl me over. That happened to me only a few days ago.'

'Wi' the compliments of the postman?' said Fergus.

'No, with the assistance of a Scot who's now in Edinburgh,' said Alice.

'You cannot trust some of these Scots,' said Fergus, 'they're a braw and bruising lot. And you're a fine and tender young lady. I willna keep you longer—'

'Fergus, you can take your time.'

'And I would, but I can hear a pair of hobnailed boots coming this way. The duty sergeant's. So guidnight, Alice, and thanks again for your letter. Have you caught the evening news?'

'No. I can catch it at nine, in five minutes.'

'Then you'll catch a report about an attempt to assassinate Germany's hound of hell,' said Fergus. 'I'll be writing you, Alice.' Down went the phone. Alice hung up at her end, then

317

rushed to turn on the wireless.

Up and down the country, people were listening to the calm mellow voice of Frank Phillips, unsurpassed as a newscaster. There was no official confirmation yet of an attempted assassination of Hitler, but there were rumours and reports from various sources of a bomb explosion at his headquarters in East Prussia. German radio so far had issued no communiqué either confirming or denying the rumours.

Chinese Lady, Mr Finch, Sammy and Susie were all listening, Chinese Lady in hope that Germany's warmonger had gone to the devil, Mr Finch with his thoughts on Trudi Lemberg. He experienced a little note of pleasure that he had believed her, and that she was now in London, her chosen city of asylum. He had an instinctive certainty that the assassination attempt had been carried out, but felt the lack of confirmation from German radio suggested the Nazi leaders had not yet made up their minds how the result should be presented. It also suggested confusion. Confusion about what? Hitler's death at the hands of one of his own people? That would not go down well with millions of Germans who still saw Hitler as their saviour. Or was he still alive but badly injured?

Patsy, Daniel, Vi and Tommy were also listening. Tommy had asked if they could catch the nine o'clock news before he and Vi left.

Patsy was listening awestruck.

'Oh, my stars,' she breathed, 'if Hitler's dead could that bring an end to the war?'

318

'I hope so, I really do,' said Vi.

'If he's been blown to bits, it won't grieve your grandma, Daniel,' said Tommy.

'What's it like, I wonder, suddenly finding yourself flying about in bits?' said Daniel.

'Daniel, don't make me puke,' said Patsy.

'Oh, I think you can sometimes be sick in a good cause,' said Vi, whose equability only failed her when she thought of what Germany's *Fuehrer* had done to her world.

Frank Phillips announced that further news would be given at ten o'clock.

Tommy said he and Vi could catch that at home, that they didn't want to outstay their welcome.

'Oh, stay until then,' said Patsy earnestly, 'and we can all catch it together.'

'We'll stay,' said Vi, who was developing a warm liking for the girl she and Tommy were going to take care of.

'Shall I make a pot of tea?' suggested Patsy.

Daniel liked that. Patsy was coming to understand what was most welcome to English people in certain circumstances. A pot of tea.

'Well, I won't say no,' said Tommy, for long an admirer of Patsy for her sterling work during an air raid. She had helped Daniel in an attempt to get a trapped couple out of their overturned car at the foot of Denmark Hill. Tommy himself and Sammy, out on ARP duty, had arrived in time to lend an effective hand before the car blew up.

'I'd love a cup of tea,' said Vi.

'I'll put the kettle on,' said Patsy.

'I'll help,' said Daniel, and went into the

319

kitchen with her to set out the cups and saucers on a tray.

'Daniel,' said Patsy, filling the kettle, 'I just know I'm going to like living with your Aunt Vi and Uncle Tommy.'

'And they're going to like having you,' said Daniel, loading the tray. 'And who wouldn't? You're a bit of all right, Patsy.'

'I've heard that expression on one of your radio shows,' said Patsy. 'ITMA, I think. There's a cockney character in it, a Mrs Mop.'

'She's the scrubber.'

'Daniel, no,' said Patsy.

'No what?' said Daniel.

'A scrubber's a – well, a street floozie.'

'Oh, one of those,' said Daniel. 'I don't think I know any myself.'

'I should hope you never do,' said Patsy, waiting for the kettle to boil. 'Daniel, am I really a bit of all right?'

'You sure are, sugarbaby,' said Daniel.

'Get you, cowboy,' said Patsy. 'Daniel, could Hitler really be dead?'

'If he is, Patsy, not many people in this country are going to send funeral flowers. Let's see what the ten o'clock news comes up with.'

By Bere Regis in Dorset, Rosie and Felicity were keeping compulsive company with the wireless. So was Polly. She and the twins had arrived in the morning to spend a few days at Rosie's home. The twins and Rosie's children were all abed and sound asleep, after an exhausting day scampering about in the garden. Rosie's chickens were pretty worn out too, having spent hours running and squawking to save their feathers from Polly's twins.

At ten o'clock, the BBC news led with the latest details on what had happened at Hitler's head-quarters, German radio having confirmed that a foul and traitorous attempt had been made on the *Fuehrer*'s life. The attempt, however, had failed and the *Fuehrer* had survived. Proof of this would come when he addressed the German people. But so far, said the BBC announcer, that address had not been made, and the German radio went no farther than asking the people to stand by.

'Are these wretched Nazis playing for time while they decide on the right thing to do?' asked Rosie.

'You think Hitler didn't survive, that his death is being kept quiet?' said Felicity.

'Everything about the news is so sketchy that it could mean mad Adolf is now a corpse,' said Polly, 'and that the fat one and the poisonous one are running about like headless cockerels. Well, I ask you, duckies, why haven't Goering and Himmler made statements on their radio? And why hasn't Goebbels, who's noted for his ever-open mouth? Perhaps all three of them are busy stabbing each other in the back. I'm going to bed now in the hope that by morning I'll wake to a world minus that frightful *Fuehrer* and his mobsters.'

'Bed?' said Rosie.

'Exactly that, ducky,' said Polly. 'I'm electing for optimistic shuteye.'

'I'm an admirer of your talent for making good decisions,' said Rosie. 'Bed, then. How do you feel about that, Felicity?'

'Frankly, I've come to dislike an empty bed,' said Felicity. 'But there it is, we're all without our men, curse it.'

'Matt has a Dorset saying for that,' said Rosie. '"Men be off when their blood be red, leaving their women to an empty bed."'

'If all I know about the Prussians is true, Rosie, that probably originated in Prussia,' said Polly. 'Discuss how it reached our lovely Dorset, but not now. Tomorrow.'

'When tomorrow pops up, I hope we'll be able to discuss Hitler's funeral arrangements,' said Felicity.

They all went up to their beds.

The wireless, switched off, was silent.

322

Chapter Twenty-Five

'Well, we don't know any more now than we did before,' grumbled Chinese Lady. It was gone ten-thirty, and she and Edwin, with Susie and Sammy, were sitting around the kitchen table. They were still listening to the wireless, to learned experts on the Nazi regime giving their opinions and making their assumptions about what appeared to be a traumatic development in the affairs of the Third Reich. Whether Hitler was dead or not, Mr Finch thought the confirmed attempt on his life must have been of a dramatic and devastating nature for Goebbels to allow the German radio to admit it. Goebbels was behind every important broadcast relevant to the fortunes of the Third Reich. Such broadcasts in these days of total war were usually of a kind to boost the morale of the people. If Hitler had gone, Goebbels would probably be digging deep into his facile mind to come up with a communiqué that would encourage the German people to expect a resurrection.

'If Hitler really is going to speak on the German wireless,' said Susie, 'what's stopping him doing it now?'

'It's all a bit dubious, if you ask me,' said Sammy. 'What I'm in favour of is a broadcast of his funeral. I've never liked the bloke. Too much mouth. Blind O'Reilly, what a cakehole.'

323

'Sammy Adams, must you talk common?' said Chinese Lady crossly.

'Sorry, Ma,' said Sammy, 'but–'

'And how many times have I told you not to call me Ma?'

'Well, old lady–'

'Don't call me that, either,' said Chinese Lady, fidgety, 'it's bad enough Boots always doing it.'

'All right, I got you, Mother dear,' said Sammy.

Mr Finch coughed, Susie clapped a hand to her mouth, and Chinese Lady eyed her youngest son suspiciously.

'Carry on, Sammy,' said Mr Finch.

'Right you are, Dad old cock,' said Sammy, a blithe spirit even in the face of dark maternal suspicion. 'I was going to say that Bert at the factory reckons even if Hitler's north-and-south was full of six cream buns, he could still wallop the ears off a herd of elephants. You ever seen an elephant's ears, Ma?'

'Sammy Adams, if–'

'No, honest, you ever seen an elephant's ears, Mother dear?' said Sammy.

Chinese Lady glanced at Mr Finch for help. He straightened his face and gave her a sympathetic look.

'I think Sammy's doing his best, Maisie,' he said.

'I never know if his best is any better than his worst,' said Chinese Lady fretfully. 'Him and Boots, they're a pair together.'

'Yes, and if you're trying to make us laugh, Sammy, it's not working,' said Susie, struggling to keep a straight face of her own.

324

'Susie, I concur, don't I, that this is all a bit serious,' said Sammy.

'Not much you don't,' said Susie.

'Daniel's not back yet,' observed Chinese Lady.

'Gone to Hitler's funeral, I expect,' said Sammy.

'Sammy, I'm warning you,' said Susie. From across the table, he gave her a wink. That Sammy, still incorrigible. He wasn't taking any real notice of what was now coming out of the wireless. Well, it wasn't news, it was just talk. No wonder Chinese Lady was fidgeting, although Grandpa Finch was listening with keen interest. The specialists on Hitler's Germany were commenting at length on the possibility of the Third Reich disintegrating if Hitler had been killed and not merely injured.

'I hope that wireless isn't going to carry on like that all night,' said Chinese Lady.

'There'll be another news bulletin at eleven, Maisie,' said Mr Finch.

'I'm not waiting up for more talk,' said Chinese Lady, 'I'm going to bed. If that man's got what he deserved, he'll be where he's always belonged, in the devil's parlour and shaking hands with him.'

'I wonder what the devil will be saying to him, Maisie?' murmured Mr Finch.

'I know what,' said Susie.

'What?' asked Sammy.

'"*Heil Hitler*,"' said Susie.

Tommy and Vi were saying good night to Patsy. Vi said she hoped they hadn't stayed too long, and Patsy assured her she'd enjoyed having them, and that her Pa had enjoyed meeting them.

'Well, it could've turned out a good evening all round if only the news hadn't told us Hitler's still alive,' said Tommy. 'Still, they might've got it wrong.' On that note of optimism, he and Vi departed, leaving Daniel to say his own good night to Patsy. He did so with a kiss.

'Hey, that was another peck in passing,' called Patsy, so he came back and tried again. It was such an improvement on the peck that she said, 'Daniel, should you kiss me like that when we're only friends?'

'Not half,' said Daniel. 'Come round tomorrow evening, meet me in the garden by the potatoes, and if Hitler's dead and not alive, I'll do it some more.

'Daniel, if your parents see you kissing me like that, they'll think we're more than just friends,' said Patsy.

'Well, we've got a year or two to make up our minds about that,' said Daniel.

'Oh, sure,' said Patsy. 'About what exactly?'

'You're right, Patsy, yes, exactly what, might I ask,' said Daniel. He looked her in the eye. Her lashes quivered. He was tempted to commit himself. No, better not. Well, he couldn't honestly tell her Pa he was a great catch for Patsy. He might be after the war if his position in the property company really did pay off, and he was a responsible bloke of twenty. 'Oh, we'll know when we get there. See you tomorrow, girl guy. Glad you like Aunt Vi and Uncle Tommy. So long.'

Patsy, closing the door after he'd gone, stood

with her back against it.

I guess that's it, she told herself. I guess I must be in love, or I wouldn't want my fun guy all to myself for better or worse. Oh, well, like he said, we'll both get to know for certain sometime.

The fate of the conspirators in Berlin was sealed. Hitler, shaken and singed, limbs trembling with creeping illness, shock and uncontrollable rage, had issued a foam-flecked spate of revengeful words.

'These criminals will be given short shrift. No military tribunals. The People's Court will deal with them.' The People's Court was notoriously biased, its judges a disgrace to the principles of justice. 'No long speeches from the accused. The Court will act with lightning speed, and two hours after the verdict, all sentences will be carried out. By hanging, hanging without mercy.'

Which meant not a rope, but piano wire.

Von Stauffenberg, his young aide Haeften, and two other officers had already been seized by the SS and shot in the courtyard of the Reserve Army headquarters. Von Stauffenberg, just before the volley of bullets riddled him, called loudly, 'Long live our sacred Germany.'

To him, Nazi Germany was the antithesis of sacred.

The Gestapo went after Dr Gordeler. He fled. General Beck, however, was finished off after unsuccessfully trying to kill himself. Others died, all without trial. The rest of the conspirators and many of their associates were arrested to face the appalling consequences of appearing before the disgusting People's Court.

Field Marshal Rommel, when fully recovered from his injuries, was to be offered the option of committing suicide. In due course he took that option, and Hitler, not wanting the German people to know that the nation's most popular war hero was against their *Fuehrer*, allowed him full funeral honours.

When Chinese Lady, Susie, Sammy and Daniel had all retired, Mr Finch phoned a certain number in the bowels of Whitehall. What is known, he asked, of the true events in Germany?

'Hitler definitely survived.'

'And?'

'The Gestapo and the SS in Berlin are on the warpath.'

'Do you know who was responsible for the attempted assassination?'

'According to the underground information we're receiving, a Colonel Count von Stauffenberg. He placed a bomb in Hitler's conference room.'

'Has he been arrested? If so, God help him.'

'He was shot out of hand between eight and ten this evening in Berlin.'

'Then perhaps God did help him,' said Mr Finch quietly. 'Do you know the present situation of our informant, Trudi Lemberg?'

'Oh, we've brought the lady over, and placed her in a safe house with the caretaker and his wife.'

'How is she?'

'At the moment, I rather fancy she's indulging

328

in "I-told-you-so-stuff". Other than that, she's been making requests to see the sights of London and to meet rich Americans.'

'I see.' Mr Finch smiled. 'Good night.'

Hitler addressed the German people by radio at one in the morning, his voice harsh and hoarse.

'My German comrades...'

It was an address of accusation, reassurance and vengeance, and he left his people in no doubt that, by the grace and intercession of Providence, he was not only alive but would lead them on to their destiny, while overseeing the destruction of the small military clique of criminal officers responsible for the plot to kill him. His people would expect him to deal mercilessly with these and all other enemies of National Socialism.

It was possible that the listening German people heaved a collective sigh of relief at the survival of their beloved *Fuehrer*. Immersed in the Prussian cult of glorifying a leader, perhaps they believed their destiny under Hitler's continuing control would be Utopian, despite the existing omens of defeat and disaster.

On his way to the factory with Daniel in the morning, Tommy said, 'Did you listen to the breakfast news?'

'Yes, and I found out Hitler's still alive,' said Daniel.

'What a let-down,' said Tommy. 'Ruddy mess-up. Ought to have given the job to your cousin Tim and his Commandos. Here we are, you and me and thousands of others, getting chased to work by Hitler's buzz-bombs all too frequent, and there's Hitler himself sitting up and eating soft-boiled eggs or German kippers for his breakfast, on account of some bloke called Stuffemberg not placing the bomb right under his fat backside.'

'Did you get all that on the early morning news?' asked Daniel.

'Some of it,' said Tommy. 'I'm imagining the rest, and it all amounts to a lousy disappointment. No more Hitler, no more war, that's what I reckoned on. What did your grandma have to say?'

'That if Grandpa bought a new wireless, it might come up with news that didn't aggravate her so much,' said Daniel.

'She's still a character,' said Tommy. 'I tell you, me lad, Tim and his Commandos could've done the job easy. They wouldn't have mucked it up.'

'Uncle Tommy,' said Daniel, 'I've got to point out one or two difficulties—'

'Daniel, I'm admiring of you,' said Tommy, 'you're a credit to the family, but I know about difficulties, don't I? Me and your dad have had a cartload over the years. What you do with difficulties is get the better of 'em the best way you can. You listening, me lad?'

'I'm all ears,' said Daniel, eyeing a girl boarding a bus at Camberwell Green. She was just like Patsy in her spring-heeled motion. Patsy. What a girl. 'Yes, I'm all ears, Uncle Tommy.'

'Well, there's no difficulties the Commandos couldn't get the better of,' said Tommy, 'and if they'd been asked to they'd have planted the

330

bomb just where it hurt most.'

'Hurt most, right, got you, Uncle Tommy,' said Daniel.

'You're welcome,' said Tommy. 'Listen, if I haven't mentioned it before, your Aunt Vi and me want to compliment you on finding a girlfriend like Patsy. Very choice, Daniel.'

'Yes, I know,' said Daniel.

'Before I started to appreciate your aunt, I knew a few girls meself,' said Tommy, still a handsome man.

'Choice ones?' said Daniel.

'I've got to admit I don't recollect any as choice as Patsy,' said Tommy, frowning at the clutter of traffic in front of him. 'Look at that, makes you wonder where all these car drivers get their petrol from.' He had an official allowance himself for his daily journeys to the Belsize Park factory, and if he ran a bit short, well, brother Sammy always had some coupons to spare. Tommy, honest and straightforward, never asked where they came from in case the information pained his integrity. 'Your Aunt Vi thinks a lot of Patsy.'

'So do I,' said Daniel.

'Might I ask if you've got intentions?' asked Tommy with frank interest.

'Yes, I intend to make a good go of my post-war prospects,' said Daniel.

'Got you, me lad,' said Tommy, travelling behind a lumbering Army lorry. 'You're waiting till after the war. But suppose Patsy does go back to America, after all?'

'I'll have to fight my hard luck,' said Daniel.

'Ah,' said Tommy. 'Ah, well,' he said. Then,

331

'Any perishing doodlebugs about this morning?'

'Haven't heard or seen any yet,' said Daniel, 'but I'm expecting a few hundred any moment.'

'Why?' asked Tommy.

'Well, Hitler's still alive, but I don't suppose he's in a very good temper,' said Daniel. 'It's my belief that as soon as he's finished his soft-boiled eggs or his German kippers, he'll bawl for up to a thousand flying bombs to be aimed at us in one go.'

'Didn't I tell you?' said Tommy. 'Didn't I say out loud and twice over that Tim and his Commandos ought to have been given the job?'

He knew nothing of the fact that Tim's group, 4 Commando, to which Colonel Lucas also belonged, was about to undergo long-term training for an assault that would free the approach to the port of Antwerp, so necessary to the Allies in the event of a successful thrust into Belgium.

The first V-1 of the day came rocketing over then, to dip, nosedive and explode in the ruins of Wapping.

In Normandy, Montgomery's army and the Cherbourg Americans had been either repelling desperate German assaults or smashing forward German strongholds prior to the forthcoming Allied offensive. Montgomery was aiming to strike his hammer blow on the twenty-fifth of July, and General Omar Bradley aiming to launch his American forces in concert. General Eisenhower, Supreme Commander, was keeping an eye on both of them. Monty and Omar were rivals, each hoping for the top place in history.

Which was side by side with Napoleon.

30 Corps headquarters was buzzing, but Boots and Captain Ben Reynolds found a few moments to spare for each other when they met outside the Corps Commander's conference room. Captain Reynolds referred to the failed assassination attempt.

'Colonel, the bugger's still on his feet.'

'What can I say?' said Boots. 'That the devil looks after his own?'

'It's a feather in your cap that you believed Trudi Lemberg,' said Reynolds.

'A temperamental young lady, but worth a medal or two,' said Boots. 'Or a rich American husband.'

'General Bradley might have a few on his staff,' said Captain Reynolds.

'Not the time to ask him,' said Boots, turning to enter the conference room. 'Wait till we get to Berlin.'

That was typical of the man, thought Captain Reynolds as Boots disappeared. Cool and dry. One of a family of cockneys, so I hear, and got himself a grammar-school education. Made sergeant in the last war, and colonel in this. Not bad going. Married to General Sir Henry Simms's daughter. Even better going. I've no idea how he managed that, but he's got my best wishes. Bloody decent type, in my book.

Polly would have told him she'd never been interested in Boots as a decent type, that what mostly captivated her from the moment she met him was the amiable but exciting devil she sensed lay beneath the surface of his good humour. Decent types were for grown-up Girl Guides, and she had never been a Girl Guide herself.

Chapter Twenty-Six

The 22nd of July

The troopship docked at Liverpool early in the morning. Disembarkation was a slow process, and it was not until ten o'clock that Sergeants Freddy Brown and Dusty Miller, showing their railway warrants, boarded the waiting London train. Their warrants were for third-class travel. They ignored that on the reasonable grounds that the country and its rail systems owed them something better, and they entered a first-class compartment. Freddy stuck a prepared label on the inside of the window.

'RESERVED'

It was a good imitation of the real thing, and it kept out the riff-raff. A porter coming along stopped to take a look, then opened the door as soldiers and civilians surged over the platform.

'I'll have to–'

'No, don't bother,' said Freddy, and showed him five bob in the form of two half-crowns. Army wages had been paid in sterling aboard ship.

'Rightly, I shouldn't,' said the porter. 'Rightly, I can't. And not for that amount of brass. One of them half-crowns'll do.'

And he settled for that, leaving them to deal with any ticket inspector during the journey.

None turned up. Freddy and Dusty travelled all the way in style.

Outside Euston station several hours later they took in the old familiar look of London, bashed about a bit during these years of war from the air. All was very familiar, the grey brick and weathered stone of buildings, the dusty windows, brisk people, dawdling people, cockney women still favouring old-fashioned hats, old blokes still favouring flat caps and chokers, an evening newspaper vendor standing beside his propped pavement placard bearing the headline, LATEST WAR NEWS, and buses of bright red that splashed the scene with colour. They stood in observation, two lean and hard-looking men in khaki, the pallor of the exhausting and brutalizing campaign in India and Burma no longer evident after their sea voyage.

Dusty said, 'I like it, not a Jap or a swamp in sight. We're home, mate. You catching a bus here?'

'Not till I'm sure you're going to do what I've suggested,' said Freddy.

'I said I would, didn't I?' growled Dusty.

'Which is?'

'Leave it to me old man and a couple of his mates to catch the fornicating Yank and do him over,' said Dusty.

'That's only half of it,' said Freddy.

'I know, I know,' said Dusty. 'Next, I've got to talk to me loving wife and explain to her that on account of her committing bleedin' adultery behind me back, I'm chucking her out, bag and baggage, and that she can whistle for a divorce.'

'Can I be sure you'll stick to that, that I won't have to worry about you landing yourself at the Old Bailey in front of a hanging judge?' asked Freddy.

'You've got my word,' said Dusty. 'I'm bleedin' touched, ain't I, that you care?'

'Don't get lippy,' said Freddy.

'Listen, mate, me dad's a foreman at his factory, and can take a phone call there,' said Dusty, 'so you can ring 'im if you feel you need to find out whether I kept me promise. Right?'

'Right, what's the phone number?' asked Freddy. Dusty gave it and Freddy noted it. 'Right, then, you catch your bus, and I'll catch mine, and I'll see you here in two weeks time.' Dusty lived in Barnsbury, just north-west of Islington. They shook hands, shouldered their kitbags, and parted.

On his way home, Freddy encountered something he had only heard about, the arrival of a V-1. At a stop in Kingsway, a hell of a noise in the sky brought most of the passengers off the bus, Freddy and the clippie joining them on the pavement. All heads turned upwards, and Freddy had his first sight of one of the black monsters. High above, it emitted a huge buzzing drone, and Freddy watched it travelling north-west at speed.

''Orrible packet of trouble for 'Appy 'Ampstead, I shouldn't wonder', said a woman who was rubbing elbows with Freddy.

Freddy took note of an absence of panic in this woman and the passengers generally, as well as

337

among other people in Kingsway. He sensed they were on edge, but no worse, as they watched the flying bomb disappear. Freddy could hear them talking, not shouting in alarm. He guessed these were people who had adapted to the menace of Hitler's terror weapon.

'That's the first one I've seen,' he said, as the passengers began to climb back on the bus.

'Oh, yer been overseas, 'ave yer, ducks?' said the woman.

'That's a fact,' said Freddy.

'Well, you'll get used to 'em. Mind, you might 'ave to start running sometimes, but I suppose you're used to getting out of the way of all kinds of nasty stuff from the Germans. Talk about a troublesome lot, I never knew worse. Well, good luck to yer, soldier.' She got back on the bus, and Freddy followed, returning to his seat and his kitbag.

He arrived at his home in Wansey Street at five-thirty. The railings and the gate were missing. Like all others in Walworth, they had long been taken up by the council for use as scrap in the munitions industry. Approaching his front door, his emotions were very close to the surface, his thoughts not only on his family, but also on everything that had turned Dusty sour and bitter.

A large woman stopped in her walk to stare at him. A soldier with three stripes. A sergeant.

'Excuse me a minute,' she said.

Freddy, dumping his kitbag on his doorstep, turned.

'Yes, missus?' he said.

Mrs Hobday regarded him in curiosity. Cassie

338

had spoken a lot about her husband, what a cheerful bloke he was, and how he kept her in giggles all through her young years. Well, if this was him he hardly looked a cheerful character. His face was lean and sort of starved, and there wasn't even a tiny bit of a smile. Still, he was all of a man; he looked as if every muscle was as hard as iron.

'Excuse me,' she said again, 'but could you be Cassie Brown's 'usband from Burma?'

'That's me,' said Freddy, fishing in his pocket for his door-key, something he had always held on to for good luck. 'I'm home on leave for a couple of weeks.'

'I'm Mrs Hobday, a friend and neighbour, but I don't know that Cassie knew you was on your way home. The last thing she told me was that she 'adn't heard from you for Lord knows how long.'

'The last thing since when?' asked Freddy.

'Well, it was these 'orrible doodlebugs, yer know,' said Mrs Hobday, 'she–'

'Jesus Christ,' said Freddy, 'don't tell me something I don't want to hear.'

'Oh, it's nothing sorrerful,' said Mrs Hobday in hasty reassurance, 'it's just that she didn't like what might 'appen to the children, so she took them back to 'er dad's sister in Wiltshire, and 'er dad went with them. Only a few days ago, and I know she wrote telling you. It'll upset 'er, you coming home to an empty house, but she didn't know you was on your way.'

'I wrote, but forgot to get the letter posted,' said Freddy.

'Oh, I'm that sorry for both of yer,' said Mrs Hobday, heart as large in its way as her bulk was in its own way. 'Well, you could get a train tomorrer down to Wiltshire. Mr Brown, if there's anything I can do? There won't be nothing in your house, not a bite of food – 'ere, could I bring yer some tea and milk, and a bit of sugar so's you could make yerself a cup or two? And I could cook yer something, like sausages and mash, for a bit of supper. It ain't much, but I got some spare sausages. Oh, and some spare tomaters, now I come to think. It won't be no trouble.'

'Mrs Hobday, if you're a friend of Cassie's, that offer makes you a friend of mine,' said Freddy. His stiff face muscles relaxed, and something of a smile appeared. It was enough to put a little warmth into his eyes, and Mrs Hobday thought she could just detect the man that had been. A bustling and hearty woman, she wasn't unperceptive, and it was no effort to imagine what fighting Japanese devils in Burma could do to a soldier.

'Oh, Cassie's a blessing, Mr Brown, I'm missing 'er now she's gone back to Wiltshire, and it'll be a pleasure to do a little supper for yer. I don't suppose Burma's been much like a Bank Holiday.'

'No not much,' said Freddy, beginning to warm to this neighbourly woman, 'but I think we're winning. I'll catch up with Cassie tomorrow, you bet, and thanks again for all you're offering.'

'I'll get a bit of tea and the other things, and do the sausages and mash in about an hour. Would that suit yer?'

'Not half, missus,' said Freddy, and Mrs Hobday bustled back to her house.

Freddy slipped his key into the lock, opened the door and stepped in, hefting his kitbag into the passage. He closed the door and went through to the kitchen, the place where he and Cassie had spent so much time together. It was in perfect order, clean and spotless, but so empty, so silent. He felt cheated by circumstances. His mouth tightened, and he stood there reflecting on the bitter savagery of jungle warfare, and what it had done to thousands of 14th Army men. It made him realize just how much Cassie and the kids meant to him. Home was a lifeless place without them.

The knocker sounded. It was Mrs Hobday, with a little tray on which rested a bowl containing tea, an eggcup of sugar and a small jug of milk. There was also a slice of plain cake.

'Here we are, Mr Brown, you see you make yerself a nice pot of hot tea,' she said, 'or I'll do it for yer, if you like. It won't be no trouble.'

'You're a good sort, Mrs Hobday, but I can manage.'

'Well, all right,' she said. 'Me old man'll be in from 'is work in just a bit, so I'll do his supper and mine now. I'll see you again later.'

Freddy sat at the kitchen table drinking his tea, dwelling on past times with Cassie when she was a riotous, scatty and bossy young girl, and later when she was his wife and had given him his lovely kids, Muffin and Lewis. Forgetting to get his letter posted was consistent with everything

341

else that had been on the minus side for the squaddies in Burma. Cassie's Aunt Win didn't have a phone, so he couldn't ring her. That was another bloody minus.

So was the emptiness and silence of the house.

Mrs Hobday brought another tray just before seven. A covered plate of hot sausages and mash, with fried tomatoes, was presented to him. Freddy felt frankly touched. Mrs Hobday, overflowing with neighbourly goodness and generous bosom, cut off his words of thanks and told him to get the food down him before it turned cold.

'It's a pleasure to know you're a neighbour,' said Freddy.

'Well, we've all got to stand together and 'elp each other,' said Mrs Hobday, 'or it wouldn't be no use fighting this war. I'll leave you to yer supper now.'

She hadn't made the mistake of insisting he come and eat with herself and her husband. She guessed, correctly, that he couldn't fit himself into company just yet.

'How's he feeling now?' her husband asked her when she got back.

'Still a bit quiet, but he'll be all right once he's caught up with Cassie and his kids,' she said.

'Yerse, course 'e will, me old kipper.'

'Here, who you calling old kipper?'

'Forgot meself. Mind, I like kippers, only you can't get 'em now.'

'Well, try bringing home the next pair that fall off a waggon at your works.'

Freddy heard the occasional flying bomb hurtling through the night sky over London when he went to bed. Each passed on northwards. Some poor bleeders are suffering, he thought. No wonder Cassie took Muffin and Lewis back to Wiltshire.

He didn't know it, but there would have been a regular succession of the infernal invaders had it not been for the fact that watchful fighters over the coastal area of Kent and Sussex, together with batteries of ack-ack guns now using shells fitted with the proximity fuse, were blowing an increasing percentage of these rocket bombs to bits in mid-air.

He dropped off. He'd thought his sleep would be restless, but he slept like a log. There were no crazy dreams, no nightmares. When he woke up to a rainy morning, he wondered what kind of a night Dusty had had.

At eight-thirty, good old Mrs Hobday turned up with some hot grilled bacon and scrambled egg, the latter made from the powder being imported from America.

'Bacon?' he said, having brought her through to the kitchen.

'Well, me old man works at Nine Elms depot,' she said, 'and he sometimes gets 'is hand on stuff that's fell off one of them goods waggons, and as I mentioned to Cassie, it don't make sense to try and put it back. So he brings it home. He's a bit aggravating at times, but he's still got some sense, which saves 'im from being useless, like.'

'Give him my compliments for being useful,' said Freddy. 'And thanks again, Mrs Hobday,

343

you're a welcome friend.'

'Hope this rain stops for yer journey,' said Mrs Hobday.

'I can stand an honest share of home-grown rain,' said Freddy.

'Course yer can, Mr Brown, after all that Burma muck. We get our share of rain all right, but we get spring daffodils as well, don't we?'

'So we do,' said Freddy.

'Did you see any in Burma?'

'Not one,' said Freddy.

'Fancy, no daffodils,' said Mrs Hobday, and departed disbelievingly.

Later, with the rain clouds disappearing and the sun breaking through, Freddy returned clean crockery and utensils to the good lady, and when she said that was nice of him, he said nowhere near as nice as she'd been.

'Well, good luck, Mr Brown,' she said. 'Give me best wishes to Cassie and 'er dad.'

'I will,' said Freddy.

Before he began his journey to Wiltshire by train, he used a public booth at the railway station to phone the factory where Dusty's dad worked. Mr Miller, called to the phone, said 'Hello, hello, who's that, might I ask?'

'Freddy Brown, a mate of Dusty's.'

'Well, I've heard of you, of course.'

'Is Dusty all right?'

'Our George?'

'I know about his wife and her Yank, and I–'

'Bleedin' brimstone, I suppose what you don't

344

know is that me upset son found out the Yank was a reg'lar guest of Lily's, and that the cowboy turned up while George was having to talk to her about chucking her out. I was there, y'see.'

'Don't tell me he blew it,' said Freddy.

'Blew it?' said Mr Miller. 'Not half he didn't. Well, Elmer – the Yank – brought a bunch of flowers, a jar of peanut butter and some canned American fruit with him. And on top of that lot, his American pyjamas. Before I could stop him, me upset son, a lot more upset, jumped the cowboy, and the fight spilled out of the happy home into the street. Lily ran out after 'em, and George left off booting Elmer to clout her. What happened next? Well, I'll tell yer. The coppers arrived, carted George off to the station and charged him with assault and battery. But he'll only get seven days, I reckon, him being a Burma campaigner, but it's pained me, I tell yer.'

'It's pained me,' said Freddy, 'I told him not to tackle the Yank himself.'

'I know what you told him, because he told me, and what you suggested made sense, but he saw flaming red. Still, he won't mind seven days too much, not after what he did to Elmer.'

'That's seven days off his hard-earned leave, so tell him I'll knock his head off when I next see him,' said Freddy.

'Couldn't help himself, yer know,' said Mr Miller. 'It was the bloke's American pyjamas that did it. Still, all told, he'll be better off without that Lily. Any bloke sweating his guts out in Burma deserves a decent wife, not a tart. Got to go now, Freddy, glad to have had this little talk.'

Freddy, some of his kit and belongings stuffed into a valise, caught a train to Swindon, from where he could get a bus ride to the village in which Cassie, her dad and the kids were living.

It was afternoon, the sunlight warm and mellow, cottages and houses fronting the village green. The little school was closed, the children on summer holiday. A number of them were playing on the green. They watched the departure of the local bus and the approach of a soldier carrying a valise. A young girl stared, her eyes opened wide and she gave a delighted yell.

'It's Daddy! Lewis, it's our Daddy!' Away she went, little Lewis scampering after her.

Freddy saw the girl running, coming towards him, curling hair dancing, a small boy following. He knew himself to be physically changed, much thinner in body and face, but that hadn't prevented his daughter Muffin from knowing who he was. She was running joyfully.

'Muffin?'

'Daddy, Daddy!'

Freddy went down on one knee and swept her into his arms.

Up came Lewis, four years old.

'Crikey, is you my dad?' he asked.

'I told you and told you that we both had a dad, didn't I?' said blissful Muffin.

'Crikey,' said Lewis, and Freddy cuddled them both.

A woman came out of a house to call her children in for tea. She saw them in the embrace of a soldier down on one knee beside the green.

She put a hand to her throat, and then she too began to fly.

Freddy looked up and spotted her. There she was, his Cassie, skirt of her dress whipping to her run, children on the green staring.

'Cassie?'

'Freddy!' She arrived in a rush of gladness, and all the minuses, all the bitterness of Burma, all the hatreds it had fostered, and all the sourness he had felt towards Dusty's wife, fell away. He stood up, his children clinging to his legs.

'Hello, Cassie me love, how's your Sunday lace?'

And the smile he had for her was the smile of a man who knew life had been good to him in the way that counted most.

Ruddy good.

If some GI's had helped wives like Dusty Miller's to go off the rails, there were a great many others of a wholesome kind who, now fighting in Normandy, had young women in the UK waiting and praying for their safe return. They were the young women, civilians, Wrens, Waafs and ATS, destined to become GI brides, unless they had lost their loved ones in the battles of air and land.

Chapter Twenty-Seven

Saturday afternoon, the 23rd of July

In Normandy, the Allied armies were straining at the leash, General Eisenhower prepared to allow his field commanders, Montgomery and Bradley, to let loose their dogs of war at the throats of the Germans in two days time, when all preparations would be complete. The Germans, without their idol, Rommel, who had apparently died of his injuries, and knowing a mighty assault was due, were still mounting desperate attacks in an effort to unsettle Allied dispositions. All were beaten off, some at heavy cost to the Americans, British and Canadians, but at even heavier cost to the Germans.

In the West of England, Sammy and Susie had covered two hundred miles on their journey to Cornwall. In the car with them were Paula, Phoebe, Bess and Jimmy. They had stopped in a Devon village to pick up sixteen-year-old Bess and fourteen-year-old Jimmy, both of whom, as evacuees, were staying on to complete their schooling away from the flying bombs. They were happily excited about spending a fortnight's holiday with their family in Cornwall.

In the thundering Cornish Express from Paddington were Chinese Lady, Mr Finch, Daniel

348

and Patsy, Patsy having earlier said goodbye to her Pa, who was leaving for France with other war correspondents.

Both parties were due to spend the fortnight in a house in the little coastal village of Trebetherick, which overlooked the Camel Estuary and offered a view of old and quaint Padstow across the water. Patsy was looking forward to enjoying invigorating days in company with her English fun guy and his likeable family. She was not quite sure how she had come to identify so closely with them and their quaint English ways. His parents, his grandparents, and even his young sisters, really did seem incurably old-fashioned. Everyone wore best clothes all day on Sundays. At home in Boston, kids and teenagers slipped into jeans whenever they could. Except for a fridge, a Hoover and an electric steam iron, there were no really modern labour-saving devices in Daniel's home, only talk about getting some, which Daniel's attractive mother said could only be obtained in wartime if her husband Sammy came across a business friend who knew a man with the right connections, and even then no-one could be sure that Grandma Finch would be in favour. Daniel said his grandma didn't go in for new-fangled things. She was convinced that most new-fangled things would either blow a body up or electrocute her. In fact, she was still suspicious of what the phone might do to her. When Patsy asked him if he had jeans, he said he'd never heard of them except on cowboys, and didn't a feller need a horse if he had jeans? Somehow, none of this caused her irritation or exasperation, just a feeling that she wanted to laugh at this family of slowcoaches, and anyway, the Victorian granny was a cute old lady who was obviously very fond of Daniel. She called him upright and respectable, which in American terms meant a stuffed shirt.

'Daniel, do you like being upright and respectable?' she had asked him one evening when they were in the garden of his home.

'Well, it ought to keep me out of prison,' said Daniel.

'Daniel, I don't think you're upright and respectable.'

'Why not?'

'Because you're not stuffy.'

'What am I, then?' asked Daniel.

'Cute,' said Patsy, and Daniel sort of growled.

'Patsy,' he said, 'd'you want to be mercilessly tickled?'

'Oh, no, don't. I'll go crazy. Daniel, please don't ever tickle me.'

'Who's cute, then?'

'You are,' said Patsy wickedly, and ran for her life.

She thought about that, a dreamy smile on her face as from her corner seat in the compartment she took in the panorama of fields and farmlands forever passing by. Daniel just hated being called cute. Well, of course he did see himself speeding towards enlistment almost as fast as this train was speeding towards Cornwall. He'd enter a different world, meet up with a different kind of people, live a different and more demanding kind of life. She was sure, however, that he wouldn't

350

fail himself, or his family, or his country.

His country. Everything visible from the window was so much smaller than the landscapes of New England, except in those places that had associations with the Pilgrim Fathers who had come over in the *Mayflower*. They seemed small too, those well-preserved old places, with their clapboard houses, little churches and village stores, everything unspoiled by modern development, except, sensibly, an acceptance by the inhabitants of modern amenities. Imagine, Daniel's family still lit coal fires in the winter.

'Daniel, where are we now?' she asked.

Daniel, sitting beside her, with his grandparents opposite, said 'Devon, and you've been dreaming, Patsy.'

'Oh, I guess I enjoy watching the passing scenes,' said Patsy. 'I did get to know your countryside when I was at that stuffy boarding school.'

'Dream on,' said Daniel. 'We'll be catching up and passing the family car in about an hour.'

Sammy had left at seven, the train at ten.

'Will we see them?' asked Patsy.

'Not unless this train takes to the road,' said Daniel.

Patsy rolled her eyes.

They were travelling first-class. Mr Finch had booked and paid for reserved seats. Chinese Lady demurred about the expense, but gave him one of her affectionate little pats for his thoughtfulness.

Sharing the compartment with them was a major of the Royal Engineers and his com-

351

panion, an ATS captain, and both showed visible amusement at the dialogue that periodically went on between Patsy and Daniel.

'Daniel's a comic,' said Patsy to Chinese Lady in the opposite window seat.

'He gets that from his Uncle Boots, my only oldest son,' said Chinese Lady, 'but where Boots got it from, I'm sure I don't know. It wasn't from me. Mind, Daniel's dad isn't much better. Still, Daniel's turned out nice and respectable gen'rally.'

'Very,' said Mr Finch.

'Sweet,' murmured Patsy.

'What was that, dear?' asked Chinese Lady.

'Something that'll earn her a tickle as soon as the train stops,' said Daniel.

Mr Finch smiled. The RE major and the ATS captain smiled. The train rushed on towards Cornwall. They were to alight at Bodmin, and catch a local train to Wadebridge, and from there a bus to Trebetherick.

The train crossed the border, steaming for Liskeard. The countryside opened up to present a view that was rugged and undulating, Patsy delighted with the blue sky and the sunshine, not a constancy in the United Kingdom, even in high summer. The seat and the compartment seemed to surge and vibrate then. Iron wheels grated, rasped and shrieked. The train shuddered under the increasing application of brakes. Couplings clanged, coaches jerked, passengers rocked, and the whole became a juddering complaint of wood, steel and iron as the express was forced to a stop.

'Lord,' gasped Chinese Lady, hanging on to Mr Finch, 'what's happening?'

Mr Finch, as calm as ever, said, 'An unscheduled stop, Maisie.'

'Did it have to be so noisy and sudden?' asked Chinese Lady. 'It's shaken my every bone, and not done my nerves much good, either.'

Throughout the train there was a commotion of agitated voice. Outside, there was silence. Daniel came to his feet, let the window down, and put his head out. He could see nothing except the standing train, its engine letting off steam.

'Anything visible?' enquired the RE officer.

'Not a thing from here,' said Daniel. 'From here you can't see what's ahead of the engine.'

Along the corridor came a ticket inspector.

'Keep your seats, ladies and gentlemen, keep your seats.'

The major pulled the door back.

'What's the problem?' he asked, and the ticket inspector, noting his uniform and rank, bent to deliver a whisper.

'I'm Royal Engineers,' said the major. 'I'll take a look.'

'Go up to the engine, sir,' said the ticket inspector, and went on his way down the corridor to urge all passengers to keep their seats.

'What is it, John?' asked the ATS captain as the major came to his feet. He looked at her, then at the others.

'We'd like to know,' said Mr Finch, always impressive in his looks and demeanour.

'UXB on the line,' said the major. 'Unexploded bomb.'

'You're not going to–?' The ATS officer looked concerned.

'Just to take a look,' said the major, and disappeared.

They waited. The whole train waited, every open window showing craning heads, every passenger in ignorance of the cause of the hold-up, except those in a particular first-class compartment.

Patsy and Daniel both had their heads out, but neither could see what was happening beyond the stationary, steam-hissing engine.

'Oh, my stars, Daniel,' whispered Patsy, 'if we'd run into the bomb–'

'Thank the driver that we didn't,' said Daniel. 'What I'd like to know is how a bomb got on the line.'

'Daniel, they're usually dropped from bombers,' said Patsy.

'Swipe Mother O'Reilly's bloomers,' said Daniel, 'is Hitler dropping them on Cornwall now? It wasn't a Cornishman who tried to blow him up, was it?'

'Daniel, listen,' said Patsy, and they listened. From way down the track came the faint sounds of men laughing.

'Can't be a serious bomb,' said Daniel.

Ten minutes later, when the train was moving again, the RE major returned to the compartment.

Chinese Lady, unable to contain her desire to know, 'Begging your pardon, but has it been exploded? Only we didn't hear anything.'

'I'm sure you haven't,' he said, showing a grin

of amusement, 'it was a drum, not a bomb.'

'A drum?' said Mr Finch.

'A long cylindrical metal-grey drum with a ruptured skin,' said the major. 'From the driver's cabin, it could have looked like a bomb, and neither he nor his fireman risked taking a close look. They were thinking, in fact, about reversing the train to get farther away. If someone left the thing there as a practical joke, he needs his head examined. On the other hand, it did raise a laugh when I took it to the cabin and showed it to the driver and fireman.'

'I think we can all join in now,' said the ATS officer.

On steamed the train to Bodmin, Patsy with her arm tucked inside Daniel's.

Sunday afternoon

Lizzy and Ned were at Lewes Hospital, sitting beside Bobby's bed, Lizzy not sure she liked the look of the thick bandage around his head. She and Ned had been informed by the matron that their son had suffered a fractured skull. Ned said he understood it as due to a car accident. Matron Wellings, professionally able to keep a confidence, said car accidents could result in very serious injuries. However, she said, Captain Somers had responded well to the very delicate operation necessary to relieve any pressure on the brain, and would be up and about in a week's time. Lizzy asked how Helene was. Recovering splendidly from a fractured shoulder blade and a broken arm, said Matron Wellings, and Ned said they'd like to see her too. Matron Wellings said she'd arrange that, then took them to see Bobby.

Bobby, despite a head that still felt tender and eyes that looked as if he'd fought a bout with a bruiser in a boxing ring, received them cheerfully, invited them to sit down and asked if they'd brought any grapes.

Lizzy said she was ever so sorry, but the war had made grapes disappear.

'Never mind,' said Bobby, 'you and Dad have brought yourselves, and it's good to see you. You're looking younger than springtime, Mum. How'd you do it?'

'Spinach,' said Ned. 'We've got a huge garden crop this year, and your mother eats most of it.'

'No, I don't,' said Lizzy, 'just modest helpings.'

She was a naturally healthy woman, and at forty-six her figure was blooming. Buxom lines were creeping up on her, but her rich chestnut hair was still a crowning glory, her brown eyes still reflective of a youthful spirit. She was never going to grow weary of life, thought Bobby, any more than Chinese Lady was. If everything else around these two became dispiriting, there would always be the unchanging value of the family. And his dad would always be there for his mum.

'I don't think I'm too partial to spinach,' he said.

'Well, give thanks, old lad, that we didn't bring you a ton of it,' said Ned. 'Exactly how does your head feel under that turban?'

'Hollow,' said Bobby. 'I hope my brains didn't escape under the operation. Tell me about everybody, tell me about Annabelle, and Emma and Edward.'

'Oh, but you know that Edward's walking out with Leah Goodman, Rachel's younger daughter, don't you?' said Lizzy.

'I think I heard about it way back,' said Bobby, while Ned, observing his son, wondered just how the car accident had happened, if it did. He was inclined to connect Bobby's injuries and Helene's broken bones with something else, something that could be associated with under-cover work. Ned was sure the two of them were not engaged in the conventional side of war. And there was one factor that didn't make sense. A car accident in Sussex, close to Lewes? That would have meant Bobby and Helene were in England, in which case Bobby would almost certainly have been in touch with home, even if only by phone. So exactly how and where did they come by their injuries?

'Bobby,' said Lizzy, 'Edward and Leah are talking about getting engaged next year.'

'Well, lucky old Edward,' said Bobby. 'If I remember right, Leah's a raving young beauty.'

'It'll mean there'll be a mixed marriage in the family,' said Lizzy.

'Frankly, I'm against calling it a mixed mar-riage,' said Bobby, thinking of what Pétain's pro-Nazi officials had done to the Jews of France, and what he and Helene had come to believe about Himmler's concentration camps.

'Oh, I don't mean anything disagreeable, Bobby,' said Lizzy earnestly.

'Leah will be a welcome daughter-in-law, you

357

can believe that, son,' said Ned.

'Invite old Eli Greenberg,' said Bobby. 'Ask him to drive Leah and Edward in his pony and cart, if his pony's still frisky and his cart hasn't lost its wheels. Old family custom.'

'Bobby, that sounds a lovely idea,' said Lizzy.

Nurse Wickford appeared then, and with her was Helene, in a dressing gown, its left sleeve hanging loose. Her plastered arm was in a sling inside the gown, and above the elbow it was strapped to her body to prevent the kind of movement that would disturb the fracture of her shoulder blade. The fracture was close to the point of her shoulder.

'In you go,' smiled Nurse Wickford, and Helene entered. Her dark hair with its auburn tints had been brushed and burnished for her. She did not have the look of an unwell patient, she was flushed with healthy pleasure at seeing Bobby's caring parents. Beneath the dressing gown, her robust figure was coursing with life, the life that had been spared.

Her smile was vivid.

'Madame Somers – Mrs Somers – Mr Somers, I am so happy to see you.'

'Oh, my dear,' said Lizzy, gently patting Helene's sound arm, 'we're even happier to see you, and we do hope you're not in any pain.'

'No, no, no pain at all now,' said Helene.

'I'm so relieved that you're both recovering,' said Lizzy, while thinking how much more she would like it if these two were husband and wife, and not unmarried lovers, which Ned was sure they were.

'Listen, parents, we've news for you,' said Bobby.

'Good or bad?' asked Ned, up on his feet and offering his chair to Helene.

'We haven't won a fortune,' said Bobby, 'but on the other hand, we haven't lost one, either.'

'There, his jokes are still terrible,' said Helene.

'Bobby, what news?' asked Lizzy.

'It's my pleasure, parents, to inform you that as soon as we're up and about, my French lady friend and I will be arranging to get married,' said Bobby. 'Helene has decided to make an honest man of me. Have a word with the vicar, Mum, about reciting the banns, would you?'

Lizzy melted with happiness and relief, even though it meant another mixed marriage, Helene being French Catholic and Bobby Church of England.

The family was going to spread its wings.

Chapter Twenty-Eight

The house in Daymer Lane, Trebetherick, belonged to Mr Blenkinsop, a Civil Servant with the Air Ministry. His relationship with Sammy, solely to do with contracts, had become a very human one, and when he offered Sammy the use of his Cornish house for two weeks, Sammy accepted with grateful wordage.

The house was large and stone-built, and Daymer Lane led down to Daymer Beach, a magnificent expanse of golden sands washed at each high tide by the Atlantic rollers. Here, however, they surged in gently compared to the thunder of their booming charge over the sands of Newquay and Polzeath.

Sammy, Susie and everyone else had walked down the lane to the beach this morning. With only a few other holidaymakers in evidence, the sands were inviting, the tide outgoing, and the sun turning the sea a deep blue.

'Oh, gee whiz, isn't it lovely, Daniel?' breathed Patsy, the breeze causing the skirt of her cotton dress to flirt playfully around her bare knees. Her feet were also bare, Daniel carrying her sandals and his own. Everyone was bare-footed except for Chinese Lady and Mr Finch.

'I'm glad you're here,' said Daniel, sporting skimpy shorts and a flapping, unbuttoned shirt. 'When I woke up yesterday, I said to myself,

Daniel Adams, I said, I wonder if that girl Patsy will remember she's coming with us?'

'That girl? That girl?' said Patsy. 'That could mean any girl.'

'You're not any girl,' said Daniel.

'I should say I'm not.'

'I'm saying so as well. Patsy, look at that.'

They stopped at the water's edge. Ahead of them were Bess, Jimmy, Paula and Phoebe, all in shorts and tops. Bess at sixteen was still slightly plump, but it was gradually slipping away, much to her relief. Well, what girl of sixteen wanted to be an advertisement for lingering puppy fat? Incurably jolly, Bess's frequent shouts of laughter at the antics of brother Jimmy were caught and blown about by the sea breezes. Farther on were Sammy and Susie, Sammy in shirt and slacks, Susie in a light cotton dress. To one side, on a drier reach of the sand, were Grandma and Grandpa Finch, Grandma formally dressed and wearing a hat, Mr Finch in a blue blazer, light blue flannels and a white Panama.

Across the shimmering expanse of the estuary, Padstow and its fishermen's sheds came clearly to the eye.

'Everything's kind of picturesque and un-spoiled,' said Patsy, 'like Cape Cod. That's where everyone goes for summer weekends, and you have clam chowder and lobster for lunch, and a clambake on the beach at night.'

'What's clam chowder?' asked Daniel.

'A rich creamy soup made from clams.'

'What're clams?'

'Well, a kind of sea slug, I guess.'

361

'I pass,' said Daniel.

'Oh, you don't have to eat them,' said Patsy. 'If you're a bit fussy or delicate, you can just make chowder from them. It's delicious.'

'I'm not known to be fussy, but I might be a bit delicate,' said Daniel.

'Oh, poor you,' said Patsy, giving him a look of caring sympathy. He didn't need any, of course. He wasn't delicate. He didn't show pale or puny, just lean and fit. His open shirt exposed a firm chest, and just as firm were his bare legs. A little flutter arrived as she noted how his brief shorts exposed the strong supple lines of his thighs. Oh, gee whizz, my fun guy's sexy. 'Daniel, you do look freedom-loving.'

'Well, I favour democracy, of course,' said Daniel, 'but I didn't know it showed.'

'I mean, you look a free spirit in your shorts and shirt.'

'Just something old I chucked on,' said Daniel. 'You look like summer yourself. By the way, what's a clambake?' he asked, as they resumed their walk, feet dipping into wet sand.

'Oh, you bake clams on hot stones, with layers of potatoes, fish, maize and anything else you might fancy,' said Patsy.

'If you eat it—'

'Well, of course you eat it, you kook.'

'And when you've eaten it, what happens to your stomach?' asked Daniel.

'It gets kind of happy,' said Patsy.

'You sure?'

'Sure I'm sure. A New England clambake on the beach rates high as a happy social event.'

'Well, we can't have one here in Cornwall,' said Daniel, 'so make do with mackerel.'

'Mackerel?'

'Yes, local fish, and Grandma's giving us some freshly caught ones for lunch,' said Daniel. 'She says you've got to eat them fresh, or they go off like last week's bananas. Patsy, I really am glad you're here. When I woke up yesterday morning, I said to myself, Daniel Adams, I said–'

'Excuse me, but we've had all that,' said Patsy.

'Oh, right,' said Daniel.

'Daniel, isn't it just great to be here and away from the flying bombs?'

'It's great, Patsy,' said Daniel.

He took her warm hand. She applied a squeeze to his fingers, and they walked on amid the sounds of Bess's laughter.

Afternoon

They were all out again, although Chinese Lady and Mr Finch only ventured as far as the garden, kept in trim condition by an obliging old local twice a week. Chinese Lady and Mr Finch made happy use of deckchairs, while the rest of the party, finding the balmy weather and the sea breezes irresistible, took the cliff walk from Daymer Bay to Polzeath. From the grassy cliffs, the view was of sun-dappled blue waters stretching to the horizon. Below, on a little rock-strewn beach, some happy kids were paddling about in pools and trawling for trapped shrimps. Sammy and Susie kept close company with Jimmy and their three daughters, making sure

363

no-one strayed too close to the edge.

Daniel and Patsy dawdled, much as if hurry would steal minutes from them. The air was pure, the clifftop breezes brisk. Daniel stopped to gaze at the sea. Little white ripples ran towards the sands of Polzeath, hidden from the walkers.

'I wonder, would any German U-boats be prowling around out there, Patsy?'

'There's not much we could do if one poked up its periscope and took a look at us,' said Patsy.

'We could try the "V for Victory" sign and see if that made the captain mad,' said Daniel.

'If it did, how would we know?' asked Patsy.

'Well, I suppose he'd fire a torpedo,' said Daniel.

'Oh, sure, and I guess it would climb up the cliffs and keep coming,' said Patsy. 'Daniel, it's so lovely and peaceful here that I don't think I want to talk about the war. Before I said goodbye to Pa yesterday, he told me to fix my thoughts on peacetime. He said peacetime's going to come for sure, and that it won't be too long because Uncle Sam's gotten the bit between his teeth. Daniel, wouldn't it be great if the Allies finished Germany and Japan off real quick? Then you might not have to enlist.'

'That's a happy thought, Patsy, peacetime just around the corner,' said Daniel, sauntering on with her over the green turf. 'You'd think about going home then, would you?'

'Oh, I could go home anytime then,' said Patsy, 'but Pa told me a little while ago that your country's going to have a hard time recovering, and I did tell you I just don't see how I could turn my back on it, not when I've been so happy here, even at that stuffy boarding school.'

'Patsy, I never knew any girl like you before,' said Daniel.

Patsy did a little swallow and turned to observe the few houses built on the high point of the cliffs, each on a spacious plot, their roofs of Delabole slate glittering with sun-bright colour. They had to be the holiday homes of the affluent, although only one seemed occupied. After the war, Patsy could imagine all of them being full at this time of the year. The views they had of the sea, the estuary and Padstow must be breath-taking.

'Daniel?' She looked for him and was just in time to see him disappearing over the edge of the cliff on her left. 'Daniel!' Her scream was a choked one. She rushed to the edge, and there he was, standing on a lower ledge, reached by cut-out steps. He looked up, saw her wild eyes and white face, and he climbed back at once.

'Patsy?'

'Oh, I thought you'd gone, that you'd slipped over,' she gasped, winding her arms around him. 'Daniel, please don't ever do that again, don't ever go away from me.'

Daniel held her close, his warm body a reassurance.

'No, never, Patsy love.' Patsy love. That was a commitment, if anything was.

In Wiltshire, Freddy's reunion with Cassie and his children, and with Cassie's bluff and good-natured dad, was like a rousing day-to-day carnival. If there were moments when Freddy fell silent, reflecting on the atrocious nature of the Japanese soldier in war, a touch and a squeeze from Cassie told him she understood, and there were always Muffin and Lewis close by to let him know the laughter of children still existed, even in war-weary Britain. There was little laughter among the children of Burma.

Chapter Twenty-Nine

The 25th of July

The Americans, British and Canadians opened their offensive with a great roar of guns, their objective to liberate France, Belgium, Holland and Denmark, and take them on to Berlin.

And the concentration camps.

It was the beginning of the great break-out, the Americans heading for Paris, the British and Canadians for Belgium and Holland. The Germans were resolute, courageous and formidable, and every battle was ferocious and costly. Progress was sometimes merely yard by yard in the streets of shell-devastated villages, where cobbles ran red with blood. The going was especially grim for 30 Corps, helping to spearhead the advance of Montgomery's army, while the forceful Canadians took their full share of casualties during the many occasions when they were required to reduce and destroy German strongpoints.

The Americans, smashing through desperate and fanatical opposition, broke right out and their mighty legions of armour and infantry swarmed over the fields of France. Checked by Panzer reinforcements, they fought decimating battles that covered the fields and roads with broken guns, burned-out tanks, and the dead, dying and wounded of both sides. The Germans were eventually forced into serious retreat, and the Americans, with reserve divisions and new armour strengthening their front, swarmed again.

One evening in late August, Chinese Lady addressed her husband.

'Edwin, am I listening to good news on this wireless?'

'Maisie, my dear, you're listening to communiqués that suggest Paris is going to be liberated in a day or so,' said Mr Finch.

'Well, I suppose that's good news for French people,' said Chinese Lady a little fretfully, 'but what about us being liberated from these aggravating doodlebugs that never stop coming over? Susie, what's that noise?'

'Not one of the aggravations, Mum, just Sammy seeing Paula and Phoebe to bed,' said Susie, applying herself to her favourite homecraft hobby, embroidery.

'It has just been confirmed,' droned the announcer, 'that the American forces are within thirty miles of Paris, the enemy divisions are still falling back and their occupying troops are preparing to evacuate the French capital.'

'Splendid,' murmured Mr Finch.

'I might of known what those ructions were all about,' said Chinese Lady. Upstairs, Paula and Phoebe were in fits of laughter. 'I don't know that ructions help them little girls to go to sleep. Still, they always do, and I must say it shows Sammy enjoys being a father. Like I've often said, he's got his good points.'

'It's making me a back number sometimes,' said Susie. 'Sammy's very special to Paula, and Phoebe adores him.'

'Oh, you mustn't mind that, Susie,' said Chinese Lady, 'lots of little girls do get specially fond of their fathers. My, young Phoebe, she's growing so pretty she could go on the stage, which I hope she won't. Well, you know what some stage people are like, and we wouldn't want none of that in the family.'

'None of what, Maisie?' smiled Mr Finch, as the news ended.

'Now, Edwin, you know what I mean,' said Chinese Lady, 'and when this blessed war's over, you can help to make sure we don't let Phoebe go anywhere near a stage. Oh, and by the way, I want you to retire before the winter comes, so I'd be grateful if you'd have a word with the Government about it.'

'I did decide I'd see the war through, Maisie, before I–'

'Yes, I know, love,' said Chinese Lady, 'but I'd like to have you home with me for good. It's time you stayed at home, and I must say you've always been nice company.'

'Ah,' said Mr Finch.

Susie leaned and lightly patted his arm.

'I never knew nicer company than you, Dad,' she said.

'Yes, and when me and Susie go shopping,' said Chinese Lady, 'you'll be able to come with us, Edwin.'

'Well, Maisie–'

'You can speak to the Government tomorrow,' said Chinese Lady.

'Ah, h'm, excuse me a moment, dear ladies,' said Mr Finch, and retreated to his study to concentrate without interruption on the problem of how to stave off speaking to the Government, and how, when retirement did arrive, to avoid spending it in grocers' shops, all without upsetting a wife of whom he was exceptionally fond.

A small whisky accompanied his deliberations.

A solution came forth.

Treat the matter as if it had never been mentioned.

There was one subject he did mention to a colleague the following day, that of the welfare of Trudi Lemberg.

'Happy to bring you up-to-date, Edwin. She's met a rich American officer, and is working up to being proposed to.'

'The lady has flair and initiative,' said Mr Finch.

'In abundance. Join me in a prayer for the American.'

The 25th of August

With Montgomery's army driving into Belgium, this day saw the liberation of Paris by the dynamic Americans in unison with a Free French force, much to the great joy and fervent acclaim of all Parisians except those who were known to be collaborators. General de Gaulle disdaining to acknowledge he owed anything of importance to Churchill, his staunchest ally, or to Britain, his refuge for four years, ensured there was no official UK presence at the Liberation Day parade of Americans and Free French along the Champs Elysees. He walked at the head as the tall, dignified saviour of France.

The 4th of September

Two separate thrusts by the British 30 Corps effected the liberation of Brussels and Antwerp, where there was every kind of rapturous and hilarious welcome for the 'Tommies', seen as the sons of the men who had fought in Flanders in the 1914-18 war. Since 1940, the Belgians had endured the rigours and privations of German occupation. Today, the people of Antwerp and Brussels flooded into the streets, swarming over tanks, guns and every man wearing a khaki uniform, and happily ignoring the odour of the sweat-stained khaki. Flowers were thrown by the citizens, and in return cigarettes and boiled sweets were handed out by the squaddies. Embraces and kisses were bestowed by delirious Belgian females, tears of joy shed.

Some squaddies took advantage. 'Parley-voo Anglais, darling?'

'Yes, yes.'

'Good-oh. Where can I meet you tonight?'

'Anywhere you wish, Tommee.'

'Okey-dokey, in your mum's parlour about twenty-hundred?'

'Happily. What would you like me to wear, please?'

'Nothing very much, darling.'

371

The next day, Lieutenant-General Brian Horrocks, the energetic and dashing commander of 30 Corps, entered Brussels with his staff. The people were still out on the streets, still celebrating, and they gave Horrocks and his officers a tremendous welcome, running towards the cavalcade of open staff cars. In one car, Colonel Robert Adams found himself, along with other officers, besieged by clambering girls and women, all ardent to deliver kisses of gratitude. They expressed admiration for Boots who, it must be said, looked very spruce and personable in his best uniform.

'Ah, so handsome.'

'So brave.'

'And exciting, I think.'

Boots, in danger of being smothered, said in French, 'That's all very well, but am I to die a death without a single German in sight?'

They shrieked with delight.

The motorcade, forced to halt, became swamped by happy Belgians of the female gender. Boots received a score of kisses and about the same number of offers.

His wife Polly would have understood, and might even have laughed, providing he did not take up any of the offers.

On the darker side, the retreating Germans were forming new lines of massive defence in Holland and France, and the Allied armies had months of war still ahead of them.

On Sunday, Daniel and Patsy were strolling in

Ruskin Park again.

'Oh, my stars, Daniel, isn't it exciting, Paris liberated by our American GI's, and now your armies chasing the Germans right out of Belgium? Did you see the pictures in the papers of the people welcoming them? Imagine, the war could be over well before Christmas. I've had encouraging letters from Pa. He's real proud of General Patton and the GI's, and can't see anything stopping them.'

'I can't see anything stopping the Russians,' said Daniel, 'Hitler's going to get squeezed. What'll he do when he's as flat as a pancake? Slip down a drain, I shouldn't wonder. That'll please Grandma, Hitler ending up in the sewage.'

'Oh, you bet,' said Patsy. 'Daniel, won't it be great if the war's over quick and you don't have to enlist?'

'I've been thinking about volunteering,' said Daniel.

'But you don't have to do that,' said Patsy.

'No, but suppose later on I've got grand-children and they ask me what I did in the war–'

'No, don't do it, Daniel, stay with me.'

'Right, Patsy.'

Patsy hugged his arm, while asking herself when he was going to tell her he loved her. I'll sock it out of him one day, I just know I will.

Down in Devon, where the people of the villages had exercised a large amount of patience and goodwill in putting up with the precocity of untamed evacuees from bombed cities, harvests were being gathered. Close to the village of

Ashleigh, a reaper was at work on a field of barley, the field part of the farm and estate belonging to Squire William Grierson. Driving the reaper was David Adams, elder son of Tommy and Vi. David and his young brother Paul had been living with the Goodworthy family in Ashleigh since being evacuated in September, 1939, five years ago. Well past eighteen now. David was eligible for call-up, but Squire Grierson had applied for and secured a six-month deferment for the young man who had been working for him since leaving school at sixteen.

David hadn't been too sure that he ought to accept deferment because so many of his relatives were doing their bit in the Services. However, Squire Grierson and Mr Goodworthy had convinced him his work on the farm was as important to the war effort as anything he could do in uniform. In love with the land, he said all right, deferment for six months, then, to see how it goes. He had become so attached to the rural way of life that he'd given up his earlier ideas of emulating his Uncle Sammy in some kind of business venture. Easy-going, personable, and tall in the way of most adult Adams males, he was presently a free spirit. His erstwhile girlfriend, Kate Trimble, now in the WAAF, had let him know sometime ago that she was being regularly dated by an American Army officer. She assured him in her letter that he would always count as her very best friend because of how wonderful he'd been when Aunt Hilary, her guardian, was arrested on a charge of espionage. David took the blow like the son of his resilient dad, although it hurt a bit. He knew Kate had always had a thing about the glamour of wartime heroes, and she probably saw her American officer as excitingly heroic.

Spring rain and summer sunshine had brought about a bountiful harvest all over the extensive farm, and here there was a lovely sound of the crisp barley falling under the reaper. In the distance, he saw the large dairy herd pasturing. Mr Goodworthy, looked upon as Uncle Jake by David and Paul, was the squire's chief herdsman, general farm foreman and the salt of the Devon earth. He and his wife, Aunt Beth, had been the kindest of guardians over the years, and David held them and their children, Posy and Abel, in deep affection. They represented his second family.

A horse and rider approached the field gate. The rider, a girl, dismounted, flipped the reins over the gatepost, vaulted the gate like a young Amazon, and walked along the path at the edge of the field. She eyed the moving reaper as it pursued its straight line. She waited until it reached the hedge and made a turn. Then she gestured peremptorily with her whip. David came to a stop, and the girl walked up to him.

'Hello,' he said.

'What-oh, worker of the world,' said Miss Penelope Grierson, seventeen-year-old daughter of the squire. Mr Grierson also had two sons, both in the Army. Penelope, having recently finished her time at boarding school, had been interesting herself in the estate and farm. David had come to know her and to treat her with caution, for although she could be fun, there were times when she was very much the squire's daughter. She was dressed today in a brown jersey and light brown breeches. Her cap of brown leather was worn over a mass of raven-blue hair. She was quite as pretty as Kate, but she wasn't Kate.

'What can I do for you?' he asked.

'Do I need help, then?' She had a posh voice.

'I don't know,' said David, 'I just thought I'd ask.'

She looked up at him. He was bareheaded, his shirt unbuttoned, face, neck and chest tanned. Old corduroy trousers covered his long legs, and he had the dark brown hair and grey eyes of his dad and his Uncle Boots.

She ran her tongue over her lips, and said, smiling, 'I say, you're pretty good, aren't you?'

'Well, I went regularly to Sunday School as a kid,' said David, 'so I suppose that helped.'

'No, not that kind of good, you clown,' said Penelope. 'I meant you're good at keeping the reaper in a straight line. I'll come up with you now, and we'll cut some straight lines together.'

'Sorry, Miss Grierson, nothing doing,' said David.

'Now look here, you stuffy beast, make room, and give me a hand up.'

'Excuse me,' said David, 'but I work for your father and he pays me fair wages. He won't pay me a farthing for letting you ride around with me, he'll more likely read me the riot act, and you know that as well as I do. Sorry and all that,

376

Miss Grierson, but it's not on.'

'Wow, what a lot of stuck-up, mealy-mouthed piffle,' said the young lady.

'Lot of sense, you mean,' said David.

'I'm coming up, so make room,' said Penelope.

'Look, don't you have a feller you can go horse-riding with?' said David.

'Several, but they're all riding tanks or some other gruesome iron stallions for our King and country,' said Penelope.

'Well, can't you find a bloke who's not doing anything for anybody? Some bloke who's spare?'

'Oh, very funny,' said Penelope, keen in fact to ride pillion, to get her arms around him and her hands inside his shirt. 'Look here, you cheeky beast, don't you realize that with so many young men of Ashleigh away fighting the Huns and the Nips, you're the only one for miles around I can chum up with?'

'No, I hadn't thought about that,' said David, 'but what about the Land Army girls, can't you chum up with them?'

'Girls don't need other girls, you loon, unless they're a bit freakish,' said Penelope, 'and pay attention when I'm talking to you.'

'I'm stopping for my lunch break in ten minutes,' said David, 'I'll have to get going again until then. You go and ride Dobbin.'

Penelope laughed and put herself in front of the reaper.

Chapter Thirty

A bus pulled up outside the Post Office Store in Ashleigh. Aircraftswoman Kate Trimble alighted and began walking. She looked trim in her blue WAAF uniform, and well able to be of service to her country. She had certainly owned ideas of becoming some kind of a heroine, but on the day she entered a training unit, she was unable to offer anything notable in the way of scholastic or career achievements. And she made the mistake of saying she was a good cook, which resulted in her being trained for the catering branch of the Service. Subsequently, she found herself cooking for the ground staff of an RAF station in Somerset. However, she was an adaptable and optimistic young lady, and from her station she was able to spend her leaves at home. Home to Kate, who had lost her parents in the London Blitz, was the Dorset cottage in Corfe Castle village, rented by Colonel Robert Adams and his wife Polly for the duration of the war. To her they were Uncle Boots and Aunt Polly, having taken her in when her Aunt Hilary, a bit of a Bohemian and secretly pro-Hitler, was arrested in 1941 for an act of sabotage. Kate spent over two years as companion and help to Polly, particularly helpful when Polly became the mother of twins.

She was on a week's leave, staying with Polly, and had come from there to Ashleigh to see

Uncle Boots's nephew David, of whom she was very fond. They'd spent some hilariously hectic times together in 1941, and there'd been a kind of understanding that pointed to a future together... But she'd met Captain Glyn Walters, an American officer, and he'd begun dating her. He had all the dash and vigour that appealed to her. Polly suggested that if the relationship was becoming serious, Kate should let David know. Kate, very straightforward, wrote to him about her American. She hoped, she said, that he would understand.

David wrote back saying yes, he understood, and that a girl like her was bound to have admirers. He was one himself, he said, so if she ever needed help of any kind, to let him know and he'd come running. The letter made Kate feel uncomfortable and a little guilty, but Captain Glyn Walters fascinated her.

Yesterday, on the second day of her leave, he asked her to marry him. Kate, thinking of life in America, that great land of thrust, drive and energy, was overwhelmed, but retained a little note of caution. While she was fascinated with Glyn and with all that America could offer, she wasn't sure she was actually in love. So she said she'd give him her answer before her leave was up.

She told Polly, of course, and Polly said great American gophers, it really was serious, then. So what are you going to do about David now? Tell him, said Kate. I'll go and see him, she said. That's fairest, as it might be the last time I do see him, and he's been such a lovely friend to me that

I don't think a letter would be enough. I like you for that, said Polly.

One thing about the girl that Polly sometimes found disconcerting was her similarity to Emily, Boots's first wife. She had the same kind of dark auburn hair and striking green eyes, and the same kind of appetite for life. If she married Captain Walters and departed to America, thought Polly wryly, perhaps she'd take the ghost of Emily with her.

It was nearly noon when Kate reached the Goodworthy's cottage. Beth Goodworthy answered her knock. Beth, thirty-eight, was brown-haired, rosy-faced, and distinctly comely.

'Oh, hello, Mrs Goodworthy,' said Kate, 'remember me?'

'Ah, that I do,' smiled Beth. 'David's young lady friend that summer three years ago. Now look at you, in that uniform and all. Proper grown up, you be, Kate. So's David.'

'I don't suppose he's here just now?' said Kate.

'No, nor young Paul, who's at school. David's up at the farm along of the barley field and reaping,' said Beth, who knew from David that he'd been supplanted in Kate's affections. 'Squire's daughter be after him, I hear.'

'Is she?' said Kate, daughter herself of Camberwell cockneys. 'He's never mentioned that to me in his letters.' She and David still wrote to each other. Not often. Occasionally, and only as good friends.

'Squire's daughter won't get him, I reckon,' said Beth. 'Regular young flirt, and not the kind David would take up with.'

380

'I should hope not,' said Kate, 'David's too nice for that sort.'

'That he is,' said Beth. 'Kate, will you come in and have a bite with me, seeing it's near to eating time?'

'Thanks ever so much,' said Kate, 'but if I go up to the farm now, I'll be able to see David in his own eating time.'

'So you will,' said Beth, although she thought the meeting might reopen old wounds for David. Still, he was a man now, good as, and wouldn't bleed for all to see.

Kate felt a twinge of nostalgia as she began her walk to the farm. That summer of three years ago, when Devon had opened its green horizons to her, and David had made her days carefree and hilarious, still had a happy place in her memory. And David himself did too, didn't he? Did he mind very much that he'd become second in her affections? Well, he wasn't mean-minded, he didn't bear grudges, he might even be pleased for her when she told him she was thinking of saying yes to Captain Walters, a man ever so alive and exciting.

September's air, gentle and balmy, caressed her as she walked over fallow fields, shoulder bag swinging a little. Then her mood began to change because so much was reminding her of the summer that belonged to her and David. Perhaps she shouldn't have come, after all. A letter would have been easier than a visit, even if less courageous. No, blow it, it was right to meet him, especially as it really might be the last time she would see him.

She entered the farmland through one of its many gates. Away to the right she saw the dairy. Outside, on benches, Land Army women were sitting, eating their midday rations and pouring tea from flasks into enamel mugs. From a distance, they watched her heading for the large field of barley, where a young man, seated on the reaper, was having his lunch of sandwiches made for him by Mrs Goodworthy. Beside him stood the young madam from Ashleigh Hall, the home of the squire. She was laughing. The faint sounds floated.

Kate saw the girl. The squire's daughter, she supposed, who Mrs Goodworthy had said was after David. Not to marry him, thought Kate, not her, daughter of the wealthiest man for miles around. Drawing closer to the field, she saw a tethered horse. Neither David nor the girl had noticed her yet, and nor did they until she swung herself over the gate. At which point, David stared.

'Who's that?' asked Penelope, still having trouble in her attempt to enslave him for a couple of months or so, or even three months or so if he didn't get too boring.

Kate made a kind of brisk advance.

'Hello, David,' she said.

'Kate?' David, up against the totally un-expected, was lost for other words.

'You're trespassing,' said Penelope to Kate, 'so do you mind letting me know who you are?'

'A friend of David's,' said Kate, 'and I need to speak to him, so could you go somewhere else, like?'

'Do you know who I am?' asked Penelope.

'Well, I know you're not Queen Liz,' said Kate, 'and she's the only one I bow down to. Look, I don't want a fight, specially not while I'm in uniform, so could you be nice enough to leave me and David alone for ten minutes?'

'Some people,' said Penelope, and left with a grinding of her teeth.

'Well, David?' said Kate, and he took a good look at her, uniformed, trim, and all of a young woman.

'I think we've met before,' he said. 'Written any good stories lately?'

'Good?' said Kate, who had put her imagination to work during that summer of 1941, and come up with all kinds of melodramatic war stories. 'Silly, you mean.'

'Entertaining, though,' said David, and slid from the reaper to stand before her. Crikey, what a lovely bloke, thought Kate, I'd forgotten how I used to like looking at him.

'You're older,' she said.

'I think we both are,' he said, 'it's something to do with the passing of time.'

'Your education's showing,' said Kate. 'I never had your kind, just some years at my Camberwell elementary school.'

'What's that got to do with anything?' asked David.

'Blessed if I know, blessed if I even know why I said it.' Kate was fighting nostalgia. The day, the lovely sharp smell of the barley, the memories of David mowing the lawn, and of herself, a town girl, coming awake more gladly each morning, even if the crowing of cockerels was never going to be as popular with her as the clang of a London tram. 'David, you still on your six-month deferment?'

'One more month to go,' said David, curious about why she had come.

Her green eyes flickered.

'Then what'll you do?' she asked.

'Apply to join the RAF,' he said. 'I can't live a comfy life any longer.'

'But farm work's not comfy, is it?'

'In one way it is. You don't get shot at. Kate, you said you needed to talk to me. What about?'

'Well, I did want to see you and not just send a letter,' said Kate.

'Why?'

'Well, you remember Captain Walters, don't you?' she said.

'As matter of fact, no, I don't,' said David. 'I've never met him. He's the American date you've written about?'

'Yes, and he's a dream bloke, David. I'm sure you'd like him.'

'Don't be too sure,' said David.

'Anyway, I wanted to tell you he's asked me to marry him,' said Kate, watching David's expression. His mouth tightened for a moment, then he forced a smile.

'Well, I thought it might come to that,' he said, 'I thought it might.'

'I told him I'd give him my answer before I finished my leave,' said Kate. 'I've got seven days with your Aunt Polly, and this is my third day. So I thought I'd come and see you and tell you about being proposed to, like.'

'I understand,' said David.

'I hope Glyn does, because I'm going to have to say no.'

'What?'

'I think something stopped me saying yes when he asked me,' said Kate. 'It was like being on the brink and feeling giddy, but not actually feeling sure. David, can we start again, you and me? Can we?'

'I can,' said David.

'From now, this minute?'

'Yes. Have one of Aunt Beth's egg sandwiches with me.'

'Oh, not half, I'm starving,' said Kate.

'Well, there's two left,' said David, 'have them both.'

'Both?' said Kate. 'Crikey, that's the best start anyone could've made just now. And besides–' She paused, a happy smile on her face, the smile of a young lady now sure of what was right for her.

'Besides what?' asked David, up in the air at the result of this reunion.

'I want to save you from that girl, the squire's daughter,' said Kate.

Sergeant Freddy Brown was back in Burma, where the bitter-hard men of 14th Army, engaged in continuous battle with the Japanese, were driving them back and opening up the roads to Rangoon and Mandalay. Freddy was using every trick of his barbaric trade to stay alive. To survive.

Bobby and Helene, fully recovered, were married on the last Saturday in September, and they went to Torquay for a week's honeymoon. On their first night, Helene asked Bobby to take a little walk while she undressed for bed.

'Take a walk at this moment in my life?' said Bobby. 'Are you serious?'

'Of course,' said Helene, 'so you must go away for ten minutes.'

'Why?'

'I'm a bride,' said Helene, 'and must undress by myself. It's the custom.'

'For blushing virgins, I suppose,' said Bobby, 'but could I point out that–'

'No. Go away. Walk about and fidget.'

'Fidget?'

'Yes, bridegrooms fidget and brides are shy and anxious,' said Helene.

'French brides?' said Bobby, and shouted with laughter. Helene seized a pillow from the bed, hit him with it, and thumped him out of the hotel room.

'Out, out,' she said, and closed the door.

'Listen, shy and anxious,' said Bobby through the keyhole, 'women are a rum lot, and that's a fact, especially if they're French.'

The door opened and the pillow thumped him again.

'I heard that,' said Helene.

'Just a passing comment,' said Bobby. 'All right, I'll go down and have a drink.'

Helene laughed and dropped the pillow.

'Come here, husband,' she said. She took hold

of his jacket and dragged him back in. She kicked the door shut.

'Now what?' said Bobby.

'Bobby, I'm enchanted to be your wife and to have you do as I say.'

'Hold on,' said Bobby. Like his Uncle Sammy, he had fixed ideas about who should wear the trousers, and since he knew Sammy was still having trouble with Susie about that, his suspicions regarding what might happen to his own status in the years to come required him to stand his ground right here and now. 'I'm afraid you've got things the wrong way round.'

'No, it's best my way,' said Helene, 'and I demand your agreement.'

'Demand it?' said Bobby. 'Look, could we have a discussion?'

'Yes, like this,' said Helene. She gave him a push and he fell on the bed. Helene jumped on him.

'Stone my marbles,' said Bobby, 'isn't this supposed to be your shy night?'

'I was teasing you. Lie still, *cheri*, we're married and are going to be very happy.'

'I'm all for being happy,' said Bobby, too much the son of his mother to get rough with his newlywed, 'but something tells me I'm going to have problems. As a start, could I ask what the hell's happening now?'

'I'm taking your trousers off.'

Jesus give me strength, thought Bobby, I'm married to a French Susie.

Three days later, Jacob and Estelle Aarlberg, who

had a farm a few miles from Dunkirk, received a visit from a member of the French Resistance. It was no furtive visit, for the occupying Germans had gone, beaten into retreat by a force of Canadians, Poles and British troops, the British returning with grim satisfaction to the scene of their disastrous defeat in 1940.

The Resistance man stayed long enough to drink a glass of wine with Jacob and his wife, and to tell them that their daughter Helene was now married to a British officer, Captain Somers. He assured them that both were well and presently in England.

'Are you pleased, Jacob?' asked Madame Aarlberg, when the visitor had left.

'I would have been happy to know they were still alive,' said Jacob. He and his wife had given Bobby help and refuge following the Dunkirk evacuation of British troops in 1940. Bobby wounded, had been unable to reach the beaches. 'I'm happier to know they're married and, therefore, very much alive.'

'I suppose the marriage means Helene no longer regards Bobby as an idiot,' murmured Madame Aarlberg with a reminiscent smile. One could smile these days, when four years of occupation by the Germans had ended.

Chapter Thirty-One

November

The bitter battle for Arnhem had been fought and lost, the Dutch citizens rendering heroic assistance to men of 30 Corps and the Airborne division who, against overwhelming odds, fought the Germans street by street and house by house.

Now a special task force that included 4 Commando attacked the German concentrations along the Scheldt that were preventing the opening up of Antwerp to Allied shipping. The fighting was savage. It cost 4 Commando their heaviest casualties to date.

Colonel Lucas, always to be found in the thick of an action, was leading a detachment which, after some ferocious engagements with the enemy, was faced with the necessity of reducing a German pillbox. With Tim, his second-in-command close by, his detachment dug deep into the cover of sloping ground some twenty yards from the pillbox. Tim wondered what the hell he himself was doing here, risking life and limb once more when he had a blind, pregnant wife waiting at home for him. But his hand plucked automatically at an assault grenade. So did other hands. Up came heads to take quick stock, pins were pulled and a dozen grenades sailed at the objective.

They exploded, one after the other, and the detachment leapt from cover. For a moment it seemed that the defenders of the pillbox were too stunned by the explosions to use their firearms. But as the Commandos made their charge, the muzzle of a machine-gun glinted at an aperture of the pillbox. Colonel Lucas and Tim, sixth sense at a peak, flung themselves down and the venomous burst of fire killed men behind them. One Commando rushed on in a crouching run, straightened up and flung a grenade through the aperture. Seconds later, the pillbox rocked and shuddered to the explosion which, in the confined space, blew the German defenders to bits.

In the grey murk of the wintry morning, the assault continued until the banks of the Scheldt had been cleared of Germans, and Antwerp's port made available to Allied shipping. Only then did Colonel Lucas and Tim realize they had arm wounds that sent them back across the Scheldt to a field hospital for a few days.

Tim declared it was a small price to pay. Colonel Lucas said a small price didn't alter the fact that because of previous wounds they'd both end up leaking like colanders every time they sank a glass of beer. Count your blessings, said Tim. To hell with that, said Colonel Lucas, I don't fancy going back to Eloise full of holes. Felicity won't notice mine, said Tim, and they both laughed. Well, they were lightheaded with relief at having survived one more battle.

The Russians were making life hell for the German armies on the Eastern Front, the Americans were threatening to enter Germany itself, and Montgomery's army was hammering at the enemy's stubborn defences in Holland.

In December, winter arrived, an appalling European winter of snow, ice, slush and leaden skies. It halted any prospect of a major Allied advance, bogged their armies down and grounded their warplanes. The Germans began to build up for a mighty offensive of their own. They were helped by the fact that the icy slush on the Eastern Front had slowed the now magnificent Russian fighting machine.

Down in the winter wilds of Dorset, Felicity was carrying all before her.

'God, I'm enormous,' she complained to Rosie one evening.

'Just a little on the stout side,' said Rosie, reserving one ear for Felicity, and the other for soothing radio music.

'A little?' said Felicity. 'It doesn't feel like it. Thank God I can't see myself, and I'm also thankful to some extent that Tim's not here to see I've turned into a balloon.' She actually wished fervently that he was. She never lost sight of the possibility that his luck might run out one day. 'Tell me something to cheer me up.'

'I'll pick something out of a hat,' said Rosie, who had her own worries about husband Matthew in Italy, where German resistance was still at its most dangerous and lethal. 'You're glowing with health, how's that?' she said.

'Kind words are good for fat ladies,' said Felicity.

'It'll be all over in a couple of weeks,' said Rosie, 'and you'll feel as free as a bird then.'

'Don't be too late, infant, you're supposed to arrive before Christmas,' said Felicity, patting her bulge. 'Let's hope your imminent arrival co-incides with the end of the war. Are you listening?' The infant kicked. 'Can you believe that, a kick, Rosie? It's telling me to shut up.'

'They all complain a bit at that age,' said Rosie. 'They sense the approach of the stark light of day.'

'Well, when I wake in the mornings, I know for myself that there's light out there somewhere,' said Felicity. 'Rosie, thanks a thousand for being a lovely sister to me, for letting me share your home and your infants.'

'It's a pleasure, Felicity old thing,' said Rosie, 'you're family.' Which could have come straight from the lips of Chinese Lady, the matriarch.

In the snowbound headquarters of 30 Corps, Boots received a letter from Polly.

Dear old Darling,
I'm chuffed that you managed to arrange the sending of that beautifully-dressed Belgian doll for Gemma's birthday and the lovely painted wooden railway engine for James. And Belgian lace panties for me, you lovely man. Lace of any quality has almost disappeared here, and panties have become progressively more unlovely. I'd be ashamed to wear them in the presence of your discriminating Lordship,

I'd feel like something the cat brought in.

Gemma and James, three years old, can you credit that? Three years. Time's running away. But I look at them and think there they are, my greatest achievement. Darling, I grieve that you're missing so much of their young lives, but I promise you, they know who fathered them. Is there just a small chance you could be with us for Christmas? My father and stepmama will be here, and I know they'd love to see you almost as much as I would.

Your nephew David has joined the RAF, training for his wings, and Kate who, as I told you, threw herself back into his arms, looked very happy about her day of decision when she was last here on weekend leave. And I have to tell you that Bobby and his wife Helene drove over on Sunday. They arrived in a battered old heap of a car, but with a great deal of good spirits. It seems they're now on the staff of a training establishment in Hampshire. They weren't very forthcoming about what kind, but something Helene said about the area told me it was in the New Forest. What do you know about training establishments in the New Forest? I thought the pair of them a little secretive about it. Apart from that, they enjoy a very animated relationship, although Helene says she's crazy to have married a man who makes terrible jokes. By the way, Eloise phoned yesterday and we had quite a heart-to-heart, in which you and Colonel Lucas received favourable mentions. Some husbands do get talked about in a complimentary way.

Write soon to let me know when you anticipate the Corps will be in Berlin. Gemma and James send you love and thanks for their birthday presents, and I send

you my devotion. I miss you painfully. Take great care every hour of every day.
  Yours ever and always,
  Polly.

The Germans began their massive offensive in the Ardennes on the sixteenth of December. The Americans, not anticipating any offensive, especially one so formidable, were taken by surprise, and with Allied warplanes still grounded by the weather, the Germans made gains that threatened to split the Allied armies. The fighting GI's rallied, however, reserves were rushed up to help check the enemy, and the British 30 Corps, together with one of Montgomery's available airborne divisions, further strengthened resistance. The offensive petered out and the Germans, suffering a huge loss of men and armour, retreated behind their own borders. It was to be their last offensive of any kind on any front. From now on, Hitler was forced to fight a defensive war.

Christmas came and went, with neither Boots nor Tim, neither Horace Cooper nor Matthew Chapman, able to get home from their battle stations in Europe. And in the Far East, Freddy Brown was still engaged in helping to purge Burma of the Japs.

In the New Year of 1945, Hitler's scientists launched the huge V-2 rocket projectiles at London. These and the V-1's constituted Germany's final attempt to destroy Britain's suffering capital and to force Churchill to ask for peace terms. Churchill did not even consider making that request, although the V-2's were infamously destructive of life and buildings. His greater concern was with a victory that would bring the Americans or British into Berlin ahead of Stalin's Russians. That concern was politically motivated.

Churchill could see ahead.

In early January, Felicity was delivered of a baby girl, whom she named Jennifer, and if she experienced her own kind of pain at knowing she could not see her child, and never would, she did not show it. She only seemed at first to be intensely grateful at the successful delivery that unburdened her body, and then to enjoy a spell of self-congratulation at her achievement.

With 4 Commando back in the UK and at temporary rest, Tim was able to get leave and to see for himself the perfection of his daughter with her baby blue eyes. His delight in the child was matched by his emotional admiration for her mother.

'Puss, you wonderful woman.'

'Well, I feel a lot lighter after my hours of struggle, and that's something. Is our infant lovely?'

'Gorgeous.'

'Can she see?'

'Not at the moment, she's got her eyes shut.'

'But she can see, can't she?'

'She can see, believe me.'

'God, I wish I could.'

That was Felicity's only reference to her inner pain.

Aside, Tim had a word with Rosie.

'Rosie, are we sure that she's going to manage?'

'Well, I am, aren't you?' said Rosie.

'I can see the problems now that the baby's actually arrived.'

'Don't worry, Tim old lad, Jennifer will have two mothers until her daddy's home for good,' said Rosie. 'And remember one very important fact—'

'Which is?'

'That no-one's surer she can manage than Felicity herself,' said Rosie.

'Thanks for reminding me of that,' said Tim. 'You're a treasure, Rosie. One of the best things our dad Boots ever did was to keep you when he found you on his doorstep.'

'That, Tim lovey, was the day that gave me a life of happiness.'

Somewhere, a baby began to yell.

From the maternity ward came the sound of a woman's voice.

'That's mine.'

Felicity's voice.

Chapter Thirty-Two

'Daniel?' It was a cold but crisp Sunday in March, with the British and Americans engaged in forcing a crossing of the Rhine. Patsy and Daniel, warmly wrapped in coats, were in Ruskin Park, walking briskly.

'Well, Patsy?'

'I'm loving my time with your Aunt Vi and Uncle Tommy, they're sweet. Did you hear the midday newscast? Daniel, we're over the Rhine, and the Russians are making huge advances. Hitler surely must ask for an armistice now. Won't it be great if he does? I heard from Pa yesterday, and he's never written a more optimistic letter. And he sure is proud of our GI's.'

'Personally, I'm proud of you,' said Daniel.

'Are you?' said Patsy. 'Why?'

'You're still with us,' said Daniel, 'you're facing up to everything Hitler is slinging at us. These V-2's, they're fiendish twice over. Hitler, the lousy stinker, ought to be tied to one, and it ought to be launched straight into his backyard.'

'Daniel, you're losing your English manners,' said Patsy.

'Sorry about that, Patsy.'

'Oh, that's OK,' said Patsy, 'I've heard real fiery stuff from Pa.'

'Black mark to your Pa, then,' said Daniel, 'for

burning the ears of an innocent girl.'

'Innocent? Me?' said Patsy. 'Daniel, I'm not ten years old.'

'Glad about that,' said Daniel, 'or there'd be a copper on my doorstep asking questions.'

'What questions?' asked Patsy.

'Oh, something like, "Now then, now then, what's all this 'ere, eh? Do I understand you been seen with a little girl on your lap, and kissing 'er, what's more? Under age is against the law, so comerlong with me, me lad."'

Patsy shrieked. The leaves of Ruskin Park's evergreen trees rustled. Passing people looked.

'Daniel, oh, you kook, be my–' Patsy stopped. She'd been going to say be her fun guy for always, but she remembered her Pa's sincere advice. Don't throw yourself at Daniel, let him make the running. But when was he going to do that? He must know why she was staying on and on despite all the hideous flying bombs. 'Daniel, you're a hoot.'

'No, seriously, Patsy, if you were only ten–'

'I'm not, I'm in my eighteenth year, and you'll be in the Army in a few days.' Daniel had received his call-up notice. 'Oh, my stars, this war just has to be over soon.'

'It'll wear us down to the ground if it isn't, Patsy,' said Daniel soberly, and they walked on, faces tingling in the crisp cold.

Commando groups were playing their part in the crossing of the Rhine and in the fierce battles with the Germans now east of the river. Colonel Lucas and Tim, veterans of assault tactics, came up against the still dangerous remnants of a German infantry brigade. Leading their detachment, with British infantrymen on their flanks, they maintained the impetus of attack, but ferocious return fire forced them back into cover. Overhead, RAF Beaufighters swooped in support of the British troops. For ten minutes the usual kind of hell erupted, the Germans scattering. Following which, the British came out of cover to indulge in a headlong rush.

The Germans weren't finished, however. Rapid rifle fire and bursts from a machine-gun sprayed deadly bullets. Colonel Lucas staggered under the impact of hot lead striking his right arm and shoulder. At the same time, a German stick grenade exploded close by. Tim had gone to ground, flattening himself, and from there he saw Colonel Lucas fall like a smitten log.

'Oh, Christ,' he breathed.

For the next ten minutes, the resistant Germans kept the British attack in check, when up came a reserve company to actually launch a counter-attack. The fighting was bitter over trampled and smoking ground, RAF support planes unable to intercede when friend and foe were locked.

Finally, a British tank unit arrived and cleared the locale of the enemy within minutes. Tim, exhausted, drained himself of reserve strength by going on a long search for Colonel Lucas among the grounded casualties. He failed to find him.

'MISSING BELIEVED KILLED IN ACTION.' The War Office telegram stunned Eloise. It took her long, suffering moments to come to terms with what it meant and what might follow. Confirmation.

She was given immediate leave, but did not make an immediate move for home. She left the depot to walk blindly along country lanes in the cold air of March, tears streaming.

No, it couldn't be. Her great, courageous soldier, born for exultant life and magnificent endeavour, had gone? I'm asked to believe it? I'm asked to believe I shall never see him again? How can I believe anything so impossible? I can't, I won't, not unless some faceless official at the War Office is instructed to send me confirmation. Do such officials carry out these kind of confirmations unemotionally and while drinking a cup of office tea?

There has to be hope, there has to be.

But her tears still ran.

At home with Grandma and Grandpa Finch, she received comfort and sympathy from them that was quiet and understanding. Other members of the family might have rushed to crowd her, might have descended on her in a pack, but did not. After all, there had been no confirmation, and Mr Finch wisely saw to it that people called only in ones or two's, and that they expressed hope as well as sympathy. It ensured the family embrace was sensitive rather than suffocating.

Boots, receiving the news from home, also received details from Tim, who was nagged by a certainty that his French sister's husband was dead. Boots wrote to Eloise, expressing his great regret that Colonel Lucas was missing in action. However, despite knowing what Tim's feelings were, he recommended that nothing should be considered definite until the full facts were known.

In her reply, Eloise included the following passage.

If I receive confirmation, Papa, if Luke really has gone, I shall always be glad that I knew him, always be glad that he became part of my life. But I think perhaps I eventually came to feel there was a greater chance of losing him than keeping him. I told him many times he would be the first soldier into Berlin, the first to reach Hitler and hang him, but I knew months ago that because of his chosen way of fighting the enemy, it would be a miracle if he lasted as long as that. There will be consolations, Papa, the best of which will be knowing that he loved me. But despite all that, I still refuse to believe I have definitely lost him.

'Edwin,' said Chinese Lady in their bedroom one night, 'isn't Tim one of them Commanders?' She meant Commandos.

'Yes, Maisie.'

'Well, after what's happened to Eloise's husband, something's got to be done to make sure the same doesn't happen to Tim.'

'We've yet to receive confirmation of the worst, Maisie.'

'But it's hard to look on the bright side, Edwin. Can you talk to someone about Tim?'

'I'm afraid there's no-one,' said Mr Finch.

'Edwin, there's got to be someone. Tim's been five years fighting for his country, and didn't ought to be asked to still put his life in danger, not after all this time. He's done his share and more, so see if you can think of someone to talk to. It's bad enough that Eloise might be a war widow, but think of how much worse it would be for Felicity.'

'It isn't easy, Maisie, to obtain exemption from battle for any combative soldier.'

'Still, think about it, Edwin.'

'Yes, of course, Maisie.'

'You haven't done anything yet about retiring.'

'No, Maisie, not yet.'

On March the thirtieth, with the unstoppable Americans swarming into Germany, 30 Corps, spearheading Montgomery's Army Group, began a headlong drive for Bremen, the second largest port in Germany. Lieutenant-General Brian Horrocks commanded the Corps in stirring fashion, supported by his staff, his adherents to a man. Boots did not omit to write the occasional letter to his father-in-law, General Sir Henry Simms, now on the retired list. The letters enabled Sir Henry to read between the lines, and to relish the achievements of 30 Corps and the leadership skills of Horrocks.

German resistance was broken again and again under the impetus of the drive north, and among the more formidable units of the Corps was the 51st Highland Division, packed with fighting Scots, one of whom was Fergus MacAllister, who carried with him, as a lucky charm, a quite affectionate letter from Alice Adams, under-graduate at Bristol University.

It was the Scots who overran a prisoner of war camp holding hundreds of captured British soldiers, officers and men. Conditions there had deteriorated due to the desperate situation in which the Germans found themselves. However, the camp doctor had treated wounded British prisoners conscientiously. It was he who drew the attention of a Scots officer to a British Commando, a colonel badly wounded in the assault following the crossing of the Rhine.

'His right arm has been amputated, you say?'

'For his own good,' said the German MO in excellent English. 'It was less of an arm than a limb of shattered bone, and a condition of gangrene was imminent. He also has a broken leg and a head wound.'

'Christ Almighty. How is he?'

'He's alive, yes, but his broken leg is not to his liking, and he spends much time swearing at me.

'We'll ambulance him out, with other wounded, right away. Major Herschel, my thanks for all you've done for him, and to the German soldiers who picked him up from the battlefield. Not everything about a war is totally bloody.'

By mid-April, Montgomery was able to report that his leading infantry and armoured divisions were within sight of Bremen, and preparing to invade it. The driving onslaught of 30 Corps had carried them a hundred miles, and on the way German civilians had hung white flags from their windows, and thousands of exhausted German soldiers had been taken prisoner.

Much to the sorrow of Patsy and the whole of the USA, President Roosevelt collapsed and died at this time, and at a moment when his great efforts to ensure victory for the Allies seemed about to be rewarded. The vice-President, Harry Truman, a homespun son of Missouri, accepted the burden of office.

With Daniel now in the Army, Patsy was missing him in a way that made her quite a lonesome young lady. So Tommy and Vi took her to a midweek Evensong service at the local church, at which the passing of President Roosevelt was mentioned and 'Abide With Me' sung in commemoration. Patsy, a Baptist, didn't mind Church of England in the least, and after they left she spoke feelingly to her temporary guardians, now regarded by her as an aunt and uncle.

'Aunt Vi, Uncle Tommy, thanks a whole lot for being with me.'

'We like being with you, Patsy, in good times and sad ones,' said Vi gently.

30 Corps resumed the drive north to capture Bremen and advance on Hamburg. In Burma, the 14th Army had the Japanese in disorganized retreat and Rangoon in sight. Sergeant Freddy Brown, wounded in his right thigh and left leg, was in hospital in Mandalay, and glad to be there. He reckoned, rightly, that he'd done his share and more. He wrote a happy letter to Cassie and his kids.

In the Pacific, the Americans were wiping the

Japanese off the face of the ocean, and the only effective weapons the enemy could throw at their warships were bomb-carrying fighter planes under the control of suicidal kamikaze pilots.

'Lieutenant Lucas?' An ATS sergeant called from somewhere.

Eloise, back on duty and trying to turn her work into a palliative for her suffering and her fading hope, called, 'Here.'

Into the office of one of the depot's vast sheds came the sergeant.

'Two telegrams for you, ma'am,' she said. She was experiencing an awkward moment. All the ATS personnel knew that Lieutenant Lucas's husband might be numbered among the men killed in action. The telegrams together possibly meant double confirmation.

Eloise looked at the proffered buff envelopes, her lips compressed, her face stiff.

'Thank you, Sergeant Moore,' she said, and took the telegrams. 'Yes, thank you.'

The sergeant readily took the hint and left.

Eloise hardly knew how she managed to slit the first envelope and extract its contents. The words danced before her dizzy eyes. The message was from the War Office, yes.

THIS IS TO INFORM YOU COLONEL LUCAS RELEASED FROM PRISONER OF WAR CAMP STOP WOUNDED NOW HOSPITALISED IN BELGIUM STOP FURTHER DETAILS TO FOLLOW.

Eloise, heart jumping, blood racing, tore open the second envelope. More dancing words.

DEAR WIFE STOP LOST AN ARM STOP BROKE A LEG STOP GOT A FAT HEAD STOP BELGIAN HOSPITAL BUT THIS MESSAGE WILL BE SENT FROM PORTS-MOUTH STOP HOME IN A WEEK DYING TO SEE YOU BUT STAYING ALIVE STOP LOVE FROM LUKE.

Eloise's dizzy eyes closed, opened again, scanned again and grew huge.

Alive. Coming home. Alive. What did an arm matter? Oh, dreadful, of course, but she was sure she would have sacrificed one of her own in return for his life.

Alive.

She sat there reading each telegram again and again, until the succession of readings made her feel she was on a winged bicycle and soaring high into a clear blue sky.

Wonderful. But why a bicycle? She had no idea. All she did know was that she didn't have to use the pedals.

Later, she phoned home. She phoned Rosie and then Polly. She followed with calls to Grandma and Grandpa Finch, Lizzy and Ned, Sammy and Susie, and Tommy and Vi. Eloise rarely did things by halves. Everyone received the glad news as exuberantly as she gave it.

Captain Naomi Wilkes of the ATS entered the office.

'Lieutenant Lucas, you're monopolizing the phone and jamming the switchboard.'

'Oh, am I?'

'Have all those calls been private?'

'Yes, all of them.'

406

'Eloise, look here, you're very flushed. Has something happened to make you unwell?'

'Unwell? No, I'm flying a bicycle.'

An explanation followed, of course.

Chapter Thirty-Three

'Edwin?' Chinese Lady was about to make one more request for information from her husband. It was the evening of the last Sunday in April, and they were in the parlour with Susie and Sammy. Tommy, Vi and Patsy were also present, visiting for the evening. Paula, now ten, and Phoebe, now eight, had just been put to bed, although not without a few girlish complaints that at their ages they ought to be allowed to stay up a bit longer.

'Yes, Maisie?' said Mr Finch, detaching himself from a homely chat with Vi.

'I was just thinking about these flying bombs,' said Chinese Lady from her fireside chair. Hitler's projectiles had almost disappeared from the skies. 'Who was it you spoke to about them?'

'Ah,' said Mr Finch, which was his well-known way of being all things in answer to one of Chinese Lady's imponderables.

'Whoever it was, it's done some good,' said Chinese Lady, 'and I'm sure we're all grateful.'

'I think we can mostly thank the Allied armies,' said Mr Finch. 'These bombs, you see, Maisie, are launched from rocket sites, and the sites are now being overrun and destroyed. That's why they've stopped worrying us.'

'And what a blessing,' said Chinese Lady.

'It's certainly a blessing for Paula and Phoebe,' said Susie. For too long the young girls had had to suffer their worries, while still insisting they didn't want to be sent to the West Country. They were happier now, and sleeping better.

'Well, I'm sure it helped, you speaking to someone about it, Edwin,' said Chinese Lady. 'I won't ask who it was, as I know the Government likes names to be kept private, but we're all thankful that we've got a bit of peace for a change, and that the wireless is more cheerful.'

'Someone must've fed it a glass of port,' said Sammy.

'Well,' said Chinese Lady, 'something must – wait a minute, did you say glass of port, Sammy?'

'Not half, and out loud,' said Tommy.

'I heard him too,' said Patsy, wondering what Daniel was doing right now in his training camp.

'Edwin, no-one's poured port into our wireless, have they?' said Chinese Lady.

'I shouldn't think so,' said Mr Finch.

'Could've been whisky,' said Sammy. 'Did you do it, Susie, feed it whisky?'

'Ha-ha,' said Susie.

'Oh, it's great to hear all the encouraging newscasts these days,' said Patsy, seated in the middle of the semi-circle facing the fire. She was finding old-fashioned firesides kind of cosy and friendly, except that they drew in draughts. She was dying to tell Tommy and Vi about the advantages of central heating. 'Pa wrote to say he heard there's a hundred million Russian soldiers rolling up Germany.'

'A hundred million?' queried Tommy. 'You sure he said that?'

'Sure I'm sure,' said Patsy.

409

'A hundred million?' gasped Vi.

'Are they anything to do with Stalin?' asked Chinese Lady. 'Only if they are, I don't know I'd like even a thousand of them Bolsheviks getting any closer. I don't trust Bolsheviks, specially not Stalin. They've always been a trouble.'

'Your instincts aren't wrong, Maisie,' said Mr Finch, who knew that General Eisenhower and the late President Roosevelt had agreed weeks ago to leave the capture of Berlin to the Russians. He knew too that Churchill and Montgomery were appalled by such a decision. Crafty old Joe Stalin was delighted. The American generals were so tickled that Smartmouth Montgomery wasn't going to grab the kudos by marching his Army Group to Berlin that they overlooked the obvious, that Stalin would communize all that his armies held of Germany and Eastern Europe. Churchill saw how the post-war situation would develop, almost wholly in favour of Soviet Russia. Their armies were now investing Berlin itself, and Montgomery was kicking his heels in North-West Germany. 30 Corps was at a virtual standstill.

'Still, if it helps to finish the war quick, I suppose we'd better not complain,' said Chinese Lady.

'Granny,' said Patsy in her blithe way, 'could we catch the next newscast?'

'Well, let's see if it's still cheerful,' said Chinese Lady.

The parlour wireless set stood on the sideboard. The time was just nine o'clock as Sammy got up and switched it on. The BBC pips were heard and then the announcer himself, who opened with the sensational news that Hitler had committed suicide in his Berlin bunker.

'Jesus Christ,' said Sammy.

'We won't have no blasphemy, Sammy, especially not in front of Patsy,' said Chinese Lady, who hadn't turned a hair. 'Let's just be respectfully thankful that that man's gone where he should of gone years ago. To purgat'ry.'

'Where I wouldn't put it past him to put one over on Old Nick himself,' said Sammy.

'Meself,' said Tommy, 'I'm blowed if I don't feel a bit sorry for Old Nick if Hitler's in his parlour.'

With the death of the *Fuehrer*, Germany collapsed and accepted unconditional surrender. On the day of victory in Europe, the centre of London became a mass of swarming, exhilarated people. Soldiers, sailors and airmen of Britain, America, Poland, France and Norway mingled with surging seas of delighted civilians, and thousands crowded into Whitehall to await the expected appearance of Prime Minister Churchill on the balcony of the Ministry of Health. A huge roar of welcome assailed him, a roar that was repeated again and again, but silence became his due the moment he began to speak. Among those who heard him were Patsy and Daniel, drawn irresistibly to London Town on this day. Daniel, now in khaki, had been given three days victory leave from his training regiment, along with the rest of the recruits. He and Patsy listened with deep respect to Churchill.

'My dear friends, this is your hour. This is not a

411

victory of any party, it's a victory for you. Every man, every woman and every child in the country had never a thought of quitting the struggle. We came back from the jaws of death, out of the mouth of hell, while all the world wondered. When shall the reputation of this generation fail? In the long years to come, never. We have emerged from our deadly struggle with a terrible foe, and so I say the victory is yours and that of our gallant allies of the United States.'

Daniel and Patsy were also in the great sea of people who later saw him appear on the balcony of Buckingham Palace, with the King and Queen, the Princesses Elizabeth and Margaret Rose, and old Queen Mary, granddaughter-in-law of Queen Victoria. The acclaim was tremendous, King George visibly moved, the Queen animated, Churchill responsive. Patsy felt so emotional that she was choked.

Swallowing, she whispered to Daniel, 'Do you think I can count as one of Churchill's people?'

'Of course you can, Patsy. You are one, and will be for certain if, say in a year or so after the Japs have been knocked out, you'll marry me.'

'Daniel, d'you mean that, really mean it?'

'I sure do,' said Daniel.

'Oh, my stars,' breathed Patsy, lightheaded and delirious, 'could we talk about central heating sometime?'

Daniel laughed. His arm tightened around her, and they stood there, lost in a crowd of thousands, lost amid the waving hands, the waving flags and the tumultuous sounds of the people of Britain and of other nations celebrating victory over the monstrous regime of Hitler and his Third Reich. But they were lost together, their eyes on the man of the hour, the chubby man with the smile and the big cigar.

Polly, returning home with her twins from an exhilarating visit to Rosie, Felicity and the new baby, found a letter from Boots on the mat.

My very dear Polly,

Since last writing you in answer to your letter about the family and the survival of Colonel Lucas, I have discovered something even worse about Germany than I expected. I have been to a place called Belsen, a concentration camp in Germany, and have seen vileness at its most vicious, horrifying and depraved. I have seen a pit of corpses, and walking skeletons that were once innocent men and women of the Jewish faith, and I have smelled the worst kind of death. I feel defiled, and accordingly have an intense need for the civilized clean lines of home, and I will be there and with you quite soon.

If, as you tell me, you have these times when you miss me, does it help to tell you how much I miss you? Do I actually need to tell you? You have given me everything that's been worthwhile to my life since Emily went, your love, yourself and the twins, and what man could ask for more? What is any man's life without a wife, a home and children? Nothing. War is a destructive obscenity that tears men and their women apart, but out of it comes a man's greater longing for his home and family. We shall have our years of peace together, Polly, you and I and our children, never doubt it, and if you live to be a

413

hundred I hope to be with you all the way. Going back to your encounter with that German prisoner of war, I wish him well in that although he made a nightmare of your time with him, he didn't harm you or the twins. I have to be grateful for that, and I salute you for your courage in facing him out.

All my love, and give Gemma and James a big hug and a kiss for me. Tell them I'm coming home.

Boots.

'Mummy?' said Gemma.

They were there, Gemma and James, looking up at her.

She cleared her throat and said, 'Darlings, do you know how lucky we are, and why? No, you don't know, do you, my angels? So I shall tell you. We three, all of us, belong to the finest of men, your father, and woe betide you if you ever forget that.'

The publishers hope that this book has given you enjoyable reading. Large Print Books are especially designed to be as easy to see and hold as possible. If you wish a complete list of our books please ask at your local library or write directly to:

Magna Large Print Books
Magna House, Long Preston,
Skipton, North Yorkshire.
BD23 4ND

This Large Print Book for the partially sighted, who cannot read normal print, is published under the auspices of

THE ULVERSCROFT FOUNDATION